Mercy's Ransom

Text Copyright © 2024 SL Thorne
4th Edition
Original copyright @2004

ISBN: 978-1-961615-12-0
Imprint: Thornewood Studios

Mercy's Ransom

By S L Thorne

TRIGGER WARNINGS

This book contains whippings, forced prostitution, one
scene describing the initiation of SA but not the full act,
gaslighting, frequent sexual scenes with detailed and
occasionally aggressive foreplay but no graphic
depictions of intercourse or organs.

This book is not appropriate for anyone under the age of 17.

Dedication

To my muse, Clio:
who wouldn't let me think of anything else until I
wrote this down.

To Ron Kirkpatrick
who insisted that it was publishable.

Far beneath the sea-sky foam,
facing the deeps, but never alone.
Your crown of gold to light the way,
a joining of souls where dark holds sway.

Chapter the First

"Margaret, I will not have you defying me," he warned.

Captain Ambrose Price glanced over the shoulder of his reflection at the woman being cinched into a new corset on the other side of the room. Her white-blonde hair caught the dying light from the window and coloured it with deeper shades of gold and red. He decided he did not like the colour on her. Though, with the silhouette she was cutting in her undergarments as the maid worked, he was tempted to forget her mission and ravage her himself.

"Jeanette, tighter," he ordered. "I want to be able to wrap my hands around her waist and meet my own fingers."

Margaret gasped as the girl pulled back hard in response to the order, nearly lifting her off her feet. She thought she was going to be cut in half. "But, sir, I can hardly breathe as it is," she protested, as the new steel busk pressed uncomfortably whilst the whalebone forced her body into the shape he desired.

He turned away from adjusting his wig and crossed the room

to her. He shoved the small black girl out of his way and began to manhandle Margaret's breasts into place to present the most appealing vision. "Get the dress," he ordered, without looking at her. "Now," he said, his voice deceptively pleasant, "I have told you to call me Captain, haven't I?"

She hung her head, "Aye, Captain," she breathed.

He touched her chin in what began as a tender gesture, then moved her head rudely out of his way. "Now make certain that you bring up the subject of my promotion with subtlety and a casual, but calculated, glimpse of this," he said, giving her décolletage a light pat. He set his hands around her waist until his middle fingers touched and frowned to note the quarter inch gap between his thumbs. "It will have to do ...for now," he added with considerable menace.

Jeanette wisely approached from behind and climbed on a short stool to be able to get the dress over the girl's head without messing up her elaborate hair. Margaret wiggled to help, but frowned as the bloomers chaffed against her thighs.

"Must I wear these accursed things between my legs?" she pouted.

He cupped her chin and squeezed hard enough to hurt, but not enough to leave a mark. "One: Do not frown, it mars your beauty. Two: You *must* be wearing drawers when he undresses you or you will be seen as a wanton and all my carefully laid plans will be for naught, which will cause you considerable pain. Three," he added, cutting off her next thought, "you will not question me. You *do* remember your dear brother, don't you? And what your obedience to me means to him?"

She lowered her silvery-grey eyes in submission, and it seemed to please him. He let her go, paced back to the vanity and allowed Jeanette to finish working her magic. He opened a drawer and returned with a three strand rope of pearls spread between his hands set with a brilliant sapphire the size of a Spanish doubloon surrounded by diamonds. He set it at her throat and handed the clasp back to Jeanette to fasten.

Margaret ran her slim white fingers along the gleaming ropes. They were breath-taking, and they made her think.

"Captain," she ventured.

"Yes," he mused, as he adjusted a curl that was blocking the view of her earrings.

"What news of *my* pearl?" she asked.

He glanced down at her, and then went back to making his minute adjustments. "It never made it."

"Sir? ...Captain?" she corrected quickly.

"The ship carrying the bulk of our belongings was attacked by pirates," he answered, as if its loss meant nothing to him. "It was the *Mercy's Ransom.* No doubt it is even now gracing the neck of some pirate's whore. I wonder if she knows what she has?"

His smile was cold and cruel.

From outside there came the sound of a carriage and he shooed Jeanette away and pulled Margaret into the hallway.

"But... the *Mercy's Ransom* takes no survivors. How do we know it was her?"

He paused on the top of the stairs, his hand tightening on her elbow. "Because another ship saw her leaving the wreckage but was unable to catch her before she vanished. She was sighted, and you will drop the matter. I have not allowed you to use that pearl for some time now. Its absence will hardly be missed. You will forget about it, and keep your mind on the task at hand tonight. Vice Admiral Trask will be waiting for you."

With that he half dragged her down the stairs to the front door. He stopped in front of the butler and got himself under control, his face once more the nonchalant mask it always was, looked her over for signs of dishevelment, then looked back at the butler. The man nodded minutely, serving as mirror in absence of one, and only then did the Captain signal him to open the door. He was the picture of gentility as he handed her into the black coach and watched them drive into town.

Captain Jack Wyndlam stood up in the rough native dugout and reached for the underside of the bridge. He steadied himself, then began climbing precariously up the side. He had gotten one bare foot up on the plank arches and was pulling himself over the rail when a black carriage charged over the narrow bridge and veered too close to the side. He felt the lantern glass shatter against his hand and lost his grip. He fell, struck the side of the dugout and flipped into the broad stream.

Swearing, he tried again, looking both ways this time before throwing his leg over the rail and standing rather unsteadily on the planks. The ground was painfully still, but his head insisted it wasn't. He swayed, tried to steady himself, cursing dry land.

He did not wait to get his land-legs. That was a pointless endeavour. They were something he had never in his life been able to reacquire, not even in the four years he had languished on that damned island. The sooner he got moving, the sooner he could 'acquire' a ship and be back on water. Sopping wet and wringing out the tattered gold sash at his hip, he rolled into town.

One the first street, he passed a fruit vendor folding up his wares for the night and handily filched an apple, slipping it up his sleeve as he volunteered to help the man pull down the heavy planking that closed up his cart. The old man thanked him, then got a look at his tattered clothes, bare feet, and questionable appearance and hustled away with his cart without another word.

Jack shrugged and walked the other way, taking a deep bite of the russet apple. He savoured it, sucking on the bitten piece to get the most of the flavour before chewing. He headed toward the docks and the taverns that were livening up as darkness approached.

Vice Admiral Trask was a portly man, getting on in years and heavily pock-marked. "So tell me," he was saying, "what *is*

your relationship with Captain Price?"

Margaret swallowed her distaste for the man, and smiled coyly at him over the dinner table. "He is a friend of the family," she beamed shyly, tilting forward as if she had no clue the view this presented her host. "When my father died and my brother went off to sea he took me in."

"You are what, seventeen?" he asked.

She blushed, and responded with a diversion of long practice. "Not quite, Vice Admiral. But that is not exactly a proper question for a lady."

"I apologize, Miss Margaret, truly. I was just curious why you have not been married off as of yet."

She toyed with her food, staring at her fork as she turned it. "I suppose he is waiting for word from my brother before he makes such plans. I... I really would not know of such things. He has never discussed it with me."

The Vice Admiral seemed to approve as a servant entered with a stack of documents on a plate. "Thank you, Morton. Now, I know you came here with an eye out for your benefactor. You want to know how he stands for my job, seeing as I'm retiring fairly soon." Margaret looked up in shock. "Oh, don't play coy, my dear. I know how this game plays. Come, sit closer whilst I go over these papers."

He waved for Morton to clear away the remains of the meal, and reached over to pull Margaret's chair close. "That will be all, Morton. ...Unless, of course, you want dessert?" he asked, turning to her.

She shook her head. "No, thank you. I... couldn't eat another bite." It was not really a lie. Though she was still quite hungry, the corset's tight laces guaranteed she could not eat a single grape more than she had. "What, what are these papers? If you will forgive my rudeness?"

"Oh, it is not rude in the slightest. This is what you came here for, after all. These," he said, leaning in uncomfortably close, "are Captain Price's records of service."

"All of them?" she asked, seeing the thickness of the stack. She was aware where his eyes were and could almost feel the heat of his pheasant-laden breath on those ivory mounds, though he made no move to touch her.

"Yes. I can't even think of taking his offers into consideration if his records do not come close to justifying him for the position. I would love to recommend the man, but I need to cover my own assets. You understand, my dear. Now, let us see.... Here's the list of pirates he's hung, both here in Port St. Charles and at sea..." he muttered as he set it aside.

"Personally?" she asked, her eyes widening. The list was long.

"Yes. While under his official command, anyway. Those hung when he was on board, but in temporary command are over here." He fished for another document.

Margaret picked up the parchment and glanced down its length. There were nearly forty men, along with ships and dates on the first page alone. As he turned back to her with the other list he knocked over a glass of wine and she jumped back with a squeak, the papers clutched to her for safety. The chair clattered as it fell over and she tripped on the outstretched leg as the dark red liquid ran across the table and splattered onto the floor. She managed to catch herself before she fell, but the papers scattered. She began apologizing, and dropped to her knees to pick them up.

The Vice Admiral bellowed for Morton to come and clean the mess, then pulled Margaret gently to her feet, away from the spill. "Are you hurt?"

"I am sorry, I... I'm..." she began, still clutching the few pages she had rescued.

He gave a dry chuckle. "It is all right, my girl. *I* spilled the wine, not you, and I have servants for that. But thank you for saving them. You did not get any on your dress, did you?"

Margaret did not hear him. She had seen the name on the bottom of the page in her hand: Marcus Taft. The date next to his name was five years ago. She felt weak. She became aware of hands on her, arms wrapping around her. "Miss Margaret! Are you all right?"

She looked dumbfounded up at the Vice Admiral. "Pardon? I ... I am sorry, I... I must have eaten far too much of your fine dinner than is good for me."

"If you ask me, you ate far too little, but no matter." He took the papers gently from her and passed them to the servants who were cleaning up. "Come, sit down. You look faint."

"I think... I think I shall be sick," she said, managing to think again. Her mind raced.

"Oh, dear. Henrietta!" he bellowed. A tall weed of a woman answered his call. She bobbed a curtsey without a word. "Take Miss Margaret to the privy. She is feeling ill. Then find her a place to rest a moment."

Henrietta bobbed another curtsey and took hold of her. The woman was almost strong enough to carry her as she helped her down the hall and into to the small room where chamber pots were kept for the convenience of guests.

"Just... leave me a moment," she gasped. "I'll be fine. I'll... let you know when I am... recovered."

The woman nodded and left. The instant the door closed, Margaret looked about for a way to escape. There was nothing, not even a window. She leaned back against the door and tried to breathe. A noise came from down the hall, followed by shouting. Another moment passed and she heard the maid's heavy footsteps walking away and ventured a peek out the door.

The hall was empty and she took the opportunity to slip out, heading in the opposite direction of all the noise, searching for a door out of the manor. It took her a few moments before she found the servant's entrance in back and slipped out into the streets, pausing to snatch a cloak from a nail by the door.

Everyone was headed to the front of the house in a hurry. It took her several precious minutes before she found a servant's entrance that opened onto the washing yard. She snatched a

cloak from a nail by the door, and plunged into the darkness towards the back gate she had glimpsed, hoping it opened into the
streets.

Jack sat in a tavern with his head over a mug nursing his
second pint of sour, watered beer. He had managed to pick a
pocket or two, 'acquired' a pair of ill-fitting boots off a man in an
alley too drunk to need them any more, and a new coat to cover
his weather-worn shirt. The coat was a faded indigo and set off
the blue part of his eyes nicely. Though in the dimness of the tavern nothing remained but the brown rims as he surreptitiously
studied the denizens of the tavern. At the moment, all he had to
do was not call attention to himself, and he should be able to
commandeer one of the smaller ships in the harbour without too
much trouble. He flexed his injured hand, now wrapped in a
dirty rag and soaked in the bit of whiskey he had allowed himself
to buy. The light burn hurt more than the cuts, but the pain gave
him focus.

Around him sailors talked of their ships and their women
and he kept a tally of which ships' names he heard the most,
telling him which ones were most likely to be easiest to take,
having less men on board. He was also listening for word of a
particular ship, but was disappointed to hear nothing of her.

He flashed a grin that was less sober than his head at the
wench who brought him a third beer. When she smiled back he
reached out and pulled her into his lap. She giggled, seemed
more than willing.

"Cor, yor' an 'andsome one. Though a bit worn. Whatcha
need, duckie? A bit of company?"

"Mmm," he rumbled, deep in his throat. "Maybe later," he
purred, slurring his speech, though it did nothing to change the
warm, silk-like quality of his voice. It was huskier than it used to
be from long disuse and abuse by the sun and sea, but it was sultry and seemed to inflame her to genuine desire.

"You sure? I might not even charge you," she cajoled.

"Don't tempt me, luv, it's been too long. But I'm lookin' more to... information, you might say, rather than company."

She snuggled into his lap, laying her head on his shoulder and her mouth next to his ear, and played with his hair. "So, tell ol' Darla what ye want to know."

He rubbed his unshaven cheek against her expansive breast, and placed a light kiss on the high swell. "Ah'm lookin' fer a ship."

"There are quite a few hirin', luv. What are ye lookin' fer? Merchant, man o'war...?"

"Pirate," he whispered with another kiss.

She gasped, both from the touch and the words. "Oh!"

He grinned, continued to wrap around her, his hands wandering quite artfully. "Oh, not just any pirate ship, luv. One in particular."

He moved to her ear, and whispered a name. She was off his lap in seconds, knocking over his mug, whether by accident or intent he could not be sure. While she was picking it up she hissed hastily at him.

"Ye best be fergettin' that death ship, luv. Ye'll live longer. An' ye'd best be makin' ye'self scarce, and quick. I'm thinkin' ye'll not be wantin' naval attention?" She waited until he gave her a minute nod. "Cap'n Wellington's men'll be comin' off the evn'in' watch shortly."

Jack nodded, doing a quick calculation of how long it had been since the seventh bell. He stood, hoisted his breeches, then swept Darla into a passionate kiss before he strolled out of the tavern, leaving her breathless with three pence in her cleavage and no idea how it got there. He sauntered down the walk toward the docks with someone else's unattended mug, staggering from time to time.

He did not get far when he saw a troop of off-duty navy men headed straight for him and spun on his heel, hiding his face in his cup. They went past without incident. Unfortunately, turning back toward the docks, he slammed into a lieutenant who had been lingering back from his men and spilled half a pint of sour grog all over his uniform. Jack grinned, and spread his arms in way of a drunken apology. However, the lieutenant was brighter than most, and noted his attire beneath the pilfered coat.

"In a bit of a pickle, aren't we, thief?" he snarled, staring pointedly at the coat.

Jack gave a half-chuckle, wavered on his feet. "Oh this? T'were borrowed, actually, ...from a close... -hic- personal friend. Didn' want me walkin' about all soppin'. Catch a death 'at way."

"And why are you wet?"

He waved an airy hand inland, "Some tawdry farthing pushed me in th' drink." He stared at the wet stain on the lieutenant's chest. "Not tha' drink, though. Th' salty can't drinky kind." He seemed to be having trouble focusing on the lieutenant's buttons.

"Well, why don't we go find this friend and ask him, shall we?" he suggested with false friendliness and reached for Jack's arm.

"Certainly," he crowed. "He's right down there by the bridge thingie in the -hic- dinghy," he slurred, pointing toward a random bridge over one of the town's numerous streams and canals.

The moment the soldier turned his head a fraction, Jack tossed the remaining contents of his mug in his face and bolted in the opposite direction down an alley. Behind him, he heard the lieutenant yell for back-up. Risking a glance, he tripped over a drunk who complained unintelligibly as he recovered. He ducked, dodged, bobbed and shot out of the back end of the alley with two batches of soldiers in pursuit. Ever cagey, he doubled back up the next alley toward the docks instead of the way he had been running and shucked off the coat, throwing it to a surprised and pleased rummy who had been sleeping there.

The docks were busy and well lit. He darted in and slowed down as he neared the crew of a merchantman that was unloading its cargo into a warehouse. They were grumbling that it could wait until morning. He scooped up a small crate and slipped into the line. Someone complained it was just as well, as they would not get paid until the next day anyway, and Jack couldn't resist commenting. "Aye, we cain't be drinkin' on credit, now can we? Or we'll be dealin' in dead horses by mornin' fer sure."

There were mutters of assent and the grumbling grew quieter. Jack was able to blend in amongst them with fair ease, though he had to dodge a few more soldiers as he aimed haphazardly toward the smallest ship in the harbour. Occasionally, he would walk on board unloading ships and walk off with boxes and crates, marching them into the warehouses, or loading supplies onto soon to be out-going vessels.

He had finally manoeuvred toward a less well-lit part of the docks where only small dinghies were currently moored. He was looking for somewhere to dump the large bundle of bananas he had removed from one of the warehouses when he heard a voice calling out, "Hey, you there!"

He spun to look, hitting something with the long back end of his load. Just as he realized the caller was speaking to someone else further down the dock, he heard a grunt and then a dull splash. He looked over the edge and saw a long white arm flailing in a mass of dark cloth, slowly sinking from view. There were few people on this end, and no one seemed to have noticed. He set the bananas down, and started to curse just as a sailor halfway down the dock saw him looking in the water and asked him what he had dropped.

"Me hat," he said, without thinking. "Me favourite, lucky hat."

"Bad bit of luck, that," the man muttered, then looked up, hearing a disturbance back by the nearest of the warehouses. "Wonder what they lookin' fer? Been all of a rumpus all night."

Jack did not even stop to look. He just dove in.

Chapter the Second

Margaret could not believe the irony. *She* was about to drown, and in less than thirty feet of cold, black water. The water was clear enough. She could see the pinpoints of light above her and shadows blocking most of them, but with no moon, nothing else was visible. She tried desperately to break the surface, but that damned dress was like an anchor wet, and the cloak she had stolen was worse than a net: it was a death trap. Fighting it only tangled her up worse. The best she could hope for was to unfasten it, but it was hopelessly wrapped around her arms. She had wanted to escape, longed for home for so many years, but this was not exactly how she had in mind.

The salt water caressed her skin like a true lover, unlike Captain Price. It slid over her body like a silk shroud and into her all too human lungs, where it burned. There was no point in struggling. No one had seen her fall in, or they would have gone in after her by now. Even the man who had hit her must not have noticed.

The sounds of the ships in the harbour hummed dimly through the water; a thick, comforting sound. Soon the few lights above were gone, blocked by the fabric, or the fact that she was slowly blacking out. At the moment she did not really care which. She was free.

There was a sharper noise above just as her shoes touched the harbour floor. She tried to get her footing, but the ground was slimy here, where unpleasant things were dumped from ships' scuppers, and she continued to drift downward. Just when she expected her head to hit bottom, something pulled her upward. She tried to see, but all was black. Then there came a tearing sound, and a light shone above her. It was a man, glowing a pale, but intensely brilliant, gold. His features were clear to her, every crease, every scar, hair billowing out like a cloud around his head. And he had a knife in his hand.

Jack saw her hands the moment he got enough of the fabric away from her. They were long and white; in fact, a lot about her was silvery as he pulled at the cloak that was drowning her. He watched her hands fumble at the hip of her heavy brocade gown, desperately at first, then slowly, then stilled. He yanked away the last of the entangling garment and sliced the waist. Forty pounds of skirt and petticoats drifted to the harbour floor.

Putting the dagger in his teeth, he wrapped one arm around her narrow waist and kicked for the surface, aiming for the shadows beneath the dock. By the time he broke surface, she was unconscious and no longer breathing. There was slightly more commotion above than there had been when he dove in, where the sailor he had spoken with was calling for aid. He looked around for some place to bring her ashore, preferably secluded.

Just at the end of the dock, a scant sixty feet away, was a small flat-bottomed dinghy used for ferrying cargo from ships too big to dock. He swam for it, aware that every second counted.

Tossing his knife into the bottom of the boat, he heaved her in before climbing after. He moved her hair out of her face, silvery white and nigh onto glowing as the moon made an appearance at last. He paused a moment, struck by the flawless delicacy of her face, nearly as white as her hair except for the smeared paint of her lips and the bleeding khol that lined her eyes. She was like a statue lying there and just as cold. Then he turned her onto her stomach and began to pound her back and squeeze her belly to get her to expel the water and take a breath.

"Come on, luv. Start breathin', dammit! I did not dive in to ruin a near perfect escape to fish out a dead woman," he muttered.

"Oh, I wouldn't call it perfect," came a voice from above. "In fact, I wouldn't even call it an escape. More like a momentary delay of the inevitable."

Jack looked up to see the lieutenant with the beer stained uniform standing on the end of the dock with six soldiers aiming their muskets at him. Thinking quickly, he grabbed his knife and pulled the girl in front of him, held the blade to her white throat.

"I'll slit her open in a heartbeat if ye don't tell yer dogs ta' stand down."

"I highly doubt that, pirate. As you said, you didn't dive in to spoil a perfectly good escape if you were going to kill her. If you will forgive my paraphrasing it?" the lieutenant asked, with the air that he didn't care if he was forgiven. "Now, if you will put her down?"

At that moment, Margaret began vomiting up salt water, writhing as she choked. Drowning is indeed the softest of deaths, once you get past the panic. But it is the resurrection from drowning that makes one long for the velvet oblivion. The burning in her lungs was intense and her reaction so violent that Jack had no choice but to drop her. The moment she was out of the way, there came the clicking of muskets.

"Come along now, Mad Jack." The lieutenant grinned as Jack scowled and ground his surprisingly good teeth. "Yes. I know who you are. I didn't believe it at first, of course, but the facts are irrefutable. You see, your sash gives you away."

They both looked down at the tattered and faded gold silk

wrapped around his hips. Jack cursed inwardly. Of all the luck to run into the one junior officer on the whole damned rock that noticed details. "Maybe I stole it," he offered. "Like th' coat ye liked so much."

"The description fits," he said, shaking his head. "A small, insignificant man, permanent stagger, muddy hair, exotic eyes… though you *are* supposed to be dead. No matter, we'll rectify that come morning. No sense in waking the governor at this hour."

Two of his men grabbed Jack by the arms and hauled him to the dock, clapping him in irons and dragging him away.

"Now let's see if this tawdry bint is a wanton or an accomplice," said the lieutenant as he hopped down into the boat and pulled her to her feet.

She looked at him, saw him mostly as a bright blur of pale red in a redder uniform and tried to gesture toward the man they were arresting.

The moment he realized that the soggy mass of white curls was not a wig, he flushed. "Miss Margaret!" he exclaimed, and took off his jacket, wrapping it around her to preserve her modesty and to try to warm her up.

She resisted weakly, and then promptly fainted. The lieutenant passed her up to his men, before pulling himself up onto the dock. He then swept her into his arms, and strode off toward the home of Captain Price.

Margaret awoke in her own bed, in her nightdress, with Captain Price sitting on the edge of the mattress smoking a pipe and glaring at her. She groaned, coughed, and sat up.

"Well, I see you've had a bit of an adventure this evening," he muttered.

She looked at him, seeing nothing but a black, hazy glow, then things began to shift and settle and the features of her 'benefactor' came into view.

"What happened? What did you learn? I know you did not have the opportunity to bed the man, so we shall have to repeat this little exercise again soon. *And* you lost the bottom half of a very expensive gown."

She gave a half growl, and rolled out of the bed. "Your stinking promotion will more than likely be possible. He was pleased with what little he saw of your record whilst I was there."

"And then you became ill and were kidnapped by that pirate while the Vice Admiral was tending to an emergency with the governor's son," he stated flatly, daring her to contradict him.

She turned on him, cold fire burning in her silvery-blue eyes. "No. I was not 'kidnapped'. And that man risked his neck to save my life."

"Literally," he said casually, moving off the bed and closer to her, setting his pipe aside. "He'll likely be hanged in the morning, when the governor gets around to him."

"For saving me?" she gasped.

"No, for engaging in robbery on the high seas and kidnapping. The man's a notorious pirate. Granted, one no one's heard a whisper of in four years, but a pirate nonetheless. And you know what I do with pirates," he ground suggestively.

"Aye," she snapped, her fury removing all sense from her head. "You make them promises and exact heavy ransoms for their lives, and then hang them anyway!" she screamed.

She hit the floor, her face on fire before she realized he had moved. He seized her by her nightdress and a careless handful of hair and hauled her to her feet, pulling her close to his face. "You had best rethink your manners, girl. Lest your brother pay for your insolence."

She slapped him, raking her nails along his cheek from eye to lip. "You've already hung him, you filthy, honourless shark! You've degraded me and used me as hostage against his life when he has been dead by your hand for five years!"

The Captain dropped all pretence, grabbed her by both wrists, and shook her violently. "How do you know this?"

She sneered in his face. "At dinner with the Vice Admiral, I saw his name, ship and date of death on the list of those you've *personally* hung. I wasn't kidnapped. I ran away!" She knew it was the wrong thing to say even as the words flew from her mouth, but she had no more control over it than she had over the tides.

He flipped her hands behind her back, and held them in one as he dragged her to a chest that he rarely opened. "You will re-member one thing, whore. Your brother sold you to me to secure his life *once*. There was no guarantee should he continue his ca-reer 'on the account'. Your brother is dead, yes; but you are still mine. Behave like an obedient young lady and I'll treat you thus. Behave like a recalcitrant negro slave and, by god, I'll treat you like one!" He threw her to the floor and began pulling a pair of long chains from the chest.

"You've never treated me like a lady," she spat. "To you, I was always a captive whore!" She finished with a shrill scream that swiftly rose in pitch and volume.

He cut her off by stuffing a cloth in her mouth, and tying it in place. "I'll have none of that. I treasure my hearing, thank you," he snarled, wrapping his fist in her hair. "And my glass. I have educated you, taken you everywhere with me, fed you, clothed you, draped you in jewels. I have treated you better than a Captain's mistress has the right to be treated. But since you choose to abuse my hospitality, I shall truly treat you like a slave."

He hauled her to her feet by her hair and seized one of the manacles, clapping it over her wrists with practised ease. She fought him to no avail, as he slipped the links of the chain over a pair of lamp hooks in the ceiling. He then opened the door and bellowed for Jeanette.

"Yes, Captain-master?" she said when she arrived. She gaped in horror as he stepped out of her way to let her into the room. "Braid her hair," he ordered. "One plait, down the back. And if it is not done by the time I return she won't hanging there alone."

He left the threat open as he exited and the girl hurried to obey, brushing back tears. As she fumbled with the long, silky locks, she apologized in three different languages, shifting between English, French, and Malagasy, crying all the while. Margaret would have comforted her if she had been able to speak, but she knew the girl would not dare remove the gag. She was just tying off the hip length braid when the master returned, a horsewhip in hand. With a squeal of remembered pain, Jeanette fled from the room.

Captain Price closed the door and crossed the room casually. He had come from a wealthy family and could afford the best of everything; was more than used to handling slaves. In fact, he took great pleasure in punishing them personally, and never left those duties to an overseer. He came up behind her and caressed the back of her neck.

"I have always loved your hair," he sighed. "Like spider silk, soft and white. I would not have it cut off by an errant lash. Best to lay this out of my way," he said, draping it tenderly over her shoulder.

"You seem to have a soft spot for pirates," he continued. "First your brother, now this would-be-rescuer. Tell me, had you planned to run away with him? Or did he just happen upon you drowning?" He laughed at that, leaning in close enough to smell the sea on her skin. "You, drown? Don't you just love the poetic irony?"

He played with the short hairs on the very back of her neck. "There is only one problem with this," he complained, softly in her ear, giving a light tug on the tails of the gag. "I can't hear you scream this way. And I do so love it when they scream."

His sentence was punctuated by a crack, and a stifled cry as he stepped back and began to lay into her.

Chapter the Third

It was barely morning when Jack heard the noise of someone entering the jail, but chose not to react. He remained sitting on the stone bunk with his back against the corner, eyes closed but listening keenly. It was not the jailor. This man was young, or just slender and light of foot... though he did have the keys. He walked the length of the cells, inspecting the occupants before stopping at Jack's.

"What do ye want, lad?" he breathed, still refusing to open his eyes.

"Are you the pirate they call Mad Jack?" The accent was odd, and the voice barely out of puberty. No doubt it still cracked now and again.

"That's *Handsome* Jack, me bucko. Now go away. Don't a condemned man get a last nap? Or some such rot?"

"Only if he wishes to remain condemned."

The way the boy said it caught Jack's attention. He slowly

turned his head to look at him. He was barely Jack's height of five foot six, and might have weighed in at seven stone and ten. His features were obscured by a broad brimmed hat and he wore what might have been his father's clothes from the ill fit: a simple pair of brown breeches, a linen shirt worn untucked, and a plain brown coat.

Jack rolled off the bunk and sauntered over to the cell door, leaned on the thick iron bars. All he could see of the boy's features was a dirty, shadowed jaw. But the manner of speaking called lie to the commoner's hand-me-downs.

"An' just what interest would a whelp like you be havin' in a pirate like me? Did I kill someone ye loved?"

"No. I need your help."

"And what makes ye think I be willin' ta help?"

There was no hesitation. "Because you are a good man."

Jack laughed. He couldn't help himself. He'd been called many things in his life, but that wasn't one of them. That and the boy's voice had cracked slightly in that moment. "Not quite enough, boy."

"Is your life enough? In two hours time, Captain Price will be dragging the governor down here to authorize your execution. So, unless you want a dance with Jack Ketch you'd best accept my help."

Jack sighed. He had been looking for a way out of the noose. "Aside from pilfering the keys, do ye have a plan, boy?"

With that the boy turned and began to open the doors to the other cells. The moment the occupants realized what was going on they rushed up the stairs and out into the still, dark morning, overpowering the two surprised guards fairly easily. As he came back to Jack's cell, and put the key in the lock, something caught Jack's attention. His eyes spun a darker brown for a moment before the blue spread again in the dim light. The instant the door was opened he stepped out and put his hand on the boy's, pushing back the sleeves to reveal clean arms in sharp contrast to the dirty, brownish hands.

"Ye've soft, white arms, *lad*," he said quietly, then grabbed both of them and pulled him close. "Or should I say... Miss Margaret?"

He grinned, tipping back the hat to expose the delicate beauty from the night before. She had gone so far as to rub ashes on her face to enhance her disguise. Her silvery eyes danced grey in the weak torch light.

"My name, Captain, is Sirene. And if you want to save your neck, you should come with me *now*."

"By all means then," he said, suddenly letting her go with a lopsided grin. "Lead the way, *boy*."

Sirene pulled her hat back down over her face and led him cautiously up the stairs. She peered out first, saw the coast relatively clear, and beckoned him to follow her. They stepped over the two fallen guards and slipped around the side of the building. There was no sign of the escaped prisoners and nothing usable as a weapon had been left behind. Jack headed left toward the docks, but She grabbed his arm and pulled him to the right, away from the town.

He untangled himself from her grip and gave her a saucy, slightly unsteady bow.

"I thank ye fer springin' me, lass, but I need to commandeer me a ship to get off this rock. And th' ships be that way."

"Correction," she said. "Death is that way. The horse is this way."

"Horse?" he choked. "I'm a sailor, lass, not a bloody cavalryman! I needs a ship, not a short-eared mule."

She gave an exasperated sigh. "A frigate limped into port an hour ago; she was attacked by pirates ...with the Governor's son on board. Every solider and navy man in town not otherwise engaged is down there in the harbour. Why do you think there were only two men guarding the jail? You go down there and you'll be dancing the gibbet in short order if you're not peppered with lead on sight."

"But how th' hell am I supposed ta do anything... *inland*?" he snarled with a shudder.

"You don't. Get on the horse, and I'll explain on the way," she insisted, grabbing his arm and pulling him toward a small stand of trees.

He groaned, but allowed her to lead him. "I don't know how t' ride, lass," he warned.

"That's quite all right," she said more cheerfully as she grabbed the reins of the bright bay stallion that stood waiting in the brush. She gave his neck a loving pat before she grabbed the saddle and vaulted aboard. "I do. All you have to do is hold on," she added, turning the animal sideways and offering him her hand.

With a final growl he grabbed her arm and swung himself up behind her on the saddle. He was aware of the tiniest whimper from her as he shifted closer in an attempt to solidify his seat. He grinned and wrapped his arms around her slim waist. He noted, even as she adjusted his grip, that it was not quite as narrow, nor as stiff, as it had been when he pulled her from the harbour-bed.

As she kicked the horse into a gallop he swallowed and closed his eyes. Pressed close against her body, his senses were overwhelmed by the fragrance of her, buried though it was by the sharp stink of ashes. It was cool like dew-kissed lilies, faintly musky from recent exertions with an undertone of something that stirred more than his loins, something that reminded him of an ocean breeze. He diverted his mind by trying to calculate the difference in her waist size. By the time the sun rose and began to burn off the morning mists he guessed she had been cinched in by six full inches and was not at this time wearing a corset.

They continued at a full gallop until the sun was well up. By the time it had cleared the tree-line, he was more accustomed to the rolling gait of the beast. Before the sun had reached its sum-mit, he was aware that the girl was weakening, though she struggled to give no sign. Pressed to her back as he was, he could hear minute grunts and whimpers as the horse trod over uncer-tain or loose ground. Finally, he reached around for the reins and pulled the animal up.

"Avast, ye hulkin' beastie, avast! We need to stop." She half-turned in the saddle to protest, and he could see the paleness of her lips. "No, lass, I insist. The brute needs a rest and so do m' legs. As I am sure do yers," he added, giving her thigh a pat. He grinned as she flinched. "Now, how do we get off th' ruddy thing?"

Sirene was privately grateful he had suggested it and nodded, certain pursuit would not be coming in this direction, not for a while yet anyway. "Just hold on and throw your leg over, then drop."

He started to slide off the right side, which caused the horse to shy. She stopped him. "No, Captain... larboard. On and off to larboard, not starboard."

"Oh," he answered, and reversed his dismount. He grabbed the bridle and pulled the horse's head around to face him. "Sorry about that, ol' salt. I don't know th' ropes when it comes ta' horses. Nothin' meant by it." The horse pulled away from him, snorting and wrinkling his nose, causing Jack to laugh. He moved back toward the saddle and held his hands up to Sirene.

"I am fine where I sit, thank you," she said.

He frowned. "Madam, you are far from fine. Yer as tired as th' beast and we need to talk."

She shook her head, holding firm to the reins. "Walk off your legs while you can. We should not stop for long. I will be fine, though I thank you for your concern."

He squinted up at her, but her fine face was shadowed by her hat. "Don't exactly trust me, do ye, luv?"

"Not until we have come to an accord. You may be a good man, but you are still a pirate."

"Well put, lass," he nodded with approval, turned out his hands in surrender, and backed off. He wandered for a minute until he found a tree to lean against. "So, since yer holding all th' cards, ...and th' helm as it were... *and* know where th' blazes we are... what sort of accord are ye looking fer?"

She took a deep breath. There was no wind here, and the heat beat down uncomfortably on her dark hat and coat. "On the far side of the point there is a tiny, private harbour. Captain Price comes from a wealthy merchant family and he owns a good parcel of land near there."

"He's rich? So what th' hell's he doing in th' King's Navy?" He frowned, tipping his head back against the trunk of the tree. He grinned broadly, noticing several ripe papayas above him.

"An attempt to improve his social standing," she explained. "A naval career could do that. And he wasn't the heir until his older brother was killed in a pirate raid *after* he joined the navy."

She watched as he attempted to climb the straight trunk to reach the fruit. He amused her as he tried to rub the sticky stuff from the bark off his palms. She gave a tired smile and guided the horse over to it, neatly plucking one of the fruits and tossing it down to him.

"Thanks, luv," he grinned, using his thumbnail to slice the flesh, and pulled the fruit apart. "So, what's he got stashed at the family digs that I need?" he asked, greedily eating, spitting out the black pellet-like seeds.

"*We* need," she corrected. "There is a small ship there."

He swallowed, and gave her an apologetic grin. "See, ye're obviously not a sailor, an' I'm not in th' habit of takin' passengers aboard. Why would I take ye with me ta sea?"

"Because I saved your life. Simply put: you owe me."

Jack laughed, pushed off from the tree, and cast off the empty skin. "On th' contrary, my dear," he said, gesturing with the remaining half of the fruit. "I saved yer life in th' harbour, thereby endangering my life which ye then rectified by springing me from th' brig. We're square, savvy?" He offered her a bite, which she politely declined with a small shake of her head. "Suit ye'self. 'S no wonder yer s'thin," he added.

She leaned forward on the saddle. "I beg to differ. I saved your neck by getting you out of Port St. Charles. Anywhere we go from here is a new deal."

He stopped with his teeth buried deep in the orange fruit, glared up at her over the rim of it as his face dropped into a frown. Without taking his eyes from her, he scraped the flesh from the skin and chewed it, delicately wiping the juice from his thin, barely-there moustache with a thumb and sucked it clean. He regarded her a long, silent moment, watched the rigidness of her back as she sat up, waiting patiently. Her face was delicate, yes, but there was a strong set to it, a fiery mien and a keen will. He had to admire her wit and daring. Finally, he grinned.

"You are a very savvy woman, Miss Sirene. Where do ye hail from? Yer accent is... odd."

"There will be time enough for stories once we're on board and clear of Barbados. And, if you're a good boy, I might even tell you the *whole* story."

He shrugged. "Fair enough, Miss. I shall be looking forward to it. I do love a good yarn. Exactly what do ye have in mind?" he asked, returning to the remains of the papaya.

"I am looking for the *Mercy's Ransom*. I want you to take me to her."

He regarded her warily. "Hmm, fancy that. I, too, am searching fer that particular vessel. Though most don't throw her name out quite so casual these days. Never did really, but nowadays no one wants to hear those words. What would ye be wantin' with my ship?"

"Your ship? Oh, that's right. You're her original captain. Captain Fenning took her over when you vanished at sea, or so they said." He gave her a furrowed look. "I read a lot of the captain's reports," she explained.

But it was something else that had his ruff up. "*Fenning* took over? That dog! He wasn't even th' bloody quartermaster!" He threw away the rest of the skin, pitching it angrily into the jungle and wiped his hands on his trousers. He stepped closer, his hands on his hips in a stance that might have been impressive had he been standing on higher ground. As it was, with his head tipped back almost drunkenly and squinting against the glare it looked comical. "And what, pray tell, would a lovely piece such as yerself be wanting with a scab'rous dog like 'im?"

"He stole something from me. He robbed a vessel carrying a grey pearl in a silver cage. He either has possession of it, or knows where it is, or where it sank. Either way, I would have it back."

"And how will ye be convincing him to accommodate yer request? Providing he even can. Ye'll not likely be snarin' him as ye did me..."

She leaned forward again. "That is where you come in. You want to get back to your ship, am I right?"

"That... *was* my intention when I came ta port," he confessed with a few half-hearted, half-completed gestures of nonchalance.

"To do that you need a ship. I will give you a ship and help you reacquire yours. And, if I am pleased with your services, I might be inclined to sharing a prize with you."

He perked up. "What prize? *You've* taken a prize? Yer a naval captain's sister, or niece, or daughter, whatever. What prize might you 'ave taken? Or 'ave access to?"

She shrugged off her annoyance at the implication she was of any relation to her former captor. "Have you heard of the *Ana Maria Salvador*?"

"Everyone's *heard* of her!" he raved. "Problem is, luv, she's sunk in a hurricane over a hundred years back and lost. How are ye goin' ta' share a prize long sunk?"

She smiled a deliciously wicked grin. "Because, my golden buccaneer, I know where she lies. And what rock she blew up under. I know where she is and how to get to her. And I will share her with you in exchange for a single, solitary pearl."

Jack furrowed his brow. "Equal shares with me an' th' crew when I get back to 'er," he bartered.

She shook her head. "You and the crew get sixty percent to divide according to your articles. The rest is mine. And considering I've just abandoned my only means of support, I'll been needing it to set myself up somewhere. So, it's fair. You get your ship and a sixty percent share of the richest galleon ever to sink along the Spanish Main. I get my pearl back, and freedom."

"And forty percent o' th' richest galleon ever to sink along th' Spanish Main," he added, with a grumble. "That's not gonna sit well with th' crew, ye know."

"We just won't 'recover' the part that's mine."

He looked at her, as if she were totally daft.

She dismissed the look with a shake of her head. "You'll understand later. For now, all that matters is that you agree."

It sounded so easy, though he knew there'd be more to this. It was *never* as simple as it sounded. But the treasure of the *Ana Maria Salvador* was said to be vast, one of the largest ever lost. Surely it was worth one little pearl ...and he *did* need a ship.

"You'll *give* me a ship?" he asked suspiciously.

"Just on the other side of that ridge is a small harbour which is the secret berth of Captain Price's private toy; a brig he keeps for personal use. She's small, she's fast, and she'll run a skeleton crew of four. If anyone will catch your *Mercy*, it's the *Ambition's Price*."

"But we're only two, luv."

"Leave that to me." She held down her hand. "Are we in accord?"

"I must say, I have to admire yer dauntless personality. Aye. We have an accord." He took her hand and shook it, before trading it for her other, grasping below her elbow and allowed her to guide his momentum as he leapt back on the horse. "I know I will eventually come to regret this agreement, but I like th' way ye think." He waved his arm in a mock imperious gesture. "Onward, Miss Margaret... er, yer pardon, luv, Miss Sireeene," he corrected, drawing out the name playfully.

He had to grab hold of her quickly as she kicked the horse into a full gallop. She stifled a grunt as he slammed into her and bent low over the animal's neck.

Less than an hour later, Sirene pulled the horse up and got

down, gesturing for him to follow suit. She led the horse to some tall rocks near a cluster of sparse, dry grass and pulled off his bridle. She unbuckled the saddle and shoved it off the far side of him and gave the animal a last pat before leaving him to graze. When she was done, she found Jack sitting halfway up one of the boulders admiring the view.

"Breath-taking, isn't it?" he mused, as she gingerly climbed up next to him.

"Aye," she breathed, drinking deep of the ocean air. "I have always loved the view out here."

"I was referin' to yon vessel, but th' view is fair enough. My preferences have always been t' th' open sea with land *behind* me. Don't get me wrong, I enjoy various ports o' call, but... only fer th' necessaries."

Sirene regarded him with a restrained smile. "I know what you mean."

There was movement near the docks below. Jack quickly rolled onto his belly to observe without being observed in turn, and Sirene pointed to a more or less permanent canopy near the dock.

"He always keeps three men with her to guard and tend her. She's kept ready to sail at a moment's notice."

"This captain of yours strikes me as th' paranoid sort," he mused.

"To say the least." Sirene concentrated on the figures below, letting her eyes unfocus and see them in a different manner. "The tall one is Edmonds," she said, pointing to the lanky, dark grey one with bits of black in his glow sitting at a table under the rough shelter. "He's usually in charge. He's a cagey one and you'd be best served finding an excuse to be rid of him. Use him to get us out of the harbour and then push him overboard. He'll be more trouble than he's worth, if you don't.

"The heavy one," she said, pointing to a shorter, more heavy-set man who had just walked out from under the shelter. "That is Marklain. He's a bit... wobby, but is definitely someone you want on the ropes. He gets peculiar around me, but sweet. He'll toe the line right enough with judicious application of the proper leverage."

Another figure made itself seen next to Marklain, a man who glowed a darker blue, but was only a few inches taller and at least a decade older. "The last one is Penn. He's quiet, a decent pilot, and a more than fair gunner. He'll follow Marklain's lead. He hasn't much liking for Edmonds, either."

Jack looked at her, incredulous. "Are you suggesting I run a three man crimp crew from here to Tortuga on a brig that needs twelve hands?"

"No. I am suggesting you run a crimp crew of two quasi-willing men. They're not navy men. They are in the captain's private employ."

He rolled onto his back and admired the view she was unwittingly presenting. "So, ye obviously have a plan?"

"Aye." She gracefully slid down off the rock and held her wrists out to him. "You hold me hostage."

His eyebrow went up. He hopped down and landed like a drunken cat, but rose fluidly, if a bit off-kilter. "Ye want me... to hold you... hostage," he echoed, walking around her in lazy circles. "That is a bit trusting of ye, luv." He came up from behind her, spoke close to her ear. "Fairly risky even."

"We have an accord," she reminded, not looking at him.

The timbre of his voice sent a shiver down her back. He rolled away with a grin she did not see. He had noticed the hairs on the back of her neck rise.

"Well, it's a lovely theory in all, but it lacks one vital element," he said with a mocking bow.

"And that is?" she asked, with a grin of her own.

"I have nothing with which to threaten you." He turned his back to her, and gestured to where the horse's tack had been abandoned. "Unless ye want I should chew th' leads off the horse's head thingy and wrap it around yer pretty throat as a garrotte."

"Would a knife do?" she asked, pulling a dagger from her boot.

He threw up his arms in exasperation. "A knife would be bloody perfect, but it's a bit moot considerin' we don't," he swung around and saw the knife flash in the sunlight, "...have one."

She stood stock still, in an almost military manner. He walked over and set his hand on hers, but did not take the knife, gazed hungrily at it. What he would have given for one of these the past four years.

She met his gaze evenly. His eyes were by far the most odd and strangely handsome thing about him. They were deep, with irises of a brilliant sky blue, rimmed impossibly by a band of dark, amber brown. They were reason enough for men to call him 'mad', for what normal man had eyes of blue *and* brown?

"This is a serious act of trust, darlin'," he said quietly. "Are ye sure ye don't want to rethink it? Last chance."

She gave him a sad smile. "You cannot hurt me, Captain Wyndlam."

"Oh, really? Invulnerable are we?" he teased.

"In a very real way, yes. It is amazing what adversity will do. Though it cannot take away your ability to feel pain, surviving enough of it can remove its power to affect you."

There was a seriousness in her eyes that chilled him to the bone for reasons he could not fathom. Unable to guarantee his reaction to it, he chose to take the knife and walk away. Very little disturbed him, but the dead cold in her eyes at that moment did.

She watched him walk over to where she had tossed the bridle and pick it up. She smiled as he used the knife to cut the reins off and brought them over.

He saw her grin and shrugged with one of his own. "It was still a good idea... though better on me teeth this way." He held up the makeshift leash, and twisted a quick slipknot into the end. "If ye'd be so kind, luv?"

She held her hands out, crossed at the wrist. He looped the end of the reins over her dirty hands then turned them palm upward before tightening the leather. Pulling off her hat, he set it between his teeth as he gathered her hair more tightly, twisting it in a knot before wedging the hat securely over it. He stepped back to inspect the whole package, frowned and buttoned up her coat. She stood frozen, causing him to chuckle as he did up the button over her breast, lingering a moment to be sure they weren't obvious.

"There, that's a bit better. We keep th' brim low an' no one'll be th' wiser until we have to reveal all our cards. Now," he added, moving close beside her and setting a hand on her collar, his forefinger stroking the pulse of her bare skin at her lovely throat and running his other down her sleeve to her bound hands. Once again the hairs rose on the back of her neck. "How much do ye trust me?" he purred, close in her ear.

She felt the heat of his breath on her cheek and could smell the papaya barely masking the reek of foul prison food and sour dockside beer. Even so she could not help the shiver that threatened. It was swiftly followed by a feeling that she had never felt under Price's hands. Not trusting her voice, she just nodded.

"All righty, then," he rumbled. He gently bent her arms up until they were within four inches of her throat, then looped the leather around her neck to measure, tying small knot before fastening a slipknot just below it. He gave the loose end a light tug, was satisfied when it tightened but stopped at the knot, eliminating the threat of strangling her for real. Standing behind her, he slid his hands suggestively down her arms then up to her wrists, his face pressed close to the side of hers and breathed deep of her natural fragrance. He held her hands, tipped them, spreading them gently apart.

"If it becomes necessary to slip th' binds, just cross yer wrists like this. That'll loosen things enough ye should be able to wriggle out," he advised.

She nodded and he tightened them again. He wrapped the loose end around his left hand and set it on her shoulder, then gestured down the rocky path with the knife in his other.

"Now, after you, my dear. Step ginger, though. Th' way be less than shipshape."

They worked their way down until they were just around the bend from the ship. They could hear the water lapping against the hull, and murmur of idle chatter just out of sight. Jack whispered in her ear.

"Feel free to scream if th' moment calls fer it. But turn yer head and mind me ears if ye be so kind."

"Trust me," she whispered back. "You don't want me to scream."

He did not get the chance to respond as they heard a chair move and one of the guards call his friend. "Mawkl'in, 'at wot I fink i'is?"

Boots trod over the planks. "Where?"

"Up'n th' ridge."

"That's... that's one of the captain's horses. You think he's come home or for the ship?"

"Dunno. Wha'sit mean when th' 'orse is naked... as it were?"

"It's got no tack? You sure about that, Penn?"

"Shore as yore standin' 'ere."

"Maybe we'd better go check. The captain might be hurt."

There was a flip of a card onto a table behind them and an authoritative voice cut them off. "Or he might be with his mistress. That is a nice little tryst point, and one of his fav'rites."

Beneath his hand, Sirene shuddered. Jack took note of the reaction with keen interest.

There was a moment's pause as they made up their minds what to do. "We'd might want to at least go half way, Penn. If we hear something then we know he's otherwise occupied and not lying there broken from being thrown."

"I guarantee you will regret it," came the snide voice.

"As do I, gentlemen," said Jack, as he stepped into view with the knife in his bandaged hand pressed uncomfortably close to the underside of Sirene's jaw.

Chapter the Fourth

Penn started to surge forward, but Marklain held him back with an arm.

"Don't do anything stupid," Jack warned. He pressed the knife tighter against her throat, causing her to stand on her tiptoes to avoid getting cut. A low whimper escaped her.

'Nice touch', Jack thought. He eased her back down so her feet were flat on the ground and took a step forward to mask the act, pressed her back tightly against him in the process. This time she yelped. He pressed slowly forward. "Now, gentlemen, if you would be so kind as to set down yer arms and back toward th' vessel, I'd be much obliged."

"To what end, sir?" asked Marklain, unbuckling his pistol.

"It is my intention to commandeer yon brig, and I need a temporary crew. Now step lively lads, lest something nasty happen," he snarled with a wicked grin.

The man at the table playing with a deck of cards had yet to move. He looked up, measured the situation, and decided to play it cool. "So you kill some farm boy unlucky enough to get snatched." He shrugged, turning another card. "It will just be one more crime on your list to be read at the gallows. What does his life matter to us?"

Penn glared at the other man, but said nothing. Marklain voiced objections for the both of them.

"A life is a life, Edmonds."

Edmonds slammed the deck down. "We are paid to protect the *Ambition* from theft and nature. *Not* to safeguard the local peasantry," he snarled.

"It's the only decent thing to do," Marklain insisted.

"Th' Christian fing," Penn added in a mutter.

"You want to save lives, then go join the navy. Me? I'm staying right here, as is that ship," he pointed, "until the captain calls for her and damned be to bloody hell any fool who says otherwise."

Penn started to move on Edmonds and found himself staring down the barrel of a pistol. "Don't be stupid, Penn. I'll shoot you just as readily as I'll shoot this pirate through whatever poor sot he's using for a shield."

As the gun began to swing in their direction Sirene bucked. She gave a low, guttural cry and slammed her head back against Jack. In the process of knocking her hat loose, she clipped his chin, and took a razor scrape along her cheek from the knife. She doubled over, dislodging her hat completely, releasing a cloud of silvery-blond hair. Jack bent and grabbed a fistful, pulled her back up to show her face to the guards.

They all reacted with recognition, but it was Marklain who exclaimed, "Miss Margaret!"

"Damn ye, girl," Jack snarled. "Ye went and spoilt my little surprise."

To play it safe, he pointed the knife downward over her heart. It was not as secure, but less risky should she try something like that again. Even Edmonds froze.

"Ah, I see I have something ye *do* care about, gentlemen. Is yer answer still th' same?" he asked, with a triumphant sneer. "Or are ye gonna play along now?"

Edmonds started to lower the pistol, then a thought occurred to him as he raked his eyes over her. In response, he cocked the pistol, taking aim at Jack's head. "Why, if she *is* your hostage, is she wearing men's clothing?"

Jack switched sides, still using Sirene as his shield, shifting his grip from her hair to the strap around her throat. "Because, dim wit, I *had* hoped to sneak her on board without anyone th' wiser that I were stealin' a woman. But things got a little complicated," he hissed. He gave her 'collar' a jerk to punctuate his point. "Someone had to give up the game. Now, if you gentlemen will climb on board, we'll be underway and it will all be over in a few days, weather willing. Then ye kin return home none th' worse fer...."

"I simply cannot allow you to steal the captain's ship," Edmonds insisted, though the muzzle of the pistol had lowered a full half-inch.

Jack snarled, shifting his position again. "I'm not *stealin'* th' damned thing. I'm *borrowin'* it. Ye can even bring 'er back to port yerself when I'm done with 'er. It's not like she's big enough fer my line of work. Maybe when she grows up," he grinned. The comment did not sit well with Edmonds and the pistol resumed its bead. "Make up yer mind, man. Which do ye think yer captain treasures more? His bonny wee boat, or his silvery lady?"

Edmonds hesitated. The other men watched him desperately.

"I am not a patient man, Mr. Edmonds," Jack warned, and bent Sirene back against his body so she couldn't fall, and shifted the point of the knife below her chin.

Sirene cried out. It began as a simple, feminine scream of pain or fear, but the pitch was uncomfortably high and rising, and Marklain jumped toward her, hands up, begging her not to scream.

"Miss Margaret, please. No! I beg you!"

Jack, uncertain what was going on, backed the knife off a hair and took a step away. His ears were ringing. His hand slipped up and over her mouth, silencing her.

"Please, sir pirate. Set her down. We'll do what ye want, just ...don't make her scream," Marklain pleaded.

Behind him, a scuffle ensued. Penn had jumped Edmonds and was wrestling him for the pistol. Jack jerked his head in the direction of the scuffle.

"Ye'd best end that in my favour, Mr. Marks, or things'll end badly here."

Marklain jumped to help, but Penn had already wrenched the pistol away and tossed it. Marklain picked it up and held it on Edmonds. "There's something just not right about you, Mr. Edmonds," he exclaimed. "Willingly endangering the captain's mistress for a few timbers and sailcloth?"

A new light went on in Jack's head as he absorbed that titbit. "Mr. Marks," he began, shifting Sirene so that she was on her own feet, leaning of her own will against him. He wrapped his arm around her waist, as it seemed she might faint, and shifted the knife to the hand holding her, pressing it flat against her belly. He held his bandaged hand out to Marklain. "Th' pistol, if ye would, mate."

He turned it around, grabbing it by the barrel, but hesitated to hand it over. Edmonds struggled in Penn's grasp, but Marklain ignored him.

"Please don't hurt her, sir. She's a right sweet woman. Take me for hostage instead and leave her here. Penn and I'll sail you wherever you want to go."

Jack sighed. "That's mighty kind of ye, but I fear she's a tad more valuable than you. Th' pistol?" Still he wavered. Jack was losing patience. "I assure ye, man, that if it comes to th' worst, th' pistol would be a swifter, kinder end than my knife. Especially if it should open her belly."

Edmonds shouted unintelligibly as Marklain closed his eyes

and passed the butt into Jack's waiting grasp. "May God forgive me," he prayed.

"I'm sure he will," Jack answered, and shifted Sirene to put the dagger into his belt, holding the pistol near her head. "Now," he said, straightening. "Mr. Marks."

"Marklain, sir," he corrected politely.

Jack nodded. "Marklain then. I think my first order shall be for ye to find something with which to restrain th' wicked and heartless Mr. Edmonds."

Marklain nodded and trotted onto the ship. Jack led Sirene to an empty chair and sat her in it. He sauntered to where Penn stood over the kneeling Edmonds. Penn's arms were tucked under his, and his hands were locked behind Edmonds' neck.

Jack looked over the contents of the table, at the order of the cards, then began to inspect the troublemaker Sirene had warned him of. He saw something sticking out of the man's sleeve where they waved ineffectually above his head. Jack grabbed his wrist with a grin and pulled a card out of the sleeve.

"Cheatin'? At solitaire, no less? Tsk tsk. Yer truly a dishonest man. I wonder what else ye've been stuffing up yer dirty little sleeves."

Edmonds struggled and snarled, flailing his arms back at his captor. "Now's your chance, you idiot. Jump *him* not me!"

Jack chuckled, turned the last chair around backwards and straddled it. As he crossed his arms over its back and leaned forward on them, he made sure the muzzle of the pistol was pointed in Sirene's direction and that the arm was free to change targets if need be.

"I don't think he will. Ye see, unlike you, Mr. Penn... it is Penn, isn't it?" he asked. Penn merely nodded. "Mr. Penn is a smart man. You... yer a selfish man. He knows I could, at anytime, simply shoot th' lady. If, say, he were to have taken yer advice," he said civilly, pausing to pick something out of his teeth, "and attempted to jump me, I would have swiftly shot him and stabbed you. And whilst this would mean Miss Margaret over there would be safe, she would have to work twice as hard, as would Mr. Marklain, to get me where I'm goin'. And ye wouldn't want to see that delicate flower of womanhood hauling capstan lines, now would ye? Oh, right, of course. Ye wouldn't care a whit. And not just because ye'd be dead."

Marklain returned with a length of heavy rope.

"Ah, just in time." He frowned, as he looked from rope to ship to the stout man. "That wouldn't happen to be something we'll be needin' on our voyage now is it, Mr. Marklain?" He frowned, twitching one side of his sparse moustache and managed to stare imperiously down his nose at the taller man.

"No, sir. This was a bit of extra. What it was cut from was replaced months ago. I just never got around to splicing it in."

"Hmm, very well then. Tie 'im up. And see that it'll be a while afore he can manage to wriggle his way out of it."

He watched the process with a lopsided grin of approval as the two men were less than gentle with their chore. He also noticed that Penn left most of the tying to his friend. When they were done, he inspected the knots to make sure they would hold and was surprised to note they had used knots that would hold in the roughest weather. Poor Mr. Edmonds was going to have to be cut loose. With a swagger, he crossed to Sirene and picked up the end of her leash.

"Come along, Miss Maargaret," he drawled, as he gave the line a tug. "There's a good girl. Mr. Penn, be so kind as to fetch th' lady's hat on yer way aboard. Mr. Marklain, I'll be takin' yer pistol belt and ye'll be leadin' th' way."

He handed over the belt without a fuss, which Jack looped over his shoulder, and walked onto the gangplank followed closely by the pirate and his hostage. Penn trotted behind, pausing to undo the mooring before leaping aboard.

Once on deck, Jack took Sirene to the quarterdeck, lifted her up the stairs, and set her by the wheel before he let go of her leash. Tucking the pistol into his sash, he took hold of the helm. He began giving orders and the two men scrambled to drop the sails necessary to leave the small harbour.

Sirene sank gratefully to the deck and leaned her forehead against the rail attempting to regain her strength. Jack kept half an eye on her and half on his shanghaied crew. As they began to pull away from the dock, he couldn't help himself and jumped to the rear railing to wave to shore.

"Do give my regards to yer master, Mr. Edmonds. Be sure to tell him that Handsome Jack came to call and thanks him for the use of his pretty little coracle, ...*and* his lovely mistress."

He laughed as Edmonds jumped up and down in his chair, cursing foully as he tipped over in his impotent rage. Jack gave him a saucy salute and hopped to the deck. As he turned back to the wheel, he scowled to see Marklain bent over Sirene.

The man jumped when a dagger embedded itself into the deck beside him, a hand's breadth from Sirene's knee. "I was making sure she was alright, sir...Captain," he choked. "She seemed..."

The scowl on Jack's face silenced him. Sirene watched in amazement at the presence the small man commanded when he wanted. Of course, her current point of view could be skewing her impression.

Jack was silent for a few seconds more.

"Mr. Marklain. Release th' lady and help her to th' lower deck. Ye both kin earn yer keep."

"You want *her* to help with the rigging? But sir..."

"That's *captain* sir, Mister," he roared. "And bear in mind, I'll shoot at th' first sign o' mutiny from any one o' ye. Once we've put in at a useful port, everyone can go their merry way and none to harm. We've few enough hands at th' moment and I need them all, savvy?"

"Aye, Captain. Though I still think the lady'll be of no use. She'll only get in the way," he mumbled as he cut the reins from her wrists and loosened the loop around her neck.

Sirene set her hand on his arm before he could note the fail-safe. "It's all right, Mr. Marklain. The captain is right. We need all hands... even his," she added, glaring at him over her shoulder. "I may not know the ropes, but I can be of other help. Just tell me what to do," she said, slipping the rein over her head.

He helped her to her feet and, still grumbling about it 'not being right,' led her down to the main deck and set her to work helping drop the rest of the sails.

Jack grinned, most pleased with himself. He was on a real deck again with the wind at his back and the horizon open before him. The broad ocean beckoned to him like the open arms of an eager lover and he was not going to disappoint. He spun the wheel with intense joy, bringing the ship full around and aiming her prow to the open water.

Sirene paused from fighting with a stubborn knot she had no idea how to undo. Her hair continued to whip into her face, though she tried to capture it beneath her hat. She sighed, closed her eyes and drank in the salt air and the heaving waters, then exhaled slowly to calm her frustration. A deep, almost painful longing washed over her, leaving her as cold as if struck by a re-ceding wave and left standing in the wind. She opened her eyes, found herself looking up at the bridge deck where the captain stood, feet spread and rock-steady, hands to the wheel, surveying the ship and the sea like an ancient pirate god.

His head was thrown back drinking in the wet, briny air, and the wind spread his hair before him. However, it did not seem to be bothering him as hers was. The sunlight gleamed off the brown locks, flashing coppery in places and gold in others. His clothes were old and looked like a shipwreck, as did the faded yellow sash that waved from his hips, but the body beneath them was lean and wiry and permanently tanned from years at sea. She knew that from the few times she had been up close and per-sonal with it.

There was no sign of scurvy or other seafarer's diseases, and his teeth were remarkably good. His face was timelessly young. He could easily be mistaken for mid-twenty when rumour alone dated him more than thirty. His beard was short and sparse, lying close against his chin along his jaw and, as she remembered, was soft enough he must never have shaved a day in his life. Gone was the rolling gait of the drunkard, replaced by a perfect ease with the pitch and swell, and a confidence that was undeniable. Somehow, she did not find it arrogant, as she did on Price. On Jack it was absolute freedom.

She was distracted by Penn's approach. He bobbed his head and asked with a gesture if he could be permitted to help her. She nodded, grateful. He showed her which end to pull to release the knot with minimum effort. He kept his head bent to his work, showing her the next thing that needed to be done, but questioned her in a low voice.

"Ye's all roight, Miss?"

She realized that her eyes were tearing, and she hurriedly wiped them on her sleeve, nodding as she answered. "I am fine, thank you, Penn. It's the wind. It keeps whipping my hair into my eyes."

He nodded, but there was a look of disbelief on his face. "'e 'an't... 'urt ye, 'as 'e? 'r oferwise..."

She cut him off with a choked laugh. "No, he hasn't."

"No doubt is on 'e mind, though," he mumbled. "Way 'e looks at ye."

She helped him haul on a line to bring up the main staysail. "I confuse him," she explained.

He gave a snort. "Don' all women any man?" he muttered. "Try t' stay out o' 'is attention, Miss. We'll do as 'e say so long's 'e don't lay an 'and t' ye. Not be standin' by 'at."

He might have said more, but the captain walked by, dancing across the deck as he dodged ropes and swinging booms, having the time of his life. Penn moved to drop the top gallant sails, but the Captain's voice stopped him.

"Avast, Mr. Penn." They looked up to see him balanced with one foot on the gunwale and one hand on the ratlines. "We'll run on the mains and the tops at best fer speed, but should we run up a squall, the gallants'll be too much for four hands to furl in time. Leave 'er as she is."

"Aye, sir," he responded curtly, and promptly retied the line.

"I'll thank ye t' man yer post, pilot," he added. "There's shoals and reefs afore open water and ye'll be knowin' 'em better than I. I'll see t' th' lass's education."

Penn ground his teeth, but nodded and headed to the bridge. Jack jumped to the deck, enjoying himself. As he crossed the planks toward her, he noticed a shift in the ship and the wind, and looked up into the sails. A great rippling ran across the canvas as they began to spill.

"Smartly, Mr. Penn. I like me sails full!" he shouted, jumping into action. "Mr. Marklain, brace that mains'l!" He pointed Sirene to a line not far from her. "Third pin larboard there. Unhitch the line and pull 'er back 'til th' sail fills!" he ordered, running farther ahead of her to grab the line on the topsail.

Sirene fumbled with the line, but managed to unhitch it in a reasonable amount of time. She hauled back on it as hard as she could, drawing the boom around to catch the changing wind. It was a fight, but she slowly began winning it. She was just reaching for the belaying pin to wind her down when Penn bellowed a warning.

"Comin' about, larb'ard!"

She had no time to ask what that meant before the rope she had hold of went slack, sending her tumbling toward the deck. She never landed as the wind caught the sail in the last second and flung her up the deck into the captain's arms. He stared down into her ice-blue eyes and chuckled.

"Just can't resist me, can ye, luv?" he teased, wrapping an arm around her back and ducking the both of them in time to avoid the swinging boom.

Jack reached out and deftly snagged the line with his other hand. He braced his foot against a raised hatch to keep it from tossing him as well and grinned down at her, as she had yet to let go. His smile faded instantly. Her eyes were glassy and her lips, parted in a gasp, were whiter than her hair. There was blood on his shirt where she grabbed it, and the hand on her back felt a cold dampness under her coat. Just as he noticed there was no sweat on her brow, her eyes rolled back, her hand lost its hold and she began to slip to the deck.

Jack held her tighter, bracing her with his knee to keep her from falling, and bellowed for Marklain. He strained against the pull of the wind until he saw the man from the corner of his eye and tossed him the rope. Mr. Marklain had no choice but to stop to tie it to the belaying pin.

The moment his hand was free, Jack grabbed Sirene and lowered her gently to the deck. He made sure she was breathing, however shallowly, and that her heart beat evenly, if a little weak. He ran his hands inside her coat and up her back to make sure she was not wearing some binding he hadn't noticed before that might have caused the faint. Her back was bare but for the shirt, and drenched with a cold sweat. He pulled his hand out, gently brushed a lock of hair from her brow ...and gaped in horror at the red streak his middle finger left behind.

"What the devil," he began, turning his hand over. The palm was painted in a thin layer of red. "Bloody hell?"

Jack leaned her limp body against his chest and began to strip off the dull brown coat. Her shirt was plastered to her back, stiff here and there with dry blood and very wet most everywhere else. There were even places along the back of her sleeves that were dotted red. He looked up to see Marklain standing near, staring down at her in blank shock.

Jack swept her up and over his shoulder with deceptive ease and stood, paused to issue orders.

"Snap to, Mr. Marklain! I shall need water, cleaning cloths, and possibly bandages."

Marklain stirred, shaking his head. "Aye, Captain," he answered numbly, and scurried forward to acquire them.

Jack made a beeline for the aft cabins. "Mr. Penn, you have the helm for now. Think you can handle it for a while?"

"Aye, sir!"

"Very well then. Ring the ship's bell if you need a hand. I shall be below."

"Whot be th' bearin', sir?" he asked just before the captain disappeared from his field of vision.

"Guadeloupe," he answered, and vanished below.

Chapter the Fifth

Finding the captain's cabin was not difficult. It was the centre door in the aft housing and clearly labelled. The luxury of the room was almost criminal and easily took up two-thirds the width of the ship. The other cabin would be painfully small. There was a curtained, four-poster bed set for the best view out the massive stern windows. The glass in them was expensive, nearly flawless. There were cabinets with glass and bright-work doors, and a mahogany wardrobe, as well as a large sea chest.

He carried her to the bed and sat her on the edge of it, carefully working the shirt off of her. He winced whenever he had to pry the fabric loose from spots of dried blood. He ignored the snow-white mounds of her bare breasts and eased her down, laying her on her stomach. Marklain came in with the medical supplies as he was trying to get her hair off her would.

Marklain set the bucket and cloths at the captain's feet. He handed the captain a small bottle of whiskey. "For inflammation," he said weakly, pointedly not looking at the figure on the bed.

Jack noted his reaction and paleness of face, and accepted the bottle. "Thank you, Mr. Marklain. Return atop and help Mr. Penn."

Marklain left swiftly and gratefully. Jack set the bottle on the bedside table and began to gently wash Sirene's back. As the nature of her injuries became known, he began to grind his teeth.

Sirene woke to the tender ministrations of Jack's hands. She kept her eyes closed and tried to relax. She knew she should not have done as much as she had today, but there had been no help for it if she wanted to escape. It had been mostly all right even on the horse ride, but the deckhand activity had reopened the worst of her wounds. Even though her entire back was on, fire she could feel his touch on every single stripe. She became aware that he was cursing under his breath in one of the island languages, one she was only cursorily familiar with, as he followed the wickedly thin lines on her lower back to where they disappeared into her trousers. As he hesitated to figure out a way to get them off without hurting her further, she spoke.

"Just cut them off." Her voice was low and husky.

He looked to see those eyes the colour of an English sky looking back at him weakly. "Then what will ye be wearin'? I can't have ye paradin' around deck half-naked. That Marklain is already gettin' a bit peculiar with just ye bare back. I swear that man'd blush if he saw yer ankles, let alone naked thigh."

She started to chuckle and then stifled a sob of pain. "I have clothes... in the chest," she breathed.

Before Jack could move, he heard the door open and the cocking of a pistol. He saw Sirene's lips move to form Penn's name as she glanced behind him to the door.

"Mr. Penn, I sincerely hope yer not lettin' us run aground on some shoal while ye stand there threatenin' me like a fool. Ye've only one shot. And if I move, ye *will* hit th' lady."

"Ye do 'at to 'er?" he growled, through his teeth.

The look that crossed Jack's face explained the reason he was called 'Mad Jack'. He slowly turned his head, and affixed one blue-brown eye on the older Penn. There was danger in those unpredictable orbs.

The pistol never wavered. "I ask ag'in, sir. Ye do 'at t' Miss Marg'ret?"

Sirene waved to Penn to put the pistol down. She lifted her head from the mattress. "No," she said hoarsely. The barrel wavered. "Captain... Ambrose... Price."

All colour left his face. He shook his head in disbelief. "Naw... can't be. Th' capt'n wouldn' do this to ye."

"Believe me," she whispered. "It's not... the first time."

He hesitated a full three seconds before he lowered his arm and spun the pistol in his hand, held it out butt first. "Sorry, Capt'n. I stan' ready," he said stiffly.

Without hurry, Jack crossed and took the pistol. He stared up at the sailor for a long moment, taking in every wind-whipped crevice and grizzled grey hair. Then he set his hand on the man's shoulder, and spoke confidentially.

"Yer a good man and a fair decent sailor. I need every hand, including hers and I'm now short that. I may be mad, but I ain't no fool. I'll not be punishin' a man fer decency. I respect loyalty, sir. Just don't let it make ye stupid."

"Penn," she wheezed, gesturing for him to come nearer. He waited until the captain nodded before crossing to the bed and kneeling beside her. She set her hand on his. "Jack didn't... kidnap me; he saved my life. I ran away. You and Marklain can go back if you want... weave whatever story you please. But I beg you... help us. I would have asked you outright, but..."

"Edmonds," he said, nodding.

"And this way... you aren't exactly lying."

He grinned, showing poor, but clean teeth. "No' *exactly*. I'll inform Mr. Mawkl'in at once. We'll get ye to Guadeloupe safely, Miss Mar..."

She squeezed his hand, and gave a tiny shake of her head. "It's Sirene. Margaret is what Price named me. I'll not use it again."

"Aye, Miss Sirene," her corrected quickly. "Can I get ye's anyfin'?"

She nodded. "Seawater."

He bobbed his head and stood to go. "Cap'n," he said, with a nod in his direction.

Jack held him back. "Seawater?"

"Aye, Cap'n. Burns loik 'ell, but she's good fer burnin' out impurities; bettern 'at rot-gut whot's on th' table. Might want ta consider some fer yer 'and, sir."

Jack dismissed him and returned to the bedside. He crossed his arms and glared down at her. "Risky that, tellin' 'im th' truth."

She seemed unconcerned. "It was time. I can trust him."

"That were still some'at we should've agreed upon. *I* am captain, my word is law on shipboard," he growled.

She laughed softly. "Hear me roar," she mocked gently. He scowled. "We are partners in this, Captain Wyndlam. I am not part of the crew. Though, as soon as I can get up from here, I will gladly go back on deck and help as I can."

"That'll be some time, judging from that mess," he sneered, nodding at her injuries. "Why th' bloody blue blazes did ye allow me to bully ye into all that work, knowing ye were injured?"

"Because it needed to be done," she shrugged, wincing as she did.

He roared in exasperation, throwing up his hands and pacing around the cabin. The woman was infuriating; her logic, infallible. She was right, but that didn't make it *right*. Here he thought he was going to get even with her for blackmailing him into their accord, and she goes and turns it back on him, making him feel a worse cad than the man who did this to her. His internal rant was interrupted by Penn's return with a bucket of seawater. The sailor set the pail down and left. Jack brought the water to the bed, and pulled out the knife.

"Now, ye might wish ta hold still," he said, as he began to cut the trousers off her body as gently as he could.

He was surprised to discover she was not wearing anything under them that ladies normally wore. He blamed it on the marks that crossed down her back from shoulders to ankles. Though the heaviest and deepest were across the blades of her back and her hips and thighs. He went to work cleaning the wounds of dried blood with the fresh water, applying pressure only where he had to in order to stop the bleeding he had caused by peeling the fabric off.

"Shame," he mused, as he worked. "Such a nice arse, too."

When she chuckled, he frowned, not realizing he had spoken out loud. He looked over to see her regarding him with a weak smile. He bent back to work.

"So, ye want to tell me what kind of a man whips his mistress, and why?" he asked, with a calm that surprised even him.

She flinched under his hands, and he apologized. She took a long, deep breath.

"I *did* promise you a story."

"That you did, Miss," he agreed as he worked.

"My mother fell in love with a fisherman. She lived with him off the Carolina coast for a great many years. When I was born, she had to leave him. They were agreeable to the parting and mother took me home with her. After I grew up, I had a longing to see my father and mother agreed, telling me where to find him and gave me the means with which to go to him."

He frowned. She was being deliberately vague and it annoyed him. He let her continue for the moment.

"I found him, still fishing off the same islands in the Carolinas as when Mother met him. He was old by then, had a family: a wife and a son who was a sailor. She was told I was the child of his first wife, which was partly true, and took well to me, having always wanted a daughter. I lived happily enough with them for a couple years until she died. Then my half-brother Marcus came home. He and my father fought a great deal, mostly over money and careers. Before father died, he told Marcus the truth about me and my mother. He asked me to make sure he stayed under fair winds as best I could. Marcus," she paused, not sure what she felt about him any more, "was on the account, as they say. A pirate."

"What ship?" he asked, interested.

"The *Bloody Horizon*."

He nodded with appreciation. "Under Captain Halloway. I always like th' cut of her. She used to be th' fastest in th' Caribbean until yer fiendish Captain Price snuck up on her and sank her."

"Aye, but not before he captured most of the crew and hung them on their own yardarms. Not one for prison sentences, is Price. My brother, however, weaselled out of things by promising the captain a valuable treasure if he'd spare his life."

"An' that treasure, I take it, was you?" he asked, dropping the bloody rags into the bucket and sat back to listen. He was very much not pleased.

"Aye. He told the captain my secret. Gave me to him as hostage against his life. Or at least that was the story I was told."

"And what might that secret be, lass?"

She studied his face a moment before she answered. "First, dip a rag in the seawater and wash my wounds; each and every cut. Then I will explain."

He hesitated. "Are ye sure ye want this, luv? I've seen grown men withstand a dance with th' gunner's daughter without a cry only to faint dead away when seawater's thrown on."

She gave him a weak grin. "Afraid I'll faint and not tell you the rest of the story?"

He snarled. "Have it yer way, lass."

He snatched up a clean cloth in his injured hand and dipped it into the salt bucket. He grit his teeth and ignored the stinging across his knuckles and slopped the water across her back. She gave a tiny gasp, then relaxed, rubbing her cheek against the bedspread as if it were warm, soothing water rather than cold salt he was bathing her with. He frowned, but dutifully finished the job, down to the smallest scratch on the back of her arm and the nick at the top of her left ankle.

"Ye were sayin'?" he asked, tossing the rag into the remaining water.

She gave a catlike moan and stretched. She reached up and grabbed a pillow, hugging it in her arms as she lay her head upon it. "My secret is... that my mother is a mermaid, ...and so am I."

His moustache twitched. He raked his eyes down the length of her glorious, naked body with a raised eyebrow. "Ye expect me to believe those milky white legs ar' th' tail of a mermaid?"

She smiled. "It is not necessary that you believe me. Only that you complete our accord and get me my pearl. You see, it was my mother's, and she gave it to me. It is what allows me to walk on land. Without it, I am stuck in whatever form I was in when it was removed."

"Fascinating," he muttered, and dragged over a chair. "Wholly unbelievable, but fascinating. And they call *me* mad. But, fergive me... do continue."

She gave a chuckle. "Take a look at my back, mon capitane," she purred. "There are some things which thankfully do not depend upon my form to work."

He glanced at her back, and nearly missed the chair as he tried to sit. He forgot about the seat and reached out, touched where the worst of her stripes had been and now were only half as deep. The lightest of the marks were gone completely. Even the knife scrape on her face was healed. He ran his finger over her cheek.

"I'm sorry about that, by the way."

"Wholly my fault. Forget it. As you can see, the sea is my life. For you, she is a mistress; for me, a mother. I was born in her embrace and I hope to die there. She heals me. But that is about all without my pearl."

He straddled the chair, taking it all in. "So this pearl that Fenning stole... this what gives ye yer tail?"

"It is what takes it away, and returns it," she corrected.

"Does it... work on others? Or just yer kind?"

She frowned at him. "That's the same question my brother asked when he found out about it. I don't know. It's never been tried."

Jack crossed his arms, thinking rapidly. "It would explain how ye'll get me th' *Salvador*. So, how did Price abuse th' knowledge?"

"He didn't at first. He took me in, explained, in front of my brother, that I was a hostage against his life and would be living with him. I was dressed, most uncomfortably, I might add, educated, both in book learning and etiquette, how to behave like a 'lady of quality'. I was already learning everything I could about life on land, though I was loathe to go anywhere I could not see the ocean." She curled up around the pillow, crossing one leg over it to shield her snow white modesty. "For the first few years he let me wear the pearl and go swimming when I chose, though always under his careful watch. Usually in that harbour, or while he was on the *Ambition's Price*. So long as I kept him pleased, he left my brother alone.

"After a while, he began to see how he could use me to further his career, which was going nowhere. At the time he made the bargain with Marcus he was captain only by field promotion, as the real captain was deathly ill when they took the *Bloody Horizon*. He remained a lower officer for the longest time and felt he wasn't moving up fast enough. He used me to discover things he couldn't learn otherwise and to keep him abreast of matters on the sea."

His eyebrow went up in question. "How?"

She gave a laugh. "Well, for one thing, I speak at least a dozen languages."

Jack whistled. "That's a lot fer a girl yer age."

She blushed. "I'm actually closer to fifty than twenty." He gaped. "The Mother is kind to her favourite daughters."

"So ye'll be seventeen ferever?"

"No, I'll age. Just slowly."

He shook his head in disbelief. "What languages d'ye know, out a' curiosity?"

She ticked them off on her fingers. "French, English, Spanish, Malagasy, Jamaican, Polynesian, Portuguese, a little Dutch, Dolphin, whale (of which there are four major dialects), shark (though that's largely a waste of time), and various of the fish body languages." She laughed at his reaction. "Let's just say I was damned useful and got him his captaincy." He raised an eyebrow at her use of language. "It was not long after that that he began to abuse his privilege with me. He bullied me into submission the first time, using my brother's life and my promise to my father to take my maidenhead. It... just escalated from there," she finished, her voice trailing off.

She shook her melancholy off and continued. "Needless to say the bastard became accustomed to abusing me, treating me more like one of his slaves than a valuable hostage. Things became much worse five years ago, when he started to send me to seduce people he needed things from. Including the governor of Jamaica, whom he barged in on in an outrage whilst we were... in the throes... and blackmailed him mercilessly for 'corrupting his ward'. That is how he got his current command. Something went wrong near the end of last year, though, and we had to leave. He claimed he was transferred. Our things were shipped after us, including the pearl, which was locked in with his possessions. It was that ship which Fenning attacked, and why I am hunting him for the return of my pearl."

"I can see why yer hot to have it, if it does what ye say. An' why ye'd have a serious hate on fer yer captor. But why'd ye choose that night t' leave him?"

She sat up, curling the pillow strategically before her. "I found out that he hung my brother for piracy... five years ago."

He gave a sucking whistle through his teeth. "Were I you, I'd've slain him in his bed afore fleein'."

"I didn't want to sleep with the Vice-Admiral. Which was where I was, in the process of securing the captain's promotion, when I found out about Marcus and lost my head. I just ran. I was looking to stow away on one of those ships when someone knocked me into the harbour."

He shifted uncomfortably in his seat. "So, why can't ye swim? Human or no?"

"That is the drawback of the human form," she said, ruefully. "Though I *can* swim, I cannot breathe water with human lungs. I was drowning because of the forty pounds of brocade and wool I was sewn into. When I am naked or in lighter clothes I can swim as well as any, better even."

He stared hard at her, not quite sure how much of what she was telling him to believe. Behind her the sun was setting, changing the water into a sea of flames and bathing her in a russet-pink glow that gave her an unworldly appearance. He forced himself to think about something other than the naked body on the bed before him.

"So what happened to ye between my arrest and yer daring jailbreak? Why'd he do that to ye?"

She lowered her head, fiddled with her fingers on the pillow, concentrated on pulling out the little feather bits that were sticking out of the fabric. "I confronted him about Marcus. I clawed his face, told him that I had run away and called him a few things I shouldn't have while still in his power. I... I just couldn't stomach bowing to him again, submitting to his... touch another minute. He quickly put me in my place. Told me that I was never a hostage, I had always been a slave. That he was willing to treat me like his mistress so long as I behaved like it and when I still defied him..."

Jack swallowed his rage, swearing he would kill the man if he ever had the chance to cross swords with him. "Tell me about th' escape. How 'd ye get away from him?"

She took a deep breath and pushed the whipping out of her mind. "It pleased him to have his way with me afterwards, as he always does. He left me on the bed and weak early that morning to tend to naval matters, that pirated ship I mentioned. I slipped out of bed, went to a stash of salt water I kept behind the wardrobe, and sprinkled what little remained of it on my back to give me some strength. Then I stole some of his clothes, slipped into the laundry and borrowed a jacket and hat from one of the servants, took a horse and went to the jail." She shrugged up at him. "Nothing miraculous."

"The keys?"

She gave a chuckle. "There was a drunken argument out in front of the jail that amused and distracted the guards. They didn't see me slip past and lift the keys."

He scratched his chin thoughtfully. There were still some things he wanted to know. "Why me? Ye never saw my face. Why not just follow through with yer previous plan and stow away?"

"One, the ship I intended to stow away on sailed an hour after the incident on the dock, not to mention, was the ship that had been attacked by pirates. And two, there were no other ships available that wouldn't have sent me right back again the moment they found me. Too many people are in Price's debt."

"Ye didn't answer the first question," he countered.

She lowered her head. "There is another gift I have that made me invaluable to him," she said mysteriously, looked up through her lashes. "In the deep depths, visibility is next to nothing ...in those places where there is no light. So we call upon inner lights to guide our way: the soul of that which is before us. They shine to our eyes in terms of colours and hues and shades of bright and dark, deep and light, and tell us what manner of danger lies before us. With the fish and the reefs, it is a simpler thing, but with men.... Oh, you are complicated beings. More so than the most grand and complex reef I have ever explored."

She rose, set the pillow aside, and slowly crossed the five feet between them. The light was fully behind her, casting her in a haloed silhouette that obscured the details of her nakedness, but he could smell her; the salt and the sea, and the sweat of the horse and her own blood. He sat stock still, looking up at her as she approached, afraid to move lest his will to resist seizing her escape him. She bent slightly, her silvery hair brushing the tops of his hands where they were crossed on the back of the chair.

"You, my noble young porpoise," she breathed, "shine to me. I saw you when you rescued me. You glowed: a soft, brilliant gold. When you faced me in the jail I *knew* it was you. And I knew you were a man I could trust once I had your word to help me. Once I had your name from Price I knew you had the savvy and the sheer will to accomplish the task at hand. No other would have done. And you were *a good man.*"

He swallowed, clenched his teeth and flexed his injured hand. "Madam mermaid, if ye don't stand down and back away or at th' very least wrap yerself... I shall be forced to kiss you."

She laughed softly. "And what is wrong with that?"

"I am afraid I shan't be able to stop," he confessed.

Damn the woman! He had never resorted to rape, nor needed to, but that was exactly what she was about to drive him to if she did not cease to tempt him. He could not believe how quickly she inflamed him. She moved alongside the chair, ran her fingers along his arm from the tips of his fingers to his shoulder. Standing beside him, the dying light was finally able to reveal her luscious details.

"Damn it! I don't want to force ye, Sirene," he growled, grinding his fists in an effort to control himself.

"So don't," she whispered, drawing aside the curtain of his sun-streaked locks, running her finger down his bare cheek to the fine, downy beard at his jawline. He grabbed her hand; turned to look at her, giving her one last warning. He was already breathing heavily.

"I would like to know the touch of a man I *want* to be with; a man of *my* choosing," she insisted. She took his hand in her other, pried it loose and drew it toward her, opened it and touched it to her breast. "I want to know a good man, as my mother knew a good man. To be possessed by a man who understands that a possession is only what the sea lets you keep. I want you to teach me what it is supposed to be like between a man and a woman."

He felt himself melting as the heat from his hand transferred to her breast, warming her chill body. His own began to react painfully. He jerked his hand back, knocking over the chair as he hastened to escape, began pacing the far side of the room. In his frustrated rage, he grabbed a small chest from a table and threw it across the cabin, scattering ropes of pearls and a few pieces of men's jewellery.

She pulled back, startled by the violence of his rejection. She suppressed a shiver and turned away, pulling the spread from the bed, and wrapping it around her. Trying to swallow the lump in her throat, she crossed to the ancient sea chest at the foot of the bed, and sifted through its contents.

Jack heard the rattle of chain, and spun, saw her kneeling at the chest, placing a set of irons on the floor beside her. 'Gods, what is she thinking?' he thought. He crossed to her.

"No, luv, I..." he said, as she looked up, a pale blue dress in her hands. "Oh, I..."

She set the dress beside her on the floor and turned back to the chest, took out a simple white shift. The look in her eyes was as good as a slap in the face, though there was no anger or malice in her expression, only hurt. He took her by the arms gently, drew her to her feet, and turned her to face him.

"Sirene," he began, then stopped to reset the blanket on her shoulders. He paused to steel his will before looking her in the eye again. When he did there were unshed tears in their silvery depths. "Listen, luv. It's not tha' I don't want. Hell, it's been four long years since I've *seen* a woman much less... well, th' chief's sister don' count 'cause I weren't... sane per se. She said it were fer healin' an' power... an' ...an' other hoodoo nonsense. But... it would be unconscionably remiss o' me t' be down here enjoyin' th' company of a beautiful, *injured* woman, an' leave all th' work t' them two, handy though they might be," he explained, gesturing to the decks above.

Her mouth fell open, shocked by her own thoughtlessness. The tears she had held back so intently began to fall. She took a step back.

"Forgive me," she breathed. "I... I wasn't thinking."

He stepped closer, knowing it was perhaps not the wisest thing he'd ever done. "Luv, th' moment we have a crew o' even half decent size, I'll take ye up on them lessons. Until then, I beg ye not t' tempt me." He tipped her chin up to look at him. "Though, if ye are what ye say ye are it's what ye do." He flashed her a lopsided grin when she gave a choked laugh. "Now, slip inta somethin' and get t' bed. I'm goin' up top ta relieve one o' those two an' stagger watch," he said, turning away. "Though it'll take much longer now that we're only running half sail."

She clutched the shift to her chest and watched him cross the rolling deck with catlike ease, as if it were lying still. His clothes had seen better days, but he glowed through them like a golden firefly, only a little tarnished in places.

"*Mon Capitane?*" she offered.

He turned. "*Oui, Madame Sirène?*" he answered in the same tongue.

She gestured to the wardrobe. "Why don't you at least get one of Price's shirts? I'd offer his breeches, too, but they would not fit you."

He could barely see her white arm gesturing to the starboard wall in the growing dark. "I..." He looked down at his tatters, took a sniff of the sleeve and made a face. "Why not? I've helped meself to th' rest o' his things already. Though ye might want t' light th' lamp."

She moved to find it as he crossed to the opposite side of the room. She heard the wardrobe doors open as she struck the match. Once it was lit, she paused to throw the shift over her head and settle it about her body. It was one of her favourites; flared nicely from her rounded hips and flowed outward toward the floor, but never quite made it. It fell short somewhere around mid shin. It was scandalous, but that was part of why she loved it. She carried the lamp over to him, hanging it on the hook, and helped him fish through the wardrobe.

Ambrose's shirt was more than a little big on him, but with a pair of cuff-links to pin the sleeves closed and a broad belt she found, it made do nicely. She smiled as she knelt to fasten the wide leather strap around his hips, giving a tug to the hem of the shirt. He saw her wry little smile and grinned.

"I said later, luv." She blushed and moved quickly back to the dresser, which was what he wanted. "I'll say this for yer bonny captain..."

"CapTOR," she corrected.

He made a rather effeminate, dismissive gesture with his hand, watching the lace flop limply as he did. "-Tain, -tor, whatever. I'll say this for him: he has nice clothes."

He frowned at the cuffs, trying to get the lace to not block his manual dexterity. Finally, he pulled the knife and cut the lace off, using his teeth to hold it while he sliced. He looked up to find her laughing at him with those silvery blue eyes, holding a heavy coat.

"It may be all well and good fer hidin' th' filchin' o' small bits and bobs while in port, luv, but it ain't suited fer climbin' rat-lines."

"I did not say a thing," she protested, trying to suppress the smile.

"Didn' have ta," he snarled, with the lace in his teeth. "Wha's 'at?" he asked.

"A coat. It's getting cold out."

He stowed the knife and spat the lace aside. "Turnin' inta me mother now?"

She grinned, as she helped him in it. "I'm old enough, to be sure."

"It's goin' to swallow me," he frowned, changing the subject. "Yer blighter's near six feet and built like a bull."

"Bull shark, maybe," she snorted, as she folded back the cuffs.

He raised an eyebrow, but let her dress him. "Am I yar?" he asked mockingly, when she was done.

She sighed. "You'll do. You'll not be wantin' a hat, I suppose?"

"Not one o' his," he sneered, sweeping from the room. "But yers'll do nice." He set hers on his head and turned in the doorway. "Rest yer fins, lass," he teased. "We'll be in Guadeloupe in two days, wind willin'."

She stared at the closed door a moment before turning her gaze out the stern windows to the cold black ocean. She sighed and crossed to the great windows. Opening one of them, she perched on the bench seat, and leaned back against the wall. The salt spray barely reached her here, but she could see the roaring wake of the ship and hear the wind in the sails above. From time to time the captain's voice drifted down to her, filling her with odd emotions.

She closed her eyes and listened to the world around her: the wind, the waves, the timber of Jack's voice singing an old sea shanty about navigation and the stars, and far off she could almost hear the call of whales. Pressing her head against the window frame, she fell asleep.

Chapter the Sixth

Sirene woke to something squirting her feet. She realized her leg was hanging out the open window and something belong was spitting water at it. She pulled her foot in and leaned out, saw a pod of dolphins below. She grinned and squeaked at them. They clicked and squealed back. She laughed, answered in their own tongue.

"No, I cannot come down to play. I don't have my pearl."

They chattered, half-rising out of the water. *"Sing for you?"* She sighed. *"Let me get up on deck. Then we will see,"* she clicked.

Climbing out of the window, she closed it and left the cabin in higher spirits than she had felt in years. Going up onto the deck, she tied her hair in a queue with a red ribbon and took a deep breath of the salty air. From behind her, she heard the captain's voice call.

"And what are ye doin' out of bed, lass?" he growled.

She looked up to the helm where a worn-looking Jack stood glaring down at her from under her hat. "Have you even been to bed?" she countered. She glanced about at the shrouding and across the deck. "Where are Marklain and Penn?""Sleeping. Where you should be," he said curtly.

"And you," she snapped. "What do you plan to do? Do without for two days?"

"If necessary," he replied, turning the wheel. She sighed, crossed to the starboard rail and leaned over. "Sick?" he asked doubtfully.

She laughed, a high ringing sound that echoed through the sails with a haunting quality. "See for yourself."

"I don't have time," he ground through his teeth, turning the wheel the other way. "I have bigger problems."

She looked over her shoulder at him. "Like?"

Before he could answer, she heard a great rattling of canvas as the wind died. A moment later it was dead calm and the sails hung slack. Jack began cursing as he secured the great wheel with a loop of rope and leapt to the ratlines. He ran nimbly up to the first platform and on to the top gallant looking for the barest breath of wind. There was nothing.

"Anything?" she called. His curse was all the answer she needed.

Jack heard noises below and looked down to see dolphins sporting along the starboard side. They seemed to be chattering at Sirene. Stranger still, she was chattering back. He swung down one of the ropes to the deck just as she headed for the hold.

"Where are ye going?"

"To call us a tow," she cried and dropped below.

Confused and intrigued, he crossed to the hatch and looked in. "What?"

She dug through the few stores and items in the small hold. "Prepare a line."

"Fer what?"

She laughed again, came up with an old barrel mug, which she promptly knocked the bottom out of. "You'll see. Just prepare a tow-line and keep your eyes larboard astern," she advised, and promptly vanished from view.

Frowning, Jack returned to the helm. His eyes were burning from lack of sleep and his body wanted nothing more than to curl up and hibernate somewhere. But he refused to yield to his body's needs. He was still too close to Barbados to allow himself to be caught floundering. Any naval ship that Price would send after him would have oars and the hands to man them. So unless he wanted to be right back where he started this venture, he could not afford rest. There were nearer ports of call, but he knew of one in Guadeloupe where he could find a temporary crew willing to overlook a woman on board.

He became aware of a strange noise from below his bare feet. The very ship seemed to vibrate and resound with a bizarre humming and bellowing squeals.

"What the devil is that woman doing!" he roared, looking down into the hold through a different hatch. She had the mug pressed against the hull below the waterline and her face pressed to the newly opened end.

Marklain poked his head out from the fo'c'sle, asked sleepily, "Have we sighted whales, Captain?" he called.

It finally hammered its way through Jack's fogged skull. "Since yer up, man, ye kin prepare a towin' line," he ordered, swiftly figuring out her plan.

"Aye, Captain," he mumbled, coming up on deck. Penn was not far behind him. As he crossed to the bowsprit, Marklain looked around. "Where's the ship that's going to tow…"

"Whales, sir!" Penn shouted from near the quarterdeck. "Breach broad t' th' larb'rd quarter!"

Jack whirled, shocked to see the fountain of whale spray glistening in the sunlight in the distance. He turned back and glared down at the white beauty sauntering up on deck.

"Damned useful, damoiselle," he snarled. "But how're ye gonna get 'em to take th' ropes?"

She smiled as she crossed the deck to the steps and spoke to Penn who had the tow rope in hand, "Make sure you toss a long loop off the bow. Secure both ends, one to starboard, one to larboard, like reins."

He nodded. "'Bouts 'ow long, Miss?"

"Fourteen fathoms should give us plenty of leeway without danger of the fluke breaking the bow," she answered and headed to the quarterdeck. "Then ye might consider hoisting the sails lest we get back-winded."

Jack glared at her. "I asked ye a question, wench. And instead of answerin', ye deign to order m' crew around," he growled.

She smiled. "I think I've told you this before." She chuckled, sashaying up to him and tipping back the hat to look into his eyes. "I am not part of your crew." She kissed him, a deep, drawing kiss that left his body demanding more and woke him up better than black coffee. "And if you are going to be in the habit of ordering me around, you'd best figure out how to use those chains in the sea chest. Savvy?" She pulled away, laughing at his reaction.

Jack scowled as she darted out of his reach, her skirts swirling around her shins as she leapt lightly to the stern railing. "Avast, wench! What'd ye think yer doin'?"

"Going for a swim, mon captiane!"

"What if there be sharks?"

"Ha! There be dolphins in the water, luv!" she mocked. "No shark in its right mind'll be anywhere within a nautical mile o' here, blood in the water or no. And besides, they've asked so nice, and been so patient..." To which several of the dolphins below squealed a response. "Don't worry. They won't let me drown."

She pulled the ribbon from her hair and tossed it to him, then leapt into the air. He ran to the rail and watched her graceful arching dive, slicing into the water with barely a splash. The dolphin pod gathered around, laughing and jumping as she breached the surface. She chattered and squeaked with them a moment before grabbing one of their dorsal fins and waved up to

Jack.

"I'll be back. Make sure they have the towline ready! And furl those sails!"

He pounded his fist on the rail, cursing under his breath, and crossed forward to where Marklain and Penn were securing a length of rope to both sides of the bow. They seemed to have everything in hand and were taking this in better stride than he was. He stood with his hands behind his back, rocking on his heels, trying to figure out what he was angry about. This was the fantastic... the kind of stuff legends were made of; what fantastic reputations were built on. What was he complaining about?

Still grumbling to himself, he moved to help the others. Between the three of them, they had almost all the sails furled when Jack heard Penn muttering behind him.

"Holy Mary Mother o' God."

Both Jack and Marklain turned to see Sirene standing on the water, arms out, knees bent, maintaining her balance as he had seen the South Pacific natives do. She was laughing and the dolphin pod was leaping and cavorting in the water around her and the great beast skimming the surface below her.

"What is she doing?" Marklain asked, crowding the rail next to his companion.

Jack frowned, twitching his sparse moustache. "He'e nalu. Wave ridin'. Only she's ridin' a whale."

As if in answer, the great beast breached. The creature was nearly a fifth the size of the *Ambition,* and a dark bluish-grey with a large patch of white by the blow-hole. It raised its head out of the water, flashing a pair of tusk-like teeth on its lower jaw. Jack leaned back from the rail gingerly. "Aye... ahoy to you, too," he answered, a little unsure what to do. "Well, girl, is he goin' t' tow us t' port er not?" he asked, trying not to get close enough to get splashed when the beast went under.

"No!" she called. "He's going to tow us within sight of the island. We can catch the trade-wind there. He's a little nervous about getting too close to man places."

"Fair enough," he conceded. "Get him... moored up, or whatever," he replied, trailing off into a mutter as he headed back to the helm.

Sirene hummed to the great beast below her, rubbing one of his many scars. She took a deep breath as the creature dove, hung onto his dorsal, and rode him below the keel of the *Ambition* and up again at her bow. The rope was already lying in the water. Above her, Penn and Marklain watched, fascinated, as she took the rope in hand and swam it to the beast's mouth with the less than useful help of some of the younger dolphins. She rubbed his beak and he opened his massive maw. She slipped the rope in, placing it as comfortably as she could.

"Are ye comin' back aboard, milady?"

Sirene looked up and saw Jack on the bowsprit looking down at her with his arms crossed. She turned back to the whale, dipped her face below the water's surface and sang the question to him. His reply was a deep hummou that had the dolphins squealing and the youngest spitting up at the man on the ship. She laughed, looked sheepishly back up at Jack.

"He wants me to stay with him. He is still not convinced the spar isn't a harpoon... and the pod wants me to play. I'll be fine. They will keep me abreast of the ship ...if they don't out run it."

Jack sighed. "Very well, then, here's th' ladder if ye change yer mind."

He kicked a rope ladder sullenly over the side. She was disconcerted at his manner when he walked away, but did not have time to think about it as the whale moved off and the dolphin she was holding onto dove.

Jack left Penn at the helm and stood at the bow watching Sirene play with her dolphin friends and the goosebeak whale towing the ship. As if his miraculous 'return from the dead' wasn't enough, this just might make him a legend. Depending on what people saw, the stories would either be that he sailed into harbour on a ship without sails, or that he rode in on the back of a whale; possibly both. The dolphin pod would certainly exacerbate matters. Though you had to be careful when encouraging such tales. They tended to get away from you, out of control, to disappoint. Of course, now that he was thinking about it, all this just lentfurther credence to her story.

But why not, he thought. Ye've seen stranger things, mate. Hell, the chip log read sixteen knots, nearly twice the ship's speed under full sail.

Just before midday, Marklain sighted ships, then land, in that order. Jack snapped out a spyglass and scanned what he could see of the port. There were no ships he recognized, and only a small naval presence and that French. There was only one English ship as far as he could see, and it was no threat.

The *Ambition* slowed. With a last singing call, the whale raised its head from the water, let go of the rope, and sank straight down. A moment later, Jack heard the dolphins complaining, and the ladder rattle against the ship's hull as Sirene climbed. He grabbed the coat she had worn the day before and wrapped it around her the moment she set foot on deck, as the white linen plastered to her body revealed everything below it. She accepted it graciously after wringing out her hair.

He called the tiny crew together on the fo'c'sle.

"All right, gentlemen," Jack addressed the two men. Sirene perched on the bowsprit and let the wind dry her lockes. "It is my intent, upon reaching Basseterre, to go ashore and recruit a reliable crew. With what, I've no idea," he added in a mumble, "but I'll manage."

"Do you know a jeweller over there?" she asked.

He looked back at her. "Aye, why?"

She pulled the pearl and sapphire necklace from her coat pocket. "Then we have money."

He stifled his greed as the jewel flashed in the light. He had a greater jewel to chase, and the promise of so much more. He forced himself to turn back to Marklain and Penn.

"Now, when I return with said crew, you two will have a choice: remain aboard as senior hands, or, say th' word and I'll have ye rowed ashore. Ye should be able to work yer way back t' Port St. Charles easily enough. However, I need to know now."

The two men tipped their heads toward one another, gestured, and mumbled in half words and fractions.

Then Marklain asked, "What do you intend to do when you get this crew?"

Jack glanced at Sirene, confused.

"They were never told," she explained

He sighed. "I've no intention whatsoever of committin' piracy in this little... teapot, if that's what yer worried about. She's a pirate *chaser*, not a pirate *ship*. My intentions are ta chase down a particular pirate ship, board her, and claim my rightful place as her captain. Once I've done that, th' rest is rather superfluous, as will be th' ship that brought me to her and her crew, who will then be free to sail on their merry way and do with her what they please."

Penn and Marklain put their heads together again. Finally, Marklain turned.

"If it please you, sir, Penn and I'll stay at least that long an' safeguard Miss Sirene."

Jack frowned, not sure if that was a good thing or a bad thing.

Sirene laughed lightly. "Mr. Marklain. I was under the impression your loyalty was supposed to be to your employer, not his... not me."

Penn tipped his chin up, flared his nose and crossed his arms with a frown. Marklain rubbed his neck looking sheepish.

"Well," Marklain said. "We're in agreement that we can hardly be loyal to a man that treats a white woman like a slave."

Sirene jumped off the bowsprit. "As far as he was concerned, Mr. Marklain, I was his slave; bought and paid for with my brother's life, which he then took. I appreciate your loyalty. Captain, if we are to go ashore without you being arrested, we'd best get our costumes on," she said, heading for the aft cabins.

"Costumes? What th' devil are ye talkin' about, lass?"

She laughed. "Gents, if ye'd be so kind as to prepare us to enter port as best ye can, he'll be back shortly to help ye."

Jack chased after her, grumbling about her ordering his crew around. The moment he closed the cabin door and took a breath to bellow his displeasure, she spun around and threw a lace trimmed shirt over his head.

"If it helps, think of those two as *my* men and this new crew yer fetchin' as yers."

He pulled the shirt off his head and changed tracks as she peeled out of her wet shift. He cleared his throat.

"Yer startin' t' lose yer high falootin' manner a' speakin', lass. Talkin' more like a low-born pirate. What am I supposed to do with this?" he waggled the shirt.

"It happens," she shrugged. "I tend to pick up what I hear the most. I blend. And what yer supposed t' do is put it on. And these," she said, gesturing to a pair of dark blue trousers she laid on the bed. "They'll be a mite big, I know. But I can fix that temporarily and have a story in mind to cover it," she added, pulling out a dry shift and getting dressed herself.

This enabled Jack to focus on the task at hand. "What exactly *do* ye have in mind, lass?" he asked, narrowing his eyes at her.

"How's your French?" she asked, smiling.

"Terrible," he lied.

She picked up the blue dress and wiggled into it. "Hmm, think ye kin take orders from a woman, then?"

He gave her a warning look. She sighed and crossed to him. "You do not want to be noticed, do you?" she asked, taking her hat off his head and straightening his hair with her nails, trying to clean him up a bit.

"Not particularly," he admitted.

"Well, servants are invisible. All eyes will be on me."

He twitched his lip, intrigued. "Hmm," he rumbled, slipping his hands around her waist and over her ample hips. His fingers swiftly found their way into the open back of the dress. "What exactly do ye have in mind, milady?"

She grinned, spun in his hands, and lifted her hair, looked over her shoulder at him. "You can start by lacing me up," she said with a flash in her silvery eyes.

They limped into the harbour at Basseterre under quarter sail and dropped anchor out of the way of other ships, but close enough to row to the docks. Sirene stood by the longboat waiting to be handed in. She was a vision in the pale blue dress, cut low in the front and full at the hip, though it was cleverly made to give the appearance of layers upon layers as was proper, yet remain light and cool as was the necessity in the Caribbean. She snapped her white fringed parasol open to shield her from the sun and primped her hair.

Jack gave the last of his orders as he helped drop the anchor and raise the sails. "All right, Mr. Penn, yer m' pilot. Yer to remain on board to receive what's shipped over in supply and crew. Make sure nothin' happens to her, and ye know th' story as it'll be told if yer approached. No one else, but th' new crew and ourselves are to come aboard. Handle matters as ye think best. Meanwhile, I'll thank ye t' chart a course up th' chain to Montserrat fer starters."

"Aye, sir," he mumbled.

"Mr. Marklain!"

"Aye, sir!" He snapped to, coming to stand at attention in front of Jack.

"You, sir, will come with us, Master Bosun," he added pointedly. Behind him, Sirene smiled. "Ye'll wait with us until we have th' money, and then ye'll be given what we'll need to acquire supplies."

"Aye, Captain!"

At which, Jack stepped into the longboat and turned to offer his hand to Sirene. "Madame," he said, with a sarcastic grin.

She let him help her into the boat with an imperious air and sat in the prow. Penn lowered the small vessel with Marklain's help once Jack and the lady were aboard, and then lowered Marklain by rope ladder.

The harbour-master was waiting for them with two men who were prompt to help them to tie up. As the tides were not completely in yet, the boat bobbed several feet below the surface of the pier and the dockhands aided Jack and Marklain in getting the lady onto the boards.

Jack staggered when he set foot on the still planks. He hated being on land, especially docks, where the world around him moved but not the ground beneath his feet.

The harbour-master bowed, and addressed them in French. *"Good afternoon, Madame, and welcome to Basseterre. How may we be of service today?"*

"Oh! To hear my mother tongue," she simpered immediately, *"I am here to provision and crew yon vessel for my return home."*

"Crew, Madame? You have suffered casualties?" he frowned.

"Oh, my word, how I've suffered! First, my wretched husband drags me to Barbados, then gets himself killed! Then, pirates attack Port St. Charles and I barely escape with two crewmen and my servant! I don't even have a lady's maid! She disappeared with most of the slaves the moment we were told there were pirates attacking." She brushed the back of her fin-

gers tenderly along Jack's downy jawline. He tried to remain stoic as she purred, *"Only my loyal Jacques, here, remained at my side to spirit me to safety on board my husband's boat. We barely escaped, and the trip here was terrible. I had to dress him in what clothes my husband kept on board, ill fitting though they are, as we fled with virtually nothing."*

The man coughed. *"I am frightfully sorry, but there is a cost to dock, even if for a little while."*

She waved her hand dismissively. *"Oh, I am aware of that. If you would be a patient man, I intend to sell a bauble or two to pay for the... re... re..."* she looked impatiently at Marklain, who was just standing up from securing the boat. "Monsieur," she called. "What ez ze word... to supply...what we are 'ere for?"

"Refit, Ma'am?" he asked, confused.

"Oui, dat eez eet. Refeet."

"Your men are Eenglish?" He frowned again.

She sighed. "Unfortunately, when you live on an Eenglish is-land eet cannot be 'elped. 'E speaks no French. Eef you would be willing to wait a mere 'our or so, we will be able to pay you before we disembark. For a fellow countrywoman desperate to go 'ome?" she added, with an irresistible pout.

He sighed, yielding. "Oui, Madame, but of course. May I at least 'ave a name for my book?"

"Oui. Margarite Valencouer du Prix."

The man wrote the name down, and permitted her and her men to pass.

"Come alon'," she said imperiously, and marched off to-wards the tiny town.

Jack followed diligently, a half step behind and to the side until they left the docks, at which point he told Marklain in a low voice to keep a weather eye out for trouble behind and stepped in front. He kept his eyes open, watching beside and ahead of them as he led her to the watchmaker-jeweller's small shop. He held the door for her, and asked Marklain to wait outside unless there was trouble, then followed Sirene within.

The shopkeeper was overjoyed to see a woman of her quality enter his store. She accepted his pleasantries and launched immediately into the story of woe and tragedy she had told on the docks. Jack kept his eyes and ears open while standing, inconspicuous, behind her near the door. He had to admit, she was a damned fine actress. Even he might have believed her if he hadn't known better. It made him wonder.

"So you see, monsieur, I find myself in ze lamentable position of selling some of ze jewels my late 'usband gave to me. Would you be willing to buy one of my smaller bagatelle?"

"Certainly, Madame. Let me see ze piece and I will see what we can do," he answered, fetching his loupe and appraisal equipment.

Sirene snapped her fingers and held out her hand. "Jacques, ze box."

Trying not to grind his teeth at being ordered about, he pulled the long thin box from inside his shirt where he had put it for safe keeping, and pressed it into her hand. He noted the greed that crossed the man's eyes when the box was opened. No other emotion touched his face.

"Eet eez a most lovely piece, madame, to be sure. Your late 'usband 'ad excellent taste," he admitted, as he put the pearls to the test and the gems under his loupe.

She gave a sad sniffle. "Eet waz 'is gran'mozzer's."

He mumbled to himself, nodded, and jotted a few things down. Finally he put his tools away and laid the necklace back in its box. "I can give you an 'alf million livre, but zat, I fear, eez all eet eez wort'."

Sirene's face went hard. "Monsieur, I may be desperate, but I am no fool. Zat bagatelle eez wort' an eazy fifteen hundred Gold Louis," she said coldly. "I understand zat may be a beet much for you, which is why I chose my smallest piece to sell. 'Owever, I will not take a sou less zan an' 'undred t'ousand."

"Louis?" he choked. "But... but madame. I simply do not 'ave zat kind of money! Nor would I 'ave a market for such 'ere!"

She gave a short laugh. "Monsieur, you do not 'ave a market for anyt'ing you 'ave 'ere on zis wretched island. But I know for fact you do trade, and some of eet wit' pirates like zose what keeled my late 'usband." He paled. The information Jack had given her was painfully accurate. "You 'ave a market somewhere or you would not steel be in business."

His eyes narrowed. "You are a very shrewd woman, madame," he complained.

She loosed a ringing laugh. "My 'usband did not marry me for my physical assets," she replied, giving her stomach a pat. "'E preferred more meat on 'is weemon. Now, eef eet eez truly an 'ardship for you, we can perhaps remove ze pearls an' trade for ze pendant?"

He seemed more willing now, and leaned on his counter. "Well, ze trouble eez, zat eez what makes eet so valuable. I could steel 'ave trouble raising even seventy-five t'ousand."

She leaned in, knowing very well what kind of view was being presented. Jack noted that the jeweller was professional enough to keep his eyes on her face. "Zen perhaps we can make up zee difference in ozer goods? Pearls, per'aps? I 'ave a fondness for pearls," she purred.

The negotiation went on for nearly a half-hour as she proved to the jeweller that she knew her pearls. When they left, she had a small chest filled with pearl ropes and pearl earrings and even a pearl drop tikka from India. This she left Jack to carry and kept the money purse in hand. Outside, she removed a handful of coin in various denominations and nationalities and put them in a silk purse tucked safely in her bosom. The rest she handed to Marklain.

"Use zes for ze refeet."

Jack felt something give at his hip, the subtle snapping of precariously basted threads sewing him into the breeches. His hand shot out and snagged a small, bony wrist. He spun it around and tossed it to the ground in front of Sirene, scowling down at the thin boy.

Sirene refocused her eyes a moment. She was amused to note dirty patches in his faintly blue glow, subtle shiftings of less than honest amid a general good nature.

The boy, seeing a well-dressed lady standing over him, scrambled to his feet, bowing profusely and begging her pardon in poor French, weaving a sob story about starving and thinking she could afford a sou for bread. His hair was a shocking red and stood out like a poorly bundled haystack. His eyes, though a fierce green, were bright and sharp, missing nothing about her as they scanned her surreptitiously.

"Ye were pickin' *my* pocket, not hers," Jack growled.

The boy didn't miss a beat. "A' carse. What lady o' her quality carries 'er own money? Ah figured ye'd be carryin' it." His accent was Irish and light.

Sirene shifted to English once she realized how difficult French was for the boy. "So, why didn' you ask for eet?" she demanded, keeping her 'act' up.

He snorted, straightening clothes that were outgrown years ago. "Beg? Ah 'ave me pride, ma'am! 'Sides, they're 'ard on beggars 'ere. An' ah'm small enough t' escape notice most times." His voice was high and cracked from time to time and not from puberty.

"Do you 'ave a name, chil'?" she asked.

"Oui, madame," he squeaked. "Seamus. Though most folk call me Hare."

"'Are," she mused. "Short for O'Are?"

He blushed. "Nay, ma'am, ...or ah don' know ma'am. Been orphaned as long as ah kin remember, ah have."

"So why d' they call ye Hare, boy?" Jack asked, stepping to Sirene and draping his arm on her shoulder.

His eyes danced over Jack's form, taking in the false servility and the intimate manner between them. "'Cause o' m' feet, sair," he answered, showing off a pair of bare, dirty, and unusually large feet. "An' m' speed. Kin ah help ye?"

"Orphaned?" Sirene smiled. "'Ow fortunate."

"Fer you, madame?" he asked, suspiciously.

"Oh, non, for us bot'. Jacques?" she asked sweetly, leaning over to him. "We could use a cabin boy, oui?"

"Mais oui, madame," he answered, with a hard glare at the child in question. "That we could."

A ginger eyebrow arched.

"Are you willing to go to sea, Monsieur 'are? To make an 'onest living?" she asked.

"At least for a while," Jack muttered, twitching his moustache.

"Oui, Madame. Ah knows me ropes at least."

"Looks like he's been practising them in his hair," Marklain muttered, from nearby.

Sirene suppressed a smile, and was pleased to note, so did the boy. "Very well zen, Monsieur 'are. Go wit' Monsieur Marklain 'ere an' do as 'e says. 'E eez our bosun, si vous plais?"

The boy stood his ground. "'ow much?"

"I beg yer pardon?" Jack ground, though he was beginning to like the boy even more.

Hare didn't flinch. "Ah said, 'ow much?"

Sirene smiled. "I t'ink manners will need t' be learned, as well."

"Oh, ah knows me manners, ma'am," he grinned. "An' when they apply. This ain' social, this's business. An' ah don' work for yous yet."

"Ye'll get th' going rate fer cabin boys," Jack snarled. Then he lowered his voice, and inspected his nails absently. "An' a quarter share in any prize we take should ye turn out t' be worth yer salt."

The boy's eyes lit up, as did his glow. "A half," he countered.

Jack threw back his head and laughed. "A third. And when ye' turn fourteen we'll talk about more."

"'At's four years, sair," he squeaked.

Marklain chuckled. "He even sounds like a rabbit."

The boy ground his teeth, glaring at the unseen bosun, then stuck out his hand to Jack. "We have an accard, Captain, sair."

Jack shook the hand, but didn't let go. "What makes ye think *I'm* th' captain, boy? Maybe *she's* th' captain," he said, nodding at Sirene.

Now it was the boy's turn to laugh. "'Cause ye' don' lean on yer captain like 'at, unless yer either married to 'er or otherwise related. An' neither seems t' be th' case 'ere."

Sirene turned around to face Marklain. "And you said *I* was savvy," she murmured to Jack as she moved. "Monsieur Marklain, I would you take ze chest back to ze *Ambition* and place eet safe in ze cabin. Take ze boy wit' you to supply an' pay ze 'arbor-master. While you are out, get 'im some proper clothes an' grooming supplies, oui?"

"Aye, milady," he said, accepting the box from Jack. "Come along, Mr. Hare. We'll get you squared away."

Sirene was further amused when Hare gave her a proper bow before trotting off with the bosun. She listened to Marklain making idle conversation on the way. "So, what part of Ireland are you from?"

The boy sighed. "Ah haven' th' froggiest, sair. Orphan, remember?"

Jack led Sirene to a different part of town, walking closer to her than before. They passed through open-air markets of fruits, vegetables, and dry goods. He hoped Marklain would have the sense to buy weapons, as well. He needed a cutlass. By the time he stopped at the door of a tavern, Sirene's attention had been diverted.

"All right, luv," he said, in a low voice. "I need ye t' stay close, but out of th' way, and watch yerself. They's not exactly," he paused, "purple frogs and dancin' girls, but they'll spit at ye as soon as lift yer skirts," he spouted, to see if she was paying attention; which she clearly wasn't.

She reached into her bosom and fetched out a single livre. "'ere, 'ave a drink or two, an' maybe some dinner. Do what you can to 'ire a crew. I shall meet you back on board later."

He grabbed her wrist instead of the coin, though it somehow found its way into his possession anyway. "Madame, it's dangerous to wander th' port unescorted."

She laughed, and gave his cheek a fond brush with the back of her free hand. "Do no' fret, my golden one. Zey can 'ardly do worse to me zan I 'ave already suffered. And should zey try... I shall simply scream."

He twitched at that. He could not understand why she seemed to think that was a serious threat.

"Besides, eet 'as been ages since I went shopping!"

She gracefully untangled herself and sauntered toward a merchant selling bolts of fabric. He watched her finger a length of white cloth with a pattern of thin red stripes. Hopefully, he thought, she'd buy something to wear on deck that wouldn't cause a riot when she got it wet.

He grumbled and entered the darker interior of the tavern. It was crowded, but not as packed as it would be in a few hours. He had missed lunch and was too early for dinner. He settled for a pint and stood near the side of the bar to survey the lay of the land, leaning on a post as he drank. Behind him, he heard a clattering, and turned to look. Unfortunately, not in time to avoid the ample rear end of a woman backing out of the kitchen door while trying to keep precariously stacked tar-jack mugs balanced on a tray. Her wares hit the floor with a dull clatter. His drink went all over his shirt. She spun to shriek at him and stopped cold, all colour draining from her dark, narrow face.

He apologized profusely, even though he was the one drenched, then tipped his head as he recognized her. Her mouth worked uselessly and her light brown eyes where opened wide and dilated.

"Cca... ye, ye... dead... yahr," she choked.

"Anjali?" he exclaimed. "What're ye doin' *here*, luv?"

"Kkkalimata! Yahr alive!" she finally managed, and grabbed him.

Chapter the Seventh

Jack struggled to breathe. The woman was a hand and a half taller, and quite a bit stronger than he, and beginning to crush him in her exuberance. *"Blessed goddess, you are alive,"* she chanted in singsong Hindi.

"Not fer long, luv, if ye don'... let... me... breathe!" he gasped, trying to untangle himself.

She released him as suddenly as she had seized him. "Sorry, Captain," she said.

Then she noticed his drink all over his clothes and his mug on the floor. She left it where it lay and disappeared behind the bar, ignoring the barkeep when he gave her a hard time about shirking her duties, and poured two drinks.

"Get back to work, you Punjabi whore!"

She shouted back, "What de customah want, de customah get, right? Well, he want me!"

She handed Jack a rum and dragged him to a dark corner, ignoring the barkeep's cursing complaints. "What *happened*, Captain? Oh, Tortuga is going to be so happy!"

Jack shifted to Malagasy, a language they both knew. "*First things first, lass. What the devil are you doing on Guadeloupe?*"

Her smile faded, "*Well, best to start with the night you disappeared.*"

"*Very well, there then,*" he answered, sitting back to drink. He nearly choked on the taste. "*Wait, what is this?*"

"*He cuts it with water and flavours it with lemons. He says it's to fight scurvy; I say it's because he's cheap and doesn't want it known how little rum he uses. Calls it grog.*"

"Oh." He frowned, and took another sip. "*Tastes more like frog.*"

She leaned forward on the table over her mug. "*When we hit the hurricane's eye, everyone ran atop to tend to the damages. We found no one on board but Fenning, slumped at the wheel. He claimed he had come atop and caught Westing before he went overboard, but that his hand slipped when a wave hit. Showed us deep claw marks along his inner arm as proof. Of you, he said he saw nothing, claimed you must have washed overboard in the same wave that took Westing. The lifelines had been snapped by a falling spar. He couldn't ring the bell, 'cause that'd been lost with the spar and he couldn't make himself heard over the wind and seas, and didn't want to leave the helm lest we flounder. Tortuga saw something floating by and fished it out. It was your gold scarf. We had no choice but to believe him. We had to elect a new captain, and... I'm afraid, he was it.*"

Jack frowned. "*Why wasn't your husband elected? He was the bloody quartermaster!*"

She scowled, her strong, almost masculine features turning dangerous. "*He was still a bit in shock, and when he insisted we look for you and Westing, Fenning and his friends spread it that he was mad with grief and would get them all killed for one man. That, and that he was the one what brought the ship safely to the eye. The men followed him,*" she apologized.

Jack sat flicking his thumb across the inside of one of his fingers where he normally wore a ring. He was reassessing his plans. *"And you on Guadeloupe?"*

"Pregnant."

He started to smile. *"Now, that's the first bit of bright news I've heard in four years. Where is the little nipper?"*

Her expression said everything. Jack deflated. *"I am sorry, luv."*

She shrugged, brushing it off. *"Fenning insisted that a woman on board was bad enough, but a pregnant one was unconscionable. He would not be responsible for anything that happened to me, or the child. ...Like he cared... There was agreement from the crew that I should be set ashore. They didn't really like having a woman on board, anyway, kept blaming me for everything what went wrong, and that was plenty.*

"Tortuga was torn. He wanted to stay with me, and yet he knew that he should leave the Mercy, *he'd never be able get back aboard and we needed the money. That, and he still believed that your luck would hold somehow. I let him set me up, and insisted he return to the ship. He was supposed to check up on me frequently, but he never did, which is why I started working here. I lost the baby a few months after they left. He doesn't even know."*

Jack was sullen. He did not like the events as they had unfolded in his absence. Anjali, on the other hand, perked up as she drank.

"But all that changes now that you are here. You are going after her, aren't you?"

He nodded. *"Aye. I have a pirate chaser off the coast waiting for a crew. I have a pilot and a bosun, ...oh, and a cabin boy. I need everything else."*

"How many hands do you have to have?"

"She crew's fourteen. I need at least twelve more. Know a few?"

"Aye," she answered. *"That I do. That is, if you don't mind*

some of the hands bein' less than manly?"

He laughed. *"Have I ever minded women aboard? S' long as they're worth their salt at sea and don't cause distractions. Any of them have an eye for the sweet trade after we catch the ship?"*

She laughed. *"Ye didn't say ye wanted honest hands."*

"I honestly don't care what their predilections are, though I may be needing to replace some of Mercy's *crew when I retake her. Those that don't want to stay on can have the* Ambition."

"That makes things a bit easier. There's a sight more honest men on this rock than not. Well, you know what I mean." She stood. *"Come on. Follow me up to my garret so I can change and get my things and we'll go get your crew."*

He nodded his head toward the barkeeper. *"What about your job, luv?"*

She snorted, walked toward the kitchen door, and picked up one of the tarjack mugs still lying on the floor. Without warning, she hurled it at the barkeeper, beaning him squarely on the side of his head. "Dat is what I t'ink o' yahr piss-watahed rum, *and* yahr hog's wallow, whorehouse job, ya frog eatin', razorbellied lubbah!"

"What ze 'ell's in your bonnet, ye dark-skinned cow?" he shouted, bracing in case she was of a mind to throw another one.

She dropped a sarcastic curtsey, her accent thickening. "why dank ye kind, Mastah Franc. I do b'lieve dat is de nicest ding you evah said to me." Before he could recover from his state of disbelief, she grabbed Jack's arm and dragged him out the back door.

Sirene was already on board when Jack returned with the new crew. She stood at the rail of the quarterdeck in front of the wheel, and watched as Jack delivered his initial address from the top half of the narrow steps.

Penn was at the helm, and Marklain stood on the main deck

at the foot of the staircase. Slightly behind Jack was a woman of distinctive features: sharply angled face, but with high, round cheekbones, deep, kohl-lined eyes and really dark skin. She was a good six inches taller than Jack, emphasized by her position on the step above him. While there was a certain handsome quality to her, she was by no means beautiful and seemed built for hard labour. She wore a pair of bloused trousers that tied at her ankles and a scandalously short-sleeved top that was snug, low cut across the bosom and cropped at her ribs, all in a dusty brown trimmed in gold. Her dull black hair was twisted and pinned in a neat bun at the nape of her dark neck. Sirene's attention was drawn to her, to the familiar way she stood behind Jack surveying the crew below with a protective, jealous glare.

This thought brought her attention around to more important things, and she also surveyed the crew, but with a different eye as Jack laid down the laws on shipboard. He paid extra-close attention to the 'meddling' of the male crew with the women on board. 'Meddling' was not forbidden entirely, but was only to be at the consent of said woman and not at a time when either party was on duty.

"Anything which wilfully interferes with th' runnin' o' this ship will be dealt with appropriately," he growled. "Now, yer officers be as follows. Quartermaster: Anjali," he said, pointing to the tall woman behind him. "An' ye'll address her as 'sir' if ye know what's good fer ye." There were a few grumbles from the gathered men. "Bosun: Marklain." Marklain nodded. "Mister Lambert: first mate," he went on, indicating a rail-thin man of middle years in the front. "Mister Hare be cabin boy, and that," he finished, as a large white cat with patches of black over most of his body, including his left eye, leapt lightly to the ship's rail and waltzed along it with his black tail streaming like a banner straight up in the air, "be Mister Flagstaff, quartermaster's mate: our ratter. Any questions?"

One of the men indicated Sirene. "What about 'er, Capt'n. Where she fit in?"

Jack looked over his shoulder at her, and thought how best to state matters. Her attention was not on him or the crew, but on the cat who had just noticed her. "The Lady Sirene is... our financier, fer now," he decided. "If she gives ye an order, ye'll obey it as if yer life depended on it. 'Cause it might. She is essential to our cruise and off limits for meddling. Any man, ...or woman," he added, glaring at one in particular, "who makes an improper advance best be prepared to deal with Mr. Penn, th' pilot, or Mr. Marklain. Or gods ferbid... me."

There was a bit of mumbling, but it seemed to satisfy them. With that he bellowed orders to make ready to sail and the crew jumped into action. Sirene had been watching the cat with near terror from the moment he had jumped onto the railing. He started to move toward her, but when the captain began issuing orders, Hare grabbed him and dropped him down into the hold out of the way. As Jack headed up the steps to the deck to survey the work, she heard Anjali whispering to him in Malagasy.

"I thought ye don't take on passengers, or women not worth their salt at sea?"

Jack laughed. *"Oh, she's worth her salt; many times over. And she's not a passenger."*

"Still, Captain," she insisted, but not in a tone that could be thought she was contradicting him in front of the crew. *"It looks bad with the insistence we made about Mary and Genevieve."*

Jack took the helm from Penn, but did not look at the woman directly as the men began dropping the sails. His eyes were on Sirene's back, whom he knew understood every word.

"That woman is solely responsible for our timely arrival in Basseterre. Without her, we'd still be floundering a day out and probably caught by now. You'll understand later. For now, play nice."

Anjali looked almost insulted. *"What would I do, Captain?"* she gasped.

He looked deep into her dark brown eyes. *"Lots of things, luv. I know yer religious predilections. Mr. Marklain!"* he called,

"Did ye manage t' arm us as well as feed us?"

Obviously dismissed, Anjali left the captain and went to work, though Sirene could feel her eyes on her back.

"Aye, Captain," Marklain called from ratlines where he was overseeing the security of the rigging.

Jack sighed, grating his teeth. "I'd like a cutlass o' me very own," he ground sarcastically.

Sirene laughed softly. He glanced at her, but said nothing.

"Your new gear is in your cabin, laid out on the bed according to orders, Captain," Marklain answered, without looking. "The other way, you lubber!" he shouted at one of the men. "Don't you even know your ropes?"

"I did, sir!" the man complained.

"Whose orders?" Jack bellowed.

"No, you didn't, man! It's bloody backwards!"

In answer to the captain, he looked down at him, glanced over to Sirene then went back to work straightening out the crewman.

"Sorry, sir," the crewman was saying. "It looks right to me, but I gets things backwards now and agin."

"Mr. Lucas," Marklain said, through his teeth. "Get out of my rigging. Ye've been demoted to gunner's mate."

Jack turned to Sirene, had to move to the steps to see her face. She was wearing a mischievous smile. He headed down to the cabin to see what was about. The moment he was gone, Anjali took the opportunity to approach her.

"What are you to him?" she hissed. "What hold do you have ovah him to make him break his own rule?"

Sirene watched the work on deck around them. "He owes me a debt."

"What kind?" she insisted, glaring down at the smaller woman. Standing next to each other, the differences in colouration were stark, black and white.

"Life," she answered, and turned to look the woman over. She watched the colours shifting in her glow. She was dark blue at the core, red at the edge, with the fringe so dark she was al-most black, and blending into a deep purple in-between. "I re-turned him to his way of life. He is going to return me to mine."

Anjali digested the information, uncertain how she felt about it.

Sirene saw the colours alter in degrees, watched the blue and the red battle for dominance. They settled somewhere in a stronger purple range and the Hindi woman moved away, and Sirene went back to watching the crew.

Several of them were struggling to wind the capstan to weigh the anchor. In a high, carrying voice she began to sing. She had spent enough time on ships and near them to know the right songs for the right work. She sang the first stanza of 'Drunken Sailor', an old capstan shanty. It got the crew's attention quickly.

After a few awkward seconds at the end of the first chorus, one of the sailors threw in the next stanza, joined by the rest on the second line. And so they sang. After each chorus, someone else would offer up the next way of dealing with the drunken sailor and the rest would sing along. Some of the lines were fairly risqué, perhaps in an attempt to embarrass the females. That ended, however, when the worst of the lines was offered up by Genevieve.

Sirene sang with them, even the less polite ones. She me-andered off the quarterdeck and crossed amidships to the prow, staying out of the way as the sails dropped one by one and caught the wind. The song continued this way until the work was done. She sang the last stanza alone as the ship turned her nose to the open seas and north-northwest to Montserrat.

The crew was delighted to see dolphins sporting off the prow, racing the ship into open water. It was a good omen they all could appreciate.

Jack stepped out on deck done up smartly in his new clothes. Even his hair had been trimmed. He stood, feet apart and perfectly balanced on the rolling deck, one fist on his hip and the other draped over the hilt of his new sword. He wore slightly baggy trousers that tied below the knees in a faded white with widely spaced thin red stripes. These were tucked into a pair of new black boots that folded over at the knees, from the cuff of which gleamed the hilt of a dagger. His shirt was a typical linen garment that laced from mid-chest to throat, though it was left untied, and the sleeves were full, but plain cuffed. Over this he wore a long vest in a dark amber leather, cincheded at his hips with a new gold silk sash with fringed ends. His scabbard was woven into a fold of it. He had a belt diagonally across his chest with his pistol and powder supplies, and on his head was a smart new hat that matched his vest with red and gold ostrich feathers. Beneath its brim, his eyes flashed at Sirene from across the deck.

She smiled softly.

He doffed the hat and bowed with a flare. He then stood, wedged it back on, and roared. "Why're ye muckin' about, lads? I want this island in me wake!"

"Dolphins, sir!" some one yelled, though they quickly busied themselves again. "We've got dolphins off th' larboard side!"

"An' ze starboard!" Genevieve called.

"They'll be there all day most like," he replied. "Mr. Penn, are we on course?" he asked without turning to look to the deck behind him.

"Aye, sir!" Penn shouted, sounding like a mumble even at that volume.

"Then steady as she goes, man!"

Sirene turned back to the sea, began to sing to the dolphins below as they had begged. It was a wordless song, part whale melody, part wind, an echo of the rising seas and the sun lowering itself off the larboard prow. The sailors were quiet. Those who needed to be, remained working; those that did not, stopped where they were, on deck, in the rigging, and listened to the haunting voice singing to their souls. There were more than a few eyes that were less than dry when she finished. Then she silently went to the cabin.

She did not stop to light the lamp in the darkened room, heading straight for the window. She opened it and leaned out, squeaking at the dolphins that had followed her, playing in the wake.

"Send out word, scour the seas, find me a ship the colour of a shark's belly and then lead me to it. ...Why? Because that ship has my pearl. With it I shall be able to truly play with you again."

At that they scattered, swimming at full speed and calling through the waters to all who could hear them.

As Sirene closed the window, she caught a glimpse of movement. Glancing out of the corner of her eye, she recognized the glow.

"Evening, Anjali. What answers may I provide you?"

"What *ah* you?" she whispered, the barest hint of fear touching her glow.

Sirene sat on the ledge and watched her, smiling. "I have been called a witch before, if that is what is running through your Hindu mind. But I have no intentions of harming your captain." Anjali raised her head in defiance, her hand drifting to her pistol. Sirene laughed ironically. "Perhaps that was a poor choice of words."

"I do not feah witchcraft," she snarled. "I have dealt wit' de priests of Haiti and Trinidad, and laughed at t'eir puny magicks. I truck in powah greatah dan dead chickens, so do not cross me... witch."

Sirene watched the red swell, all but snuffing the blue core and realized how dangerous the woman could be. It was best she discover how to manipulate her blue heart and quickly. "So," she asked, with outward calm, "tell me what hold the captain has on *your* heart?"

Anjali stared at the silvery woman in the window, noted her calm fearlessness and the intent blue-grey eyes. She decided there was no harm in the woman knowing, and the knowledge might stir fear in her at last.

"I am loyal to th' captain for many reasons. I was th' daughtah of a street sweepah in Kotte so many years ago I've forgotten how many. I was a young t'ing, dressing up in a wealt'y woman's clothes while she was away and my fathah was sweeping de walks and my mothah cleaning t'eir privies. Th' village was attacked by corsairs, and they grabbed me t'inking I was th' rich man's daughtah. when it were discovered who and what I was... an Untouchable... and that no one would be paying for my safe return they decided to make use of me."

She was genuinely surprised to see understanding in this delicate, pristine beauty; real, been-there understanding. "They were selling me to a slave tradah when they saw the *Mercy's Ransom* sailing out o' th' night like a ghost-ship, glowing under a full moon. Captain Wyndlam had his whole crew painted up wit' white half-skulls on t'eir faces and bones on t'eir arms like th' Haitians playing wit' Baron Samedi. They were in grey tattahs and glowed like real ghosts where th' moon struck th' paint.

"Slavahs are more superstitious dan othahs and fled. Th' corsairs were torn between fight and flight and underwent a mutiny. Full scale civil war on deck. They were easy picking. I found myself in Tortuga's arms and never left dem."

Sirene gave a soft smile. "Painted up like the very devil, he must have been a frightful vision."

She laughed. "You obviously ain't seen Tortuga. But at that point, anyt'ing that put those slant-eyed yellah devils to the sword was a right handsome sight. ...And he was tendah. I miss him terrible."

A thought occurred to Sirene. "Why did Jack attack the corsair and not go after the slave ship? Usually more valuable..."

Anjali shook her head. "Not once he realized they were runnin' empty and th' slaves were on th' corsair. Th' captain has this special place for slavahs." She smiled wickedly. "And a special knife to stick in it. He don' tolerate it. Indenture is one t'ing, that's willin', but he could never sit by an' not do... somet'ing. Saved my Tortuga from it," she added proudly.

Sirene noted that the red had blended with the blue and the woman was now glowing a pleasant purple in the darkness. She decided to take the gamble. "He has saved me from slavery as well."

Anjali snorted with contempt. "White Woman's slavery? Dat what you call it? Bein' forced to marry whatever fat pig yore faddah Wants?"

"No," she answered calmly, rising from her seat and crossing the room. "That is not slavery, not the way we know it. Slavery is being used for a man's pleasure who is neither your husband nor your choice, being whored out to advance his career and whipped for your trouble whenever he is displeased with life in general. Slavery is being tormented by the promise of life for another so long as you behave and having the life you knew dangled before you on a silver thread just out of your reach. Being hounded and hunted by a man who has no legal claim to you..."

She was interrupted by the opening door and a golden glow filling the dark room. She was inches away from Anjali.

"Ladies... not fighting over me, I hope?"

Anjali whipped around guiltily. Jack was standing in the door, resting his arm on the jamb.

"Actually, I rather hope ye are. 'Cause that just does wonders fer th' male ego. That and wonderin' what ye two are doing in here alone in the dark..."

"I caught her squeaking and clicking in some kind of code to someone outside," Anjali accused.

"Hmm, the dolphins," he nodded. "So what did they want? Surely, they're not expectin' me to allow ye to go play with them at this hour?"

"No. I sent them to find your ship," she said, lighting the lantern.

"Whot?" Anjali gasped.

Jack chuckled. "I told ye she was no passenger. She is... a linguist, among other things." Before Anjali could press the matter, he crossed to the chart table and pulled out chairs for both women, ordering them to sit. Sirene glided into place with the lantern and sat. Anjali crossed the room sullenly, glared across the table at her. Jack, thoroughly amused, parked himself and set a paper on the table in front of them, pulled out a pencil, which he began to sharpen with his knife.

"Now, Milady," he said, with a lopsided grin. "If ye would give me yer observations of th' crew today, I would appreciate it."

She noticed Anjali shift and settle herself to hear this. "You have a largely trustworthy crew. Of the fourteen new hands, eleven have blue hearts, one white, one grey, and one red."

"How many of them might have an eye for piracy?" he asked.

"You might get six. Maybe more if you manage to earn them."

"Specifics?" he asked, putting his knife away and preparing to take notes.

"Well," she said, thinking. "One of the women, ...the redhead..."

"Genevieve," Anjali answered, confused.

"She is a hot one. She has a chunk of cobalt the size of a British sovereign that is surrounded by this spiked shell of blood red. The rest is in various shades of vermilion. There is surprisingly even a touch of pink in there somewhere, but she is a violent one. The other woman, Mary? She is a swirling mass of colours that cannot seem to make up their mind. She is a follower, without question, though. She'll follow the stronger pull, I think. Tap that one carefully."

"Whot do you mean?" Anjali asked suspiciously. "Whot is this blue heart red heart rot?"

Jack jotted notes on the list as he explained. "One of Sirene's gifts. She reads th' soul."

Sirene reached out, putting her hand into Anjali's glow. "You, my dear, are blue at your very heart, which means you are loyal, not just to others and your word, but to yourself and what you believe in. But the rest of you? The rest of you is a battle, red and blue, fighting for dominance. You blend mostly when in harmony with your desires and then you are a lovely shade of purple.”

“And what do th’ red mean?” she asked suspiciously.

“It means many things. It depends on the context, where it is, and the situation. Broadly speaking, it means passion, anger, violence. You are a dangerous woman when crossed and hell be open to take whoever comes between you and that you give yourself to. Your blue heart means you are largely honest about yourself, and what you are.”

“And you? What colour ah you?” she challenged, trying to recover her composure at being so accurately read.

“It doesn’t work that way. I cannot see these things in reflection, which would be the only way to read myself.”

“Th’ captain?”

Sirene leaned forward and rested her chin on her hand. “He is golden, bright and pure. Granted, there are places where he is tarnished a little, but he is a good man. He overflows with life and lights up a room.”

“What does that mean?” she asked.

She sighed, leaned back. “I have no idea. I have never encountered it before. I just know that it calls to me, comforts me.” She quickly shook off the mood threatening to overwhelm her and turned back to the matter at hand. “Mister Lambert is a lot like Penn, blue inside and out. He is perhaps too honest to take the sweet trade, but he will not turn you in if you earn his loyalty beforehand.”

“Th’ white heart?” he asked, making notes next to the first mate. “Who’s?”

She paused as someone knocked on the cabin door with a foot. Anjali got up and let Hare in with their dinner on a large tray.

“Thank ye kind, Mr. Hare,” Jack sighed, snagging a chunk of bread and a slice of roast pork on his knife.

Sirene smiled at him. "You cleaned up quite smartly, Mr. Hare."

He gave her a bow. "T'is nice havin' clothes what fit, ma'am. Many thanks." His voice did not seem as stressed, and his face shone from scrubbing. He had even brushed his hair into a neat queue and tied it back with a ribbon.

"You look respectable." She laughed as he frowned. "All right, you could *pass* for respectable."

This seemed to please him more, and he bowed again before leaving. The moment the door was closed Sirene nodded after him. "That one will follow you anywhere. He has an eye for the sweet trade, but I do not know how he'll handle combat. He has a penchant for larceny, but I do not see any violence in him." She reached for the fish.

Jack frowned. "That's th' last thing I expected *you* t' cat."

She looked incredulously at him. "Tell me, what other options would I have?"

He shrugged, dug into his food. Anjali frowned over hers, not sure what to make of any of this.

"The white heart," she continued, returning to their pre-supper discussion, "belongs to the man with the green scarf on his head. He's an innocent lamb."

"Green scarf," Jack mused, pouring over the list, trying to remember who that was.

"Backhand Luke," Anjali supplied with her mouth full. "He th' one th' bosun demoted 'cause he always getting t'ings backward."

Jack made that notation and added the nickname in front of his name. "And th' red one? Who does that belong to?"

"The good-looking blonde who was standing in the back."

"Towahs," Anjali nodded. "Don't like dat one."

"He has touches of green to his edges and his glow is close-cropped. He plays close to the vest and is not to be trusted at all."

"Violent?" Anjali assumed. "Not necessarily bad..."

"No," Sirene corrected. "Selfish. When at the core red does not just mean violent, it means danger. It means he'll do whatever serves *him* best and damned be anyone who suffers because of it. The kind of man who'll take a sweetmeat from the mouth of a starving babe to satisfy his desire for dessert. He'll follow you so long as you are his best interest, either out of fear or need. The moment he finds something or someone who'll do him better, he'll turn." She shuddered. "He reminds me of my brother."

She stared in silence at the food on her plate for a long minute, then: "Watch him. Manipulate him to your advantage, then find a way to be rid of him that he cannot fault you for. And he *will* fault you if he can. That man is a shark if ever I saw one in human form. Make sure you never drip blood in his water," she warned. She turned to Anjali. "You be careful, too. I saw the green flare when you were introduced. He will find a way to undermine you if he can. If he is intelligent he will be more trouble than we need."

"Noted," Jack said, reaching for another piece of fish. "Is there anything else?"

She thought. "You might want to post a reward for any sightings of dolphins or whales. I'll put one of my pearls up for it."

"What be th' importance of dolphins and whales?" Anjali asked.

"Most likely they'll be coming to report to Sirene th' location o' th' *Mercy*," Jack mused as he ate.

It was clear she still found it unbelievable. Jack gave Sirene a lopsided smile. Sirene gave them specifics about other members of the crew while they ate; nothing dire or impressive, just minor clues on how best to deal with them.

"I am curious," Sirene asked eventually. "The women."

Jack arched an eyebrow with a grin.

"It is rare to find a single female sailor on a ship," she began. "But to find three, not only willing but capable?" She gave a nod to Anjali, "Your story I know, but what about the other two?"

Anjali, having been the one who recruited them, explained. "Genevieve was a pirate's wife. She took exception to being left behind and followed him out to sea. Found out he had six wives and filleted him. None of her othah two husbands fared any bettah, so she given up on men, and violen'ly so. T'at about all I know of her. She is kind of... well... ask her to tell you and she'll do so gladly, but you won't undahstand half of it," she chuckled.

"Mary was th' sistah of a shipping magnate. She learned to sail from a young age. when her brot'ah lost everyt'ing in a hurricane, she dressed as a boy and signed on wit' th' East India Trading Company as a cabin boy. She was almost fourteen when they were taken by a pirate ship, and she was captured. She was a late bloomah, so it were two more yeahs before th' pirates discovahed th' trut'. They were of mixed mind on th' subject and finally elected to leave her on Guadeloupe. She been dying to get back to sea, but no one will take her on. She th' quiet sort, a 'good girl'. She can hold her own in a fight t'ough. Fights dirty," she added with obvious admiration.

Jack stretched, and heaved a satisfied sigh. "All right, ladies. The chatter's been lovely, but I need sleep."

"I should say so," Sirene snorted. "Seeing as you haven't had any since..." She frowned. "Did you sleep at all in that cell?"

Jack stood without answering her and put the empty dishes onto the tray, handing it to the darker of the two women. "Anji, if ye'll be so kind as t' return that t' th' galley on yer way out th' door?"

She frowned, but took the tray and made her exit graciously. Sirene started to follow, but Jack caught her by the waist and pulled her around, pinning her to the back of the door as it closed. "Ah, no, luv. School's not out yet," he purred.

She shivered, her breath caught in her throat. He had washed, so the stink of the prison was gone, leaving only the smell of seawater and the musky scent of a highly aroused man. Normally this fragrance disgusted her and this position would have sent her instincts to fight into a frenzy; but something in her wanted to submit, to be dominated, to let the golden light swell and wrap her in its blazing heat and consume her. His voice vibrated deep in his chest and sent chills down her spine. His breath was sweetened by the apples and the cloves at dinner, touched by the wine. Sirene had never felt so weak in her life, or welcomed it so much. Her chest heaved as she struggled to breathe. He chuckled.

"Is it me or yer corset that has ye so... out of breath?" he asked in a sultry voice. His left hand wandered behind her while his right toyed with the spray of lace edging her low neckline. The pads of his tanned and calloused fingers brushing over the near-white tops of her breast sent renewed shivers through her body. "Oh, that's right, luv. yer not wearin' one. Or anythin' else below decks, as I recollect. Why is that, I wonder?" he asked, as he drew torturous, slow circles across the exposed expanse and up her slim throat.

"It... it interferes... with the ...change," she gasped.

He gave a low chuckle, rubbed his cheek against hers, making sure not to stroke against the grain of his soft, sparse beard. His thin moustache tickled the hollow beneath her ear as he brushed his lips across the skin of her throat. "Ahh," he rumbled.

He gave another low laugh as she shuddered violently beneath his hands. She was barely breathing except for the occasional gasp for air, trembling and afraid to move. For a woman who had known many lovers, she was behaving like an untried maid.

He pulled back with a grin, suddenly letting her go. "Of course, if ye've changed yer mind about those 'lessons', I'll leave ye be."

It took her a full second to catch herself, to be able to react. "Jack," she snarled, seizing him by the pistol belt as he started to turn away, "if you leave me like this, I'll scale you as you sleep!"

"I'm not the one with scales, luv," he laughed.

"Ye will be when I'm done with ye," she growled, pulling him back to her.

She kissed him fiercely, as if he were the wind in her sails and she was trying to fill herself with him.

He grinned, untangling himself. He grabbed both her hands and held them still, looked deep into her eyes. Hers were nothing more than grey-white rims, fully dilated with passion and need. His were almost entirely brown. "That," he said, trying to control himself, "was all I needed to hear." She surged toward him, but he restrained her. "Ah, easy, luv. I'm the school master here."

She looked up at him in desperate wonder, her lips parted as she panted and the reasons for his actions seeped past her raging blood into her head. She melted in that second, as he pulled her close, took those quivering lips in his, stealing her breath away yet again. Crushed against him, she could feel every inch of his body as it supported her weight. She slipped her hands free, wrapped one of them around his neck, and buried the other in his hair.

His hands wandered her back from neck to hip with expert skill. Her fingers became entangled in his hair, fought against the queue. She ripped the ribbon out of it and shook his lightly curling locks loose. She was annoyed when he pulled back from her again, this time to tug on her sleeves, and was highly surprised when her dress fell obediently to the floor. Freed from the confining folds of fabric, however light, she lunged toward him, falling into his embrace again. This time he picked her up and carried her to the bed.

He clung to her, breaking their kiss only long enough to throw his pistol belt over his head and cast it to the floor. She ran her hands along the muscled thigh pressed to the bed between hers, hungrily tore at his new breeches. He caught her hands and smiled down at her.

"Ah... patience, my little catfish."

As she manoeuvred toward the centre of the bed, she heard his boots hit the floor. He pulled off his shirt and she curled upwards, rising to press her body against his, kissing the sea-hardened muscles she could reach. She could taste the acrid tang of the saltwater he had bathed with, drank in the musky warmth of him, ran her hands over every inch he would allow.

He shivered, as her fingers found places still sensitive even after years of healing. The touch of her cool lips on his hot skin was like lightning on the sea. Her hair was unwoven silk in his hands, as soft as it was white. He remained on his knees a moment, straddling her body, and pulled a handful of her hair to his face and breathed deep. There was something about her fragrance that drove him mad, brought to mind the feel of being on deck in a full storm even when he had been on land with her. The smell of horse was gone, and of her blood, but still the sea remained. He told himself it was because she had recently been swimming.

It was his turn to gasp as she found a scar on his back that ran in a spiral around his hip and down to his inner thigh, traced it with her fingers and tender, loving kisses. He had not been aware she had unfastened him. He bent, running his hands down her arms to her wrists, spinning them against her palms and lacing his fingers in hers. He pulled her hands up as he bent to kiss her again, laying her back on the bed, pinning them beside her head.

"Oh, please," she moaned, against his ear. "Let me touch you."

"Belay that, luv. Let me touch you."

He pressed his body to the bed beside her, half-pinning her, and let his hands wander over the white linen covering her luscious form. For a moment it was easy to see her with a tail instead of long white legs. Then he began pressing feathery kisses across the flesh already exposed and let his hand explore the smooth length of her. The short shift made it easy to get underneath and while his lips caressed her chest and throat, his hand caressed her thigh, inside and out. She shivered under his touch, moaned, begging for more.

He was maddening. Not like Price at all. He took his time with her body, finding what places made her jump and which quiver with pleasure. She moved the thigh pinned beneath his body subtly, expressing her need for him, paying him back by driving him to a near frenzy of desire. He moved his mouth near her ear and the crook of her neck.

"Madam, if ye don't cease that immediately, I shall dig out those chains of Master Price, put them to use, and take you at my leisure."

She shuddered, unsure why that threat filled her with pleasure instead of loathing. She rubbed her cheek against his, whimpering, begging for a kiss. He obliged, kissing her deeply as he eased her out of her shift.

Pulling back to remove the last of his own clothes, he paused to admire the vision splayed hungrily on the feather mattress before him. Her skin was perfect, unmarred by the raised, angry welts he had so carefully tended a few scant days ago. Her hair glowed by the light of the moon filtering through the windows; her silvery tones competing with the profane, amber glow of the lantern on the table across the room.

She was hungry; feeling things deep down in places she never knew could know pleasure. She wanted to feel him, for him to touch her in places she had never desired a man's touch because of Price. She thought he had tainted her forever, but this was clearly not the case. Jack stood there, naked and glistening, breathing heavily and radiating enough light to nearly blind her. ...And he was taking too long. She slipped her feet along his thighs, and up to his hips, wrapped her legs around him and pulled him down to her.

"Next time you can chain me down," she rumbled, her voice husky with desire, and kissed him deeply, lifting her body up to meet him.

$$Chapter\ the\ Eighth$$

Sirene slowly became aware of the gentle rocking swells and the sound of the ship's bell ringing three times. The feather mattress and the possessive weight of a hand on her ribs snapped her eyes open in a panic, terrified it had all been a wistful dream.

The room was bathed in brilliant golden light. She hesitantly touched the hand, felt the rings on the fingers and relaxed. On the *Ambition* she may be, but her thrice cursed master was not. She stroked the appendage softly, playing with the two rings which he had taken off to play servant and put back on when he changed into his new clothes. She admired them in his light. One of them was a large golden pearl; the other a star sapphire.

"Give me an open sea and a star to sail by," he said, wiggling the rings in turn.

She chuckled as he pulled her tighter against him. "I thought that was 'a tall ship and a star to sail her by'?"

He shrugged, laying his head on the crook of her shoulder. "Each his own. Besides, I already have me tall ship. I just have t' catch her."

She noticed several fairly deep cuts on his knuckles and a burn on the back of his hand. "Where did you get these? A bar fight?"

"A carriage," he mused, tipping his hand to squint at it in the dimness. "Was climbing a bridge when a coach nearly crushed me, dropped me back in th' river. It's not terrible serious."

She felt a chill. "In Port St. Charles?"

"Aye. The eve we met actually. Why?"

"Black carriage, silver chasing?"

He narrowed his eyes. "Maybe. I didn't see details. Too busy falling."

She moaned. "The driver was muttering something about a broken lantern when we got to the Vice-Admiral's."

"So yer th' blame, eh?" he chuckled, settling down. "Don't feel so bad about knockin' ye in th' harbour then."

She slapped his shoulder. "That was you?"

"What? Ye couldn't tell? I thought I was a 'beacon o' golden light'?"

"I wasn't looking at souls, I was trying to escape. I was trying to not be noticed. I didn't see anything I could use, so I was turning around to find another dock when I was blindsided by a bunch of bananas," she growled playfully. "Besides, I am rather glad we backed into each other. Wait... what were you doing climbing the bridge?"

"Effecting me resurrection from th' dead."

"Seriously, Jack. I'm not the crew who need the myth and mystery. I would like the truth. Hearsay is you were lost at sea in a hurricane. How did you survive?"

He sighed, rubbed his chin against her silky skin. "Me cursed father's luck."

"Your father?"

"Aye," he grumbled. "Lucky Robbie Dunn," he said, as if every syllable left a bad taste in his mouth.

She reacted just as he had expected. "Your father is Robert Dunning?"

He growled, sullen. "I ain't proud of it."

"Why? He's a legend. Luckiest man on the Main!" she exclaimed. "He's taken whole fleets without firing a shot, limped out of a storm on the only ship left intact out of the whole flotilla that was on his tail. Nothing bad has ever happened to that man."

"But nothing good ever happened to those around him," he snarled, sitting up. He leaned back against the headboard, crossing his arms. "One of th' many reasons I kept my mother's name. I actually got to sail with him onct. Wish to God I hadn't. He's so smooth it's criminal; succeeds without effort, barely givin' a second thought to those around him that he hasn't an immediate need for. That man is *cursed* with luck and doesn't even know it. He's not even that good. Biggest disappointment of my life. The legend was easier to live in the shadow of so long as I didn't know the man."

She curled up against him, playing with the sparse hair on his chest. "So how did his luck help you survive?"

"By costing a friend his life." He sighed, and told her. "Fenning came upon me that night in the hurricane. I had no reason to expect treachery. I was struggling to save our skins. He hit me from behind and shoved me over th' side. Westing attacked and Fenning threw him after me. I had been knocked half-senseless and came to as Westing pulled me above water. We struggled against th' waves, trying to get back t' th' ship when the top gallant fell. It hit Westing; missed me. That's my father's kind of luck.

"I managed to keep him from going under, but it was too late. He was already dying. I braced us t' th' broken gallant and we barely rode out the storm. We never even saw the eye. We hit an island afore it broke, weathered the rest of it out in a sheltered cove.

"I buried him there. It was strange, but he always wanted to be buried on land. Me... I was born on th' sea, I want to remain there even after."

Sirene smiled sadly. "How long were you there?"

"Four long years, or very nearly. I had food, fresh water. Would have killed for a metal knife instead of the stone chip tools I had to make do with. I taught myself spear fishing. Several times I tried to build a boat, but none of the trees were suited to it. Nothin' got me past the reefs. Finally, I got lucky."

"Passing ship?"

He shook his head. "Ye see, that island is sacred to this tribe of Caribs that live on a neighbouring one. Every ten years, they row out to worship this goddess there and collect these rare orchids that bloom only once in ten years and only on this particular island. They use them for medicines. They found me there, sleeping at the 'goddess's feet' so to speak and decided I was their responsibility.

"I got dragged down to their big luau on the beach with a bonfire that seemed to stretch to the sky and drank fermented coconut milk that they dug up what they'd buried the last time they were there. That stuff is potent! I was dancing and drinking and seeing things and hearing things.... I had an encounter with their priestess, a tantric shamaness that had to be... near fifty, but still had a body that could bend forty ways to Sunday. I don't remember much about that night," he mumbled truthfully. "I saw things, was told things I only half remember. Three days later they took me back to their island with them, gave me a dugout and sent me on my way with enough food and water to get me to the nearest civilized island: Barbados."

"That's quite a tale," she mused. "Almost unbelievable." She took note that his manner of speaking had changed a little, becoming more proper as he recounted. She didn't think he was even aware of it.

"Yea, ironic that they'd believe I was rescued by a mermaid more easily than the truth," he grumbled, jerking his thumb at the decks above them.

She chuckled. "So why the bridge?"

He glared down at her, squinting to see her in the dark now that the moon had set and the lamp had gone out. "Now I couldn't very well row me bones into th' harbour all right an' proper, now could I? I came up river in secret and was trying to sneak into town that way. But that was kind of... waylaid, wasn't it?" he teased.

"*I* didn't have anything to do with that. It's not like I was driving," she protested, pulling away.

He clung to her, rolled over to pin her down, and kissed whatever he could reach, causing her to squeal. "Methinks I'll make ye pay anyway."

"You savage," she laughed. "Oh!"

They were interrupted by a knock on the door. Jack collapsed on top of her, burying his face in her hair. "Maybe they'll go away," he mumbled, but the knocking continued. "What!" he bellowed, glaring at the door.

Hare's voice drifted through the closed wood sleepily. "Mr. Lambert says we're comin' up on Mon'serrat, sir. Like t' know which port, he would."

"Kinsale!" he growled. "I'll be on deck shortly."

He laid his cheek against her breast. She ran her fingers through his hair. "Have you had enough sleep?"

"I haven't had enough of bloody well anythin'," he snarled, and dragged his body off the bed to hunt for his clothes.

She rolled onto her belly, resting her chin on her hands. "Left. An-other foot," she guided. He followed her directions, grumbling the whole time, and found his trousers. "Why don't you light the lantern?"

"Why don't you?" he complained.

"'Cause I have you," she grinned, got up and began taking clothes out of the wardrobe.

Finding everything but his shirt, he grumbled and lit the lamp. He found it halfway across the room. Stalking over to it, he snatched it up and threw it on. As he pulled it down and saw her front-lacing herself into a dark blue dress. It was not very long, barely falling to her shins in front, though it hung longer in the back and draped low over her cleavage, which she was manoeuvring into place. Under the gown, her white petticoats fell to the floor, providing her with the semblance of modesty. "And just where do ye think yer goin'?" he asked.

"With you," she countered.

"I don't think that wise," he said.

"Wise or not, I'm going."

He was not in the mood to argue and there were certain advant-ages to bringing her. He watched as she pinned her hair up with combs so that the loose waves brushed the tops of her exposed shoulders. Yes, he thought, definite advantages.

Their trip into Kinsale was fruitless: vague, un-confirmable sight-ings and rumours, but no contacts; likewise Plymouth and Brisket's Bay. It was the same story all the way up the leeward islands of the Lesser Antilles. Jack would sail into a harbour, or anchor out of sight and enter port another way with a handful of crew, sometimes with, sometimes without Sirene. Then scour the docks and taverns looking for any information via whatever means were necessary.

He ordered a lot of drinks, though it was killing him to not drink much of any of them. He could not afford the risk; he hadn't had nearly enough sleep to safely indulge. They would return to the ship, he would give Penn a new destination, and then fall into bed, sometimes with, sometimes without Sirene.

Sirene was aware he was not getting enough sleep, tried to resist his advances, but, although he never forced her, he frequently forced her body to betray her. She could never resist for long. She made him eat, especially before going into port, knowing the more he could appear to drink, the more others would drink and the easier they would talk to him. She helped however she could, but could see his exhaustion catching up to him. They often had less than a watch's time between stops.

They were approaching Hispaniola when Sirene intercepted the quartermaster, as she came down to wake him.

"He can't keep going like this, Anjali," she told her, pressing her back to the closed door.

"Aye, but what can we do? Ordahs ah ordahs, and he is obsessed... nay, *possessed,* on dis mattah," she complained.

Sirene drew the taller, darker woman aside. "It is simple. We don't tell him this time. This time I go into port without him."

"I cannot let you go alone," she hissed.

"Fine, send someone to watch me. I might be able to accomplish something if I appear to be alone." She gave a little turn. She had done her best to look cheap. "Do I look like a strumpet?"

Anjali snorted. "You look like a rich lady slumming."

Sirene sighed, frustrated. "Then help me fix that and have me put ashore."

Anjali looked back at the closed door behind her and took a deep breath. Then she grabbed Sirene's arm and dragged her into the cabin she voluntarily shared with Mary and Genevieve. The two women were on forenoon watch and were currently playing cards on the floor of the small quarters.

"Ladies, we need to cheapen dis liddle bit," she announced. Then explained.

Genevieve jumped up with joy, dug in her possessions for her small box of cosmetics. Mary pulled out a chest to use as a chair and bade Sirene to sit. Between the three of them, they primped, propped, prodded and painted her up until she looked like any well-worn woman found at the dockside taverns. Genevieve even spritzed her with a cheap French perfume on the verge of going rancid. Sirene sneezed, but otherwise bore it well.

Anjali decided that Genevieve and Hare would accompany her: 'Vieve to keep an eye on her and physically handle any threats, and Hare to keep an eye and ear out for other words or problems and to fetch help if necessary. Sirene rowed ashore with just the two of them in the deepening night. 'Vieve was similarly decked out, and the two women strolled into the town arm in arm, headed for the taverns. By the time they reached the Scuppers, the seediest dive in Santo Domingo, Sirene had managed to copy the staggering, half-drunk walk of the thirty-year-old woman. They were laughing when they entered the bar, and Sirene ordered drinks for them in Spanish.

Jack stirred, groaned into his pillow. He reached out next to him and found the spot empty. He sat up, squinted into the darkness.

"Sirene?" he called.

There was no answer. There was something wrong. Her absence had not awakened him, he was getting used to that. She did not understand yet that she was half of what enabled him to keep going. She was still of a mind that she was keeping him from getting the sleep he needed, not realizing that the depth and quality of sleep he got after their 'meddling' was far better than without. That and there was something about her that....

It hit him then what had awakened him: the ship wasn't moving!

He shot off the bed, grabbing for his shirt. He was still shrugging into his vest and pistol belt as he charged up on deck. Staring off the starboard bow, he saw the torches and fires of Santo Domingo and scowled. He marched up onto the bridge deck and confronted Anjali, leaning against the starboard rail with a spyglass, watching the city.

"Just what the devil is going on, Anji? Where's Sirene, where's th' longboat, and why've I been left sleeping whilst we sit at anchor?" he demanded.

She closed the glass, set the hand on her hip, and regarded him calmly. "You *said* t'obey hah ordahs, as if they were yore own."

"Don't play with me, woman," he snapped, his voice dangerous.

Anjali backed down. "You need more rest than your allowin' yourself, Captain. We acted in your best interests. Th' crew is getting' moah sleep dan you," she protested.

As he glared up at her, she folded and told him everything. His mood did not improve.

Sirene was sitting in a pirate's lap, her drunken behaviour less of an act now than when she had come in. She laughed as she tried to sing a song he was teaching her. The man sported a braided moustache, but a bare chin and his hair was a greasy mass slicked back in a tarred pig-tail. He thoroughly disgusted her, but the strong drink she had shared with him helped immensely, as did the need for the information he might have. He was entertaining her by flexing his arm muscles to make the lady tattooed there dance and entertaining himself by count-ing the crumbs that had fallen in her cleavage. In the end it wasn't much different than things she had been forced to do for Price.

Genevieve was not far away, chatting up one of the barmaids, keeping an eye on Sirene and ready to step in the moment she seemed uncomfortable. She saw Hare signal from the door a moment too late. There came a loud bang and Jack suddenly filled the doorway, looking larger than life in a dark amber coat edged in gold, his new hat on his head, sword in one hand and a smoking pistol in the other. Those sit-ting near the door quickly vacated, and whispers of "the Ghost of Mad Jack" spread like a pox throughout the room. His eyes were smoulder-ing as his face darkened with rage. His presence filled the tavern, mak-ing him seem six feet tall.

Sirene squeaked, her eyes going wide as she saw him, and tried to wiggle off the man's lap, but he had decided to dive after the crumbs. He froze at the sound of a pistol cocking and turned to stare down the barrel of Jack's second piece, his tongue still buried in her cleavage.

"Un-... hand... my... bird," Jack growled.

The man's visible paw went up instantly, his mouth working use-lessly as he tried to come to grips with the identity of the man before him. The arm that was holding her on his lap let her go, and Sirene tumbled backward onto the floor. It was obvious then that the man had freshly lost his other arm halfway above his elbow.

No one made a sound. Anjali and one of the other sailors stepped in behind him, flanking him and keeping an eye on the room. Both hands were braced with pistols.

The one-armed man finally found his voice.

"Ccaptain Wwynwyndlam. I...I 'ad no way to know..." he choked. "She didn't say she was.... yer... I... oooh.

Sirene, still feeling the effects of the alcohol, staggered to her feet holding her head. She looked at Jack, took in the tightening of his hand around the pistol, at the hard look in his cold blue eyes, all traces of brown gone. She threw herself at him, getting in the way of the shot. She was sobering up, but still had enough wit to improvise.

"No, Captain! Please, don't. *He was Fenning's mate,*" she added in a lower voice in Malagasy before returning to full volume. "I'm sorry! I... I had too much t' drink... I'm..."

He snarled, gave her a look that sent a moment of real fear into her belly. grabbing her with his pistol hand as she reached for it, he threw her behind him into Anjali's waiting arms. He then took a step toward the pirate and back-fisted him with the hilt of his sword.

Patrons scattered out of reach of the fight. The man was taller than Jack, but rolling on the floor trying to escape the cutlass hacking after him had the opposite affect. He managed to get off the floor, flipping a table as an obstacle. Jack's sword embedded deeply in the edge of the table and he left it there, pulled out his pistol and fired, deliberately missing. The pirate got past Anjali and the other sailor, and escaped outside. Jack stormed after, his coat billowing out behind him.

Sirene tried to stop him, but Jack swept her up in one arm, snatched one of the pistols from Anjali's many belts, and disappeared into the darkness outside. Behind them, Genevieve pried the captain's blade loose and followed the fight, tailed closely by Hare with his pockets full of other people's valuables.

Outside, the pirate had fallen into a net of Jack's men and found himself lifted off the ground and dragged into the alley. Jack followed; Anjali and her companion closing ranks behind him. He dropped Sirene on the ground near where the one armed pirate was being held.

"Tell me why I shouldn't kill ye both!" he snapped.

Sirene rolled over to grab his leg, wrapping herself around his boot, begging. "I would never betray you, Jack," she sobbed. "Never!"

"Then tell me why ye were in this filthy dog's lap," he demanded, pointing to the guilty man with his pistol, "with his foul paws up yer skirts and 'is face buried in yer..."

The man surged against the hands holding him. "I never 'ad me 'and up anyfing! I only gots one and it was holding 'er up... quite innocent."

Jack cocked the pistol and the man yelped and fell silent. He looked down at Sirene. "So I'll just cut out 'is tongue then."

"He was on board the *Ransom* not a fortnight ago," she gasped.

Jack stared from one to the other. He handed Anjali the pistol and took his sword from Genevieve. He stepped up to the pirate, laying the sharp edge against his throat and bringing his face close by grabbing his braids. "Talk fast, dog, or you'll never wag yer tongue again," he growled.

The man spilled his guts, talking almost faster than he could be understood. "I gots set off a week and an 'alf ago when I lost me arm."

"Where were she headed?"

"South, to Grenada. Though she may be working 'er way back up by now... or not," he yelped, as the sword pressed closer to his throat. "I swear, if anyone asks I won't tell yer lookin'.'"

"Oh, on th' contrary, me bucko," he snarled, inches from the man's face. "I want ye t' tell. Anyone who'll listen. Tell them all that th' sea's tossed Handsome Jack Wyndlam back from th' depths. Tell them that I'm on th' hunt fer th' *Mercy*, and that I'll pay well fer accurate information and charge dearly fer false."

He shoved him back against the two who had caught him.

He slid his cutlass back into his sheath with a snap as he turned on Sirene. She stared at him, wide-eyed in the torchlight, her white breast heaving erratically. He stalked past her, bent, and with a flick of his wrist gathered most of her hair in his fist. She managed to grab his wrist with both hands as he lifted her to her feet by it, so that her weight was carried by her hands on his arm, not her hair, though she yelped, pleaded and begged as if it were.

The others followed along behind in silence, some wondering how much of this was an act. Not even Anjali seemed sure. Jack did not say another word. His jaw was clenched as tight as his fist, and his mind full of a black rage he could not explain. People in the streets moved out of his path without word or interference. The six hands tramping along behind him wearing multiple braces of pistols left no question whatsoever as to their occupation and no one wanted to risk coming to their attention.

Jack got to the longboats before the others, pulled her close to him and took a deep whiff of her neck. It sent a chill through her body and she could feel her own arousal beginning. Before she could react, she found herself shoved backward off the dock and into the water. This dress was lighter than the ones Price normally chose for her and had been selected with the possibility of swimming in mind, so it did not drag her to the bottom of the harbour. Though she did lose a shoe in the process. When she surfaced, flipping her hair over her head and glared upward, he was standing on the edge of the pier with one foot up on the piling, and one hand on his sword hilt, scowling down at her. She floated there a moment, uncertain. His glow never changed colour, never wavered, but remained a constant, bright gold.

The crew arrived, climbing into the longboats, and still the two remained staring at each other. Then Jack moved his other hand, throwing something into the water. She caught the rope and used it to pull herself to one of the boats where Hare and Genevieve hauled her in. Jack got into the other one and his oarsmen headed back to the *Ambition,* in an uncomfortable silence.

While they were rowing, 'Vieve leaned over with a grin.

"*I* t'ought eet went brilliantly, *ma' petite.* Could not 'ave gone better eef we 'ad planned eet," she whispered.

Sirene trailed her hands in the salty water. "*Oui,* but how do you recommend I handle *him* now?"

'Vieve laughed, though she kept her voice low. "Ride heem hard an' put heem away wet."

Sirene stifled her giggles, both at the comment and Hare's confused expression.

As they neared the ship, they could hear Jack's orders to chart to Grenada, but not the straight across. He was waiting for her when she climbed aboard, still dripping. He stood there a second, arms crossed and glaring, then turned on his heel and stalked to the cabin. She followed, meeting no one's eyes, though several of the crew were discretely watching.

Just before she disappeared from the helmsman's view, she caught Penn's concerned and angry glance and shook her head, warning him not to do anything.

She didn't know how she knew, as his glow told her nothing, but she knew though he was furious with her, he would never hurt her. He would find another way to get even. She entered the cabin with no small measure of uncertainty, expecting him to bellow at her the moment the door closed. She was not, however, prepared to be seized and the door slammed, as her body was swung violently against it.

"What the hell were ye thinkin'?" he demanded.

She stared at him in shock. "What?"

He growled, tightening his grip on her upper arms. "What th' hell possessed ye to go whoring in Santo Domingo?" Though why the thought disturbed him boggled his mind. It wasn't like half the women he was used to bedding weren't whores.

She went livid and tried to push him away. "I wasn't whoring," she spat. "I was trying to find your ship."

"That's not how it looked," he countered. "And what would ye have done if he had demanded yer favours, or anyone else for that matter?"

"'Vieve would have stopped him," she said, raising her chin defiantly. "And failing that, *I* would have."

"Really?" he sneered. "Then stop me now."

He used his whole body to pin her against the door, took a moment to sniff her: her still damp hair, thick with undried salt; her throat; her cleavage. No trace of the tavern or cheap perfume remained. Even the scent of the one armed pirate's hand on her was overpowered by her abrupt bath and the scent of arousal rising from her body like steam as she dried.

It was their first encounter all over again, and Sirene was trembling. There was violence in him now, something she could sense more than see. She closed her eyes, not wanting to be deceived by them. There was something possessive in the way he smelled her, something that changed in his scent as he did so. His hands on her body were rough, demanding. She tried to claw at him, putting up physical resistance, but he grabbed her wrists and pinned them easily behind her. He pushed her head aside with his cheek and covered the join of her shoulder and throat with his mouth, roughly dragging his teeth across the flesh, as well as his tongue.

Her instincts were to struggle, but not for the reasons she expected. Price was the last thought on her mind, as he pulled her away from the door and laid her on the chart table. He manoeuvred her hands into the small of her back and applied his weight to keep them there as he drew his knife and cut the laces in the front of her dress, spreading the water-blackened fabric open to expose her damp body. The cloth held together just below her belly button and he pinned her thighs together between his, turning his focus to tormenting what he had exposed.

He was less than gentle, pressing hard as he ran his calloused fingers from her stomach to her shoulders, noting as he passed them that her breasts were a little more than a handful. She was smaller in a lot of ways than the women he was normally attracted to: her hips were ample, yes, but the waist cut in more sharply than he liked. Hell, he could almost wrap both hands around her. And both her breasts would barely equal one of the tavern women he usually played with. And she was light, of hair and eye when he liked his women dark, and either red or brunette.

Why then was she suddenly such an obsession? Why then did the trace scent of another man on her skin send him into a frenzy? The thought of another's hands touching her, another's lips tasting her drove all reason from his head. She had used her charm in his presence before without this kind of reaction. Why now? he demanded of himself; but the taste of her skin quickly drove all rational thought from his mind.

Sirene tried to get her hands out from under her and could not; her weight and his were too much. She had gasped when he cut her laces, quivered and trembled as he laid her body open to the cooler air of the room. His own skin was hot, and his hands seemed to burn where he touched her. His fingers and lips wandered her upper body, less than delicate, yet inflaming her more than before. He bit this time, nibbling at whatever he could reach without climbing on the table with her. The more he played, the more she needed, and she began to struggle, desperate to touch him, to pull him to her and shed the rest of this cloth.

She whimpered deep in her throat, arching her back in an attempt to free herself. He responded by taking the presented throat in his teeth, sucking on the hollow. The vibrations of her flesh against his mouth as she moaned nearly made him lose control, as did her movements beneath him. She could feel him pressed against her, felt the cold, sharp edge of his pistol belt's buckle and gasped.

He stood back up, hands pressed to the table on either side of her hips and threw his head back like an animal preparing to bay. He took a ragged gulp of air, trying to get himself under control. This was not how he wanted her; to become a rapist like Price. She had only been doing what Price would have forced her to do. For him to punish her for that.... But she was there beneath him, and her fragrance was more intoxicating than a barrel of rum and as compelling as a pistol to his head. He looked down at her, at how the open dress framed her body and could easily see a mermaid. Hell, her body was still wet!

She took advantage of the moment to slip her hands free. Her body was singing for him, screaming for him. "Do you always... hesitate before you pillage, pirate," she gasped, grabbing him by the hair and pulling him toward her.

His arms stiffened, preventing her from moving him and he remembered why he was mad at her. "Is that what ye want? To be pillaged by a pirate?" he growled.

The reverberation of his voice struck a chord deep inside her. "What is your problem?" she breathed, still trying to get to him, but he was an unyielding rock. "Are you angry because I did something without your consent or because I left you behind?"

He seized her by the arms, and shook her. "Do ye have *any* idea how dangerous what ye just did was?" he snarled.

She shuddered, though she still met his gaze in the faint light. She was breathing in gasps, her freed bosom heaving. He could easily imagine the vision the other man had enjoyed of them, propped and presented as a tempting plate for God knows what. His anger was returning, starting a slow burn deep inside, and threatening to overwhelm his will.

Sirene suddenly realized why the mere thought of him taking her as plunder thrilled her: passion. There was passion in what he was doing. It was an expression of desire and life and ...love; raw, base need; not a matter of control or power over another as it had always been with Price. It was not being forced to submit to another's will. It was being compelled to yield before a force of nature; the difference between love and hate, passion and apathy.

She knew what she wanted, and in that precise moment divined how best to get it: fight.

He was surprised when she stopped pulling him toward her and shoved him violently. The moment she had her legs free she dropped off the table and her dress hit the floor with a wet slop. He was caught off guard, not certain what she was doing or what the appropriate response was supposed to be when she lunged for him, striking his chest.

"Why don't you tell me, savage?" she spat.

He caught the hand before she could slap him, grabbed her other, crossed them and twisted. He spun her back against him and held her arms across her body. She struggled, butted her head back against his, catching him in the jaw.

"That's the second time ye've clipped m' chipper, wench" he snarled.

"This time it was deliberate," she growled, struggling in his grasp. She pressed back against him as she did, making sure the state of her body was all too clear to him. He pressed his cheek close to her ear, and growled in a low voice that raised goose bumps all over her body to his further involuntary excitement.

"Hispaniola is a dangerous place fer a woman, especially one as soft an' fair as you. Ye could be taken by force and sold into slavery," he hissed.

He fought against a pain deep in his chest, and a sharper, more insistent one lower down. She pressed her head back against his defiantly.

"You think I can't defend myself?" she asked, slipping her foot in between his legs and behind his knee. She threw her weight in the right direction and they both fell to the floor. She rolled, sitting on top of him. "The only reason Price was able to keep me in his possession for fifteen years was because he held my brother's life in ransom. And he *knew* what I am capable of. *Let* them take me, *let* them think they are in control, and I will leave them deaf and bleeding in my wake!"

He bucked, throwing her off balance enough to switch places, though it was a fight to do so. "Really? I keep hearing hints at how dangerous ye are, but I've yet to see it."

She managed to get one hand past his defences and slapped him with surprising strength. "Only because I do not wish to cripple you."

He managed to regain control of both wrists, and made the mistake of sitting up too far. She rocked back, raising her hips from the floor and, wrapping her ankles around his neck, pulled him over backward. His head hit the deck with a crack and his vision swam. In that moment she was off him and on her knees in front of the sea chest, pulling out the irons.

He rolled onto his belly when he heard the rattling, and lunged for her. They struggled, each trying to capture the other on the pitching floor. She managed to get one of the manacles almost on his wrist, largely by cheating: while one hand was wrestling for possession of the iron, her other made a grab for something far more sensitive. This seemed to renew his determination and he slung one end of the chain around the foot post of the bed.

With the aid of a well-timed wave, he rolled on top of her again, and this time applied his weight more strategically, sitting on her hips so she could not use her legs again. A moment later, he too, cheated, and clapped her wrist in irons. He sat up, dangling the chain in triumph, making her wrist flop like a marionette.

"Damned useful bit of shine, this," he taunted.

She just grinned. He frowned and felt the other manacle snap into place around his own wrist. He looked down at it, then her and scowled. She sat up, leaning against the foot of the bed. "So, tell me, *pirate*. How d' ye intend t' take advantage of my rather exposed virtue whilst in chains?" she taunted.

"I'm only half in chains, wench," he growled and grabbed her, dragging her onto her back.

He pulled his end so that her hand was under the bed and unfastened his buttons. They struggled again, this time in a far more playful mood, though the intensity remained. She had stopped resisting him some time ago. Now she was simply battling for dominance in the issue. Their play was rough and heated, exciting her no more or less than their previous encounters, but in a very different way. Reaching her peak, she was forced to bite his shoulder to keep from screaming, instead causing him to cry out as she drew blood. When at last they lay mid-tangle and exhausted on the floor, it was nearly dawn.

He pulled her toward him possessively, resting her head on his arm and buried his face in her hair and the crook of her neck. He breathed deeply of her, felt invigorated by the scent of the sea, and her body and his commingled... no trace of another. He sighed, content.

"Just tell me th' keys are in th' bloody sea chest and not in th' dresser."

She gave a dry laugh. "The keys? Do you really think Price left the keys on board?"

He glowered down at her. "Ye clapped me in irons ye don' have th' keys ta?"

She giggled. "It seemed like a good idea at the time." He scowled, pressed his weight down on her again. "Hey, I had to do something. Your pride left me little choice."

"M' *pride*?"

"Yes, your pride." She tenderly brushed his hair out of his face, tucking the damp, unruly curls behind his ear. "We let you sleep because you needed it. If you'd keep your hands off me long enough to sleep solid between harbours..."

He bent his head, pressed his forehead against hers. "Do you have any idea why I've taken ye t' tumble every chance I get?"

"Yes," she chuckled. "It's been four years. I remember. ...And the chief's sister didn't count."

"No," he said, tenderly kissing her nose, "'tis because you," he worked his way down to her neck by her ear, "...do something to me.

You... inspire me. I sleep deeper after... get more rest in less time... You make me... you make me feel at home," he finally admitted.

She ran her fingers over the bite and claw marks on his back and shoulders. "It is because you are a child of the sea... just as I am. Though I think you still do not believe me," she smiled, suppressing a shiver as he breathed in her ear.

"Oh, but milady," he grinned, purring in her ear again, "it is not necessary that I believe ye. Only that I complete ar accord."

She giggled, curling away from him as his moustache tickled hypersensitive areas. He sat up, twisted himself to be able to reach into the sea chest and began rummaging inside for something useful. She rolled closer to the bedpost, wrapping her arm up under the frame and around the post to give him more length.

"What are you looking for?"

"Something long and thin, preferably fairly strong."

She reached out with her feet, snagged his pistol belt with her toes and pulled it close. She unbuckled it and held it up to him with the tongue sticking up. "Will this do?" she asked.

"It might," he mused, taking it from her and began to pick the manacle lock by feel. "So tell me, exactly how does this pearl work? I mean, do you have to say a word to change or get you wet while wearing it? What?"

"Why?" she asked, with less suspicion than she would have a week ago.

He shifted the manacle on his bare knee to manipulate it better. "It would be useful to know. If all ye have to do is get wet, it'd be unhealthy t' allow y' t' be splashed while on land or in front o' th' crew. If there's somethin' t' be done, I'd like t' be able t' activate it for ye if ye get swept overboard and can't yerself. Lots of practical reasons."

She smiled, resting her chin on her propped hand, watching him work so intently in what to him was near dark. "If the pearl gets wet, I change, but only if I do not chose not to, ...and there is nothing to interfere with it."

"Like drawers?" he said, grinning.

"Like drawers. To change back, I simply blow it dry."

He succeeded in picking the lock and threw up his hands in triumph. Sirene laughed.

"What?" he asked, pulling off his shirt at last, the only thing he had been unable to get off while they were chained together.

"I did tell you that the next time you could chain me down," she giggled.

"That, m' dear, was several 'times' ago," he leered, began reeling her in by her chain. "Though I'm not sure I'm ready t' undo these; they do so become ye," he rumbled.

Sirene took a quick breath as a chill ran down her again. "Oh, no, you don't. Not now. You need sleep, and so do I. Now, pick it and let's go to bed." She saw the look on his face as he debated between the downy oblivion of sleep and the salty sweet taste of her ivory skin. "That is... if you *can* pick two in the dark," she challenged.

With a growl he pulled her wrist onto his knee and felt for the lock, inserted the buckle tongue into it. Unfortunately, he did not miss the implications of his actions and by the time he got it unlocked he was ready to go again.

Instead of peacefully crawling into the bed once the irons hit the deck, he pulled her to her feet, swept her off of them, and collapsed onto the bed on top of her. It only took her a moment to stop resisting.

Sirene woke to a strange weight on the bed slowly moving toward her. Her eyes opened as it touched her foot. Daylight was streaming through the windows as she looked down to see Flagstaff sniffing her toes beneath the covers. Her fist tightened on the pillow. She had been avoiding the animal since he had arrived, and his unexplained presence on the bed sent her into a panic. When the huge cat pinned her foot down with his paws and licked the blanket covering her toes, she clawed at Jack, leaving new welts on his shoulder. He woke with a yelp and squinted at her.

"What?" he asked, reaching under the pillow for the loaded pistol he had strapped to the headboard. He followed her gaze as his hand curled around the butt, craning his neck to look over his shoulder. "Oh, it's just Flagstaff," he mumbled, pulling this hand back from the weapon.

He started to relax when he realized she was terrified. He grabbed the cat, pulled it to him and held him still. The animal continued to try to reach Sirene, but settled down when Jack began scratching in the right places.

"Haven't ye ever seen a cat before?" he asked, as she moved to the opposite side of the bed.

"Not... not really close. Price hates animals," she breathed.

"Then why are ye afraid of him?" he asked softly, burying his hands in the thick fur. Flagstaff slow-blinked at her through his black eyepatch, looking very piratical, and started purring.

"It's... I'm fish. Cats... I've seen them on the docks begging for fish scraps. I'm afraid... afraid it'll bite... try to eat me."

"Well there's only one way t' find out. Hold out yer hand."

"What?" she yelped, backing to the foot of the bed.

"I won't let him hurt ye. But we have to know. If he tries to claw ye I'll make sure he never wants to again. If not, then you know he likes ye and either way, ye know ye don't have to be afraid of him."

She tried to overcome her terror long enough to reach out to the animal, but couldn't. Instead she closed her eyes and curled up at the end of the bed and shivered. Jack let him go, keeping a hand close by to yank him violently back if he chose to attack. He wiggled out of Jack's arms and padded across the bed to the cowering woman and began sniffing her toes and up her legs.

She felt the tickle of whiskers and warm breath as it investigated her naked limbs. She peeked. Jack was near, talking in a soothing voice and ready to grab the beast at any second. Then she felt the rough, dry-wet of its tongue tickling her knees. She gasped, held her breath as the creature licked its lips, sniffed again with its mouth half-open, then butted his huge head against her leg and gave off a loud, coarse rumbling sound.

"Is that good?" she whispered.

"That is a purr," Jack chuckled. "They do that when they're content." Flagstaff began rubbing his cheeks against her knees more aggressively, making him laugh. "Consider yerself marked, luv."

She glared at him. "Kind of like what you did last night?" she asked.

He scratched the cat above his upright tail. The beast ignored him and continued to rub against Sirene, stopping to lick her frequently. He pulled him away from her.

"'Ey! That's my job, ye mangy..."

Sirene rolled off the bed, and fetched her dress from the floor by the table. She lifted it up, looked it over, and frowned. It was still wet in places, and stiff with salt. She stepped into it, crossing to the wardrobe as she put her arms in the sleeves. Fishing out a new lace, she fastened the front up again.

Jack watched her from the bed, lying on his belly with his elbows propped up and his chin in his hands. The cat passed in front of him, flicking his tail in Jack's face before jumping to the floor and following Sirene. She danced out of the way, laughing as he began licking her toes.

"Will you go find a rat or something?" she giggled. She looked to where Jack was observing with a boyish grin on his handsome face. "Are you sure he's not going to try to bite me as I sleep?"

"No," he sighed, forcing himself to get up. "I think he won't."

Ignoring the cat for a moment, Sirene watched as her lover stretched, admiring the cut of his naked body. She picked up his shirt, sauntering over to him. She paused in front of him, stepped up close and stroked his cheek, ran her thumb tenderly under his eyes.

"Hmm, yes, I think you've finally had enough rest," she purred.

He flashed her his lopsided grin and slipped his arms around her waist. "Is that an offer, luv?"

"No," she said, handing him his shirt. "It's a statement of your need to get back to work," she laughed, spinning out of his grasp and dancing across the room.

She paused at the chart table where someone had set a tray of breakfast some time ago. She snatched up a pair of apples, throwing him one before sashaying up on deck. He stuck the apple in his mouth as he pulled the shirt on.

"At least that dress won't start a riot if she gets wet," he grumbled to himself as he looked for his breeches; although he was afraid its length without the under-dress would still have its problems with some of the men.

He found out a few short minutes later that no one would have dared. Anjali was prowling the quarterdeck.

The next few days passed serenely. A few ships passed without incident; none close enough to identify the smaller vessel and none with the distinct markings of the craft they were hunting. Sirene sang for the crew frequently, joining them in their work songs and serenading them when the mood was on her, usually standing in the prow keeping her eyes on the seas. Her hunger for her scales was a soul-deep ache that translated itself through her singing.

Mid-morning the third day Backhand Luke sighted a dolphin speeding their way from the south-east. Sirene ran to the larboard rail, leaning way out on the ratlines to see. As soon as she confirmed the sighting and the dolphin was near enough, she dove.

Jack had been at the chart table with Penn when he heard the call of dolphins and went to fetch the pearl reward. He was getting ready to come up on deck when the cry of 'man overboard' went up. He bellowed orders to cut sail and turn about as he ran to the rail and demanded who'd been lost.

Towers answered, "Th' crazy, white-haired woman, Captain. She jumped, sir!"

Jack twitched his moustache, and calmly asked who had sighted the dolphin. Luke landed on the deck from the crow's nest and saluted.

"I, sir," he said.

The crew confirmed this and Jack handed him the promised pearl on a string. Luke thanked him and looped it around his neck, tucking it under his shirt for safe-keeping. Some of the crew gave strange looks at how unconcerned the captain had become once he'd learned who'd gone overboard. He glanced up to the quarterdeck and gave the current helmsman orders for coming about and ordered the anchor dropped. Then he sauntered to the mid-deck and leaned casually over the rail with his spyglass.

One of the female crew started to drop a rope ladder into the water.

"Avast, there, Miss Mary."

"But, Captain?" she asked, confused.

"When she wants to come back aboard she'll ask permission." He grinned, finally catching sight of her sporting with a juvenile common. He perched on the rail, half-tangled in the ratlines, and watched her for several minutes before she finally swam back. She grabbed hold of a jut of wood and held herself still. The dolphin parked next to her, staring up at Jack as Sirene was doing.

"Have a nice swim?" Jack called down to her, handing Anjali the spyglass.

"Informative," she said evasively, stroking the dolphin's black nose.

Jack kicked the waiting ladder over the side, and Sirene gave the dolphin one last stroke before climbing up on deck. The blue dress clung to her legs. The indigo turned near black when wet, obscuring rather than revealing her assets. He led her to the cabin, gesturing for Penn and Anjali to follow. The moment they were inside and the door was closed, he offered her a blanket and something to dry her hair.

"So, what'd he have t' say?" he asked.

"*She*," Sirene corrected, wringing out her hair, "says a whale sighted the *Mercy* a few days ago."

Jack's grin was replaced by an eager scowl. "Where?" he asked, spreading out their current chart.

Sirene wrapped herself up, pulling her hair back and trying not to drip on the map. She turned it so that she was looking at it from the ship's current perspective, translating the dolphin's rough directions into something they could use.

"My best guess is somewhere over here." She pointed near Dominica. "The whale said she was chasing another ship up this way, but they could have gone anywhere from there."

"Be she running north er south?" Penn asked, still unsure of the idea of talking with dolphins.

"I think north, though the directions don't translate well. She was this way is about the best I can do." She moved back from the table to wring her hair out more.

"We could run 'at way and hope t' catch 'er," Penn suggested doubtfully.

Jack tapped the map, "Or we could shift in that direction and do what we were doing before: passing inquiries at th' varied ports. Though he probably has th' word we've been looking by now," he mused.

"The question is, given that knowledge, will he run or hunt?" Sirene asked.

"You want my advice, Captain?" Anjali asked, staring intently at the map.

"I've always valued yer advice, Anji," he said. "If ye've a better idea, let's have it."

She pointed to a port. "If he's come anywhere near here, he going to stop in Jamestown on Nevis."

"Why?" Jack asked.

Sirene drifted up behind him, rest an arm on his shoulder and her chin on her wrist, looking down at the map with him. He reached back and put his arm around her waist.

"Bernadette," Anji said, smiling. "She run a house in Jamestown. He nevah passes within a day of Nevis that he don' stop to pay her a visit."

"Wife?" Sirene asked.

"No, just a fellow countryman and a long time lovah. She puts up with his tastes and catahs to his needs. He usually lets several of de crew accompany him when he go. If he has been anywhere near, she'll have seen him."

"That settles it. Mr. Penn, we put for Jamestown."

"No' a'visable, Cap'n," he mumbled. "Th' *Ambition*'s known in Jamest'n."

Sirene nodded sadly. "As am I."

He sighed. "So how?"

Penn pointed out a cove on St. Christopher's across the Narrows from the small island. "'ere at Nag's 'ead, per'aps? Be tricky wi' th' reefs, but I fink we draft shaller enough."

Anjali nodded. "She's a populah bert' for pirates wanting to go into Jamestown. That's where Fenning's always hid her. *Mercy* is a rathah distinctive vessel," she explained to Penn. "I'll lend a hand to de charting, as I know de watahs a bit. But de two of you best get ready if you are going. We can be there in... " she looked over at Penn.

"From ar current position," he mumbled, as he did some quick calculations in his head, "I'd say four 'r five 'ours. From there'll take 'bout an 'our t' row t' Jamest'n."

The pilot and quartermaster headed out of the cabin with the charts in hand and their heads together, leaving the captain and Sirene to make best use of the time.

Jack was not sure exactly how he felt watching Sirene shrink in the distance on the *Ambition*'s deck. He had five crewmen with him: Anjali, 'Vieve, Mr. Lucas, and two others. It was just past dusk as they rowed across the Narrows and into Jamestown. The port was busy, the harbourmaster easily bribable to ignore their presence, and they rolled into town like sailors on holiday. The women and Mr. Lucas spread out and headed into various bars, looking for information, while two other men eagerly followed Jack up the hill to the whorehouse.

Bernadette's was a well-lit two-story affair teeming with life even at this early hour. The crewmen went in and quickly acquired company. Jack took his time, surveying things first. The girls were intrigued by the dashing youngish man in the amber coat. They all assumed he had money and were eager to service a handsome rogue for a change. He flirted, played the dandy, but did not commit to any of them.

"I am reserving myself for the Lady of the House," he rumbled, toying with the three who were vying for space on his lap. They were all very tempting, one was even a redhead, but there was a paler wench on his mind.

Eventually he was approached by an enormous woman in a dress that was two sizes too small, cut two inches too low in front, and probably cost as much as one of the rings on his hand was worth. Her breasts were bigger than Hare's head, with a single piece of patch silk on the crest of the right one, cut in the shape of a star and her mass of crisp blonde curls was obviously a wig. She off-set her lack of real beauty with an abundance of jewellery, all in excellent taste, and one of which held his attention exclusively. 'No,' he thought. 'It cannot be this easy.'

She extended her meaty fingers to him, expecting him to kiss the be-ringed digits. He bowed as he took her hand graciously and barely touched his lips to the knuckles, making sure he lightly breathed on the space in between them. He felt the slightest reaction from her, enhanced it by stroking the length of the fingers as he released her. He noted that she smelled heavily of perfumed talc.

"Vat kin I do für yu, *mien schönling herr*?" she purred. Her breath smelled strongly of cloves, and she did not expose her teeth over-much, preferring to pout her lips as she spoke.

"Ah, such a flower *does* blossom in these waters," he grinned. "I was of half a mind to call Gustav a liar to his face. But I can see very well yer not a myth."

Her manner shifted chameleon-like from surprise to pleasure to suspicion. "Gustav Fenning?"

"Of course," he said. "Might we, perhaps, set ourselves apart from these... other affairs?" he asked suggestively. "There are issues to discuss which none involved would be comfortable having overheard."

She thought a moment. Finally, she took a deep breath and gestured to a side room. "Dies vay," she said, leading him into a private parlour designed for both business and pleasure. She settled on a divan and watched him carefully. "Now, 'ow is it yu know mien Gustav?"

He chuckled. "Right to business then? I like a woman with priorities."

"Yu clearly did not come here für a tumble. A man yur size vould have taken any number uf my little girls. Instead, yu vait für me," she said, with a disinterested wave of her plump hand.

Jack paced around her couch. "And why wouldn't I? I like a challenge. They are no challenge."

She humphed. "I vould crush yu."

He bent over the back of the divan close to her ear. "Ah, but what a way for a man to die! Suffocated in such …magnificence," he rumbled, running his hands down her arms, "such opulence, such…" he hefted the tightly bound curve of her amble breasts, "abundance!" He danced away, turning in front of her with a fancy bow. "I myself would not dream of settling for a woman less than half yer size, though I might dawdle with one. I like a woman who can strike fear into even my heart."

She primped, playing with her rings before looking up at him with shrewd eyes. "Vat do yu know uf mein Gustav?" she persisted, though he could tell she was warming to him.

"I sailed with 'im. I was lost at sea a while ago and I have something fer him. I simply wish to return it," he sighed, spreading his arms sadly.

She tilted her head, her greed sparked. "Und vat do yu vant vit me?"

"Well," he admitted. "When we talked he had mentioned ye with such," he gestured ineffectively with his hands, gave up trying to express whatever it was. "Ah, but ye know how men can be when they speak of women. I am merely gambling that if anyone would know his whereabouts, it would be the fabled Bernadette."

She snapped a fan open and applied it fervently, tipping her head back to regard him. "He does come to see me efry chance he gets," she admitted slowly. "Few vomen can satisfy a man like *das*." She kept her eyes on him as he slowly circled her, though she did not turn her head, preferring the coy impression. "Vat, perchance, uf his do yu haf? Perhaps I can hold it für his return?"

He ran his fingers along her arm, pausing at the back of her neck where he lingered, playing with the short hairs there, raising goosebumps along her skin. "I am afraid it is not something that can be left in the care of another," he frowned. He leaned on the back of the divan, focusing his attention on her mountainous bosom. His right hand stayed at the back of her neck whilst the left danced lightly over the surface of her shoulder and collarbone, threatening to stray but never quite doing so. "Something he gave me led me to a great treasure and I wish to share it with him."

Her greed was obvious now as she leaned back, enjoying his touch. "Oh. Yu must be a gut mate indeed to go t'rough so much to share dies," she challenged softly.

He slid away, gliding around to sink onto the divan beside her. "Well, truth be known, I need him to get it... well, to get all of it. I was able to escape with some bits and bob, enough to afford me these rags, but... " he conceded, "there be so much more where that came from," he said, pulling a rope of pearls from his pocket. "This bit of swag is but a small sample."

Her eyes lit and she leaned in, strategically rubbing against him, her hand finding its way onto his leg. "Und vat shall I get... für telling yu how to find him?"

He smiled. "His gratitude? Perhaps he will be as inclined to share with ye as in the past?" He rubbed the hand creeping up his thigh, turning one ring in particular as he did, a piece that had once rested in his own personal horde. "I remember how reluctant he was to sell this piece in specific. Said it would grace th' hand of none other than his Bernadette."

She chuckled. "Yu lie vell, but I like yur pretty tongue," she said smoothly, leaning closer. "I need somesing more... substantial before I risk his vrath."

"Oh, trust me, my rare and abundant blossom, he'll not be sailing yer way full of rage when I am reunited with me old mate. Though, I may be tempted to challenge him for ye," he purred, and began to fondle her.

Chapter the Ninth

Sirene was sitting side-saddle on the bowsprit, her feet dangling almost to the figurehead as she watched the distant lights across the Narrows. She was feeling a little depressed, regretted not being able to go into the harbour with Jack, though she knew she would more than likely have been sent to the taverns with Anjali. It would not have helped if he had entered Bernadette's with a woman.

The small cove at Nag's Head had a very promising reef, and, had she her pearl, she could have entertained herself for hours exploring it. Even without it, she would have braved the clear, azure waters had it been daylight. She would have been able to see fine, concentrating on the life glows of the reef, but the crew would have panicked and would not have been able to help if she ran into trouble she could not handle. Studying it from this height had an odd effect, dimly glowing in various colours through the dark water below.

Her melancholy brooding was interrupted by the insistent squeal of the black and tan dolphin. She turned around, looked behind her at the creature, who was laughing and seeking praise for what she had done. Sirene responded without thinking who might hear her. *"You did what? ...you found her? No... you led her here!"* she yelped.

She scrambled off the bowsprit and onto the deck, nearly tripped over the cabin boy in her haste to the larboard side to see if the ship was approaching. "Hare!" she squeaked. "There is still a small running boat aboard, yes?"

"Aye, ma'am," he replied, confused as he tried to untangle himself from the ropes he had fallen into trying to avoid her. "Why?"

"I need you to get in it and row to Jamestown, now."

"Why, ma'am? Th' captain said t' wait 'ere 'til he..."

She grabbed his arm and pulled him close, lowering her voice, aware other crewmen were beginning to pay attention to their urgent conversation. "Because I think the *Mercy* is about to descend on us, and the captain has to be warned."

He frowned. "Are ye a seer, ma'am? 'Cause no one sighted sail yet."

No sooner were the words out of his mouth, the lookout cried out, "Ship ahoy! Off the starboard bow!"

Her mind raced. The dolphin had come from the other direction. She scampered up the nearest ratlines, climbing high enough to see over the promontory. There was indeed a ship approaching: a large frigate flying British Naval colours. She refocused her eyes, concentrated on the souls scampering about the decks, blue and red and grey and green, as colourful an array as the reef below her, but one glow stood out from the others. A man stood amidships imperiously shouting orders whose glow dampened all those around him. It was red and black to the core, radiating darkness as Jack radiated light. When one of the blue lights passed near him and was snuffed out, only to reignite on the far side of it, she felt a stabbing pain in her heart.

"Krill," she swore. "It's too late." She jumped to the deck, hissed to Hare. "Go get Mr. Marklain and meet me in my cabin."

The boy stopped questioning, though she knew he was completely confused. He saluted and darted off to obey. Sirene headed for the cabin, stopped long enough to call up to the bridge.

"Mr. Lambert!"

"Aye, ma'am?"

"If they try to board us, do not resist," she ordered, and then disappeared below before he could question.

Inside the cabin, she went straight to the window, opened it and leaned out, calling the dolphin back. She swam eagerly around to the back of the ship and called up. Sirene asked her for a favour.

Marklain and Hare entered the cabin, closing the door behind them. "You called, Miss Sirene?" the older man asked.

"Aye," she answered, coming inside. She waved Hare to her. "Seamus, can you swim?"

He frowned, not trusting this, especially not with his Christian name involved. "A bit. Why? Ye don' be expectin' me t' abandon ship an' be left on that island all orphaned again?"

She set her hands gently on his shoulders. "No," she said, bending to his level. "I expect you to save us all by warning the captain."

"But he be on th' other island. Ah can' swim that far, an' th' cockboat'll be seen fer sure, it will."

"Aye, but a dolphin won't. Just outside that window is a friend of mine. Her name is Skilly. All you have to do is hold on to her dorsal, and she'll tow you lightning fast to Jamestown. From there I need you to find Anjali and the captain, and tell them that they are *both* here! Can you do that?"

Hare looked out the window at the black and white shape with tan cheeks waiting below. "'They're *both* here'," he repeated doubtfully. "What do ah be tellin' him when he asks whot tha' means?"

"He won't ask. Now go and quickly," she called, hearing the ship's bell calling a warning from above. "Take off your shoes and jump."

She guided him out the window and watched him drop into the water. The dolphin dove under him, pushing him to the surface and clicked at Sirene. She answered back, giving her directions.

"Oh, and Hare," she called just before they started to swim away. "If she clicks twice, hold your breath."

"Whot?!" he shouted in a moment of panic, but then the dolphin was speeding away and he had to hang on or be lost.

Sirene turned to Marklain, closing the window behind her. She met his gaze, breathing heavy, trying to think how to save him and Penn. The rest of the crew would be easy; these two.... She went to the jewel chest, taking out a set of keys hidden there, and tucking them into her hand.

"What are we to do, Miss?" he asked. "That is Captain Price, isn't it?"

She turned to him, nodded as she regarded him carefully. "Whatever happens, tell him the truth."

"All of it, ma'am?" he asked in shock.

"Most of it," she corrected, leading him out of the cabin. "The beginning. Let me do the talking if at all possible, but if that is not the case, stick to the truth."

He followed her into the quartermaster's cabin next door. She held the door, waiting for him to come in.

"Why are we here? Won't the women be a mite upset?" he asked.

She looked sadly up at him. "What is your Christian name?"

"Andrew, ma'am. But what does that..."

"I am sorry, Andrew. But I *will* save you. One way or another," she replied and then stepped out of the cabin, closed the door, and locked it behind her.

She ignored his shouting and slipped back into her own cabin, putting the keys away. She went to the window, staring out at the jut of land across from her and at the dimly glowing reef not far below. She debated whether or not to jump.

There was a banging at her door, an official sounding voice booming unintelligibly on the other side just before it was kicked in. Sirene spun as three British soldiers marched in and stepped aside, swept the room with their muskets to make sure it was clear.

As they parted, Price walked in, a superior sneer on his face and a look of disgust in his eyes. He marched up to her, paused only a moment before he backhanded her. "Bring it to the *Redoubt*. In irons, if it resists," he sneered.

Two of the soldiers took her by the arms. They were gentle, but firm. Once Price was no longer among them, she could see their glows. One was more fiercely blue than the other, but neither were anything other than ordinary. She did not fight them as they led her out of the cabin and across the deck.

The crew of the *Ambition* was lined up on both sides, being restrained by rows of soldiers in bright red coats. Lights were everywhere, on both ships. Sirene was led across a gangplank that had been set up as a bridge to the smaller vessel.

Price was standing on the deck between two other men, one of which was the Vice Admiral, the other, a high ranking British lord from his dress and manner. Trask gave her a small bow.

"I do hope you are well, Miss Margaret?" he asked.

"I was perfectly well, Vice Admiral," she retorted, pulling herself up to her full height and glaring at Price. "That is until this dog arrived in my life."

Price seethed, but said nothing. The Vice Admiral looked confused. Behind them, sailors were sorting out sets of irons for the *Ambition's* crew.

"Where is your pirate captain, Margaret," Price demanded, maintaining his outward calm, but she could see the darkness around him writhing.

She sighed, rolled her eyes as if explaining things for the thousandth time to a child. "There *is* no pirate, Ambrose. Except perhaps for me if you must label *someone*. And I suppose a pirate's *sister* is as good as a pirate."

He actually snarled. "Where is Wyndlam?"

"Excuse me, Miss Margaret?" the other man interrupted, stepping forward. "But would you care to explain that?"

"Oh, I'd be happy to, your Lordship." She curtseyed, flashing him her most disarming and submissive smile. "You see, Captain Wyndlam received a pardon from the Governor of the Carolinas some time ago. Therefore he is not a pirate."

He frowned. "Can he produce this document?"

She looked down sadly. "Alas, it was lost when he went overboard at sea four years ago. But I am sure it can be confirmed via the Governor quite readily," she lied.

The Vice Admiral sighed. "This is all well and good, my dear, but I am afraid that his appropriation of Captain Price's personal vessel cancels the pardon, not to mention stealing his horse and kidnapping his ward."

"Oh, but he didn't do either, sir."

The man frowned. Price scowled but did not interrupt, remained standing stiffly with his hands behind his back in the presence of his superior officer. "Oh? Then how do you explain..."

She smiled again, "Oh, quite easily, sir. You see, *I'm* the one who took the horse, and I gave him the ship. As Price's ward or mistress, whichever you choose to call me..." this titbit shot his eyebrow nearly into his wig, "...that isn't really stealing. Besides, I brought the horse to his other property and there were full intentions to allow the ship to be returned once we'd accomplished our mission."

"Then why did he break out of jail instead of counting on the courts to be fair?" the lord asked.

"He could not be certain they would be," she exclaimed, falling easily into the role of the wronged damsel. "Not with Ambrose so intent to have him killed because he *used* to be a pirate."

"This does not explain the events at the dock in Fairlane's Cove," Price growled. "You were held hostage while Wyndlam and two of my own men tied Mr. Edmonds up."

She waved dismissively in Price's direction. "I knew that Edmonds would never go along with our borrowing the ship, so I had Captain Wyndlam *appear* to hold me hostage. I also made certain that Marklain and Penn believed without a doubt that he would kill me if they did not do as he said. I was locked in the cabin the whole way to Basseterre, where all of those men," she pointed to the *Ambition*'s deck, "were legitimately hired to chase down a pirate ship. They are pirate chasers to the last hand, not pirates."

"You *do* know there is a woman among them?" the lord asked in a conspiratorial tone.

"She is a more than capable sailor, your lordship," she explained. "Besides, there were precious few willing to go hunting pirates, particularly the ship we're after."

"Just what ship are you after, and what is so precious you would risk your lovely white neck over it?"

Price could keep his peace no longer. "A trinket she was told to forget about."

"It was a gift from my mother, and all I have of her!" she cried, hiding behind the lord as Price took a step forward.

"Really, Price." Trask frowned, and Ambrose stood down quickly, seething in silence.

The lord turned back to Sirene. "Go on, my dear."

"If you doubt my word, you can ask any one of the men. Mr. Lambert there is first mate," she said, pointing him out.

"What about the quartermaster, or the bosun even? Higher officers?"

"I fear the quartermaster went ashore as well, your Lordship, and Captain Price will most likely not take the bosun's word for the matter."

The Vice Admiral glared over his shoulder at the man in question. "He won't, will he? Why is that? Who is the man? Another former pirate?"

"An employee of his, sir. Mr. Andrew Marklain. Who, unless you've released him, is currently locked in the quartermaster's cabin," she answered calmly.

The Vice Admiral ordered Mr. Lambert brought over for interrogation, with Mr. Marklain to be released and questioned separately. Sirene stood to the side, surrounded by sailors, some of whom were admiring the curve of her exposed ankles and calves. She stared at Price, her defiant gaze daring him to find fault in a single thing she had so far claimed.

Jack was deeply engaged in flirtations with Bernadette when he was rescued by a loud disturbance in the front room. Bernadette leaned over him on the divan.

"Hold das t'ought. Mutter vill be right back," she smiled tightly, cupping his 'package' in her enormous, be-ringed hand.

She crossed to the doors and thrust them open. Before anyone could stop him, Hare skittered into the room by taking a diving slide between her legs and hauling himself up the back of the couch.

"Nien! E's dripping on mein Persian rug!" she screamed.

Jack whipped his jacket from the floor and onto his body, spinning off the divan as Hare flipped over its back to avoid the angry madam. "This had better be good," he roared.

Hare hit the floor and scooted backward on his butt to escape Bernadette. "Miss Sirene sent me! Said they're both here!" he gasped. It was obvious the boy had run the whole way.

Jack held up his hand to stop the charging woman and picked Hare up off the floor by his shirt. "What? Why are you drenched, and how did you get here?"

Hare gave him an embarrassed grin, lowered his voice, "Th' black dolphin, sair. Th' one she went swimmin' with t'day, ah think. An' we were almost run down by th' HMS *Redoubt* on th' way, sair."

Jack frowned. The name did not ring any bells beyond her naval status. "Did they see you?"

He shook his soggy head. "Naw, Capt'n. We dove, an' they were too intent on th' *Ambition's Price*. Got here as soon as ah could find ye, I did."

His mind raced. "I haven't heard cannons yet, so that is a good sign... maybe."

"Ye shouldn't, sair," Hare explained. "Miss Sirene's orders were to let 'em board wi'out a fight. An' from whot ah saw, they did."

Jack snatched up his hat and pulled a few coins from his pocket. He led Hare to the door, gave him orders to find Anjali and Lucas, and have them meet him at the dock. He paused beside Bernadette where she had collapsed on the divan, slid his hand into her dress to cup her breast and leave the coins, purred in her ear as he pressed a kiss just below it, tugging on her pearl-drop earrings with his teeth.

"I'm sorry, luv. I have t' go. M' ship's under attack, and if m' lady's right, yer bonny Fenning's about to attack as well. And I'll have a nasty, little surprise for him."

Bernadette was so in shock at how he managed to fit his hand into her tightly laced dress that he was almost out the door before the rest of his sentence hit her. From behind him in the house, Jack heard her bellowing to raise the roof.

He ran for the docks, not knowing or caring if the two men who had come to the house with him were behind him or not. There was still no sound of cannon fire, which worried him. He tried to think of reasons why Sirene would order them to surrender. He prayed she wasn't planning on doing anything foolish. He did not know how far she would go to avoid being in Price's possession again. She kept claiming she was immune to suffering, but just how deep did that really go?

From the pier Jack could see the promontory at Nag's Head across the Narrows at St. Christopher. The small ship, ordered to rest in darkness by him, was ablaze with light, and nearly eclipsed by the larger frigate flying the Union Jack. He could see the lights, but without his spyglass he could not be sure what was what on deck. He could only tell that both ships were bustling. He was about to jump into the longboat and row across when Anjali set her hand on his shoulder.

"Don't, Captain," she warned. "Dey'll see it coming." He shrugged her off. "Ye'll only get yourself caught and hung."

There was a gasp from behind her. "What will zey do to Marie?" 'Vieve asked.

Jack threw his hat to the dock and snarled as Hare trotted up with Mr. Lucas. "None of them were pirates," he said, trying to force himself to appear calm. "If she kept her head, they may be fine. Marklain and Penn... we were careful, they have deniability. It's Sirene I am worried about. He'll kill her!"

Anjali grabbed him by the arm, stopped his frantic pacing. "Captain! I grew to like hah, too, but if th' 'hole is safe then one life is nothing. We can overtake them, find anothah ship. They were not ours. If th' *Mercy is* close then we can get word to them somehow. Tortuga will find us."

He ripped his arm from her grasp, his eyes cold and dangerous. "I had an accord with that woman. To help her escape and find her jewel, and she would help me recover the *Mercy* and lead me to the treasure of the *Ana Maria Salvador*." He pulled a silver chain from his coat pocket, dangled it in her face. "I've got it half right. It's my *honour* at stake, woman, not m'lust," he snarled.

The pearl gleamed in the faint light on the docks, swung seductive and dark in its bright cage. His eyes were drawn to it. The chain was still warm from the woman's fat neck, the silver tarnished by the oils and cosmetics she had used to cover her body odour.

Below the planks he heard a whistling call. He looked down and saw the dolphin watching him with eager eyes. He bent, dangled the pearl where she could see it. "Can ye get this to her?"

he asked.

She splashed her head from side to side, and began swimming backward away from him. She called him, as if trying to lead him.

Something Sirene had said to him clicked in his brain. He thought he was crazed for thinking it, but he had to try something. He sat on the edge of the pier, looping the chain around his neck and pulled off his boots.

"Captain, yore not goin' to swim?!" Anjali exclaimed, dodging one of the boots as he tossed it. "It is two leagues!"

"Not the way ye think I am, I'm not," he grumbled, shrugging out of his coat and laying aside his pistols. "These'll be useless by the time I get there. But I'll keep th' cutlass."

He looked across the Narrows to the pair of ships, and strengthened his resolve, then slipped off the dock into the water. He sank slowly, closed his eyes and held his breath, waiting for whatever change would come. Nothing happened. He opened his eyes and saw the dolphin inches from his face, laughing at him. She dove below him and tugged on his trousers. He rolled his eyes and shot for the surface.

"Right," he growled the moment his head cleared the water.

Above him, the others leaned over, 'Vieve holding a torch to see him. He began to unbutton his breeches, grabbing a breath as he sank, fighting with them. The dolphin tried to help, but he shooed her off. He finally got free and started to hand them up to Anjali when it happened.

His eyes went wide as he felt his lower body melting together and begin to change. There was a great deal of discomfort as his bones fused and twisted until his spine continued all the way to his flat, transparent toes. He writhed, sinking under the water as muscles reacquainted themselves with the new bones and how to move them. There was a painful, white-hot tearing at his neck, and his hands shot up defensively.

There were three narrow strips on each side which were struggling against his hands to open and flap in the water. There was a burning in his chest, a panic reflex as his body demanded oxygen from some source. The moment his fingers released them, his new gills opened and began to suck in the water, shutting off the lungs and all access to them to keep the water out of places not meant to hold it.

He looked up and realized he had sunk to the bottom of the harbour. He could see the torch above him and the shadows of the women, the boy, and Lucas panicking. He thrashed his legs to kick off the harborfloor and return to the surface, badly misjudging the strength of his new tail. He nearly shot out of the water. They grabbed for him, to pull him to the dock. Then 'Vieve saw the scales below his sash and dropped the torch.

Jack bobbed back down, holding onto the planks, but making sure the water did not go below his chest. It took him a second to figure out how to reopen his lungs to allow him to speak.

"Don... Don't panic. Anjali, ye wanted to know her secret. This is it. Find the other two, but don't tell them. This... is a tale to keep to ourselves, savvy?" He half-frowned, half-grinned. "Take th' boat an' row around th' point inta th' Narrows, but stay low. Pretend yer fishin'."

The dolphin squealed at him, grabbed a lock of hair and pulled. He shooed her off. "Gimme a minute! Just keep yer deadlights open and play it smart. Seas willin', I'll be back fer ye." At that he turned and dove, snagging his trousers and tucking them into his shirt for later.

Hare sat down hard on the dock, staring at the ripple in the water where the captain had been but a moment before.

"Did ah... ah see *scales*, Miss 'Vieve? Or is it a bit more whiskey ah be needin'?"

Anjali turned on him. "You been drinking whiskey?"

"Naw, ma'am. But after 'at, ah think ah should polish off about a fifth ar two. Ar rum. Ah hear rum's good an' strong."

'Vieve set a companionly hand on his shoulder. "*Non, mon petit lapan*, we all saw what you t'ink you saw. An' I, for *une*, am not going to leave *mon sucré* Marie to zose Britich dogs." She pulled him to his feet and walked to the longboat. She looked back, saw Hare still standing there in shock. "Well, 'op to eet, Monsiuer 'are! You 'eard ze capitane! Go get ze ozers!"

That snapped him from his stupor. "They kin rot, ma'am. Ah ain' goin' near 'at place agin, Ah an't!"

After both Lambert and Marklain related tales similar to hers, Sirene was led by Price and the Vice Admiral to the main officer's cabin, which at this point belonged to Trask. He was very much a gentleman as he led her to a chair at the table and offered her wine, which she politely declined. Trask ordered the sailor who had followed them to make certain that the crew of the *Ambition's Price* were made comfortable and fed if they had not already been.

Price waited until the door closed before confronting the admiral. "Surely you don't believe them, sir?"

"Of course not."

"So, why aren't we clapping the lot in irons as we speak?" he protested, gesturing at the door.

The Vice Admiral lost his temper. "Because some daft idiot decided to perform interrogations on the main deck!" He poured a glass of wine and began pacing with it. "Damn it, man! How many times must I say it? Appearances are everything. It doesn't matter if *I* believe them or not. Their stories are credible and cohesive. There is no reason not to believe them. Why the devil did you have to confront her on deck ...and in front of Lord Hamilton, no less?"

Sirene watched the exchange in silence. So near to Price, he was impossible to read, and she deeply regretted never having done so before.

"I had no idea the little bint was such a clever and ready liar," he snapped.

"Why not?" she mumbled. "You trained me to be."

He glared at her. "Give me an excuse, Margaret," he warned.

Trask refilled his glass, shaking his head. "She ran away from you, Price. What made you think she would so readily give up her pirate lover?"

Price twitched at that and Sirene decided to pick at the wound. She began mumbling in French, a language he only half knew. She was well aware he would understand just enough to enrage him. *"Better man than you ever were,"* she said, not looking at either man, but instead scanning the well-lit and better appointed cabin.

He whirled. "What did you say?" he seethed.

She stood. "I said," she said, crossing to him slowly. "I received greater pleasure in his bed, both forced and willing, than I ever received in yours, or with any of those barnacles you forced me to seduce or pacify." She stood on her tiptoes and sneered in his face. "I would rather lie in chains at his feet as his *dog* than at your side as mistress, ward, *or* bride!"

He slapped her, the back of his hand raising a red mark to match the one from earlier. Sirene bent under the weight of the blow but did not fall, stood straight again, as defiant as ever. She spat blood on Price's white shirt front. She was fully aware of the Vice Admiral watching from the cabinet, sampling his wine, not bothered by the display of brutality in the slightest.

"That's another thing, Price," he said casually. "Her deliberate little slip, 'mistress or ward', in front of Lord Hamilton. Not good. Not good at all. You'll have to find a way to pacify him."

"Or blackmail him," Ambrose ground, shoving Sirene back into her chair.

The Vice Admiral shrugged. "Either way. We will sit things out here until morning or until we get word from the HMS *St. George*. Then I suggest you set three or four soldiers on board the *Ambition* to run things, and send her home with her hired crew."

"That's risky, sir."

"Appearances, Captain," he warned. "If anything happens, the soldiers'll put it down and then you can hang them all."

"We could just follow them back on the *Redoubt*," he suggested. "To be sure."

"No," he sighed, moving over to sample fruit from an enormous crystal bowl. "The wreck of a Dutch Merchant was found near Antigua. You'll be staying to catch the pirates we suspect did it."

"Aye, sir. Though if Wyndlam thinks she's on board the *Ambition*, he might give chase to her."

Trask plucked a few more grapes, and snorted. "With what? Scuttlebutt is that he's been hunting for the *Mercy's Ransom* from Grenada to Puerto Rico. You've taken his ship. Though with or without one he's not likely to give chase to a skirt, however fair, with his prize so close. No, she goes with the *Ambition*."

"Sir, it's too risky," he insisted. "You don't know what she..."

"No buts. Regulations are clear on the matter. The only women allowed on board Navy vessels are official passengers and prisoners. No exceptions. And she is not an official passenger."

"Officers are allowed servants," he offered.

"Maids are not on the roster of allowable servants."

"Fine," Price ground. "Prisoner then," he said, and turned to fetch a set of irons that had been brought in earlier.

Trask shrugged, continuing to pick at his fruit. "If you want to risk your career, go ahead. I just don't see why you are so... obsessed with her."

Sirene could not afford to wait any longer. She screamed. Her voice rose and fell in pitch, the volume growing higher as she stood. Trask dropped the orange he had just selected and covered his ears. Price staggered. The crystal bowl burst, impaling the Vice Admiral in several places, sending him to the deck in agony. The windows shuddered, vibrated, then she found the right pitch and they exploded outward just as a peal of thunder rolled across the ocean. Price, trying to shield his bleeding ears, staggered toward her, and swung the chains in his other hand.

The u-shaped irons carried the momentum, wrapping the chain around her head and impacting her forehead with the locking bar at its end. Sirene crumpled to the floor.

Price staggered to his feet, was standing over her body when the door was forced open by a soldier. The man took in the scene. "What happened, sir? I heard... holy," he exclaimed when he saw the broad stern windows in shards.

Trask groaned on the floor amid the broken glass.

"Get... the Vice Admiral... to the ship's doctor," Price heaved, unsteady. He was nearly knocked to the deck as the whole ship pitched more intensely. "What the hell is going on, Lieutenant?" he demanded.

"Squall, sir," the soldier replied as he helped Trask to his feet. "I was sent to request your presence on deck. What we can see of it, it's a strong one, Captain."

Price wiped the blood from his neck and ear. He dropped the chains on top of the unconscious woman and moved away. He paused at the mirror to make himself presentable before heading up on deck to deal with the panicking crew.

Jack made the last part of his approach below the surface, guided by the dolphin as he was unable to see at all. Apparently, Sirene's gift of sight did not come with the tail. He had to assume neither did the ability to heal with salt water. The dolphin led him to the anchor chain, which he followed up to the surface. He looked upward and saw the crew bustling to batten the ship down for a serious storm. He nearly jumped out of the water when a bolt of lightning struck something across the Narrows.

He needed to board, and fast. He stayed close to the hull, looking for a place to climb up. That was when he noticed the lack of reflection on the stern windows. There were lights on in the middle cabin. It was the most likely place for her to be kept, and Price should be on deck if he was any kind of captain at all. This was his opportunity. All that remained was to manage the climb.

He noted that the gallery running below the windows passed fairly close to the anchor chain. If he could climb to that he should be able to make the jump. He looped his arm through one of the links of the huge chain. He held the pearl up out of the water, tried to remember how to undo the fins. He could hear her voice in his head.

"Simply blow it dry," she had said.

He took a deep breath of air into his lungs, held it a second, then blew softly on the jewel dangling before his face.

Inside the silver cage the pearl began to spin, then glow softly. He braced for the same pain he had experienced before, but was surprised to find the return transition less uncomfortable. The bones in his tail fused and split, the flesh ripping in half even as the skin at his neck sealed. He started to climb the chain, but the moment his hips cleared the water he remembered he was half-naked. It would not do at all if he had to fight, or got caught. It might arouse suspicions, and he did not want Price of all people knowing either that he had the pearl, or that it worked for others.

He sank back into the water, and, clinging to the chain alternately with arm and toes, he pulled his trousers from his shirt and struggled into them. Dressed, he readjusted himself and began climbing. The chain itself was easy, though there was the risk of pinched fingers and toes as the links shifted. Getting from the chain to the gallery was far trickier. The waves were growing in violence and the ship surged against them, making it next-to-impossible to reach the ledge and dangerous to jump to it.

Just when he was about to give up, lightning struck the mizzenmast, sending the whole top quarter to the deck, crushing the rails of the quarterdeck and dangling over the side, still attached to the shrouds. Jack clung desperately to the chain, praying not to be hit or noticed. A rope thumped against the hull near him, still smouldering at the end. He stared at it in disbelief, watching it move in his direction as the ship pitched. He did not question the stroke of luck and grabbed hold of it as it passed, using it to swing over to the gallery.

He found himself stepping on glass shards as they slid back and forth along the ledge. Occasionally pieces fell into the water below. He grabbed hold of the empty window frame with one hand, cutting himself on the jagged edges, but hung on, reached around to unlatch the window and step through. The rope was pulled out of his grip by sailors racing to clear the decks and salvage what they could.

Jack dropped into the room, looking around for signs of life. He saw no one. The cabin was opulent, as he had come to expect from Price. A well set table stood in front of him, though there was wine spilled everywhere and glass lay scattered across the floor he noticed. He bent to pick a large piece out of the side of his foot. There were several lamps, all lit and giving off the acrid stink of burning whale oil, and all of them had their glass broken out. Being careful where he set his bare feet, he drew his cutlass and began to search the cabin.

The room was in a selective shambles. Everything made of glass was broken and whatever it held scattered on the table and floor, rolling back and forth with the pitch and swell of the ship. Jack checked the bed, but it was empty and made, with no sign of Sirene. There was a set of cabinets on one wall facing the bed where numerous bottles of liquor and wine were kept. Only the unopened bottles of wine survived, and those in heavy cut-crystal decanters. There was a pool of smeared blood amid the remains of a glass bowl on the floor. Fruit was scattered everywhere. He turned and watched an apple roll across the deck. It hit something in the middle of the room that he could not see from where he crouched. He sidestepped the dining room table and saw silver-white locks splayed out on the floor and the sticky red liquid pooling below it.

He dropped his cutlass and skidded to her side, heedless of the glass slicing his feet. Dropping to one knee, he straddled the other leg over her body which was twisted with her hips facing one direction and her head another. There was red everywhere, and a set of irons draped across her back. He tossed them out of the way, hesitant to touch her body. He was afraid to find her lifeless; afraid to move her if she was not. The apple rolled away again, leaving a trail of red that ran much too fast to be blood. He dipped his fingers in the liquid, smelled it: wine.

He breathed a sigh of relief, pressed his brow to the back of her head. Taking a deep breath, something else caught his attention: the coppery smell of blood, not just wine. Gingerly, he ran his fingers through her hair, felt bloody lacerations on her scalp and gently lifted her up, shifting her arm and laying her on her back. He brushed the hair out of her face with salt-wet hands, was aware that he was dripping all over her and was suddenly inspired.

He grabbed the end of his sash and used it to wipe her face, dabbing at the deep purple and red mark on her cheek and the side of her eye. He squeezed the fringe, trying to wring out as much of the salt water onto her face as he could.

Her lip moved, her face leaned slightly into his hand. He cradled her, whispering, "Come on, luv. I know it hurts, darlin', but ye have to help me out here."

There was a crash of thunder and the angry hiss of the sky opening up in earnest. He frowned as he looked out the window. Rain meant the dolphin would have left, seeking safer waters. He would have to jump with Sirene or risk losing her in the dark and stormy seas. Almost as if to stress the point, water and wind blew in through the open windows, extinguishing most of the lights. He turned back to her still form, saw the glint of her eyes fluttering open in the partial darkness.

"Gods below, what did th' bastard do to ye?" he breathed, kissing her.

She melted into the moment, then her hand stiffened on his shoulder in alarm.

"Nothing compared to what I am *going* to do to her," came Price's silky-smooth voice from the open door.

Jack whipped around, still supporting her with one arm while his other fished for his cutlass. He cursed himself for not paying attention, for dropping his weapon out of his reach, for not hearing the door open because of the thunder, and not noticing the sea snake's presence not two fathoms away.

Price was illuminated briefly by lightning. He looked very unlike himself. His coat was wet and plastered against his body, his wig was gone, replaced by a bandage over one ear and a pistol gleamed evilly in his hand.

Jack slowly moved his leg from the other side of her body, gathering his feet beneath him and reaching for the chain.

Price cocked the pistol. "I wouldn't try that if I were you," he said with his usual calm, though there was something underlying it which rang warning bells to Sirene. "I do not know how much my little runaway slave has told you, but would you like to see if seawater will heal a bullet in her head?"

Her hand drifted up to his chest, pressed against him in warning. She felt something very out of place; something that almost burned her fingers with its need for her. She tried to keep her expression steady, though she knew Price could not see her face clearly. She sat up and hugged him, keeping her eyes on Price and her hand inside Jack's shirt.

"Don't hurt him," she begged, as if trying to shield him.

"Of course I am going to hurt him, my dear. And then I am going to hang him. You need only pray that I do not dangle you beside him."

Jack was confused, but did not show it. He scowled at Price over her shoulder, looking for any opportunity for escape. Then he felt her fingers fiddling with the catch on the chain around his neck.

"You need me," she exclaimed.

He felt it release and the pearl drop deeper into his shirt. She ran her hand down his chest, manipulating the jewel below his sash into his belly button. It did not vanish completely, but the many folds of his sash camouflaged it enough that if he were searched it would not readily be found. Now he understood and tried to pull away from her, to move in front of her.

"Not if you are going to try to escape at every turn and sabotage my..." Price was tired of the display. "That will be quite enough, Mr. Wyndlam. Another move and I'll shoot you both."

"With what?" Jack challenged. "You've only got one shot."

Before Price could produce a second piece, Sirene moved quickly. The sudden movement sent her head spinning and she hit the deck, still trying to reach Price.

"Please," she gasped, resisting the urge to vomit. She dragged herself to her knees and blocked his shot of Jack completely. "If you let him live, I... I'll stay with you willingly."

He actually laughed. "Did I hear you right?" he mocked, fiddling with the unbandaged ear. "Someone recently tried to blow my eardrums out, so I don't think I could have heard you correctly. You expect me to let him sail away unharmed? We've sailed that route before, Margaret. I did not take you for such a fool."

"Then send him to prison instead. It is an acceptable punishment. He's been inactive for four years," she bargained, thinking quickly. "To make sure we are both holding up our ends you can take me to the prison twice a year to confirm for myself that he is alive and guarantee you another six months of unquestioned obedience." She did not care if he ultimately accepted or not, only that the offer bought Jack time.

"I will think about it," he growled, hearing someone on the steps behind him.

"Everything all right, Captain?"

"No, it is not," Price said, stepping into the room and out of the way of the door. "It seems we have a pirate aboard, Corporal, trying to rescue his crew. See that he is made uncomfortable."

He kept his pistol trained as the corporal moved into the room, grabbing the irons lying conveniently nearby. Jack did not resist, nor did he flinch as the man cursorily checked him for weapons. He did not find anything and dragged Jack to his feet, guided him roughly out the door. Jack stepped gingerly, realizing that there was glass in his feet again.

"And Corporal," Price warned as they passed. "Be careful. This man is as slippery as an eel and has better sea legs than you. Remember, Wyndlam," he sneered in Jack's face. "If we get down there and you are not where you are supposed to be, I'll drag her into the bilge and drown her myself."

Jack's only answer was a scowl. Sirene remained on her knees, trying to still the sickening feeling as Jack's glow, vying for dominance next to Price's blackness, faded from her view. Then Price hauled her to her feet and dragged her to the table.

"Here we are again, Margaret," he said.

"How... how is the Vice Admiral?" she asked weakly, her head slowly clearing as the little bit of seawater did its work.

"It seems that his position may be opening up sooner than expected for entirely different reasons." He did not seem terribly upset by this revelation.

Sirene gaped. "But, I can't... that is not within my power!"

He forced her head around, and showed her the cabinet and the broken bowl. "It seems a shattered fruit bowl makes for excellent daggers. Belly wounds are right dreadful."

She fought between the horror at having been the cause of the man's eventual and excruciating death, and a sense of justice considering his cruel and distorted sense of morals. She did not have time to dwell on the matter as Price pulled her close, seemed to contemplate kissing her. She stared at his disgusted sneer, holding her breath as the pit fell out of her stomach at the thought of his lips anywhere on her body. She could feel his arousal against her leg, felt another surge of bile threaten to erupt. To her relief, he appeared to be having trouble getting the image of Jack kissing those same lips out of his head. Finally, he threw her at the table and walked around it to the windows.

She narrowly avoided cutting her face open on a shattered wine glass. She brushed it and the half eaten plate of roast pork away. As she started to straighten up, Price reached across and grabbed her wrists, pulling her towards him until her thighs hit the edge of the carved wood.

"Oh no," he ground. "You are not getting out of it that easily."

He snatched one of the curtain ropes and tied it around one wrist, looping it around the middle table leg on his side and then binding her other wrist to the first. It was a softer restraint than he preferred, but it would have to do. He stalked around the table, not taking his eyes off her for a moment.

The apple rolled back with the surge of another wave, hit his foot. He picked it up and forced it into her mouth. She fought the urge to throw up as she tasted her own blood as well as wine on its rosy surface. "There, we'll not be having a repeat of that performance. I'd cut your tongue out if I thought it would help, but it won't keep you from hitting that note, only articulating, and I happen to like your singing."

Sirene tried to block him out of her mind as he stood behind her, lifted her skirts and kicked her feet apart. "Still not wearing respectable underthings," he accused. "Easier access for your pirates, I expect."

She kicked back at him, connected solidly with his shin. He pressed close over her back, his hands tight around her waist. "You'll pay for that later," he snarled, then frowned deeper. "You've been neglecting your corseting."

She growled.

"We shall have to rectify that when we return to Barbados. You'll be sleeping in it again." She squealed angrily. "And I shall have to cut your rations... providing I decide to let you live that long. I could still hang you beside him."

She stopped struggling then, grabbing hold of the curtain bindings and blocked what he was doing out of her mind. She would have bitten through the apple, but she felt something sharp embedded in its skin and concentrated hard on not doing so. It helped to have a focus.

Jack had been left in the chains and thrown into a small cage in the lower hold that he strongly suspected had once housed an animal of some sort. He was alone down here, though there were a few stalls that were currently occupied by a pair of goats and three pigs who were none too happy with the current weather conditions. As soon as he was certain no one would observe, he reached into his shirt and sash, pulling out the pearl. He had to thread it back on its chain before slipping it around his neck again for safe-keeping.

He then began picking pieces of glass out of his feet. He was very grateful he preferred to walk the decks barefoot most of the time. Between that and having no shoes at all for the last four years, the soles of his feet were tough enough that the glass was only a minor inconvenience.

Eventually, he stood up, took a single stride and crossed the breadth of the cell and examined the bulkhead. If his hands were not bound by the short chain, he would have just been able to touch the planks. The boxes stacked next to his cage served some interest, as their sides were rough and splintering. If he was careful, he might be able to peel off a length sufficient to pick the locks between him and freedom. He did not dare at the moment. He remembered Price's warning, but would bide his time. Soon.

On the other side of him was empty cargo netting and across the narrow lane was another set of cages. One of them was vaguely body shaped and would not afford its occupant room to do anything but stand. Even turning around would be difficult depending upon their size.

He was curious as to why he had not been thrown in the normal brig, a deck above him. He could only imagine that it was currently full of his own crew. The corporal returned shortly with a cup and a bowl of some gruel-like substance which would not fit through the bars. The man refused to uncuff Jack so that he might be able to at least manipulate a spoon in between. He set the two objects on the ground beside the cage and quickly left. Jack might have been imagining it, but he thought the man looked a little green.

He got on his knees and manipulated the mug into the cage, drank some of the water. He did not even try to rescue the bowl as it slid across the deck to spill against another cell. To keep his mind off what Price must be putting Sirene through, he began to peel off a length of wood sufficient to pick his locks while he ran various scenarios through his mind on how best to kill the man. A bullet through the head was too good for him.

Jack lost track of the time in the insufficient light. The storm outside worsened, battering the ship mercilessly. He would rather have been up on deck, his preferred location in a storm. He could not explain why. It felt wrong to be inside while the ship was in danger, not that she was in any real danger in the sheltered harbour. Only a typhoon or a hurricane would sink her here.

He heard footsteps descending into the hold, two people, single file. Then he heard Sirene's voice protesting. "Ambrose, I..." she was cut off by the sound of flesh on flesh in violence. Jack ground his teeth and clenched his fists, but held his silence. When she spoke again there was a subservient tone to her voice. "Captain, I did as you asked, what you wanted. Why...."

Price pressed close to her. "Yes, you did. As tight as ever, I might add."

She stared in horror at the horsewhip in his hand. She watched as he opened one of the crates by the door, and pulled out a brand new set of chains with the cuff-styled manacles he preferred. "Lovely," he admired, holding them up in front of her. "And they compliment your colouring nicely."

"But why?" she choked, slowly backing away, her whole body beginning to burn as it remembered.

"For embarrassing me, of course," he replied casually. "For

running out on me and forcing me to chase you and my own ship the whole length of the Caribbean."

Jack could hear them nearing, the chains rattling, Sirene stumbling backward in fear and Price stalking her. Strain as he might, he could not see past the crates.

"For throwing my career away for some low-life sea scum," he continued, speaking louder than was necessary. "For nearly deafening me and ending my naval career. ...Because it brings me pleasure to cause you pain."

She saw his eyes flicker past a stack of crates where some cages had been set up as make-shift cells, saw the half-concealed glow and she suddenly understood. All of this was to torture Jack, to display Price's dominance to him.

"What makes you think he gives a damn about what happens to me?"

"He came back for you, didn't he? I saw how he touched you..."

"I promised him a great treasure if he helped me find my pearl and escape you," she said, slowly backing away, trying to buy time.

"Oh, really?" Greed rose to the surface. Recovered pirate treasure was always a good way to buy a promotion. "Who's?"

"I told him I know where the *Ana Maria Salvador* sank."

"And do you?"

She made an annoyed sound. "No. Well, yes, but she's not retrievable. She's at the bottom of a trench. Even *with* my pearl it would be impossible. Even I can't swim that deep. I would have said anything to get him to help me."

"He will not take that well," he replied, with a mocking smile. It confirmed that Jack was listening, and it amused Price to have his hopes and heart dashed by Sirene's 'confession'. "How ever would you have gotten away?"

She sighed. She hoped it would be interpreted as a resigned confession, but in reality it was a reluctance to keep lying, in doubt that she could convince Jack it *had* all been lies. "By then

I would have had my pearl and jumped overboard. It is not like he could have caught me. But that is not likely to occur now, is it?"

Price laughed, a chilling sound. "Your lying skills need work. Your claims belie the bargain you tried to make not an hour ago."

"Just because I don't want him hung does not mean I love him. I despised my brother, but I suffered you for him. I gave father my word."

"I don't believe you," he answered flatly, took a step forward, driving her back again. "But now, more importantly, neither does he. Or at the very least he doesn't know what to think."

Sirene looked to her right, saw Jack sitting on the floor watching with a look of pain. Their eyes met for a long moment, communicated volumes. There was no surprise in her silvery depths, only suffering. His eyes were wholly brown and dark with rage, but not directed at her. He had seen the whip in Price's hands. Sirene's eyes drifted to where the pearl was hidden, said everything he needed to know.

"Isn't that right, Wyndlam?" Price asked, looking over at him.

"Aren't ye supposed to be on deck?" Jack snarled. "There's a storm above, an' yer down here getting' yer jollies."

Price gestured dismissively, and looked around at the ceiling. "That is what junior officers are for. Besides, we are in harbour. We are safe. And I am after all on the injured list." He spotted a pair of lamp hooks. "Yes, that will do nicely. Take off your dress," he ordered.

Her hands went to her bodice. "What?"

His eyes darkened, but his voice did not change. "I'll not have you padded or protected in any way. Nor will I have you gallivanting about this vessel naked because that is in shreds. Now remove the dress." He saw the defiant lift of her chin and pulled his pistol, aimed it at Jack though he never took his eyes from her.

Jack watched Price like one watches a snake. "I'm th' one yer pissed at fer markin' yer territory, Price. Take it out on me, not her."

"That's *Captain* Price, dog," he snapped, still without looking at Jack. "And I *am* taking it out on you," he added smugly.

He cocked the pistol and Sirene angrily began to undo her laces. "You see," he continued, "your reputation as a gentleman and a hater of slavery precedes you. Once I knew who I was in pursuit of, I took the time to do my research. What I am about to do is going to hurt you almost as much as it is going to hurt her."

Sirene threw her dress to the floor by Jack's small cell, stood naked yet somehow still defiant in front of them. Her body was glorious. Her curves had filled out, her waist was not so waspish, her breasts more full and natural. Jack smiled. Price frowned.

"You've grown fat," he scowled. "As soon as this storm clears we will be going into Jamestown and buying you a new corset. I'll have you back down to a respectable twenty inches before Easter."

It was Jack's turn to frown. Her body had blossomed beneath his hands, filling out where a woman's should. A scent caught his attention as Price began to lock the manacles around her wrists: sex. It was on her and her dress, and it was recent. He forced himself not to lunge at the cage bars. He would not give Price the satisfaction. He watched helplessly as Price strung her up from the lamp hooks, facing him in the middle of the walkway. He took her hair in hand, twisting it and pinning it up with a long toothed comb he produced from a pocket.

Their eyes met, Jack and Sirene. There was no fear in hers, only sadness. She trembled in the chill air, attempted to keep her balance with the rocking of the ship in the storm. The single lantern swung wildly, casting bizarre shadows on the walls. Not far away the animals squealed and brayed in fear, huddled in their boxes. She was prepared for the pain, knew it well. She was not prepared to see the pain in Jack's eyes as he was forced to watch. It embarrassed her somehow for him to see her brought so low.

Yet she wanted him to know she would endure anything to save his life: even a landlocked life. Then the first strike fell. Her body surged against the chains as the leather wrapped halfway around her ribs.

She gasped, turned to look at Price with wide eyes. "You... aren't going to gag me?"

"No," he said, a fierce look in his eyes. "As you well know, I like to hear the screams. But your voice... now that would be problematic... Does... does he know?" he asked suddenly. He turned to Jack who was pressed against the bars with murder in his eyes. "She has this voice, you see. Lovely singing voice. Could lure sailors to their deaths on the reefs," he paused to laugh at his own joke. "But if she hits the right note, with the right volume... and she does have quite a set of lungs on her all things considered. ...Well, you remember the shambles the Vice Admiral's cabin was in? That was all her doing, with one single scream. Left one of my servants deaf ten years ago when he tried to have his way with her."

He stepped close to her, ran his fingers along the thin red line dripping blood down her ribs. She shuddered. "Normally I have to silence her in order to discipline her. Lest she forget herself and cause *me* injury," he went on, pointed to his bandaged ear. "This time however, I think I'll risk it. Because if she hurts me, she hurts you," he grinned wickedly, put his mouth close to her ear. "So scream if it pleases you, my dear, by all means! ...Hell, deafen him and I'll set him off at the next port and never think twice about him, no prison, no noose."

He pulled away, laughing. Sirene clamped her mouth shut, took a deep breath and steeled herself. Price laid into her. The horsewhip barely left her body that it wasn't digging in somewhere else.

Jack stood, hands tightly gripping the bars, his eyes locked on hers. When the lash missed and struck his hand he did not flinch, tried to keep her attention on him. There were tears in her eyes, and now and again noises would escape her throat, but she kept them as low pitched and guttural as she could. Her lip bled where she bit it in effort to keep her mouth closed.

Price was a madman, flailing away at every part of her he could reach, ignoring the pitch and swell of the deck below him. If he stumbled, he struck harder.

'Vieve crossed to the window of the burned out church and looked over Anjali's shoulder as the storm outside began to abate. "Can you still see 'er?" she asked softly, not wanting to wake Luke or Hare.

Anjali did not answer, but kept watch through the spyglass.

The moon was beginning to creep out from behind the clouds across the Narrows, casting her thin light over the still choppy waters. Directly across from them they could barely make out the HMS *Redoubt* shielding the smaller brig. The rain's trailing edge was slowly passing. In the shallow bay below them 'Vieve could barely see the little boat they had been forced to abandon half-in, half-out of the water. None of these things were what held Anjali's attention.

Her eyes were on the promontory edge at something she had sensed rather than seen lying in wait there. Now that the storm had passed, that something surged forth like a wolf from its den seeking new prey. Anjali's breath caught in her throat as the moonlight struck the prow of the caravel and peeled back the layer of shadow to reveal her identity. There was only one ship that bore a coat of pale grey paint: the *Mercy's Ransom*.

She gleamed like a ghost as the light struck her, which was the intent. Anjali passed the glass to Genevieve, prayed to her gods that this was good for the Captain and bad for the British.

'Vieve gasped.

"Beautiful, isn't she?" Anjali said, and smiled.

"'Ave you seen ze flag?" 'Vieve asked, handing the glass back.

Anjali snatched it up, returning it to her eye. The colours being run up were not the cold grey flag with the crossed sabres and black half-skull that stared at you like holes in the night that she was used to. The skull was whole and the sabres, still black, dripped blood and the field.... At night it was almost impossible to distinguish, even under moonlight, but the field was blood red.. "No quartah," she breathed. "When did we start flying no quartah?"

Hare looked out the window, sleepily rubbing his eyes. "Well, Ah'll be a cob's whisker! She were right!"

"Does zat mean zey'll keell captives, too? And ze capitane?" 'Vieve asked.

Anjali closed the glass and put it away, grabbing their things. "If they get to them before they find th' captain, aye. If Fenning finds th' Captain first, it won't mattah."

Lucas was jerked awake by the sudden report of cannon fire.

Chapter the Tenth

Sirene hung limply in the chains, no part of her body left untouched. There were even stripes upon her face. There was another boom of cannon, and this time the *Redoubt* shuddered. The ship's bell was ringing madly and on the decks above they could hear the cannons rolling out and sailors scrambling. Price pulled keys out of his pocket and went to unlock her, then realized that the keys to these manacles were still in the crate. He returned them to his coat, unhooked her, opened the nearest cage-cell and threw her in. He slammed it closed, and ran up on deck to take command. Jack stared at her, listening to the crackling thunder of cannons.

"Th' *Mercy*," he mused. "Ye were right." As he pulled the splinter of wood from where he had hidden it and began to pick the locks on his manacles he heard her stir.

"Why do you always doubt me?" she replied weakly.

He bolted to the cage door, and then took a step back when the whole thing rocked forward. Once it settled he approached more carefully.

"Sirene?" he called.

She raised her head, forcing herself to her stand. Her feet and hands were about the only unmarked surface on her body. She staggered, used the door to steady herself. Jack frowned as it swung open under her hands.

"How come he didn't lock ye in?"

She gave a dry chuckle. "Did it look like I could escape?" she asked, pulling the comb from her hair.

The damp locks tumbled over her shoulders nearly to her hips, clinging everywhere. The seawater Jack had dripped on her earlier had helped a little. She stumbled across the narrow way, grabbing for the cage to steady herself. He tried to reach out to help her, but the manacles would not allow his hands to go through the bars far enough.

She pressed her head against his cell, revelling in the taste of his lips and the touch of his salt-wet fingers. His clothes were far from dry yet, and he started to take off his shirt for her. He stopped when he heard the click of the lock and the creaking of the door as it opened.

He stared in shock, saw the keys dangling against her palm and grinned. Stepping out, he threw his arms over her, and kissed her. He tried not to press too hard, but to make as much contact with her wounds as possible with the still damp fabric.

"You... are a woman... after me own larcenous heart," he said in between kisses.

She laughed, turned in his embrace and, still weak, leaned back against him as she looked for the handcuff key on the ring. "That's not all I'm after."

"Well, aside from me salt," he purred, grinning.

He began to kiss the lines on her shoulders while she unlocked him. The ship rocked violently as she unfastened the last bolt, throwing the chains into a heap against the other cages. There was a crack from above and an eerie moment of silence. Then everything shuddered.

"You have to go," she breathed.

"Not without ye."

"Aye," she insisted. "I'll be safer here. You... need to stop them... before they sink us. Though I pray you still have men loyal to you on that ship," she said.

"Oh, I do. So long as Tortuga is alive, I have that ship." Reluctantly, he untangled himself from her. He took the pearl from his neck, and slipped it on hers. "Now yer safe. Even should they sink 'er."

She felt the silver hum and the pearl sing against her breast and laughed softly. "Especially should they sink her." She laid a hand on his arm. "I do not know where the crew is. They should still be on the *Ambition*."

He gave her one last kiss before running up top, and Sirene struggled into her dress. Thankfully, it too was still wet in places. Not enough to do any real healing, but enough to give her the strength to continue.

The animals were in a panic, as were the crew above. She staggered toward the pens and the stack of crates beside them, dragging her chains behind her. The keys should be somewhere in the crate with the other shackles. She noted, though, that these were the kind of bindings designed to fasten limbs to walls, not limb to limb and their presence on board a military vessel confused her; unless this was being used as a slave ship or prisoner transport.

The vessel shuddered again, rocking under the force of cannon fire. Everything in the hold shifted, as the bolts holding one of the cargo nets to the bulkhead snapped free. Sirene fell to the deck, covering her head.

Jack did not get very far. The next deck up contained the armoury, right beside the companionway. He went in, and found only a few weapons not yet in use. His cutlass was there, and a handful of knives, which he grabbed. As he headed out, he looked farther down that deck and noticed it was the actual brig. He was surprised to find it full. There were even a few cages like in the hold, where the regular cells were over full.

These men were ragged and tired, torn at the moment between fear and hope. They saw Jack and began begging him to let them out. He pulled out the keys he had gotten from Sirene, ran to the nearest cell and went to work.

Anjali and the others raced down to the longboat, turning it over and climbing in. She grabbed the two foremost oars, leaving 'Vieve and Lucas to man a side apiece. They were hard pressed keeping up with the larger woman. She gave orders for Hare to load the pistols, and the boy scrambled to do so in the slim moonlight.

On deck, all hands were in a panic. Some believed a ghost ship was descending upon them, rising out of hell's own waters. The officers whipped them into action as they set to repel boarders. The *Ambition* was protected by the larger vessel's bulk, though the falling mast nearly took out her own. The soldiers on board the brig used the *Redoubt*'s mast as a gangplank and raced up it to the other ship's rescue. Unguarded, it quickly became clear which of the *Ambition*'s hired crew were open to the sweet trade. About half of them swarmed after the soldiers with hostile intent, led by a screaming Mary and armed with anything at hand, including belaying pins.

Another cannon ball opened a huge hole in the side of the prison deck and Jack realized very quickly how close to the water line they were. There were renewed shouts from the men in the cells, as Jack got the last door open. They swarmed past him, racing for the top decks and freedom. The vessel listed again as the last few barrelled past. They lost their balance, falling to the deck and sliding towards the breach, taking Jack with them.

Jack kept himself and one of them from going out the hole, but two others fell in. The water seethed and the men below screamed. He saw the flailing dorsals of three sharks and clung tighter to the jagged side of the ship, trying to pull himself up. The last man managed to clear the gap and reached back for Jack. As he was about to accept the hand, he heard the angry squeal of dolphins and looked down. There were about four of them charging in. It was then that Jack noticed the black cannons protruding from the grey ship behind him, priming.

He looked up at the man trying to help him, and yelled, "Run!"

The man was not listening, shouted something about grabbing his hand, so Jack let go. He crossed his arms over his chest and plunged feet first. The man ran just before the cannonball tore into the bulkhead, tearing a wide swath in her side where they had just been standing.

Jack hit the water and sank, watching above him as the moonlight was blocked out by the approaching ship. He swam down, trying to get out of the way as the *Mercy* closed for boarding. Even the shark versus dolphin battle moved. One of the sharks was already dead and the other two were fleeing with the dolphins on their tails. His foot hit the top of the reef and he used it to push off in the direction of the grey ship.

Battle on the *Redoubt* was finished shortly after the pirate crew boarded her. The Vice Admiral lay dying in the doctor's berth. Lord Hamilton had been struck by the chainshot that shredded the mast and their captain had entered the battle wounded.

Price found the fight difficult, having one injured ear. His balance was off and the rocking pitch of a ship under fire was not helping. He issued orders more than once, being unable to hear responses over the din of combat. Deaf to reports not directly in front of him, he did not hear his lieutenant's warning, nor did he see the pistol until the ball bit into his shoulder. He fell forward onto the back of a bald-headed pirate who took one look at his uniform and tossed him overboard.

Sirene struggled against the chains. The wall of crates beside Jack's cell had spilled over, killing a goat and two pigs and landing on the tails of her chains. She tried to reach the first row of crates to find the keys, but it was several feet away. And the cargo was too heavy for her to move in her weakened state.

She lay on the floor breathing heavily and waiting for the ship to sink, hoping the water would grant her the strength to pull free. At worst, she could call Skilly back, or a whale to batter her out of here.

She heard footsteps on the companionway, and looked up to see a giant towering above her. She did not even notice the others behind him swarming to salvage what they could. All she saw was the seven-foot tall man with skin like pitch and a curious scarf of faded and frayed gold silk wrapped around the upper portion of his left arm. It could only be one man.

She raised a hand toward him. "Tortuga... I beg you. Throw me overboard."

One eyebrow disappeared out of sight.

Jack was quickly fetched by the juvenile dolphin who had guided him out here. She swooped past him, allowing him to grab her dorsal and ride her to the surface. He quickly found his way to the bow of the *Mercy*, snagged a rope from the spritsail that had been torn loose by a stray cannonball, and climbed upwards. Above, he could hear the sounds of the crew returning and the shouts of victory as they brought prisoners on board.

He reached the feet of the figurehead, a winged woman in a flowing dress falling at her shoulders, holding a king's ransom in carved gold and jewels in her outstretched hands. Real chains bound her to the prow, which were rusting from the salt and the sea and lack of care. He wondered what else Fenning had failed to attend to in way of maintenance.

The dolphin watched from below, though she ducked once or twice when it seemed he would slip. Climbing in between the *Mercy*'s open arms, Jack paused to peer into her pleading face. Next to Sirene, she was the most beautiful sight he had ever seen. He pressed a kiss to her flaking wooden cheek, telling her to have patience with him and forgive him for leaving her for so long.

On deck, the pirate captain stood in front of everyone as his men separated the prisoners into two groups, those who had fought the pirates and those who had fought the Navy. Those who had been found on other decks and had not fought at all were grouped with the British. Sirene was on the pirate's side, but to the rear and slightly off to the side in front of the steps to the quarterdeck, pressed back against the black man who had brought her out of the hold. The ends of her chains were wound in his massive fist and one large hand was set protectively on her shoulder. She got the distinct impression he would be claiming her as his share when all was said and done. She welcomed the support he provided, leaning willingly against him, which was causing very interesting reactions in his glow. This was clearly a man used to being feared.

Fenning was a tall man, close to a fathom in height, give or take a breath, and broad across the shoulders. He was completely bald, which made his long yellow beard seem out of place. It was coarse and heavily braided and beaded, even his moustache. On his head was a red tattoo of a runic arrow which ran from the nape of his neck over the crown and capped on his brow with the tip just between his eyes. He was not dressed fancy. In fact, he only stood out because of his stance, his sword and the tattoos on his body. He had no shirt, just a worn-out vest of some unidentifiable leather with the fur still inside and his boots were wrapped from ankle to knee in leather bindings. The tattoos, what could be seen of them in the torchlight, were of winged women in exotic armour riding massive wolves.

When he spoke, his voice was thickly accented German.

"Yu haf two choices," he announced. "Sign mein artikles, or be returned t' yer ship!"

One of the sailors dared to point out, "But... the *Redoubt's* sinking."

Fenning grinned and the man fell silent, the seriousness of what lay before them sinking in. He paced before the assembled prisoners.

"which vun uf ye *gemeiner hunds* is das captain?"

Sirene perked up, looking for the black nothingness amid the assembled bodies. She was amazed at how many blue hearts beat among the pirate crew. Sure, a great many were tainted, but largely they were an honest lot; not that they would not lie, cheat, or steal, but they were honest at how they presented themselves. They were pirates and few would deny that. Some had palls over theirs, a dirty coating of yellow and brown amid the red and blues of their outer glows. A good third of the crew was apparently crimped.

Not finding Price, she turned her attention to Fenning, and observed the black core that hid everything and the swirl of crimson that surrounded the rest of him. His light was strong, casting a red pall on all near him, making them harder to read. When no one answered, he pointed out one of the *Redoubt's* boys and a crewman dragged him forth, holding his knife to the young throat.

"I ask again," Fenning said.

A lieutenant spoke up. "You threw him overboard, sir."

Fenning stalked over and stared in the man's eyes. "Are ye sure uf das, pretty boy?"

The officer tried to hold his breath. "I saw you throw him over the side myself. He was shot, he fell against you and you shoved him over the rail."

Sirene could not keep her comments to herself. "Seems to be a habit with you, doesn't it, hagfish?"

She felt Tortuga's hand tighten on her shoulder and stifled a yelp.

Fenning's head went up. He waded through prisoners, seeking her out like a hunting shark.

"Vas das yu, *kleine perle*?" he growled dangerously as he stopped and glared into her face.

Tortuga squeezed again, but she resisted. "Tell me," she snapped, "did you at least make sure he was dead first?"

He frowned. Clearly this was not the reaction he expected. "Die sharks've finished him fur sure."

"Those... were dolphins," she explained as she would have to a child.

Fenning took in her weakened state, the bloody marks all over her body and face, and the chains in Tortuga's huge fist. "A white slave?" he asked. "On a Britich naval ship?" He looked into her defiant silvery eyes. "Or are yu a thief, *hure*, or political prisoner?"

"I was the captain's slave," she gasped, choking on the man's breath. It smelled like carrion.

She was aware of the mixed reactions from the *Redoubt*'s crew.

Tortuga looked down at her and frowned. His hand rest more gently on her shoulder. "Wha' did you do, *fotsy iray*, to earn such a stripin'?"

She looked up at him, bathed in the brilliant cobalt of his glow. "I took a fancy to yer captain," she said with a faint smile.

Fenning guffawed, a reaction that echoed throughout his crew except for Tortuga. "Sorry, *mien schatz*, but I like my vomen a bit less scrahny."

Sirene saw movement at the bowsprit, heard the dolphin's

triumphant whistle and laughed. "Not you, idiot. *Him.*"

She pointed to a form hunched between the back-spread wings of the *Mercy*'s figurehead. Fenning spun. As the dark silhouette rose against the moonlight, there was a collective gasp throughout the ship. Every man held his breath.

Jack stood slowly on the bow rail, one hand tight on his sword, framed by the back arch of the *Mercy*'s wings. His sash flapped in the breeze, water dripped from his body and ran across the foredeck. Superstitious, those standing nearby moved their feet to avoid the run-off, as if it would taint them.

Tortuga was the first to speak. "Capta'n!" he shouted in surprise.

The crew looked from the figure to Tortuga and back again. It could only be one man. The black giant had never called *any* man captain except for Jack Wyndlam. Some how he had always managed to avoid using the term with Fenning. Whispers spread through the crews as it had that night in the tavern.

A pirate stepped timidly forward. "Captain Jack? Is that really you or some devil-shade thrown back from the depths?"

"The sea is my mother," Jack intoned, pitching his voice so that it would carry through the sails. "This ship is my home. And no mere *man* is ever going to throw me off it!"

He jumped off the bowsprit and stalked across the deck. Sailors scattered, giving him room, though they continued to stare in awe and wonder. Fenning stepped forward, meeting Jack amidships.

"I don' remember gifing yu permission to come aboard, Herr Vyndlam," he growled.

"Why should ye? Yer th' usurper," Jack replied with perfect calm. He spread his hands to indicate the surrounding crew. "I wonder how they'll feel about yer captaincy when they find out how ye got it?"

The accusation did not fluster Fenning, but Sirene could see that it angered him. She sank back against Tortuga, weak, but feeling safer now that Jack was here.

"How did yu surfife der hurricane?" he countered. "Vat deals vit das defil did yu make?"

"No deals, no devils." Jack crowed, gave a saucy bow, leading with his sword. "I was rescued by a mermaid."

This had an interesting reaction amongst the crew. Sirene chuckled. Tortuga looked down at her, then up at Jack, suspecting there was something more to the statement, but said nothing. Instead, he picked her up and set her on the steps to the quarterdeck behind him where she could rest and still see. He took up a position in front of her, arms crossed on his naked chest.

Below, Skilly clicked and clattered, trying to get Sirene to answer or come into the water. She stretched over to the rail and saw the long boat gliding up alongside. She reached down and tapped Tortuga. He glared back at her and she pointed over the side with a broad grin. He frowned, leaned only enough to see that there was something down there and hear someone climbing the side. He scowled and moved closer just as a dark, familiar head popped up.

"Anji!" he roared, grabbing the woman and hauling her over the side in his joy.

Everyone looked except for the combatants.

Fenning lunged at Jack and the dance began. His older Viking blade did not yield so much as the newer steel cutlass, but had a tendency to take chunks out of whatever it bit into. Jack, having his sword already out and extended, easily managed to parry and retaliate. He had been waiting four years for this opportunity. He devoted all his focus to the fight.

A tight circle formed by the gathered crews, giving little room to dodge the combat when it surged too close. Then someone lost a hand to Fenning's hacking blade and those in the back moved up to the higher decks for a safer view, and those that couldn't headed into the rigging. No one intruded on the corner where Tortuga stood watching with the white woman he guarded on the steps above him and his wife tightly in arm.

'Vieve and the others slipped up behind them and kept anyone who reached the quarterdeck from getting any ideas regarding Sirene. Hare plopped down next to her and began picking the locks on her manacles. He continually reminded her to sit still as she tried to keep track of the fight.

The two captains traded nicks and cuts with no major wounds for either man for a full quarter hour. After the battle and the long swim both were wearing down, though neither was about to show it. Fenning fought like a demon, like he fought in ship-to-ship battles, using every tactic he knew to intimidate the smaller man. He was bulkier and taller and threw his weight around like a hammer on an anvil. He roared and yelled and hacked. At one point, he chopped solidly into the side rails, severing the ratline anchors and two of the shrouds on the starboard side. At least four men fell to the decks and one, unconscious, was dragged out of the way of the two men who danced across the planks.

Jack allowed his opponent to wear himself out faster with the extra effort. He concentrated on feints and darting manoeuvres that made the German throw his weight into places he wasn't and nicking him instead of slicing deep. His speed and nimbleness was his advantage, and he knew it. He did not think about what Fenning had been doing in front of Sirene, what he had been saying or planning. That would only enrage him and cause him to make a mistake he could little afford.

From the moment this man had come on board his ship in Port Royal five and a half years ago, Jack had been dreading this encounter, had studied the man's fighting skills to prepare for it. He had somehow known that eventually the man would challenge him. He had not, however, expected him to pitch him overboard in a storm. He had been exhausted then, keeping the ship steady and upright for hours. Now he had some sleep under him, and a good woman, too. Now he would not be taken by surprise and a hefted belaying pin.

He leapt to the capstan wheel, nimbly avoiding the brutal violence of the Viking blade on the spars before taking a leap to the hub. There he spread his hands, providing ample opening if Fenning wanted it. "Come on, Mr. Penny," he coaxed, turning the literal meaning of the man's name into a taunt. "Haven't ye got what it takes to swat a bee?"

"Das bee buzzes too much," he growled, refusing to rise to the bait and enter between the spars. Instead, gave one of them a shove, forcing Jack to move off or risk pinching his bare feet on the moving bolt. Jack jumped for one of the dangling lines and swung over Fenning's head. The German's eyes followed the line quickly to its source, then chopped it off at the pin with his sword.

Jack hit the deck on his back and slid aft on a patch of water. He rolled as he went and was on his feet before people had to move out of his way.

He waited, luring his opponent in. He had numerous cuts on him, places where he had failed to completely evade the sword. There had been no solid connection for either of them. The more flexible materials of the modern cutlass helped to keep the heavier iron sword from breaking it outright when they connected; but Jack had to be careful how he parried.

Sirene watched in trepidation as they battled. Her hands now free, she kept them closely clamped over her mouth for fear she would cry out and distract him. Jack had been dodging in the same direction for several minutes, seeming to favour his left side where most of the nicks had landed.

Fenning charged in like a bull, avoiding the puddle that Jack had slipped on, prepared for another left hand dodge. Jack went right. Fenning spun at the last second, nearly breaking himself in half as he twisted to avoid the cutlass that chopped off nearly eight inches of his foot long beard.

Everything stopped.

Fenning watched the beaded plaits and the unbraided strands of crinkly blond hair clatter and drift to the deck and his eyes went red. Those nearest him saw the look and fell over themselves trying to escape. They bolted down the companion-way to the aft cabins in their haste to be out of the way, cursing as they went.

Jack frowned. This could be good, and this could be bad, he thought. He paid careful attention, waiting for the mistake that was about to be made, and prepared for the force that would come behind it like a tidal wave after an earthquake.

Fenning charged him, frothing like a Viking berserker. Jack backed up, well ahead of the charge. The Viking sword was high and the power that would fall with it would be terrible. Jack stepped to the right at the last second, dropping his cutlass into his left hand as he feinted. His upper body bent low as he brought the sword upward with all his remaining strength, taking him from right rib to left ear. Fenning, however, saw the feint and twisted, though the change in direction affected the velocity and the power behind his blow. The sword caught Jack across the face as Fenning took the ship's rail in the hip. The wood screamed, snapped, and then fell away, taking him with it into the waters below.

Sirene's outcry was lost in the tumultuous shouts from the assembled crews. She launched herself from the steps to Tortuga's shoulder to the deck as Jack crumbled. She pulled him away from the open side where crewmen were peering with lamps and torches to discover the fate of their former captain. She was not overly concerned with his other wounds, only with the one that had caused the spray of blood she had seen from the steps. The sword's leading edge had caught Jack under the apple of his left cheek and sliced across the eye and deeply into the brow.

"Oh, Mother, no," she begged, trying to staunch the blood, to survey the damage. The sickly white of bone gleamed beneath her fingers.

Jack smiled up at her with his one good eye.

Suddenly, her light was blocked by a huge shadow and she looked up to see Tortuga bending down with Anjali standing proudly behind him. Jack reached a hand up, and clasped the wrist of the larger man.

"Good to see ye again, Tortuga," Jack breathed. "I... found yer wife."

"More like dat demon goddess of hah's found you, Capta'n," he said, grinning. He was rewarded by a rap on the head by Anjali, which he ignored. "God, but I am glad to see you." He leaned forward, looked Jack's eye over and pulled the gold scarf from his arm. "I hate dat I saved it all dese yeah's for dis, but..."

Sirene helped Jack sit up as he eyed the familiar bit of yellow silk. "I'm surprised ye saved it at all." He frowned as Tortuga gently, but tightly, bound the scarf around his head and wounded eye, noticing the traces of gunpowder and old blood. "Looks a little worse fer wear."

Tortuga shrugged. "It kep' me alive all dese yeah."

Jack frowned, gestured to be pulled to his feet. "Are ye telling me yer gonna die in th' next battle 'cause ye gave back yer lucky bit?"

Tortuga nearly took him off the deck, laughing. "Nah, Capta'n. Yar heah, an' das bettah dan any lucky bit."

Anjali glared fiercely up at her husband, though there was unbridled joy in her eyes. "And what de devil am I?"

"A T'uggee witch!" he growled, snatching her off her feet and kissing her into silence.

Sirene fussed over Jack, ordered Hare to find the ship's doctor. Jack held onto her, but ignored her protests that he was not up to whatever it was he was trying to do. He raised his voice to the men and women milling about on deck, some in celebration, some trepidation, and still others not sure what it would mean for them.

"First orders of business!" he bellowed. "Anyone *else* want to challenge me?"

No one answered.

"Fine. Quartermasters, step forward and separate out yer crews!"

Anjali pulled out of her husband's arms and moved off, seeking out the survivors of the *Ambition*. The *Mercy*'s quartermaster was killed in the first volley so Tortuga elected himself in his place and no one opposed him. Those that had been on board when Jack was still captain knew it was only right. The others just did not want to tangle with him.

"Jack, you have to stop long enough for the doctor to look you over. You could bleed out," Sirene complained, even though the blood had stopped running from beneath the silk. "And you are weak," she added in a lower voice.

This brought something else to mind. Jack glanced her over, noticed that she was only on her feet out of sheer will and concern for him. "Tortuga," he called. The man walked over. Behind him, the *Mercy*'s crew continued to sort themselves out.

"Aye, Capta'n?"

"Kindly throw this woman overboard."

She gaped at him, "Jack!"

The large Malagasy raised an eyebrow, but swept her up and marched towards the rail.

"...And Sirene," Jack added. Tortuga paused a moment. "Control yerself," he warned, then nodded. Before Sirene could retort, Tortuga let go.

She held her will as she held her breath, arched her body so that when she hit the water it was a smooth, clean dive. Skilly squealed in delight and dove after her, waiting for her body to twist into the change. She whistled in disappointment when Sirene just floated there, two legs continuing to scissor in the water, fussed at her.

Sirene sank and broke the surface again with her head back, to gt her hair out of her face. Glancing up, she could see the odd sailor peering over the side of the vessel. Standing on the high deck, Penn watched with a deep frown. Smiling, she waved at him as she conversed with Skilly, explained to her why she wasn't going to change and swim away with her, whilst she waited for her body to heal.

Skilly was chattering excitedly about the swim over with Jack when Sirene felt something bump her foot and ducked her head under the water. Swimming balefully past her, seeking out the fresh blood in the water, was a deep red glow that was growing more vermilion by the second. It was only a black-tipped reef shark but she knew it would only be a matter of time before bulls and whites showed up in droves. She surfaced, looked towards the ship and when her eyes made contact with Penn's she saw him make a shark-fin motion with his hand and point. She looked, saw scattered fins rise and fall, and dove.

She swam below the surface as she would have with her tail. She moved faster that way and with less noise to attract the hunters closing in. Skilly stayed with her long enough to see her out of the water and climbing the ladder Penn dropped for her.

"Meet me on the way to the Sargasso Desert," Sirene squealed after her.

The dolphin whistled an agreement and dove deep to avoid the packs closing in.

Penn helped her on deck and paused to make sure she was all right before moving into the cluster that was the *Ambition*'s crew. Sirene moved through them, headed to where Jack stood in the centre of the main deck.

Tortuga stopped her, scowling at her and the man who brought her back on board. He grabbed her arm to pull her to the rail when he looked down and saw the white skin unmarred by the cuts of the whip. He froze, eyes widening. She smiled up at him, slipping her hand free and patting his arm.

"I'm sure Jack will explain later," she told him in Malagasy, something else that caught him off guard.

Jack smiled when he saw her, and held out his hand. "Feel better, luv?" he asked, pulling her to him for mutual support.

"Much, thank you. Though I am still sore and you need to move that arm an inch more north or six south," she answered when the arm around her waist settled on one of the places too deep to heal completely.

He shifted. "Sorry, luv." He then turned to the assemblage surrounding him. He only recognized about a third of the *Mercy*'s crew. "Now," he began. "Those of ye who're pirates by desire, stand fast. Those forced to the account and wantin' out, step fore'd. *Redoubt*," he called, turning on his heel to face the soldiers and sailors gathered at the bow. "Who's standing captain?"

The lieutenant who had seen Price shot stepped forward stiffly, staring straight ahead at attention. Jack moved up to him, then surprised the hell out of him.

"Can you be trusted to see to the pardon of these men?" he asked, indicating those who had separated themselves from the *Mercy*'s crew.

The lieutenant's confusion was obvious. He had been expecting death or worse. "Aaye," he stammered, meeting Jack's eyes. "Aye, sir!" he repeated, as it sank in what was being asked and what it meant for the men behind him.

"Fine, then." Jack nodded, turning back to the others and stepping to the middle again. "Gentlemen, over there." The forced crewmen were quick to switch groups. Jack then addressed both crews. "Now, any o' ye fancy th' sweet trade under my command," he paused, looking up at the mast above him, suddenly remembering what was up there. "Mr. Falkes, get that atrocious red rag off m' top mast!" he bellowed. "Step to! Tortuga, we still got me old banner about, mate?"

"Aye, sah!" he called, gleefully. He ignored the glares from some of Fenning's old cronies. "I kep' it safe an' close."

"Well, get it up thar. As I were sayin'," he continued, turning back to the crews. "Those with an eye t' th' sweet trade, step over yon. I'm fairer than most, and I'll force none." He glanced at Marklain and Penn, waiting for them to contradict him. Penn stared stoically; Marklain grinned and gave him a little wave. "Nor am I a straight cutthroat. Ye'll be given a chance to once over th' articles afore signin'."

Fifty of the hundred and thirty men from the *Redoubt*

switched sides along with the nine from the *Ambition* who had already made their feelings known on the matter. Those whom he had freed from the *Redoubt*'s brig sorted themselves out, and divided into the pirate crews. Jack suppressed his smile for two reasons: one, it just wouldn't do; and two, it bloody hurt.

"Those o' ye left who have objections to m' way o' doin' things had best speak now. The *Mercy* don't shield those harbouring mutiny." Only three stepped forward. "Stir yer stumps, lads, or I'll have th' lady ferret ye out!" He pointed to the rail where Fenning had met his fate. "She knows yer hearts, boys. And she'll treat ye' accordin'."

Another twelve stepped up. Satisfied, he made a show of calming down as Tortuga reappeared with a flat, dirty sack. From this he pulled a carefully kept grey flag and spread it with the help of Falkes, who tossed the old one overboard.

As they ran it up the mast, Jack sighed. It was a black skull and crossed sabres with the left half of the skull missing on a dove grey field. It was terribly prophetic, he thought, though he felt his heart singing as it was run up the mast. He turned back to the men who had admitted they would not willingly sail under him.

"Ye'll be given command o' the *Ambition*. Choose yerselves a captain, and he and I'll parlay in a bit. Fer now," he growled at them, "you lot run across th' *Redoubt* to th' *Ambition*, clear her decks, and bring her around. The rest of ye kin scavenge the *Redoubt* fer supplies for both ships. An' that includes a reasonable assortment o' you dogs," he added, glaring over his shoulder at the naval crew. "Those of ye not remainin' aboard either ship will be taken ashore yonder on St. Christopher when we're ready to sail. I'm sure 'tis only a short walk t' th' nearest plantation."

The British sailors were surprised and relieved to find they were not to be thrown into the shark infested waters, or murdered, or marooned on some questionable island. The lieutenant-turned-captain saluted Jack, and then organized his men into work crews, even assigning a few to clear the decks they were standing on. Jack resisted leaning on Sirene for more support, but he was tiring fast. He looked up at the rigging, scowling when some of the lines did not go where they should have.

"Mr. Marklain! Know how to rig a caravel?" he called without looking for the man in question.

Marklain wandered over and followed his gaze. "Redonda?"

Jack glared at him. "Do you see more than one lanteen, mister?"

Marklain laughed. "Nay, captain. And aye, captain. I can make sense of this mess."

That was all he needed to hear, gestured aloft. "Fix it."

Marklain rubbed his hands together in delight. "Aye, sir! It'll take me a good week to rerig her completely, but I'll have her ready to limp to safer waters in an hour if ye'll give me the hands."

With a nod from Jack, he started to designate crewmen to go aloft with him when a lanky, greasy pirate stepped forward to complain.

"Excuse me, Captain, but I's th' *Mercy*'s bosun."

"Ye responsible for that mess?" Jack pointed.

"Uh... aye, sir," he stammered, taking a clue from the captain's tone.

"Right. *That* man is th' bosun. You... I'll find out what yer good fer later. Find something useful to do," he said, dismissing him.

Sirene heard the tired reverberations in his tone. "Jack, you need to go below."

"Not whilst there's work to be done."

"Jack," she insisted. "At least sit down and let the doctor look at your eye."

He relented. "Fine, woman, if it means ye'll stop badgering me."

She made him sit on the steps out of the way. "I'd throw *you* overboard if I thought it would help."

Hare managed to get the naval doctor over to the captain.

The man sighed, and began to unwind the scarf, telling Hare what to fetch. Sirene sat behind Jack and questioned the doctor.

"How is the Vice Admiral?" she asked.

He looked at her, surprised, and then began cleaning the wound. "He died during the storm," he answered. "There was nothing that could be done for it. He had a belly full of glass. Wish I knew what happened in that cabin," he muttered, shaking his head as he peered into Jack's eye, opening it with his thumb. "Hold his head still."

Sirene leaned him back and settled his neck between her knees, tipping his head onto her lap and held him still. She watched everything the doctor did, helping as she could. Jack took a deep breath. Pressed against her skirts all he could smell was Sirene, and the sea... and his own blood. Her hands were cold against his face, trembled with worry.

"How bad is it, doc?" he asked.

"Madam," he nodded to Sirene, pressing the scarf back to the wound, "would you be so kind as to keep pressure on that while I find my thread? Well," he humphed to Jack while fishing through his kit, "you won't lose it, may even be able to see out of it in a week or so if there is no inflammation. Though you will notice a great deal of sensitivity to light and may need spectacles afterward, if you care about that sort of thing," he added with disdain. "You were lucky. Your brow took the brunt of the blow. Any deeper, and you would have lost it. Boy, fetch me the strongest drink you can find. He's going to need it while I sew him up."

Hare darted off again.

'Vieve trotted up, followed more slowly by Mary who was holding her shoulder.

"Doctor, why don' you take ze bullet out of mon Marie, an' let ze professional sew up mon capitane?" she asked, in a tone that dared him to contradict her.

The doctor puffed himself up. "I'll have you know, madam, I am a medical physician. I am quite capable...."

"Oui, oui," she snapped, taking the needle from him. "An' I 'ave yet to meet one who could sew wort' a damn. I am a seamstress," she stated with pride.

Jack lifted his head from Sirene's lap and focused his good eye on the two women. 'Vieve was tearing the sleeve off her shirt and folding it into a bandage. Whether or not she had ever been a seamstress was not apparent, but it was Mary who caught his eye. He leaned over to see around Genevieve's hip. The woman was covered, head to toe, in blood.

"How much o' that's yers, Miss Mary?" he asked her.

She gave a shy, embarrassed grin. "Not much, sir. Just this by th' bullet."

"Over-did it a bit, did we?"

'Vieve beamed proudly. "Zey say she went be'surk. Zey are callin' 'er 'Bloody Marie'." She handed her rolled up sleeve to Sirene. "Trade me."

Sirene made the switch, handing her the silk scarf. 'Vieve washed it in a bucket of water, then took out her knife and carefully picked threads out of it.

Hare ran up with a dirty bottle of dark rum, moving out of the way of the doctor who was setting up to tend to Mary. He handed the captain the bottle while staring wide-eyed at the blood-soaked woman.

Jack snatched it, ripped the cork out with his teeth, and drank deeply. It was the first real drink he had allowed himself in weeks. The thick, sweet liquid added weight to his weakened limbs, and while it did not deaden the pain much, it helped him not to care. He was thoughtful enough to pass it to Mary.

When 'Vieve had enough threads, she set the scarf aside and threaded the finest needle in the doctor's collection and knelt in front of her captain.

"'Old 'im steel. I weel try to keep ze stitches small."

She began at the cheek, using a slipstitch with the gold silk to keep the scar thin. She paused frequently to let him drown himself before beginning the really delicate work on his eyelid.

"You think if we get him drunk enough, we might get him to rest?" Sirene asked.

'Vieve chuckled, "Ma'bee."

"Hey, I'm still cogigant here," Jack slurred. "Don' know I don't think what ye two're brewin'." The bottom of the bottle hit the steps, his hand still firmly wrapped around it. "Ye gods, I'm tired," he breathed.

Sirene set a tender kiss on his forehead where 'Vieve had cut the last stitch. "So what port would be safe? I'll tell the pilot. We can't berth here. The *St. George* should be nearing here by morning, and trust me, we can't handle her."

He struggled to sit up. 'Vieve moved over to sew up Mary's wound, as the doctor had taken out the bullet and pressed a bandage on, figuring that she would insist.

Mary was giggling. "It's all right, really. If it scars I'll... I'll just get a tattoo."

Jack forced himself to his feet, shaking off Sirene. "Tortuga!" he bellowed, swaying for a moment.

His answer came from the gangplank where the huge man was hauling a rope attached to one of the *Redoubt*'s cannon. He grabbed hold of the rail and waited until the cannon was blocked amidships for winch transfer onto the gun deck. Only then did Tortuga approach, grabbing hold of his captain's arm to steady him.

"Aye, Capta'n? Yah should go below."

"Will ye all stop bloody motherin' me!" he shouted, jerking his arm free. "I'll go below when I'm damned good n' ready. Now," he said, forcing his head to stay clear and his words straight. "We need a safe port to make repairs an' avoid any officigal findanglements fer a bit. Limp out t' th' windward side o' Barbuda an' fin' me a harbour. Crew up th' *Ambition* an' have 'em folla us thar. We'll shelter each other and divvy up crew and supply in some seconded cove."

"An' da *Redoubt*, Capta'n?"

He sighed. "Set those what want t' stay honest ashore yonder just afore we're ready t' sail, then finish th' frigate *without a column a' smoke*, if ye please," he added, aiming a warning finger up at Tortuga.

"Aye, Capta'n. A single shot below har line should reef har fast. Put har out o' har misery."

"And mine," he grumbled. He glared at Sirene from his right eye. "*Now* ye kin take me below an' let me pass out," he growled reluctantly.

Tortuga grabbed a hold of the smaller man as Sirene's grip on him failed. "I'll take ya below, Capta'n. Dough I'm warnin' ya, Jack. She not so shipshape as ya left har. Da lady might find da bert' not to har likin'."

Hare grabbed a lamp, and ran to hold the companionway door. "Taken care o' that, ah 'ave, sair. Ah brought some o' th' linens and things over fra' th' *Redoubt* and yore personal effects fram th' *Ambition* wi' me own hands."

Jack gave him a baleful glare as he staggered between the black man and the white woman. The boy was quick to deny any mischief. "Ah swear, Capt'n, ah took nuthin'. Though if ye see a sailar wit' his arms clawed t' hell, tha'd be Mr. Flagstaff guardin' yore pearl chest," he chuckled.

Jack laughed.

Chapter the Eleventh

Jack was issuing orders even as they hauled him into the captain's cabin and draped him over the freshly made bed. "Hare, make sure they make th' tattresses from the *Redow*," he mumbled. "'F'is naval appoints are anythin' like his privates, we'll appreciate... th' lushuries later."

Sirene looked at Tortuga as she threw the coverlet over Jack. "Tell me, was he always this way?"

"Givin' ordah in his sleep," he nodded. "It would be best if you stay here until t'ings ar settled. Dere be too many question-able element on board as of yet. I'll set da Irish boy to attend, and Anjali..."

"When you're done with her," she said, shooing him out. "Go, you have a lot of work to do and little time left, as well as a lot of catching up, I understand. Just get us under way as soon as possible. There is a warship out there looking for pirates and she out-guns the *Redoubt*."

He nodded. "T'ank ya for da warnin." He glanced over her head to the bed. "Take care a him."

"Wench!" Jack bellowed. "Get yer fins over here. Where's tha' bottle?" he mumbled, starting to get off the bed.

Sirene left Tortuga to close the door, she sat on the edge of the bed, cradling his head and helping him drink. "Only a little," she warned.

"It hurts, woman," he snarled, fighting her ineffectively as she took it away from him.

"That is enough. No more," she grunted, struggling to get it out of his reach. "You need to be sober in the morning. Jack!" she squealed, when he started making grabs for other things. "All right, that does it. Either settle down, or I'm leaving."

He glared drunkenly up at her. "Where ye gonna go?"

"Out the window for starters," she threatened, dangling the pearl in front of him.

He stared sideways at it like a parrot trying to get it to focus with one eye. "What about th' rest 'v ar accordin'ly?" What she had said in the hold blurred uncomfortably through his mind.

He wavered like a snake charmer's serpent, following the jewel. "Is that all you cling to me for?" she scowled. "That damned treasure?"

"No," he said, reeling her in. "There're other... reasons... soft, seawatery reasons," he sighed.

Burying his face in her cleavage, he breathed deeply. She rolled him over and climbed into the bed with him, sitting back against the wall that served for a headboard. He wrapped himself around her, pillowing his head on her belly.

Jack had a sudden moment of sobriety.

"Never ask a drunk t' explain 'mself. Unless yer jest wantin' t' amuse yerself. Though why I'm's drunk as I am on half a bootle is be-beyon' me."

"When was the last time you ate?" she asked calmly, stroking his hair.

He was silent for several minutes, then gave a soft chuckle. "That'd explain it."

"That, and you want to be drunk," she added.

"No. I want to be unconscionable... conscionanmint... damn it."

"I know what you mean," she said, laughing as she ran her fingers through his damp locks.

"Hmm, that feels nice," he mumbled. "Gonna need an eye patch fer a while." He frowned, his hand drifting to the bandage and the stitching hidden beneath. "Can't hardly call me 'and-some n'more. ...Not that noone never did."

"I'm sure the ladies did," she offered.

He rubbed his cheek against the indigo fabric of her dress. "Not really. Bloody Mary, now tha's a good name. Mad Jack? Can't say as I'm fond of it... makes me sound like a rabid dog, and now... now they'll not call me anything but. Hardly hand-some any more."

"Oh, I wouldn't say that," she answered. "I think you are still quite dashing, a bit more roguish now, perhaps, but handsome still. I never liked Handsome for a name, anyway; sounds too vain," she mused. "Not to mention it means 'slow' in sailor talk. Amber fits you better."

He regarded her with his uncovered eye. "Amber Jack?" he frowned. "Like the fish?"

She laughed at his expression. "Have you seen your tail?"

He sat up unsteadily and scowled. "Have you?"

"No," she replied, tried not to laugh. "But Skilly described the entire ...change."

"Skilly?"

"The dolphin?" she reminded him.

"Oh. ...*Skilly?*" he repeated with slight distaste.

"That's the best way to say it in the surface tongues. Well, the shortest way. It's actually closer to Skilliweha."

He rolled onto the pillow next to her and stared at the timbers above the bed, trying to gauge the distance to the lamp swinging there with only one eye. "Damn, but this is going to take some...clam, climb, acc-lim-a-ting." He stared silently for a few moments more, aware she had rolled onto her side to watch him. "So what'd it look like?" he finally asked.

She gave him an amused half-smile. "Like an amberjack."

He glared at her and rolled onto his belly, wrapping his arms around the pillow, burying his good eye so he could escape the view of her delectable body lounging next to him. Her reaction when he was wounded touched him in a way he wasn't ready to explain to himself. He was surprised that the pillow smelled of her. It must have been taken from the *Ambition*, he thought.

"Your belly is white, silver in places," she explained. She set her hand on the small of his back and ran it down toward his knees. "You have a dark stripe about a hand's width here. And right along here," she said, drawing a wide line with her fingers from his hip bone down the side of his thigh, "you have this stripe of gold that runs all the way down. But there are other reasons," she added, softly stroking his arm.

"Like what," he mumbled into the pillow. He wasn't entirely sure he was sober enough ...or was that 'drunk enough'... to discuss the colour of his tail.

"Well, your trademark, for one," she said, giving a tug on the sash at his hips. "Your glow for another."

"Only you can see that, luv."

"True. Well, we shall see what sticks. What is it they say? We can run it up the flagpole and see who salutes?"

He groaned into his pillow, fighting sleep. Something deep inside him told him it was not safe yet. There was too much to attend to and, drunk or not, injured or not, his instincts said get up and do them. The alcohol weighed him down, effectively pinning him to the bed, but it could not make him surrender the fight.

"Sing fer me?" he asked suddenly. "Make me sleep."

It was an unusual request. The last person who had asked

her to sing for him like this was her father, while he lay dying. She did not count the times Price had requested her to entertain. She made herself comfortable, pulled the blanket up to his shoulders and sang a high, wordless melody that her mother used to sing to her nearly half a century before.

Her voice was beautiful and carried easily. It filled the room, soft as the wind on a quiet sea. Jack felt it penetrate his mind, lifting it up and floating away on the lilting waves.

There was a shift of the ship and a deep report as the cannons went off, echoing against the arms of the cove's mountains. He jumped and glanced around, resisting Sirene's hands on his head, drawing him near as she sang. It was not until he felt the vessel turn and her sails fill that he lay his head down and allow her voice to carry him away.

She stayed with him for several hours, until she heard the eight bells tolling midnight. She untangled herself, peeked under his bandage, and saw the reddening edges around the neat stitches. Sighing, she kissed him and slipped away, turning to examine the cabin. It was a wreck.

It must have been a beautiful room once. There were high, wide windows from one end of the stern bulkhead to the other. No doubt they ran past the rest of the aft cabins as well. She was a large Portuguese caravel, perhaps built for some Spanish nobleman and was slightly redesigned with the luxury of aft cabins. The bed was the simplest affair in the room, and seemed to have been built into the ship itself. The ribs of the vessel ran up the outside wall and formed the frame line. There was no footboard to speak of, just her old sea chest from the *Ambition*, and there were attachments along the ceiling beams running from the ship's ribs to hang curtains, but they were torn and fallen in several places and no one had bothered to repair or rehang them in years.

There was a decidedly unpleasant smell of old rum and musty things, and other... issues she did not want to consider. The cabinets were sturdy, old, black Spanish wood and beautifully carved. They would only need minor repairs to the doors and a little polishing. There were a few musty, disintegrating books in one of them hiding a black glass bottle of an unidentifiable liquor and a woman's earring. The dust was several layers thick and gave evidence that the place was poorly used and certainly not as it was meant to be. Examining one of the lamps she was horrified to discover a mummified apple core.

Frustrated, she began cleaning.

She was interrupted an hour later by a soft knock. She paused in her dusting to open it, holding her breath in an effort not to sneeze. Seeing Anjali in the companionway, she stepped out and closed the door behind her before giving in to the sneezing fit. Anjali nodded patiently.

"It is like dat all ovah de ship. De captain's gonna be in a royal piss when he see hah by day," she said.

Sirene leaned against the door, catching her breath and took a long look at Anjali's glow. "Are you all right? Have you and..." The look on the woman's face made her stop. "Don't tell me there was another reason he did not come back for you..."

She shook her head quickly. "Th' reason I were set off de ship aftah de change o' captains... we lost..."

Sirene nodded. That explained the change in her colours. "How is he taking it?"

"As well as men do. He up on deck brooding. I came to check on you and de captain. How is he?"

Sirene sighed. "He is going to be in a lot of pain tomorrow, and I think it's getting inflamed. I haven't even been able to tend to his other nicks yet."

Anjali punched the bulkhead in frustration. "Is there anyt'ing we can do? Short of keeping him drunk? I'd ask th' doctah, but he asked t' be put ashore wit' th' othahs, an' in accordance wit' th' captain's ordahs..."

"You did the right thing," she said, placing a hand on the darker woman's broad shoulder. "He did all that can be done by man. What remains can only be handled by a woman of the sea."

Anjali stared at her in such an odd way Sirene suspected she knew something. "What can you do? Change him an' take him into th' depths?"

"*How much did he tell you?*" she asked her in a low voice in Malagasy.

"*Nothing. But I saw what he became because of that necklace of yours, and he said that was your secret. Now tell me what can be done?*"

"*The pearl does not confer the natural healing of a mermaid in the sea, nor does it grant him the power of my voice. I cannot heal him outright nor guarantee his sight, but I can help with the pain, ...and maybe the inflammation.*"

Tortuga stepped out of the shadows near the companionway door, arms crossed and a scowl on his face. "*Then do it, white witch.*"

She glanced up, wondering how she had not noticed his approach. "*I will have to get off the ship. Show me a chart of where you are headed. I will meet you there as soon as I have found what I'm looking for. And the fewer crew who know, the better.*"

Anjali nodded. "*Then you best go out the window,*" she said, and opened the door to the starboard cabin.

This room was a little larger than the other, though its appointments were more lavish. Tortuga turned up the lamp and locked the door behind them.

"This..." Sirene began.

"Is a mess, I know. I'll be fixing that shortly," Anjali snapped, mumbling in Hindi about the disgraceful condition the whole ship was in.

"No, I meant, this is the senior berth. I am curious why Jack chose the one he did," she explained.

Anjali looked at her as if it should be obvious. "Have you taken a good look at t'at bed? He always chose t'at cabin. Tortuga and I have slept in t'is one evah since we married. Captain felt it proper we have our own private bert'. T'ough it smells like Fenning's been holin' up in heah." She scowled and opened the window.

"I'll get a rope," Tortuga said.

"No hurry," Sirene replied. "I'll need one when I return, but I don't need one to get out. Do you have the charts here?"

The man nodded stoically, and laid them on the table. He pointed to a cove on the next island over. "Can you find dat, *mermaid?*" he sneered, not quite believing.

She took a close look, committing the shape of the land to memory. "I should. Hopefully it will not take that long. I'm going back to the reef near Nag's Head. We shouldn't be too far out. We've been tacking, haven't we?" He nodded. "I could beat you to the cove if I wanted. But I'll find you. Anjali, if you see any whales or dolphins, start looking for me," she instructed as she headed for the window. "I trust you'll look after the captain in the meanwhile, and fill in this giant of a man you call a husband while I'm gone?"

She nodded, but stopped her before she could climb onto the sill. "Ahr you going to go in t'at?" she asked, pointing to her dress.

Sirene looked down. "It *will* slow me down, and might catch on the reefs," she mumbled, unfastening it.

The laces were still damp and swollen from the salt water and refusing to untie or give. Anjali grabbed her knife and moved to help while Tortuga stood back with his arms over his chest and watched stubbornly. Sirene arched her back to grant access to the laces as the woman cut her out of them.

"That's the second time I'm going to have to replace those things," she sighed.

"Why do ye wear th' damned t'ing, den? Would t'ink it make fer clumsy swimming," she commented, peeling her out of it.

"It does," she agreed, not minding Tortuga's eyes over her body. "But I have to wear *something*. It is easier to hide what I am from the crews if I'm not striding naked across the decks when I come back on board."

"When you get back, I will give you some clothes," she said, in a tone that was not to be argued with.

Sirene looked over what the woman was wearing. "All right. I like this bodice," she said, running the back of her fingers over the taut fabric. "Something in this style would do. But I must have a skirt. I can have nothing between my legs, or I won't change if I fall overboard."

"Sarong," Tortuga said.

Sirene tried to picture herself in the garment, and ended up with a flash of the huge man in one and tried not to smile. "I think that would do nicely. Thank you," she said, grabbing a small drawstring bag from a shelf and sitting in the window. "He left about an inch in the bottle, less what Mary drank. So, you who have seen him drunk can gauge how long he'll be out," she said, dumping the contents of the pouch into Anjali's hands. It was several Dutch coins and a few loose gemstones.

"One bottle?" Tortuga snorted. "He should still be lookin' fahr more."

"Well," Anjali piped up, "it has been almost t'ree watches since his last meal."

Tortuga frowned at his wife. "An' why is dat?"

"He wahr spending every chance he got wit'..."

Sirene smiled and tipped backwards out the window. She was aware of the two of them sticking their heads out after her just before she was folded into the ship's wake and the change was upon her.

It was like shedding a corset. Her lower flesh melted and merged, the long, rigid bones giving way to articulated cartilage ribs and smaller vertebrae. She almost tied her tail in a knot, so glad was she to be free of her legs.

She rose to the surface, floated on her back in the moonlight and arched her tail upward just to see it again. The silver-white underscales positively glowed, even under the slim moon, fading into the darker blue of her dorsal stripe. She curled up, peering at the moon through the translucent fan of her caudal fin. She sighed deeply, expelling the air from her lungs and continued backward into a dive, plunging into the depths.

The pearl floated against her breast, the chain at her neck rolling just below her gills. She refocused her sight and searched for the nearest array of colour that would mark the reefs. Not seeing it, she stopped a passing grouper to ask. It regarded her with disinterest, spun in one direction and swam for a foot or so before turning back the way it had been going.

She sliced through the dark water, revelling in the feel of it surrounding her body completely unfettered, angling ever downward, as the creature she was looking for lived on the bottom.

It only took her an hour to return to the reef at Nag's Head. She avoided the wreck of the Redoubt, and scoured the seabed for at least another bell. She managed to snag a small parrotfish and ate it as she searched. She had forgotten how long it had been since her last meal. Other fish darted around her looking for scraps, tickling her sides, picking at her flowing hair. She spun, shooing them off with a giggle and saw the black-tipped fin and sleek, white underbelly swimming over her. She glared, watched it cautiously. Its glow showed her that it was curious, maybe even a little hungry as it circled back.

As it darted past her a second time, she slapped it on the gills, lashing her tail in warning that she was not to be messed with. The shark half turned, regarded her warily and then swam lazily off. Looking about for signs of other reef sharks, she saw a tinge of something green that caught her eye under some fan coral. She drifted near, being careful, as the creature she was hunting was dangerous.

Bending back the swaying pink lace, she saw a large brown and white snail dart out and attack a clownfish. Keeping her eyes on it, she opened the bag. Lying near the snail was a piece of the fan coral that had been broken off by some passing aggression. Picking it up, she used it to scoop the snail and his dinner from the seabed and up into the current, then snagged it in the bag as it floated back downward, tied it closed. Looping the strings on her wrist and keeping the arm as far out from her body as was feasible, she darted after the *Mercy's Ransom* at high speed, skimming just below the surface.

It was nearly dawn when she sighted the caravel and the smaller brig tagging along beside her. She swam to the stern, found a rope ladder dragging in the water from the larboard cabin and climbed up it quickly. She entered the open window and pulled the ladder up after her.

She was surprised to find Hare had made a bed by the sea chest and was sound asleep. From the look of things, he had also done some cleaning.

Crossing to the table, she set the bag down, noticing that Anjali had left a few things there for her. She dried herself with a towel from the *Ambition*. Price had always been touchy about her dripping in the cabin and kept plenty in stock for when he let her swim.

Dried, she set it on the chair and picked up the batik dyed sarong and tied it around her hips. It was long enough to wrap around her twice and fell to her shins. She then put on the light green Indian top. It was simple cotton but beautiful, with great care taken on the very basic embroidery. The choli was also a little big on her.

She sensed something moving beside her.

"Fancy a short life, Mr. Hare?"

The boy snatched his hand back from the bag. "Just lookin', ah was, ma'am. Honest!" he exclaimed.

"Curiosity killed the cat, Mr. Hare," she said calmly. She fetched a scrap of paper from the reorganized cabinet and wrote down the things she would need. "What is in that bag will kill you if it stings."

He straightened up. "Then howsit t' be helpin' th' captain, ma'am?"

"By not being the only fly in the ointment," she replied, handing him the paper. "Can the cook read?"

"Ah don' think so."

"Can you?" she returned.

"Mostly."

She pointed to the paper. "Then collect those items for me."

He trotted off, and she looked in the cabin for other things she would need. She opened the bag with a pair of knives, not coming in contact with it if she could help it, and dumped the rather irate mollusc onto the freshly scrubbed wood. It righted itself and started to feel its way across the table when she put a knife into it. With a little work, she forced it out of its shell and began to carve it into strips, which she set aside. She very carefully removed the venom sack.

Hare came in and set things out on the far edge of the table, away from what she was doing, but close enough for her to reach. She scraped the sack into the mortar he brought. She set one of the knives down, grabbed a snail strips and popped it into her mouth.

"Aww!" Hare recoiled in disgust.

"What?" she asked, offering him a piece. She laughed as he moved farther away. "The French eat them," she commented, "so I don't know why it bothers you, being raised on a French is-land."

"Aye, but they at least cook 'em farst," he said, grimacing.

"Fine, then go back to sleep or find something useful to do."

He went back to his makeshift bed and curled up. "In case ye need me," he explained when she frowned.

She went back to mixing the ointment, adding the things that had been brought from the galley in careful proportions to the amount of venom she had collected. All the while, she nibbled on the snail meat. When she finished, she had a cream that smelled faintly of fish oil, which she was careful not to touch as she scraped it into an empty chalcedony cosmetic pot she had found in the cabinets. She carried the mortar to the bedside, sat next to him, and watched him sleep.

Jack woke as the ship was working its way through danger-ous shoals to a harbour no British warship would ever be able to reach. He looked up and saw Sirene sitting on the bed looking longingly down at him. She smiled, an expression as radiant as the sun itself cresting the horizon just beyond view.

"Mornin', beautiful," he grinned, wincing as the expression pulled at his stitches.

She ran her hand over his forehead, feeling a slight warmth near the gash. He rolled onto his back as she began to unwind the bandage. He watched her face, gauging his condition by her expression. Her eyes darted over the wound, and she gave a tiny frown. Perhaps it wasn't as bad as it felt, he thought. "How is it?" he asked.

"Only mildly inflamed. How does it feel?"

"Like I was sliced open and sewn back together," he quipped.

She glared at him. "Be serious. How badly does it hurt?"

"Not as bad as ma' head," he answered honestly, sitting up.

"Hangover," she muttered. "I'll give you a taste of the dog that bit you in a minute."

"That's hair o' the dog," he corrected.

She folded a small square of cloth several times, and used it to wipe the inside of the mortar clean of the last of the ointment, and held it up to his face.

"What's that?" he asked suspiciously, sniffing.

"That," she responded, "is going to sting a little, then tingle, and then you won't be able to feel your face the rest of the day."

"Really?" He looked interested. "Where'd ye get it? And why's yer hair wet?"

"I made it. From things I went hunting for below. It is very potent. I only want you to use this when you have to, and never with your bare hand. It will numb anything it touches. Try not to get it in your eyes or your mouth, it's poisonous."

"Can it help m' head?"

She dabbed the cloth across the wound. "Nothing can help that, luv."

He gasped as the stuff began working. "Wench. I meant my

head*ache*."

"I know what you meant," she replied, grabbing the nearly empty rum bottle and handing it to him.

When someone knocked on the door, he doubled over, clutching his skull. Sirene called out, and Tortuga poked his head in.

"Capta'n?" he called softly.

Jack glared at him. "Ye be knowin' how much I had last night," he snarled. "Why'd ye go poundin'?"

"Ah barely touched it," he said, scowling with disapproval.

"What d' ye want?" Jack demanded sourly, chugging the last of the rum.

"Ya wanted t' see da *Ambition*'s new capta'n as soon as we wah safely hahbored. Well, he is heah."

Jack cursed. "Ah, gimme a bit," he groaned, preparing to roll out of bed.

Sirene helped him, holding him steady while he reacquainted himself with the sober pitch and swell. Tortuga offered his help, which was refused. After a moment he even untangled himself from Sirene.

She looked the big man over in the captain's light. He dwarfed Jack. She barely came to his chest. Then she noticed that his hair was different. The night before it had been tied in tangled chunks. Now it was elaborately braided close to his head and fell in beaded strands past his shoulders. She smiled.

"I think I like it better this way," she said.

He followed her gaze and smiled. "M' wife... didnah like da locs."

Jack staggered over to the cabinets looking for usable paper and ink. "I imagine it be impossible t' braid it the way ye like it by yerself. By the way, Sirene, what are ye doing in Anji's clothes?" He turned as he found a few pages as well as the ship's old articles. "Not that I don't like them. On the contrary. But they hardly fit."

She shrugged, clearing the things she had used to make the

medicine off the table. "About as well as Ambrose's shirt fit you. Any port in a storm," she purred, feeding him a piece of the snail strips.

He chewed, and frowned. "What was that?"

"It'll help your head," she lied. She put her things away and stood behind his chair when he sat. "Do you want me to leave while you do this?"

"Actually," he said, snagging her by the waist. "I'd like ye t' play secretary."

"She da wrong sex," Tortuga said bluntly, and left.

Sirene giggled as she sat down next to Jack and pulled the papers over to her, making sure the quill was sharp. "So what am I writing?"

"Whatever we agree ta. An' methinks we'll look inta getting ye some that fit when we arrive in Tortuga."

She did not have time to ask him to explain as the quartermaster led in two of the pirates from the other ship. They both looked up to see Mr. Towers strutting in with one of the Mercy's crew who had chosen to leave close behind him. They both glared at Sirene, but said nothing. She took note of their guarded manners and the spikes in their glows that warned they were in belligerent moods.

Jack stood, and gestured for them to sit at the table.

"Captain," he said, genially.

Towers nodded as he pulled a chair out. "Commodore," he said, watching Jack's reaction carefully.

Jack would have raised an eyebrow, except that part of his face wouldn't respond. "Please, sit down. And I'm not a commodore."

The two men looked at each other before taking their seats.

"Admiral then," he scowled.

Jack gave a half laugh. "No. I still be a captain, same as you."

Now the men were confused.

"*Then who* be th' admiral o' th' fleet? *Her?*" he sneered, pointing to Sirene.

"No one. There is no fleet," he explained.

"What? Then why ar we here?"

"To forge an accord. An agreement of non-interference and mutual assistance." They stared blankly, thoroughly disarmed. "Lemme explain how this works. Ye and me, we sign this piece of paper which'll detail our agreement."

Towers sat back in the chair and folded his arms. "Which be?"

"One: should our wakes cross, we meet in friendship ...or at least non-hostility," he added as an afterthought. Sirene began writing. "To trade information, goods, warnings, etc. Buy and sell supplies if needed. Two: simple non-interference. If one ship runs across the other engaged, we do not intercept or otherwise interfere without an agreed upon signal, say flag at half-mast or non-present? Or unless said ship appears to be in dire straights or otherwise captured, or closely thereto."

The two men conferred, giving Sirene time to catch up. Towers leaned forward.

"At which point, ye get what? Fifty percent o' th' plunder?"

"Nay." Jack frowned. "That would be inequitable. Ye do most o' th' fightin' and I get half th' prize? Nonsense. Twenty. And this works both ways, ye know."

"Twenty percent?" he echoed, in disbelief.

"Aye. O' course, injury pay fer th' rescuing crew should come out o' th' rescued ship's eighty percent. And one full share fer every man lost in th' aiding. It only be fair," he added, spreading his hands innocently.

"Aye... only fair," Towers said, stunned. Because it was more than fair and he didn't seem to trust it.

"Of course, should we enter a fight together, *that* be a fifty-fifty deal."

Towers leaned back, regarding Sirene seriously for the first time, and then glanced back at Jack. "So why d' we need th' paper?"

Jack leaned forward and indicated his eye. "'Cause the

Brotherhood of the Coast ain't quite th' brotherhood we used t' be. This way, there be no fights and no question o' what's who's when th' time comes 'cause it's all in writin' and all signed and legal-like. Or as close to it as *we* come," he laughed.

The others laughed, too.

"Lack of trust," the other man said, with a smile that had nothing to do with the joke.

"Yes and no," Jack admitted.

"Why d' ye not want a fleet?" he asked.

Jack looked the other man over carefully. He was of indeterminate race and country, a typical pirate in these waters. Probably an expatriate of some kind.

"Because I be not a greedy man. I want what's mine, and no more. I don't fancy spending th' rest o' m' days on the sea warrin' wi' me own kind 'cause ah spread m'self too thin. That's why England's gonna lose her colonies eventually, *and* Spain. 'Cause th' kind o' men that cross an ocean to make their homes don't like takin' orders from a king they can't see, not fer very long. Same goes fer them so called 'pirate admirals'. I know I would chafe under an' admiral I were forced to accept, and takin' more than half o' plunder I didn't earn seems somehow wrong. Not to mention, impossible to enforce."

Towers spoke again. "You sound experienced in th' matter."

"Boy, I been on these waters fer more'n thirty years; maraudin' twenty o' that. Name me one pirate who can boast of a career half as long." He glared with his good eye.

Towers leaned back in his chair arrogantly. "Speaks to lack o' success t' me. How can we be sure ye're not jest settin' us up fer somethin' later?"

Jack sighed. "If I wanted a continued attachment to th' *Ambition*, I'd have made me quartermaster her captain."

Both men frowned. "Ye mean that Indian bitch?" spat Towers. "And I thought yer madness were a rumor."

"Now let's keep this civil, shall we?" Jack scowled, resisting the urge to do something rash. "Will ye sign, or no?"

Sirene slid it across the table to their guests, watching them surreptitiously as they read it.

"I cannot see how this document can cause us injury, nor be t' any but ar benefit. We'll sign."

Towers took up the pen and wrote his name, and then passed it to the man with him who scrawled his mark. Jack made a point of writing his name in a neat, attractive script. Sirene then took the document, blowing the ink dry and got up, moving toward the cabinets.

"Why do *you* get t' keep it?" Towers accused.

"Because it be my idea, and as I gave ye that ship freely, ye can spare me th' benefit o' th' doubt. Now, if ye wish a copy for yer own boat, I'll be happy to ask Miss Sirene to draft us another copy."

She looked up, expectantly picking up another piece of paper. The two muttered between themselves.

"No, that won't be necessary," Towers said, getting up. "Now, unless there's other business?"

"Yes," Sirene said casually, putting the blank paper away. "You might wish to be careful. I was privy to a conversation between the late Vice Admiral and the captain of the *Redoubt*. It seems there is another warship prowling these waters hunting pirates with a vengeance. Keep your eyes out for the HMS *St. George,* likely coming out of Antigua. She's a 40-gun frigate."

Towers made a rude noise and continued on his way out the door. As he and his companion were shown off the ship, the *Mercy*'s officers found their way in. Sirene was pleased to note that Anjali was first mate, Marklain was promoted to the boson, and Penn was chief gunner with secondary duties to aid the pilot who was a graying, older man Sirene had not yet met.

"Glad to see yer still kickin' about, Mr. Forrest," Jack commented, shaking the man's hand.

The man chuckled and tapped the deck with his wooden leg. "So t' speak, sar!" he winked. He turned to Sirene as Jack introduced them. "Pleased t' make yer acquaintance, Miss," he said, bowing over her hand. "I've known Jack since he wast a pup."

"Belay that," Jack interrupted with a scowling grin. "Let's get the business over with," he said, sitting everyone at the table and laying out his orders.

Primarily, they were to get the *Mercy* shipshape again, and he was justifiably upset about the vessel's condition. They were to chart to Tortuga, where they would resupply and repair the vessel prior to 'intercepting a great prize' which was all Jack would say about it.

"Why won't ye tell us?" Mr. Forrest asked. "S'not like ye cain't trust us."

Jack sighed. "I have a ship that crews thirty hands currently supporting nearly eighty. Scuttlebutt is the reason I'll not be tel- lin' ye until we're out of port and on the way. We'll have t' thin out th' ranks, and I only want those truly loyal t' remain. I won't be havin' a repeat of history."

"Neidah will da *Mercy*," Tortuga muttered.

Forrest was quick to mutter an ascent.

"Explain," Jack ordered.

"Well," Forrest began when Tortuga nodded to him, scratch- ing his thinning hair. "Every since we lost ye, things just ain't been right. She's been... cranky ye' might say. I'd plot a course straight an' fair and even helm it meself. I'd take a bearin' a watch later an' find us off, onct by as much as twelve degrees! We've had guns explode ...perfectly sound guns, too. Ol' Betsy ain't fired onct since. Light 'er fuse, and she fizzles."

Jack smiled. "I heard Ol' Betsy during the fight. Why didn't Fenning get rid o' her when she wouldn't fire?"

"Fennin' tried t' have 'er tossed, but we couldn't get her free o' the housin' without takin' the deck with 'er."

Jack laughed.

"Ol' Betsy?" Sirene asked with a smile.

"The thirty-two that fires from below *Mercy*'s starboard wing." He grinned broadly. "We took her a decade back from a ship called the *Mary Elizabeth* out of Portsmouth. So we called her Ol' Betsy. She always was a cast iron bitch. But I never had a moment's trouble with her. Mr. Penn, ye take care of her and she won't backfire on ye."

Penn nodded, mumbling something incoherent.

"Well, it sounds like the ol' girl's missed her master. Which reminds me, do we have a length of chain long enough that ain't rusting t' high hell?" he asked Tortuga.

He shrugged. "Might be some in da crates we took from da *Redoubt*. You want to change har chains before or aftah we reach port?"

"Before, if we have the lengths. If not, I'll wait. Not sure we've th' locks. We can do any work we need to once she's un-chained. She's lookin' more ragged than I like. Could use a fresh coat."

Sirene sighed. "We have a problem with going straight to Tortuga." Everyone looked at her expectantly. "Unless there is cargo in the hold, and there isn't much by the manifest, we don't have the money to refit."

Jack frowned. "What about them pearls?"

She shook her head. "Only worth so much, and you'll not get everything you'll need to repair with them. You have timbers below your waterline to replace. She'll need careening, too."

Jack slammed his fist on the table. "Damn it! Didn't that slob do *any* maintenance?"

No one wanted to answer that, but Forrest winced and spoke up. "Captain, last person who tried t' do repair work on *Mercy* was snapped off th' swing by a mako. Hell, two months after we set Anjali off on Guadalupe she nearly gutted 'erself on a reef she was far too shallow to worry about. An' 'twas bloody deliberate, too!" he added, crossing himself. "After that, noone'd touch 'er. At night we'd hear th' damnedest noises from th' bow." he shuddered. "Fennin' were mumbling about dropping her in the drink, but that no one would sail without something up there."

"All right, so we have to take a prize before Hispaniola, then," Jack assessed. "Let's go hunting!" he said, and dismissed the officers. When he was alone in the cabin with her again, he leaned back against the closed door. "Gods below, I hope she's got another fight left in 'er still."

Sirene crossed to him, wrapped her arms around him and laid her head on his shoulder.

He slipped his around her waist and pulled her close. "Think ye and yore friends might be able to help us out in that department?" he asked softly.

She gave a low chuckle. "Aye. In fact, I'll go myself, and scout the way ahead. See if I can find us a prize we can take in our condition." They stood that way for several minutes, before she asked, "Why does this ship seem to have a life of her own? The men seem willing to believe every superstition about her. I'm surprised Fenning didn't abandon her."

"Well, one: Fenning never believed ...any of it. Except that he was invincible. He thought that tattoo of his would protect him from any harm," he explained, tapping his head. "He scoffed at any suggestion that *Mercy* would protect her own. Two..." he hesitated. "I named her for my mother."

Sirene asked, "Was your mother alive at the time?"

"No."

That explained everything. She gave him one last squeeze and pulled away.

"You're right," he said, reading her intentions. "We should go up top. Do me a favour?"

"Aye?"

"Go to the bow an' sing that song again?"

She smiled and followed him on deck.

Chapter the Twelfth

Sirene had been swimming for two days. She avoided a transient pod of hungry orca and sighted two warships at great distances, but nothing else of significance. She encountered a pod of common dolphins and recruited them to help her keep tabs on the *Mercy*, with various members of the pod switching back and forth from running with the ship to following her.

She was clearing the outer isles of St. Martin when she sighted a Dutch Flute labouring low in the water as it pulled away from an unseen port on the north side of the main island. She smiled, counting the guns along her sides. There were only five.

One of the dolphins butted his head against her hand as she hovered in the water, watching the ship. She stroked the black head, clicked a request, and sent him speeding off with three of his friends. After a moment, she turned and began to wend her way between the outlying islands and reefs toward the ship, pausing now and again to help the pod fish, never letting the vessel out of her sight.

Jack was at the helm when he heard the commotion off the bow. He nodded to the seaman behind him who took the wheel, and headed over to see what the trouble was. Several black and tan common dolphins were cutting across the bow of the ship.

"They playin' 'can't touch me'?" asked one of the sailors, leaning over the larboard wing to watch them come around again.

They sliced through the water at an angle, making a great deal of noise, and then circled back and did it again. Jack stroked his sparse moustache thoughtfully. It was odd behaviour for dolphins, towards a ship anyway. He'd seen them do it to schools of fish, herding them toward older, younger, and slower members of the pod. He turned to yell to Penn who had taken over from the seaman.

"Three points forward on the starboard beam!" he ordered.

Penn obeyed and the pirates scrambled to adjust the sails to follow. Mr. Forrest came up alongside.

"New course, Capt'n?" he asked.

"Aye. Folla that pod. They cut th' bow again, turn accordin'. Mr. Hare!"

The lad dropped the coil of rope he had in hand at the feet of the man who had requested it and sprinted across the deck, stopped with a salute. "Aye, Capt'n?"

"Penn said ye've been learnin' yer points?"

"Aye, Capt'n!"

"Fine," he said, patting his shoulder. "Yer new job is ta stand here and watch that pod. If'n they take a crazy turn like they're doin' current, call off th' adjustments t' th' helm. Think ye' kin handle th' responsibility?"

The boy lit up. "Aye aye, Capt'n!"

Forrest frowned, lowered his voice. "Why're we followin' fish, sir?"

"When th' sea sends ye signs as broad as daylight, it's in yer best interests to follow. Unless she's cross wit' ye fer some reason," he added with a gleam in his eye. He set his hand on the taller man's shoulder. "She ain't ticked at ye fer any reason, is she, Mr. Forrest?"

"Uh, no sir. None I kin fathom," he swallowed, suddenly unsure.

Jack laughed. "Relax, mate." He gave the arch of wing beside him a fond thump. "She's in a good mood."

With that, he adjusted his eye patch and headed back amidships. He returned to the quarterdeck and took the helm. As soon as the ship was pointed the way they wanted her to go, the dolphins spread out, swimming along both sides squealing, and jumping as they raced the ship. A trio of the younger ones sported in the wake, alternately jumping over and riding the waves.

Tortuga stepped up onto the deck toward evening, convinced the captain to come down to dinner. Marklain relieved Hare at the bow without anyone needing to ask, sending the boy to bed.

"Ah we goin' ta have ta get used ta dis, Capta'n?" Tortuga asked in a low voice once they were in private.

"Probably, why?" he asked suspiciously, resisting the urge to rub his eye as the ache began to return.

"Some of da crew ain't takin' it s' well. Most ahr, t'ink it good luck, but dolphins swimmin' wit' a ship be one t'ing. Herdin' it along is anoddah."

He reached for the little pot of ointment and the rag he used to apply it. "Take note of which is which, and we'll try to off-load those that're uncomfortable."

Tortuga watched Jack scrape the rag against the rim to get most of the ointment off before applying a thin coat in a tiny mirror. He was careful not to get any in his eye. He grinned at the black man's reflection, still standing behind him.

"Aye, old friend?"

"How is it you find yoreself a mahmaid, and I get stuck wit' de Kali-worshipin' she-devil?"

Jack laughed, and put the medicine away. "Strength of personality, I suppose. Truthfully, do ye really think I could handle that woman of yourn?"

A smile crossed his dark face. "No. And ya wouldn' want to, eidah." The smile faded, "...Ya really t'ink she sent dem?"

"Aye." He saw the concern in his companion's eyes. "Tortuga, while there be none but you I'd rather have at me back in a ship to ship, there be something about that woman. I can't explain it. I trust her. And I *do* have reason to. We've been tradin' tit for tat ever since she ran me over." Tortuga frowned. "Relax. She had no say in the matter and I, in all honesty, nearly drowned her by knocking her inta th' harbour."

Anjali came in after a brief knock and brought the evening meal. The conversation shifted direction as they sat down to eat.

It was late in the afternoon when Sirene dove under the keel of the *Mercy* and surfaced in her wake. She climbed the ladder that had been left hanging out the stern window for her since she left six days before. The cabin was empty as she crawled tiredly into the window and wrung out her hair. She pulled off her clothes a piece at a time and repeated the procedure, put them back on again. She sank into a chair at the table, grabbed an orange from the wooden bowl, and began peeling.

She was halfway through it when someone opened the door, looked up. Hare jumped, not expecting anyone to be there. Before she could say anything he closed the door and ran off. She pulled the chart on the table closer, turned it so she could look at it from the right angle, and finished the fruit. A few minutes later Jack appeared, closing the door behind him.

"You know Hare was sneakin' in here?" she asked.

He chuckled. "No. I sent him fer what yer lookin' at, luv." He sat down and regarded her across the table. "So, what news?"

Mouth full, she pointed to a spot a few degrees northeast of their position.

"What is it?"

She swallowed. "Dutch Flute called the *Zuiderskruis*. Eight thirty-two pounders, and two long nines if she matches sides."

"Heavily gunned for a Flute," he mused, grabbing a banana off the bowl.

"And heavily laden, too. She left Sint Maarten two days ago."

He looked over the map, frowning. "She should be farther out than that by now."

She grinned. "*Should* be."

"What did ye do?" he demanded, pointing at her with the peeled fruit.

"Oh, it's amazing what a chunk of shipwreck will do to a rudder," she chuckled, taking a bite from the banana. She tapped him on the nose. "And don't aim that thing at me. It might be loaded."

He viciously took a bite. "Any idea how many men aboard?"

"I did not get close enough to her to count, sorry. If I had, I'd have been seen. But I can tell you she is nearing her weight limit. She's riding almost to the gunports."

He did some quick calculations. "Flutes are almost no challenge. And she was alone? No escort?"

"Not that I saw."

"*Zuiderskruis*...what's that mean?" he asked, out of curiosity.

"I *think* it means the Southern Cross."

He brightened. "How fortuitous." He began charting a course to the vessel.

"She's also dragging horribly," she added. "The part of the wreck I used to jam it still had sail attached," she grinned.

He looked up at her. "How did ye manage that? It had to be heavy."

"I had help," she evaded. "At top speed you should be able to sight her by sundown and reach her... oh, before four bells."

He nodded. "If they're smart, they'd cut sail once they realize they have no control. I wouldn't be wantin' to cross th' Atlantic without a rudder."

Jack headed up top to make the course corrections and to get the crew prepared for the upcoming battle. Sirene made her way to the bed and curled up.

She was startled several hours later when something small and heavy jumped up behind her. Her hand darted for the pistol on the headboard even as she looked over her shoulder. She laughed and rolled over to pet the cat. He sniffed her fingers, licked them once, and then let her scratch behind his ear. She ran her hands along his sides, scratching his back and noted he had put on a great deal of weight.

"You're getting fat," she commented, as the beast purred.

"Apparently th' ship has a large population of rats," Jack said casually from the table. He got up and crossed to her. She smiled. His glow had been so much like the sunlight she had not realized he was in the room.

"How long did you let me sleep?" she asked, running her fingers through his hair.

"It's just after eight."

She sat up.

"Relax. We've only just caught sight o' sail. Though it won't take half as long as predicted to catch her. She's fully furled and we've got a good tailwind. Ye get enough sleep?" he asked, playing with her ankle.

"Do we have time to meddle?" she asked, removing her ankle from his grasp.

"A few hours."

"You best wait 'til after, luv," she laughed, evading him. "It'll provide you with incentive."

He chased after her. "I don' need no damned incentive. I'm a pirate."

Flagstaff suddenly found the bed too crowded and jumped down, crawling under it. "See what you did?" she challenged.

"No, but I see what I caught," he said, holding up her foot and reeling her in. "It's been six days, woman," he complained. "Ye'll not be denyin' me."

"You?" she squealed. "What about me? I've been swimming almost non-stop, dodging schools of sharks and killer whales!"

"Oh, well, in that case, let me make it up to ye."

They were twelve miles out when Jack and Sirene came up on deck. The moon was rounding out to half, and bright in the sky. Sirene was dressed in what might once have been a wedding gown. Once a pale pink, it was sunbleached to a bone white. The overnetting was in tatters, as was the underskirt. The sleeves were cut open and whipped behind her like pennants in the wind. She wore none of the heavy underpinnings and petticoats, which allowed the skirts to hang close to her legs in front, and billow out behind in a great cloud of ragged linen.

She was not the only one so attired, either. Every member of the crew, male and female, wore at least a poncho of old sailcloth cut in deep fringes that tied under the arms to keep it from interfering. Jack was decked out in a tattered, pale dress coat with dove-grey trousers and shirt. Beneath it he wore his gold sash and upon his head was the bloodied gold scarf. It had been washed as much as it could be, but there were still dark stains on it. He was not wearing the eye patch, and the scar was a livid white against his tanned skin.

A third of the crew waited below with Penn at the guns, while the remainder stayed above decks and lined the gunnels, passing about a series of makeup pots. Those that never served under Jack were being painted up by those that had. Their skulls were highlighted and emphasized by the paint and the moonlight, making them look like skeletal ghosts from a distance. There were no lights on the ship except for the moon.

Sirene was led past all of them to the bow where Tortuga stood with his wife. Anjali wore a dirty white version of her usual choli and pantaloons, with a net draped over her torso tied with bells and strips of old cloth. Tortuga turned, handing the captain the spyglass, while Sirene looked him over.

He wore dark trousers and no shirt, with the skull painted on his face and his bones on the rest of his skin. He wore a pair of braces with three pistols apiece and a large cutlass. Anjali was similarly armed.

Jack closed the glass and turned. "All hands to position!" he bellowed. "Wait for my signal. We'll give them a chance to surrender."

Anjali gave Tortuga a kiss before marking his forehead and hers with a bloody thumbprint, then scaled the ratlines to the top platform on the mainmast. The wind raked through the net, ringing the bells, which made a disturbing sound echoing off the sails. Jack reached for Sirene's hand, and led her into position just above the figurehead and right between her outspread wings. He kissed her hand.

"If ye would be so kind, milady. Sing. Sing like the sirens yer named for. Freeze their blood and encourage surrender." He backed away, pausing to kiss his fingers and brush them along the upraised wing of the *Mercy*. He then turned, and trotted to his position at the helm.

Sirene let the wind carry her haunting melody across the few miles to the helpless ship. The dolphins who had been sporting alongside obediently vanished. Her voice, so well suited for singing below the water and carrying great distances as the whales sing, had a different quality above. Without the heavy water to diffuse its power, it became dangerous. Volume and pitch combined to find the resonance in almost anything, and as a result the *Mercy* seemed to hum and sing with her.

Tortuga, standing eight feet behind her with his arms crossed threateningly, could feel a faint vibration beneath his bare feet. Below decks, the gun crews looked around in alarm as the sound echoed through the timbers around them, making the cannonballs, neatly stacked on their brass monkeys, ring against each other.

Dutch ship was in a panic. The pale grey caravel glowed like a ghost ship as she closed swiftly. There was an argument between the captain and the other officers whether they should drop sail and flee, risking the open sea with no control or if that was what the ghosts wanted- to drive them to their deaths; or if indeed this were not a ghost ship at all, but some trick. The regular seamen were deep in prayer even as they readied to repel things they were sure they had no hope of hurting, things come to spirit away their souls.

The first mate held up his hand for silence. The captain waved him off, claiming that the eerie singing had been going on for a half-hour already and was nothing new. The mate insisted, claiming to be able to hear words now. They all listened, and soon could discern words in Dutch, each drawn out so long they were hardly words any more.

"Surrender. Mercy. Ransom. Souls or lives, I can't be sure which, captain," he said.

The captain whipped out his glass, and studied the figure at the bow. It shone almost with a light of its own, luminous white skin and whiter hair that whipped about it like a nest of vipers. It stood with its arms outstretched, mimicking the angel bound to the stem, mouth open. What came out of that mouth could not have emanated from a human soul, much less a human body. Distant bells could be heard and there was a sinister vibration developing in the Dutch ship's timbers.

"It's the angel of death," gasped the first mate.

The captain raised his sights to the pennant flying from the mast. It was as grey as the vessel below it, with crossed sabres and a half skull glaring dead ahead in black, looking as if they were holes in the flag. His mind raced to remember what he had heard of that flag and its ship. Lately, the scuttlebutt had been different and far more dire, and the flag a bloodier red. But if his memory served him, this was no ghost ship and surrender was the best course of action. Even if he chose to fight, he could see the 'ghosts' outnumbered his men four to one, and she would be able to fire at will without his ship bringing her guns to bear in retaliation.

He sighed, snapped his glass closed and gave orders to strike their colours.

Standing at the helm, Jack smiled as the Dutch flag lowered. He sailed alongside the larger ship with ease, his gunports fully open in case they changed their minds. Both ships dropped anchor and the *Mercy*'s 'skeletoned' crew began to bind the two ships together, sliding the gangplank across. The twelve Dutch sailors and the four officers were standing amidships unarmed with their hands showing.

There was a considerable amount of grumbling from both crews as the pirates swarmed aboard. The Dutch whispered in fear that they were truly ghosts, and then in outrage that they were merely painted men. The pirates, mostly Fenning's men, complained that there would not be a fight. Jack was pleased that it had been so easy.

He met with the other captain, shook hands with him, and called Sirene over to interpret. He was genial, polite to a fault and the other captain seemed both confused and relieved. The Flute's crew was set in their ship's cockboat with a compass and enough food and water to get them back to Sint Maarten safely.

As Sirene slipped overboard to unfoul the rudder, 'Vieve came up top with the ship's manifest. The merchant's cargo hold was overloaded with indigo and cotton. There was a supply of tobacco and cocoa, as well as the stores they would need to get them across the Atlantic back to the Netherlands.

"Mon capitane," she asked in a low voice. "What will you do wit' 'er?"

"The ship?" He shrugged. "Assign a prize crew, haul her after us to Tortuga, and use her cargo to refit the *Mercy*."

"I mean after?"

There was a light in her eyes that made him smile. "Why?" he asked, already suspecting the answer.

"Marie an' I want 'er. We'll surrender our share for 'er if we must. But ...your quartermaster doesn' want 'er."

He folded his arms, and managed to look sternly down at the slightly taller woman. "Ye do realize that a Flute is notoriously easy prey."

"Oui!" she nodded.

Mary chimed in, equally excited. "Which makes her great bait. Just think, captain: a ship comes sailing along thinking 'what easy prey'. They get closer and see that it's manned by women!"

"'Alf naked weemon," 'Vieve added.

"Maybe," she said, glossing over what was obviously a bone of contention in the plan. "But either way they'll be so busy standing slack-jawed over the beauties on deck they'll never notice the guns until they rip their hull out from under them.”

Jack laughed softly. “We’ll talk privately later. Right now let’s get her ready to sail.”

“But I thought she was dead in the water,” Mary said with a frown.

“Sirene is fixing that as we speak,” he said, began to issue orders.

“Sirene?” Mary repeated.

Genevieve laughed and guided her companion away, being careful of her injured arm, promising to explain later.

They sailed into the port of Tortuga on the high tide and very carefully. While the *Zuiderskruis* was shallow in the draft, she was heavily laden and thus pushing the boundaries of how deep she could sail. For her protection, Jack went ashore in longboats, leaving enough hands on board to repel any idiots with an eye to taking her while in the pirate port. He did not let Sirene enter the port for the same reasons. He and Tortuga headed in with a small complement to make arrangements to sell the Flute's cargo or trade it for the things they would need. Supplies were expensive here, but anything could be bought or sold for the right price.

After some hard and fast bargaining, and no small amount of wheedling and arguing, 'Vieve convinced Jack to allow her and Mary to have the ship and even to accept the Flute's 'tagging along'. Even talked him into letting them play bait now and again. The women renamed the ship *The Widow* and recruited six women from the island to sail with them. Only two had any sailing experience to begin with, though they were all good in a fight. Six of the other pirates, some from the *Ambition*'s original crew and some from the *Mercy*, came aboard under Genevieve. While Marklain got the *Mercy*'s rigging finally squared away, he taught some of those women what they were about.

Both crews were thinned out considerably, bringing them down to more comfortable numbers. The *Widow* manned fourteen hands and four 'officers', though she only needed twelve and two. She was also refitted with four more guns including two swivels on the fo'c'sle. The *Mercy* housed thirty-five, and six officers counting the pilot and chief gunner. They hired a doctor who, for comfort's sake, chose to live on *The Widow*, though he served both ships.

The flute got more than just a new name. She got a new paint job, as well. 'Vieve and Mary painted the hull black with a narrow white trim. And even the figurehead underwent a few changes. The cross in the hands demurely folded at her breast was shaved off and her hands drilled through. A carved bouquet of white lilies with their stems chiselled into a dagger point was slid into place and secured. A black veil was nailed over her head and her gown was painted black.

One of the first things Jack did was remove Mercy from the stem and set her before the mast for repairs he did himself. The wings remained in place and were tended to separately. He scraped off the paint where it was chipping, and sanded down roughened places, all the while humming a quiet tune. No one interfered or behaved as if they saw him or the figurehead. One of the new sailors was caught watching by Mr. Forrest and was quickly advised that it was very bad luck to watch Mercy 'bein' dressed'.

"Show th' lady some manners, whether ye have any 'er not."

Sirene was the only one who dared approach. "Am I allowed to help?" she asked with a smile. "Or am I supposed to leave you two alone?"

Jack looked from maid to maid, and scratched paint from his chin. "I suppose I should introduce ye two anyway." He set his tools down and draped one arm over the statue's upraised one and aimed his other at the mermaid. "This is Sirene, no surname. *She's a real mermaid,*" he added in a whisper. "But ye probably know that already. Sirene... Mercy Ellen Wyndlam, my mother. Well, a fair enough likeness, at least."

She bobbed a proper curtsey. "Pleased," she said, as politely as if she was meeting a real woman for tea. "And for the record, the surname is Taft." Jack raised an eyebrow, and she shrugged. "Technically. My father was a fisherman in the Carolinas: Nathaniel Taft."

Jack handed her a pot of pale blue paint. "Here, ye can start on that side o' her dress."

Sirene learned that Jack was a fair hand with a brush. He insisted on painting the face himself, though only a few touch ups were needed. When they were done, she was lowered into place by Tortuga on the winch, and Jack chained her back up between newly polished wings with a brand new chain and locks.

Jack and Sirene enjoyed themselves: working on the ship by day and taking long, moonlit swims at night, sharing the pearl to change. After each consecutive time, Jack noticed it became less painful until it was merely uncomfortable. He had to admit, there was something very natural and appealing to swimming this way. Even making love was intriguing, a more complete merging of bodies as the flexible, serpentine tails wrapped around one another; though it was disturbing when the dolphins sped by.

His eye healed quickly. The nightly exposure to salt water cleared out any lingering remnants of an infection and the ointment was put to less use each day. The strong light of the sun on the sea continued to bother him, as did the patch, which he hated using.

Late one night, while drinking with the crew, he was examining the bottom of a brown rum bottle, frowning that it was empty. He put the bottle to his bad eye without thinking and aimed it at a torch to better see the contents. Unconsciously, he noted that the light was visible, but not as intense. Then he caught sight of Sirene trying to follow Anjali in a wild dance through the amber glass. He set it down, reached for a full one while watching the girls, and felt an opposing tug on the bottle. He looked over to see the new doctor, a middle-aged man of relative good nature and currently soused demeanour grinning at him over his spectacles.

Dr. Laurence apologized and handed over the bottle. Jack waved it off, indicating the man drink first. He turned back to watch Sirene's less graceful attempt to follow Anjali's energetic and rhythmic movements to the frantic drum beat of her husband; then turned back to the doctor, swaying for a second.

"Do they work?"

"What?" The doctor burped, and passed the bottle. "'Scuse."

"Those," he slurred, pointing at his eyes.

The doctor touched his face, and pulled the spectacles off as if surprised to find them there. "Oh. There they are. Been lookin' all over for these." He squinted at the girls, and then held them up to his eyes again. "Yes, very much. Can't see the deck without 'em. Prob'ly why I couldn't find 'em."

"Can they be made of anythin'?" he asked, taking a swallow and passing it back.

"Well, they have to use glass, I suppose."

"Aye, but any glass?"

He shrugged. "I suppose so. Why? Need a pair?" he asked, drinking deep.

"Why? Know where I kin get a pair?"

The doctor choked and handed the bottle back, nodding dumbly. When he got his breath, he explained, "There's a bloke in town makes 'em. Short Italian bastard."

The conversation abruptly ended when Sirene fell, laughing,

into Jack's lap, and took the bottle from him. "I'm a singer, not a dancer!" she yelled at Anjali.

As she took a deep drink of the rum and coughed violently, Anjali laughed and threw herself deeper into the dance.

Early the next morning, head still pounding, Jack staggered into town to pay the 'short Italian bastard' a visit. The man was taller than Jack, though shorter than the doctor, and not a bastard at all. In fact, he was quite accommodating. Jack explained his problem and his drunken idea lit up in the man's mind. Jack was promptly told to come back at the end of the week.

The ships were ready to disembark within a few more days. Jack took a group ashore to pick up some last minute supplies of fresh fruit, water, and perishables. The moment he was out of sight 'Vieve ran across the gangplank to the *Mercy* with a bundle under her arm, and dragged Sirene and Anjali into the captain's cabin.

'Vieve had acquired some fabrics in town the day they had arrived and she, Anjali, and one of the less sea-wise crewwomen had been sewing ever since. Now they were dressing their 'doll' with the fruits of a week and a half's secret labour. They had made two new choli and a pair of matching sarongs.

One set was made from Indian silk in a gorgeous white that faded down into rich blue and was embroidered in silver. The other was made from island cottons batiked in marbled greens and blues with dancing dolphins. This last one was the outfit they left her in, brushing out her hair and pinning it up on the sides with a spray of tropical flowers. Sirene dressed it up with the last rope of pearls, and went up top to wait for Jack to return with the supplies.

When Jack stepped up on deck he was grinning from ear to

ear. He had a new gold scarf which he wore folded in a narrow band around his head, and a new eye patch that glinted oddly in the sunlight. He stopped cold when he saw Sirene. Tortuga had to pick him up and move him out of the way so the rest of them could come on board to unload the supplies from the small boat.

Sirene was an island vision standing across the deck watching him. The wind lifted the edges of her sarong enticingly, granting him flashes of lean, long-muscled leg. She drifted over, admiring the new scarf. She was surprised to notice that the eye patch was transparent, made of a smoky amber glass. She grinned.

"My Amber Jack," she laughed.

He flashed her his lopsided grin. "And ye're absolutely, tropically delicious. Where did...?" He glanced at Anjali who was suddenly, deliberately, busy. "Never mind. I like it." He growled as he was hit by a passing crate. He swept her into his arms and carried her up to the quarterdeck. "There, now we're out o' th' way."

Forrest politely left the deck and went to help load the supplies.

"So, can you see through it well?" she asked, as he set her down.

"It filters out th' bright right nice," he answered, brushing wind-blown tendrils of silver out of her face. "I c'n see without th' glarin' pain. Actually, I c'n see a little better with it than without."

She frowned. "Was that a problem?"

"Not 'til after th' fight."

She touched his face, concerned, brushing her fingers over the glass and the scar running above and below it. "I was afraid of that."

He grabbed her hand, kissing the captured fingers. "'Tis nothin' to worry about, luv. So long as I've this patch I'm better than new. They're like Doc's spectacles." He glanced down at the deck, saw that they were ready to be underway, kissed her, and smiled. "Now, what's our headin'?"

She gave him a light pinch to get him to let go. He laughed and released her. She stood up on tiptoe and whispered into his ear.

"The southeastern edge of the Sargasso Sea."

He stiffened. "Ye're not serious, luv?"

"Dead." She grinned. "Don't worry. The *Mercy* does not have to enter the desert. And should she drift, I'll get a friend or two to help us out of it. Besides, there is a rocky island not far away where the ships can anchor. They aren't very big, but there are coves where we can drag the treasure to have it hauled up. The crews need never know where the wreck herself lies, not that they could ever reach it anyway."

He pulled her close again. "I hope yer right."

He signalled Forrest to return to the helm as he turned the wheel to the initial bearings, and shouted orders to the crews to weigh anchor and set sail. They were not the only ships setting sail with the tide, and the sun-kissed harbour was littered with sails scattered across the horizon. A few were incoming, most outgoing, none bothering them.

The *Mercy's Ransom* ran before the wind feeling better than she had in years, having cast off her mourning. Newly dressed in weeds and gamely struggling to keep up was *The Widow*, all in black with a fairly green crew. Jack had loaned 'Vieve and Mary a few seasoned sailors, taking on some of their crew to learn from his to teach them faster. He still had his doubts about *The Widow*, but was willing to give them a chance.

Sirene stood on the bow admiring the view of the open sea. Her hair was a living thing in the wind and her voice carried her joy at being ocean-bound through the sails. The sailors threw themselves happily into their work, singing along to keep the rhythms. Even Jack felt more alive now that land was behind him.

In the week they were at sea, they passed within sight of three French vessels headed for the Caribbean. Both sides kept watch on each other via spyglass. Sirene, with a whisper to Jack, slipped overboard and swam to them to investigate. She stayed in the shadow of the larger ship, above the water only enough to hear the discussion of the captain and his mate as they studied the two ships miles away.

"We are late as it is, Gilles," the captain was saying. *"Not to mention missing a ship already. That hurricane took a lot out of us."*

"But they fly no flag, Captian. They could be English spies."

"And if so, they are going the wrong way to do us harm. Besides, from the shape of them, one is Portuguese and the other Dutch, though I cannot seem to read their names," The captain mused, staring into the glass.

"I don't think they are at war, are they?" asked Gilles.

"No, but neither are they allies," he explained patiently. *"And that smaller one, the lead ship... I've not seen her like in common use for a long time. So, my guess is that they are pirates."*

"Then we should do something," he protested.

The captain laughed tiredly at his mate's enthusiasm. *"If you were not my sister's boy... We are tired, ill-fed, and at least a week or more from port. We are short on shot and powder. They are not at the moment menacing us. So unless they turn their sights in our direction, we'll leave them be."* The nephew started to say something, which the captain cut off. *"We'll mind our own business, Gilles. Just keep watch on them. If they change course or hoist a pennant, let me know. Otherwise,"* there came the sound of the spyglass being thumped against coat buttons as it was handed off, *"we mind our own."*

"Yes, captain," the nephew sighed.

Sirene dove and set an intercept course for the *Mercy*. Behind her she was vaguely aware of shouting and surfaced just enough to see what had happened. The young man with the spyglass was staring through it and pointing in her direction. Swearing, she sank immediately, calling to see if any dolphins were in the area. Luckily there was a small pod of bottlenose fishing nearby who gladly showed themselves to the ships and the sailors to discredit any who would claim to have seen a mermaid.

By the end of the week, they reached the coral island near the eastern edge of the Sargasso Sea. It was not large, less than a mile of barren rock jutting up out of the water like a beachless jetty. Tortuga and Anjali went ashore with them in the longboat, rowing around to a narrow inlet on the south side. It was little more than a crack in the rock, creating a canyon just wide enough to row into. It narrowed out quickly, forcing them to abandon the boat and climb up onto the rocky beach, to search out a more suitable place to bring the treasure.

Jack groaned and staggered as he set foot on the still rocks. He grabbed for one of the taller outcroppings to steady himself, as Sirene slipped into the water and shifted form. He gave Tortuga his orders as he stared down at the mermaid with a healthy mix of lust and envy.

"We'll need a good place to haul the treasure up from. See what ye can find. We'll be back in what…?" Jack asked Sirene, as he divested himself of his boots and trews.

"Maybe a bell," she answered, handing him the pearl.

Tortuga watched the exchange, eyebrow raised as his wife automatically collected their captain's discards.

"We'll return here, and ye can tell us where's best to haul it up," Jack finished, putting the pearl around his neck and adjusting the clothes he still had on.

"Why no' just haul dem one at a time up to a longboat, or attach lines to de chests an use da windlass ar' a winch t' pull dem up?" Tortuga asked.

Jack jumped into the water. As his body went through the change, Sirene answered for him.

"Because the wreck is nearly a thousand fathoms straight down. Every inch of line and chain on board both ships spliced together would not reach."

Jack bobbed up to the surface. Tortuga frowned as he stared down at the black dorsal stripe and long yellow lines along his captain's sides. "Amba'jack," he said, flatly. Then suddenly he burst out laughing.

Anjali growled. "Now he gets it."

Sirene swam up beneath Jack, seized him above his caudal fin, and pulled him under. He darted off after her, chasing her through the labyrinthine tunnels of the island reef and out towards the Sargasso. The matted sea of Sargasso weed was a bare quarter-mile north of the small island. She led him to the surface for a moment.

"Let all the air out of your lungs," she told him. "You won't need it deep down, and we are going deep. The pressure is going to be incredible and any air could crush you. Suck as much water into them as you can."

"Won't that..."

"Hurt when you change, yes. But it will hurt less than being crushed by the depths. You will also need to be careful going in. The wreck was on a ridge and could easily tip into the abyss."

He followed her example with trepidation as she sank below the water's surface, forced her lungs to open, and breathed in stinging seawater. It was difficult, resisting natural urges, but he managed eventually, and followed her through the edges of the thick seaweed mats teeming with life.

They passed all manner of creatures, shrimp and crabs, octopi and snails, though he did not see any fish at all. Then they dropped below the weed mats and he saw why she referred to it as a desert. Below the warm blanket was a cold, dead calm wherein floated the discards of the sargassum canopy, fragments of bone and broken shell, diffused and distorted rays of light, bits and debris of lost vessels.

Skilly sped out of the darkening water, happy to see them both. She cavorted around them, then led Jack, who was growing increasingly blind as the waters grew murky to his unenhanced eyes. Sirene knew just where she was going. After the first thousand feet, Skilly sang out. Sirene paused, taking over the guiding of Jack from the dolphin as she pulled up, the pressure becoming too much for her, the need for air too great.

The water remained a cold, dark desert for a long time, pressing in on him more than just physically. There was a mental toll being taken out on him as well, surrounded by absolute nothingness. Then something finally broke the pitch black. Lights winked in and out in the distance. At first they seemed like glimmers, figments of his imagination. Then they passed an upflow of surprisingly hot water and found themselves in a fountain of tiny, glowing sparks. The other lights sped close, jerking and snapping up the sparks. Jack could barely make out the shadows of fish surrounding the green, red, and blue lights. Sirene took him by the hand and swam down toward the jutting masts and rotting hull of the one hundred and fifty year old galleon.

The *Ana Maria* was wedged at an angle on a tower-like outcropping above one of the vents. A reef had built up around it, comprised of creatures that rarely saw shallower waters. Most of the fish were monstrous, yet moved out of their way. She took him in through an opening in the hull, guiding him down into the hold.

The inside was overgrown with phosphorescent things and wiggling tubeworms that glowed intermittently. These ghostly lights illuminated the dishevelled contents of the hold. Gold spilled everywhere. There were chests stacked on chests, some of which had broken open. Jack ran his hands through one such coffer, watched coins and uncut gemstones drift through his fingers in the heavy water. There had to be several tons of gold.

Each chest had to weigh a hundred pounds or more and there were eighty in this area alone. He was strong, but even he could not swim to the island hauling the smallest of these.

He looked at Sirene, and it seemed that the same thought had occurred to her. She signalled for him to wait, and left the hold. She did not get far before she realized that, though this place held life and she could see where the life was, it was not enough for her to see anything beyond that. Jack gave her a grin when she came back and gestured for him to come with her, needing his glow to light the way.

Outside the hold he was blind again, except for the dim and intermittent light of fishes flashing their glowing lures as they trolled for food. He let her lead him around the ship, through narrow places and open. He noticed drastic changes in the water temperatures, going from sunless cold to too hot in the space of a few inches.

She investigated several options before she took his hand and led him away from the ship altogether. No sooner were they shallow enough that the dolphin could handle it, Skilly pounced, chattering a thousand questions at once. Sirene asked her to find a small sunken boat, like a dinghy, and the dolphin sped off, eager to help.

When they surfaced where they had left their own boat, Tortuga was sitting on the slope beside it, smoking a hand-rolled cigar while his wife knelt behind him reworking some of his braids.

Sirene began vomiting up seawater, coughing violently to clear her lungs. Jack followed suit, but gestured for Tortuga to pull him out of the water. She quickly put a stop to that, telling him with gestures to keep his gills under the water. He obeyed, and found that it lessened the trauma of clearing his lungs, since his body was still able to get what it needed. Only then did she let the quartermaster and first mate help them out of the water.

She was the first to be able to speak. "Where?" she coughed.

"This is the best place," Anjali shrugged.

"An' d' treashah?" Tortuga asked, noting they were empty handed.

"Bigger than they ever claimed," Jack breathed. He lay flat on his back, eyes fully dilated as he stared up at the sky, a wide grin on his face. "An' that's th' problem."

Skilly came up, interrupting with chatter.

"Maybe not so much," Sirene said. "She found us a sunken longboat that's not so rotted it won't hold. If we had some strong rope, we could rig it up to carry some of the treasure."

He rolled onto his side and stared at her. "How much?"

"Eight, maybe ten chests?"

"Luv, we'd be hard pressed to bring up one between us. How we goin' t' manage eight, an' with th' drag a boat'll cause?" he scowled.

"We don't. Remember the dead calm?"

A smile spread across his face. "Anyone nearby?"

Tortuga and Anjali looked from one to the other, watching the exchange in confusion.

Sirene shrugged. "Near enough. She said there was a pod about thirty miles east. By the time we get set up and the boat loaded, they'd be here."

"Will they be able to go that deep, though?"

She laughed. "They could easily outdive us."

Jack looked over at Tortuga. "Is there enough rope in th' longboat?"

"How much is enough?" he asked bluntly.

"Oh... a couple hundred feet?"

Anjali climbed into the longboat. "You got twenty. You need anything else from th' ship while I am going? What do I tell th' crew, an' how many you want I should plan for th' recovery?"

"I think two one hundred foot lengths should do it," Sirene said, slipping back into the water. "Once we've got it and the boat, it'll take us maybe two or three hours to get it back here and start unloading. We don't want to bring up the longboat, itself. It would cause way too many questions."

Jack nodded. "Methinks we shouldn' need any crew, not to bring it aboard. Tell 'em to make ready for six chests on th' *Mercy* and two or three on th' *Widow*. Get th' rope and whatever ye two will need fer th' next few hours. Tell 'em what ye need to; just don't tell 'em th' truth." He looked down at the silvery white belly of his tail and gave a rueful grin. "*Please* don't tell 'em th' truth."

While they waited for the ropes, Jack followed the dolphin to the longboat and Sirene sang out to the whale pod. It did not take long to receive a response and she swam up to Anjali's boat as she returned. The first mate handed her a bundle on a looped rope.

"T'ere's th' two lengths you wanted, plus anot'ah, an' some sail."

"Why the extra?" she asked.

"Because she be a right savvy woman," Jack grinned, swimming up. "Well done. The longboat is actually a cockboat," he corrected. "The dolphin overestimated."

Tortuga reached out and grabbed the longboat's rim, dragged it to the rocky shore. His wife handed him another bundle before climbing out. Sirene smiled.

"If you two wish to join us, I might be able to arrange it."

Tortuga did not hesitate. "I t'ink not."

"Suit yourself. You two have fun."

This time, it was Jack's turn to drag her under to hurry her along. He took the bundle from her and looped it over his head and one shoulder, then led her to the boat. It wasn't far or deep down. It had a hole or two, nothing so big the chests would fall through, but enough to reduce some of the drag. He replaced the old mooring rope with a new one, handing Sirene part of it, and taking the bulk of the weight himself. They emptied their lungs of air and began to drag the boat to the shipwreck.

It took a little work tying up the dingy so it would not fall away into the abyss. Jack opened up the sail inside it, and secured the little boat to the coral encrusted rails before allowing

Sirene to lead him through the dimly lit ship to the hold. She gestured for him to begin selecting chests to take with them and she gathered some of the glowing worms from the walls. Swimming out of the hold with them, she scattered them over the deck. Unfortunately, large, toothy fish immediately swarmed, gobbling them up. She tried again, this time collecting some of the glowing anemone-like creatures and coral. She used them to light a path to the boat that Jack could see in the near dark.

When she returned to the hold, he had dragged aside six chests of normal size and was going through several others picking and choosing the items he wanted for the seventh. He had tucked a sword into his sash that was crusted over with the same hard, crunchy substance that was taking over the wreck. He looked up as she came in, swam over, and set a necklace against her throat.

It was three rows of luminous pearls that formed a choker, draped with ropes of pearls and diamonds forming a rich lattice work that framed the centrepiece, which was a blood ruby the size of a robin's egg.

She smiled and kissed him, spinning in the water as she wrapped herself around him. He managed to hold her still, and things were starting to get heated when they were interrupted by whale song. She laughed, an odd sound in the water, and untangled herself.

Together, they hauled the chests up through the hole in the hull to the secured dinghy. They made the last one fit and Jack covered the whole with the sail, tying it down with the extra rope so that the chests would not fall out. The whales arrived as they were finishing up..

There were eight full-grown sperm whales in the pod and one of them agreed to carry the boat by the ropes up to the surface. The rest, accompanied by six young of various ages, were already diving for squid and other fish that were milling about farther down.

Jack was in awe of the creature, and a little nervous as he

held one end of the ropes while the whale took it in her mouth. She was not the largest in the pod, but it was an encounter he would not soon forget. The female was longer than the *Mercy* was wide and it put a great deal into perspective for him. It took Sirene placing his hand on the creature's side to get him to dare to touch the wrinkly grey-brown hide. It was a wonderful but humbling experience.

Sirene sang out to the whale, emitting deeper noises than he thought her capable of, as she swam alongside. The whale's answer tickled his hands, and it seemed that she laughed at him when he jerked away.

It took them a bit longer to ascend than it took to get to the wreck, and only a quarter hour to near the rocky island escorted by the black dolphin. The whale, unable to enter the channel, set the boat on a shelf that led into it. She held a brief exchange with Sirene before rising to the surface to take several deep breaths prior to diving again to rejoin her family.

The two of them tried to drag the boat along the shelf into the channel, but it was too heavy. They secured it, then unloaded it chest by chest, hauling them into the channel to where the others were waiting. Skilly paused, listening to something. She whistled to Sirene and then swam off, following the call of something in the distance.

They tried handing the chests up to Tortuga and Anjali, but, beyond the small one, they were too tired and the chests too full for them to lift high enough out of the water for the others to take over. Finally, they rose to the surface and expelled the last of the water from their lungs.

Jack, still coughing, looked over at her, "All right, this part I kin do without."

She laughed at him, ended up choking. "Ah, but was it worth it?" she wheezed, as they crawled up onto the beach.

He flopped onto his back, pointing upward, exhausted. "Once."

Anjali squatted beside him. "So howzit feel t' survive drowning?"

He thought about it a moment. "Onct ye get past th' panic...
it's... rather peaceful actually. Th' real pain comes from survivin'
it," he groaned, rolling over as he coughed up what he hoped was
the last of it. "But we're gonna hafta tie off ropes an' haul 'em up
by th' onesies. Think ye kin handle it from this end?"

"Oh, aye. We kin haul up quite a bit, Capta'n. How many ah'
dere?" Tortuga asked with a wide grin.

"About seven," Sirene answered. "All we could fit in the boat
was six regular and one smaller one. But that one I think we can
hand up."

Jack snorted. "Yeah, that one only weighs a few stone."

Anjali frowned. "Why'd ye bothah then?"

Jack grinned. "It's not th' quantity, darlin'. It's th' quality,
savvy? An' that one's Sirene's to 'erself."

Sirene looked surprised. "That is not necessary."

"No," he said, rolling back into the water. "But that's me orders."

He looked up at Tortuga, suddenly uncomfortable with matters. Without another word, he dove, swimming back to the boat
for the ropes. He did not want to think about it, but the treasure
brought a great uneasiness with it. Once it was on board, their
accord was complete; nothing more to hold her to him. 'A possession is only what the sea lets you keep', he reminded himself,
parroting her words. Though she was never a possession; *obsession* maybe. He passed her in the channel with the ropes, tossed
her one without looking at her and fastened one end to the side
handle of the nearest chest.

Sirene took the rope and did the same, confused by his manner and silence. She did not have to guess what he was feeling.
He was not aware how much of his emotions his temporary body
transmitted. The way his fins flickered and waved, the manner in
which he undulated his tail unnecessarily as he worked, all told
her he was deep in his thoughts and unhappy with them. What
those thoughts were was not clear, but his reactions were as dis-

tinct as his aura.

It frustrated her that it never fluctuated, never strayed from the bright gold it always was. At least with everyone else she could use it to read them. There was only one other person she could not read, and ironically for the same reason. She shivered, and forced the thought from her mind, told herself that Price was divided up in the bellies of several different sharks, and focused on her knots.

Jack took the ropes and brought them to the surface, handing them up to Tortuga and his wife. While they pulled, he and Sirene lifted from below. It was not easy work, but it was not enough to completely distract his mind. It raced full of thoughts, schemes, plans, and ideas... anything he could come up with to entice her to stay near him. Now that she had her pearl she would probably just swim away. She had been kept away from her beloved oceans for far too many years. What reason would she have to remain near land or land-walkers? She had all too many reasons to abandon that life, too many years of abuse by too many men. And he? He had his ship, his crew, the makings of an unwanted fleet. Did he really need her?

That thought caused a violent physical reaction from him, an involuntary thrash of his tail and he lost his grip on the last chest. The handle, encrusted with barnacles and the like, sliced through the rope with surprising ease at the sudden shift of weight. Anjali was forced to let go as the rope ripped through her hands. The chest hit the bottom and cracked, the lock breaking and coins spilling out the partially opened lid as it settled to the uneven floor of the channel. Cursing, Jack swam down to recover the spilled treasure.

Chapter the Fourteenth

The lid of the chest shuddered unnoticed by Jack as he reached for it, his hands and mind occupied with keeping hold of the jewels that had spilled out of the opening. Sirene saw a snake-like creature lunge towards Jack's face as he pried the lid open the rest of the way. He saw only movement and darted back. Reflexively, she lashed out and grabbed the creature by the tail. Its three inch long teeth snapped closed a hand's breadth from Jack's nose.

It turned on her, lashing out with sharp, spiked fins and long razor teeth. The pair quickly became a tangled, writhing ball, as the mermaid battled the monster from the deep.

Jack pulled the sword out of his sash and struggled to unsheathe it from its crusty housing. He saw blood drifting upwards in the water and broke the coral growth sealing the blade to the scabbard. The light flashed off the unmarred steel as he swam nearer. The two combatants were so entangled there was little way he could attack the one without hitting the other. He waited, frantic for any opening.

Sirene clung desperately to the beast. She had no weapon, but managed to keep the teeth from ripping into her flesh. She had a death grip on it behind its hideous head, but its dorsal fins were spined and kept stabbing into her palms. It was nearly eight feet long with pale red lights that undulated along its slender length, and it was tightly wrapped around her tail as it attempted to bite her. Its main body was the size of a perch and covered with a stinging slime. It felt like she was caught in the tendrils of a giant jellyfish. There was a slow burning along her tail and in her hands, followed by an unearthly chill. As it turned its head away from her, she shuddered violently. She tried to let go, but her hands would no longer obey. She cried out, unable to control herself.

Jack winced, preparing for the deafening silence that would follow; but the sound had a different quality here. It became more of a shrill whistle, not unlike the dolphin's cries, without the devastating power it held in the air. The monster blinked its coin-sized eyes as it undulated and writhed out of her grasp. He saw the ribbon of blood flowing from her hands as it tore free and lunged for him again, its jaws wide open. He stabbed, embedding the bright Spanish blade through the roof of its mouth and into its luminescent brain. It lashed out with its tail, emitting a hissing shriek. He ripped the sword free and dodged the barbed whip, struck again, and cut it off. A few frenzied strokes and the beast drifted to the sea bed in several bloody pieces, the lights on its body fading out.

He thrust the bloody sword into his sash and grabbed hold of Sirene. Her body was hot, and writhing. Her hands were sliced across the palms and still grasping the water. There were livid red punctures and deep cuts down the length of her tail, some of which were still bleeding, all of which were puffing up. He wrapped his arms around her waist, pressing her tight against him, and shot for the surface. Her body seemed out of control, threatening to entangle their tails and interfere with his swimming. Tortuga and Anjali were watching from above and both reached into the water to help before they had broken the surface.

It was a struggle to get the flailing form out of the water and onto the rocks. Her gills closed and her lungs opened and a scream tore through her. It began low and guttural, a cry of agony, but threatened to rise. It echoed hard against the higher rocks.

"Gag her!" Jack yelled as he launched himself out of the channel and onto the rocks next to them.

Anjali pulled Sirene's head back against her own body and covered her mouth, muffling the sounds as they began to rise in pitch. The sounds were still painful, but no where near as lethal as they could be.

Tortuga sat on her tail, grabbing her arms as she struck him blindly with one half-curled fist. Jack dragged himself over.

"What happened, Captain?" Anjali asked.

"There was somethin' in th' chest, and I think it was poisonous. She kept it from biting me. Get her t' th' doctor."

"How, Capta'n?" Tortuga asked through his teeth. "She'll ova' turn de boat if we take har like dis."

Anjali looked at her husband, unwilling to look at her Captain, "We could tie her down," she suggested.

Jack thought for a moment before he slithered back into the channel. He cut through the water like a shark toward the abandoned cockboat. He grabbed the sail pinned beneath it and swam back without pausing. Behind him, the boat rolled and fell away into the darkening deep. He returned swiftly, throwing the sailcloth to the others and hauled himself after, catching a nasty scrape from the sharp coral along his fin that he did not even notice.

Her struggles had lessened, became little more than light convulsions. Anjali had uncovered her mouth and Sirene's jaw was clamped down on a bone. It did not take much to lift her onto the sail and bind her within it.

Before they tightened the ropes around her tail, Jack put the pearl around her neck, held up the silver cage, and blew on it. Inside, the pearl spun freely, initiating the change from fin to feet. Only then did they bind her legs into the sail to keep her from thrashing.

Jack put the pearl back on and changed himself, then struggled into his trousers. Anjali gathered up the remains of their picnic as Tortuga eased Sirene into the boat. Jack was frantic. His mind would not remain still, trapped in a conundrum. If she died because of him he would not be able to live with himself. On the other hand, if she died, it would have been saving him and his death would make hers a waste.

He settled into the boat, straddling her shrouded body and threw his weight into rowing. The activity helped to blind his mind, to drive out thought and worry. Almost before he knew it, they were shipping oars as they skimmed along the shadowed side of the caravel. He ordered a cargo net dropped, and he and Tortuga manoeuvred her shivering form into it.

The crew crowded the rails, looking excitedly for a glimpse of the treasure. They frowned and murmured at the sight of the silver woman, bound as if in death, being hauled up in the cargo net. Jack scaled the ladder to the deck with surprising swiftness, and ordered the first person he saw to bring the doctor, and then began moving people out of his way to get to the net being laid on the deck.

He untangled her from it and picked her up, her long silver hair plastered against his arm. The crew made a path as he carried her to the cabin. He was unaware of other people as they helped out, opening doors, pulling back the new curtains on the bed. No one else existed but the still form in his arms until the doctor walked into the room. Jack untied her, opening the sail, adjusted her sarong for modesty.

Dr. Laurence set his bag on the table and bent over her. Jack backed away, letting him examine the bright, angry wounds that covered her body. He answered questions numbly.

Jack began to wonder if there was a curse upon the treasure they brought up. He had never heard of anything, but that did not mean such did not exist. If there was, the object in question was most likely in the chest that still lay at the bottom of the channel. That chest would not be hauled up.

It seemed wrong to him, to be in possession of the treasure and not have her around to help him spend it. His heart beat so fast it seemed to not beat at all. He felt as if he were still trying to breathe through gills. She looked so still upon the pillow, her lips so white. He looked up as the doctor turned. The drawn face of the older man made his heart freeze.

"What. Is there...?"

"Any thing I can do?" Dr. Laurence finished for him. "I fear not. It is a poison unknown to me. If the wounds were restricted to her limbs I might be able to prevent the poison from reaching her heart, but they are everywhere, and I fear the poison has already travelled out of reach."

Jack staggered. "Is there no hope?"

The doctor reached out to steady him. "Son, where there is breath, there is hope. Keep her warm and dry, give her a little water now and again and maybe... she might fight it off. It happens, sometimes. She is a strong woman, in spite of delicate appearances, if half the stories I have heard are true. All we can do is keep her comfortable and pray."

The words that clung to Jack's mind were 'a little water'. He thanked the doctor and saw him out, and beckoned in his quartermaster who stood outside in the companionway keeping the rest of the two crews at bay. He closed the door behind him and gave him his orders.

"I need a bathtub."

"We stole more dan a few luxuries from da British ships, Capta'n, but dat not be one a'dem."

"Find something that will do, half a barrel, anything. She needs t' be kept in seawater."

He frowned. "Da doctor said dat?"

"No. He doesn't know about this. It will help her healin'. 'Tis all I can do for her," he ground.

"Is it wise t' have har in full scale on board?" the man added. "Even at da most careful, someone could manage..."

Jack nodded. "Yer right. An' she'll fit in a smaller space this way. Get me somethin' waterproof. Cut a barrel stem t' stern and bring it in, an' a barrel rack if we got. Send Luke and Smithe back with Anjali fer th' treasure. But leave th' chest what dropped. Th' sea wants it this bad, she can keep it."

Tortuga nodded, pleased that his long time friend was thinking clearly and not consumed by his fear for the woman. "Aye, aye, Capta'n. I'll send Hare wid a bucket on a rope ta fill it." He paused with his hand on the doorknob and looked back at his captain who was already returning to her side. "An' Jack."

He looked up. It was not often the man called him by his given name. "Aye?"

"I'll have my witch do what she can far yours."

Jack actually smiled. "Thank you. She be in th' *Mercy*'s arms now."

Tortuga left and Jack could hear hands scrabbling about on deck as the large man relayed his orders. He sat next to her on the bed, laying his hand on her chest, making sure she was still breathing. He brushed her hair back out of her face, and pressed the back of his hand to her temple.

"Don't ye be leavin' me, luv. I can't... just... just... don't." He sighed, unable to bring the words to bear. "Savvy?"

An hour later, an empty water barrel had been sawn in half lengthwise and turned into a tub. The carpenter, at Tortuga's suggestion, had even cut a half circle out of the centre of one end for her neck. They laid her inside, and set her head upon a pillowed stool to remove the risk of drowning. Hare hauled up bucket after bucket of heavy salt water, filling the tub to the neck hole.

Once she was comfortable, Jack drew over a chair and sat beside her, stroking her brow. His hand passed frequently over her lips, partly to touch their velvet softness, and partly to reassure himself she was still breathing.

"Capta'n," Tortuga ventured. "Da chests ah' on board."

"Take them and 'Vieve below," he ordered. "Open them all, but take great care in case anything else stowed away. Then divvy them up according t' th' articles, an' stow 'em respectively. Let 'Vieve decide what she wants to do with *The Widow*'s share."

"An' den?"

"What an' then?"

"What headin'? We can't stay heah long, Capta'n."

"Why not?" he sulked.

"Bloody Mary sighted a storm. An' it be t'reatenin' t' blow us int' de sargasso." He lowered his voice out of respect. "An' wit de *fotsy* as she is... how we gonna get out again?"

Jack sighed. "Fine, avoid th' storm. Pick a heading. It's no never mind t' me. Not like we'll be needin' t' go huntin' any time soon. Like as not some'll be wantin' retirement on their share o' this haul."

Tortuga left the cabin, frustrated and worried. Jack dipped his hand into the water, ran a finger over one of the punctures. There was still a hole, a raised welt that was a sharp, bloody contrast to the white of her skin. The seawater was helping some. Her skin no longer seemed so hot to the touch, but she was so still. There was a stiffness to her limbs that, if he was not so certain she was still breathing, she would have been taken for dead.

He remained by her side for hours. His meal was eaten by Flagstaff, who waited two full bells before helping himself. It was not until midnight that Jack stirred.

He went up on deck, crossing amidships to the bow without seeing anything else. The crew who were on watch left him be, giving him adequate space. He set his hand on the upraised wing. His voice was soft and choked as he bent forward on the bow, leaning on the rail and gazed down at the carved head below him.

"Mother, I have never asked fer much; only that ye be faithful t' those that're faithful t' you, that ye take care o' yer own. The rest I c'n pretty much handle. I've been extraordinarily lucky, an' not like father beyond th' onct."

He stared at the waves sliced by the keel. The wind was heavy with the storm that blocked out what moonlight there would have been. A glance behind showed him the roiling black and occasional strikes of lightning many miles back. The thunder was faint. *The Widow* loomed large in their starboard wake.

"I owe her," he said, turning back to the sea. "More than life, more than a trinket," he added, fingering the pearl hanging around his neck for safekeeping. "I... I know I can't keep her. But I can at least send her home as whole as she came t' me. She brought me home. ...I don't want t' lose her, but... the other way I c'n survive, knowin' she's ...somewhere. This way... I can't lose her *this way*."

There was a cry from the *The Widow*. He turned, and listened to the distorted exchange from ship to ship, and waited until Backhand Luke trotted up with a spyglass. "What is it, man?"

"A ship, sir, they think. We can't confirm it either, but there is somethin'... not right," he said, frowning.

Jack took the glass and looked where Luke pointed. Something flickered on the horizon to the southwest, something he could not get a good view of. He tucked the glass away and leapt to the ratlines, climbing up to the crow's-nest. The vantage here was little better. As he climbed back down, 'Vieve and Mary were standing at their prow, staring through a glass and shaking their heads. He went up to the quarterdeck and called over.

"What're yer deadlights tellin' ye?"

Mary crossed to the larboard side. "We haven't a bloody inkling, sir. But I ain't likin' th' feel of it. Not after this afternoon."

"Whatever zey are," yelled 'Vieve, joining her and putting a protective arm around her waist, "zey are not alone. I am certain I spied a second."

"Are you sure?" She nodded. Jack groaned. "They have to be ships."

"What do you weesh to do, mon capitane?"

"Avoid them fer now," he said, calling off new bearings northeast and taking the helm. He set a course that should take them out of sight of the ships or whatever they were long before morning. He turned to Penn, giving him the heading. "Though stay out o' that storm if ye can. I'll be in my cabin."

"Aye, Cap'n," he said, taking the helm from him.

Adding one more thing to his list of worries, he went below. He propped himself up on a chair with his feet up on the sea chest and fell asleep with his hand in the barrel resting on her breast.

Jack started awake. He looked around the brightening cabin, frowned at the red glare of dawn pouring through the windows. He gazed down at Sirene and noticed that she had stirred in the night. Her legs had shifted position where they were curled up to fit her into the large barrel. He brushed a kiss to her forehead. It was cooler than before, and it seemed to him that the wounds were smaller, less angry.

The sun breached the horizon and stabbed through his eye like a dagger into his head. Growling, he crossed to the desk and took his glass eye patch from its box and tied it on. Adjusting it, he glanced out the window and frowned. The heading he had ordered was easterly, toward the sun and open sea. The sun should not then be rising in his window.

He stormed toward the door, and opened it to find himself staring at an enormous black fist. Tortuga pulled back at the last second.

"We got a problem, Capta'n."

"Nay, th' risin' sun's *supposed* ta' be starboard astern!" he snapped sarcastically, as the man stepped aside and followed him to the quarterdeck. He noticed as he stalked toward the helm that *The Widow* was not on their flank any more, and was losing ground. "Care t' explain, Mr. Forrest?"

The man sighed. "I swear, Captain. The headin' is the same as ye gave Penn. I've even set the rope t' hold the course. She refuses. *Mercy*'s got the wind in her teeth an' keeps takin' her own head."

Jack surveyed the horizon. "Southwest," he mused. "What be so important southwest?" He turned back to the old helmsman. "Ye try cutting back th' sails?"

"Be my guest, Captain," he said.

Jack followed his hand to the main deck. All those on duty stood at the rails watching the sea pass before them. No one was even trying to man the rigging. The sails were full. He went down the steps to where Marklain sat on a crate playing draughts with Penn. He stood over them and watched as the older man seized several pieces in a single, long move.

"Enjoying th' mornin' off, are we?" he intoned, arms crossed over his chest.

"Nay, sir. I'm technically on duty," Marklain admitted, and took his turn. "'Tis the bloody vessel what's made me obsolete." He seemed pleased with his move, until Penn took his turn and wiped him out. He sighed, waved his hand. "Fine. You win." He got up and walked with Jack. "Captain, I had six men on one rope trying to furl that sail. She's not havin' it. The quartermaster couldn't budge it. Wherever she's goin', she's in a hurry and right determined. Just like a woman, stubborn as hell."

Jack walked to the rail and leaned on it. "At least we've lost whatever it was on the horizon last night."

Marklain scratched the back of his neck sheepishly. "Uh, I wouldn't say that." Jack looked over at the man. "I'd say it went the other way. Our current headin' is straight for whatever that was."

Jack stood up. "Well, there's no help fer it then. What th' lady wants, th' lady gets. Assign eyes fer th' horizon and eyes fer th' *Widow*. We'll not be wantin' t' lose her if we c'n help it. Jest remember that be where th' doctor's berthed." He turned and headed below. "Oh, an' alert me if ye sight any dolphins or whales."

"Aye, Captain," Marklain said. With a nod from the quartermaster, he began to issue orders.

Tortuga followed the captain to the cabin. He frowned at the food scattered across the plate and table. It was obvious who ate and who hadn't. He sighed.

"Capta'n, ya must keep up yore strengt'. I'll have da boy bring breakfast, but ya must eat. Ya cannot help har if ya be weak from hungah."

"I know, I just... I... cannot think of food."

Tortuga scowled. "I'll send da first mate in t' make shor ya do."

Jack glared up at him, as he sank into the chair. "Fine. Send food. I'll eat."

The man nodded. "Speakin' of Anji..."

Jack glanced over from examining Sirene.

"She convince' dere be blood soon. Who's she don' know. She been at her witchary all night."

"Tender me thanks. She able t' do anythin' fer Sirene?"

The look on the man's face said everything Jack needed to know. He nodded and went back to his vigil. Tortuga left quietly.

Needing to do more than just sit there, Jack began to brush out her hair. Flagstaff plopped down on Jack's feet, playing with the dangling locks. Jack paid him a little attention, concentrating on her and the thoughts racing through his mind. Was the ship sailing toward a cure? Something that would save her? And where had that blasted dolphin disappeared to now that he needed her? If Sirene survived and chose to stay with him, he swore that was something he'd have her teach him, how to understand those clicks and squeals. Maybe, if she wanted to leave, he could manoeuvre her into an accord to teach him. Hopefully, wind willing, by the time he learned, she would not want to leave.

"No," he said to the cat. "I cannot force her t' stay where she wills not. I'll offer her th' excuse, but t' force her t' stay would be wrong. All I c'n do is ask." Flagstaff rolled onto his back, paws tucked and looked up at him, blinked his patched eye. "I *am* a pirate," he snarled. "But I've never forced a woman." The cat blinked again. "Who didn't want t'be forced," he corrected. "When we got down t' that she was just as willin' as I."

He stared down at the silvery threads of silk in his hand. "Silver and gold," he muttered.

He was interrupted by Hare bringing the breakfast tray. "Jest put it on the table," he said, brushing again.

"Sorry, sair," the boy said, swapping out the trays. "But ah'm t' wait until' yer done. An' if'n ye don' eat, ah'm t' fetch th' fairst mate."

He levelled his gaze on the boy. "Who's orders do ye be followin'?"

"Beggin' yore rank, sair... ah'll not be pissin' off either o' them, ah ain't. Not when they're right."

Jack sighed, set aside the brush, and crossed to the table. He sat down and stared at his plate for several minutes before he made himself eat.

They sailed this way for nearly a week: Jack spooning broth and water into Sirene, watching her every spare moment and leaving someone else to watch her when he was not; sailing along night and day at speeds he had not thought the ship capable of even in the strongest wind. Now and again, at night, they would catch glimpses of the flashes on the horizon, never any nearer. By the fifth day *The Widow* was out of sight, though she struggled gamely to keep up.

Seven days out, Jack was in his cabin when he heard the shout of 'Land ho'! Before he could get his eye patch on straight, Hare was at the door.

"We sighted sail, sair!" he reported when admitted.

Jack grabbed his gun belt and sheathed the Spanish sword he had acquired from the sunken ship, now cleaned, and oiled, and ready for use. "Which is it, lad? Sail or land?"

"Both, Capt'n."

He nodded. "Stay with her."

"Aye, sair."

Jack reached for the door as the boy made himself comfortable at watch. "And that broth on th' table be hers. Make sure that damned cat stays out o' it."

"He's a right pirate, he is!" Hare crowed.

Jack tossed him a half-hearted grin and left the room. He met Tortuga in the bow, where the taller man handed him the spyglass and directed his gaze. Just forward of the horizon was an island, jutting green and verdant with tall, rocky cliffs. Sailing around its edge was a ship.

"Two ships," he muttered, as a second came into sight.

"Two?" Tortuga repeated, looking through the glass as it was handed back. "It jus' sail' around da island. Dere was da only da one when I sent da boy," he said, again passing the glass.

"Methinks she be givin' chase t' th' first... Wait, that's..." Jack readjusted, switching the spyglass to his left eye, focusing through the amber glass. The two figures became clearer just as a column of smoke erupted from the second ship and the thunder of cannon echoed across the water. "Bloody...!" He slammed the glass closed. "That's th' bloody *Ambition*."

Tortuga stepped out of his way. "We goin' t' deir aid?" he asked, disapproval heavy in his voice.

"What bloody choice have we bloody got?" he snarled. "They are clearly under attack, and by our accords..."

He shouted orders to the crew to prepare for battle, and stormed down to the cabin. They would be on the fight in less than a bell's time. In the cabin, he issued orders to Hare while he readied himself for the eminent combat.

"Stay in th' cabin and lock th' door. Guard her with yer life," he said, handing the boy a pistol. "Ye do know how t' use this, aye?"

"Aye, sair. But one shot won't do me much good, Capt'n."

Jack nodded. The boy was thinking. "Go t' th' armoury and tell Tortuga I said t' arm ye."

The boy took off, leaving the captain getting ready.

Jack pulled on a pair of boots. It would be safer in a ship to ship with unknown and sharp debris and still-hot lead scattered across the decks. He made sure his eye patch and scarf were snug, and checked his pistols. He loaded four and slung them on a brace across his chest. He picked up the sword he had taken from the *Ana Maria*, balanced it on his palm.

It was a beautiful piece of Spanish workmanship. Damascene inlay graced the hilt and guard in the elegant patterns preferred by the Spanish nobility. He had cleaned the hilt and the scabbard, tending to the blade with care. He had a feeling this would be the first time it saw blood, human blood anyway. The sword had been out of place where he found it, but who was he to question a gift from the sea?

Hare returned brandishing a second pistol and a cutlass.

"Ye be careful ye cut th' other man, mate, not yerself. I'll not be catchin' an earful from her when she heals fer getting' ye killed," he said, crossing to the door.

Hare gave him a smart salute, holding the door open for him. "Beggin' yore pardon, Capt'n, but should anythin' gets past me t' her, I'm thinkin' she'll not be givin' any an earful but th' enemy, sair."

"To their regrets, son. To their regrets," he replied, and headed up top.

Behind him, he heard something heavy scraping across the deck in the cabin, coming to a thudding halt at the door. He smiled for a moment, then put on his best scowl and stepped up into the sunlight headed for the quarterdeck.

The larger frigate pursued the brig around the edge of the island and the faster *Ambition* fired off a shot as she turned, making an attempt at rounding the far side of the island into shallower waters. Both ships traded shots, but nothing hit. The more he watched the combat, the more uneasy he became. There was something not right, but he could neither explain it, nor alter course.

They closed fast and the *Ambition* signalled them, desperate for aid. The frigate, flying British naval colours under the name of the HMS *Griffin's Wake,* out-gunned the *Mercy* by half, though she had little with real reach.

"Hoist the pennant!" Jack ordered as he stood beside Mr. Forrest at the helm.

Backhand Luke, standing by at the mast, ran up the flag. As it caught the wind, the frigate cut sail and paid attention to the new threat. They fired two whole volleys and only managed to put three shots through the *Mercy*'s sails.

Jack ordered them to turn for broadside and Mr. Forrest tried, but the wheel resisted. He scowled. It was clear that the *Mercy* intended to ram the *Griffin* amidships.

Jack grabbed the wheel, and snarled, "Oh, no, ye don't, luv. *I'm* th' captain. An' I said hard a'starboard!"

It fought him for only a second before the wheel gave way and spun, causing the ship to heave to. The instant they had a shot, Penn ordered the larboard guns to return fire. No sooner were the cannons being hauled back to reload, the two vessels came shoulder to shoulder and the smaller *Mercy* bullied the frigate off her intended course. The *Ambition* quickly rounded the caravel's prow and sought refuge behind her.

As soon as the two ships were close enough, Jack bellowed the order to board and the ships' decks became a roiling, screaming froth of humanity. Towers and his men swarmed over the *Mercy*'s rails from one side and then across her other.

Anjali swiftly killed the first man she encountered, ducked down, and bloodied her hands in his gut. She ran them through her hair to make it stand out wildly, and pressed a bloody handprint to her face. She then emitted a blood-curdling scream and threw herself into the fray, chanting maddened hymns to her dark goddess.

Jack and Tortuga battled back-to-back, cutting a wide swath in the enemy. Even in the heated fury of combat and pistol smoke, Jack realized that the enemy crew was as ragged and unkempt as any pirate. None were in uniform and few wore boots.

"Somethin's not right, mate!" he called to his quartermaster.

Tortuga's answer was a head thrown in Jack's direction. The head belonged to one of the old crew, one of the men who had left after the fight with Fenning. Jack scowled across the frigate's deck, assessing what he had gotten his crew into and looked up to the quarterdeck, right into the captain's eyes. His blood ran cold. For a moment, he thought he was seeing a ghost. Then his whole body ignited with an unholy fire of hate and he screamed in rage. Grabbing a rope, he launched himself, landed on the quarterdeck with the grace and purpose of a tiger jumping down from a high rock to circle his prey.

Fenning laughed. His chest bore a livid red scar where Jack had cut him when last they met, and the Valkyrie tattoos were marred by the teeth of sharks, a good many of which hung around his thick neck. His beard hung uneven, the missing chunk a little more ragged than before. He stood with an axe in one hand and a thick cutlass in the other, waiting for his opponent. The scars on the man's body told how he had survived and what he had endured.

For an interminable moment the two circled one another, gauging how their last battle had weakened the other. Fenning pointed with sword tip to Jack's eye patch, oblivious to its translucent nature.

"Lose sumting, Jack?" he sneered.

He shrugged. "Nothin' I miss. Unlike yer artwork, I'm sure. An' yer whiskers. That why they kicked ye outta Hell?"

Fenning frowned. "Ye should haf made sure ye killed me das first time, mate."

"Don't worry, *mate,*" he spat. "I have no intentions of makin' that mistake twice."

The rest of the battle did not exist; the shuddering of ships' decks did not affect them. There was only the two of them left in the whole world, staring across the space of a fathom... and then that closed. They were on each other like two sharks, fighting for the same blood. There was none of the nick for nick of the previous combat, no toying with each other. This time connections bit deep, neither combatant giving any quarter or expecting any.

Jack had to work twice as hard to defend himself from two weapons. Cutlass rang on Spanish steel, and then the axe bit deep into the ship's wheel.

Unable to pull it free, Fenning abandoned it, continuing to throw his weight into every swing. He did not try to intimidate Jack this time, to waste his breath with fierce faces and roaring. He knew they would not work, and the look in Jack's good eye was hard and unyielding. Both men were fully aware there was only one outcome to this fight. He did, however, try to use what he thought was Jack's blind-side to his advantage.

Jack let him believe it was working by feinting away and moving defensively right any time Fenning left the field of his undamaged eye. He dodged under blows more often than parried, being smaller and more agile. And, while the German's arms were longer, the length of Jack's blade made up for it. Granted, it was only a few inches, but those were valuable inches.

The ships traded cannon fire again. In his periferal, Jack noticed Mr. Forrest had taken up the helm and was fighting for control. Another volley and the ships collided yet again.

Fenning nearly lost his balance as the *Griffin* shuddered, but managed to fall into the parry, avoiding the swift tip of Jack's sword. He regained his footing and rounded on the smaller man, battering him past the wheel. He reached out with his free hand

and gave the helm a sharp turn. There was the scream of wood on wood as the caravel and the frigate battled for dominance.

Jack struck for the hand on the wheel, but Fenning moved it in time. The helm violently spun in the opposite direction, catching Jack on the shoulder. His whole left arm went numb for several seconds, and he was on the defensive once more. Before he managed to get it working again, the *Griffin* groaned, jerked, and keeled at a sixty degree angle, throwing both captains and a large portion of the fighting crews into the shallows of the beach.

Jack willed himself to keep his legs when he hit the water, wasting precious seconds before realizing there was no need. He was wearing trousers. Even so, he could feel the change wanting to come over him, could feel his body trying to merge even through the fabric. He looked up as he crawled ashore, and saw Fenning headed inland towards an obvious path cut into the jungle some sixty feet from the water's edge. He cursed, scrambled to his feet, and trudged ashore. He lurched, found himself attacked by one of Fenning's men, and cut his legs out from under him even as he went down.

He cursed fiercely again, struggling to get his land-legs before his lack was the death of him. Fenning knew he would have the advantage on land. It would be like fighting a drunken man, and gods only knew what kind of traps were lying in wait beyond the treeline. He half-ran, half-staggered after his enemy, the sound of cannons firing behind him.

He used the trees to steady himself as soon as he hit them, saw a dim path curving away, and set out to follow. The thought crossed his mind of scuttling *The Griffin*, and marooning Fenning with what remained of his crew, but it was not entertained for long. A cannonball whizzed into the brush near him, taking out several tall palms and blocking his return path. Stubbornly, Jack pressed forward, slowed down to a stumbling lope as he pursued his quarry, his boots slipping on the grass. Ahead, he could hear his opponent laughing at him.

A few hundred yards later the trail began to ascend and became more difficult for Jack. Another hundred and he could see it open up into the perfect ambush point. The jungle was so thick off the sides that he could not see what might be waiting just beyond them. He looked around, assessing the situation. The ground beyond the jungle continued to rise and then ended at sky another hundred yards beyond. There was an obvious path of flattened grasses, past which he could hear the crashing of waves against cliff.

'A native sacrifice point?' he thought, pausing to rip his boots off. It was entirely possible. And if he was not careful he could end up that sacrifice.

Nearby he saw a damaged coconut tree that was rotten and falling apart. He pulled a three-foot section of it out of the under-brush and held it in front of him. He began yelling like the mad man he was oft accused of being, and ran toward the open ground, making as much noise as he could. He did not manage a straight line, but he avoided falling, and stopped before he would have burst from the trees. Instead, he threw the tree.

As expected, Fenning lunged, hacking into the dead wood before he could realize it was not his quarry. Jack followed with an attack of his own, slicing into his thigh and staggered out of the jungle. This, he learned quickly, was a mistake. At least amid the trees he had things to fall against to keep him upright. Out here he could hear the sea more prominently, and it made the world want to move around him, which the ground was not, to his frustration. Fenning jerked his cutlass free and rounded on him.

"Cleffer, hund," he snarled.

Jack swayed on the steady ground, his toes digging into the loose loam of the hillside. He was tiring, though his opponent showed no signs of the same. But then, Jack had entered the battle long before Fenning, who had just stood by and observed. In the distance, he heard the sound of another ship's cannon and smiled.

"That'd be th' *Widow*," he taunted. "Come t' make a few more. Yer ship is as good as sunk an' yer men, too."

Fenning shrugged. "They are noffink! Replaceable! You... you und I on th' uffer hand..." He grinned, a broad smile full of golden teeth.

Jack parried the heavy blows, their dance carrying them up the slope and Fenning holding the lower ground by choice. He felt the ground grow rockier beneath his feet. He felt the air from below hit him before the rocks slid out from underfoot, threatening to carry him with them into the sea. Taking a step sideways, he closed the distance, and locked blades. He pressed close, pushing against Fenning, ignoring the reek of garlic and rotten meat. The stronger man began, with Jack's secret consent, to win the battle, getting him to give up ground toward the cliff's edge. Jack glanced down, judged locations of the rocks and what might be hidden below the white surf.

Fenning laughed. "Get good look, boy. Mutter's callin'," he sneered.

"Aye," Jack spat, slipping his foot in between Fenning's as Sirene had once done to him. "An' she wants t' know if ye kin stay fer supper!"

He grabbed hold of Fenning's coat and threw his weight backward, hammering the back of his knee with his heel to break his balance. Fenning roared, realizing too late what Jack had been up to and tried to resist. The edge of the cliff gave way first and both men tumbled through the air to the ocean below.

Jack let go, kicked off, and twisted into a perfect dive. Fenning hit the water just behind him in a messy heap, the impact taking the wind out of him. Jack was quick to shed his trousers, melting into the change and swimming to where Fenning was struggling to break the surface of the crashing waves without being thrown into the jagged rocks. He grinned devilishly as he snaked through the water. He took in the pirate's reaction with fiendish delight, savouring the stunned horror on his face.

Before the reality of what he had seen could sink in completely, Jack swam around behind him and grabbed him by the neck, wrapping his tail around his body. Fenning began to sink, struggling to free himself from the iron scaled grip and reach the air he needed.

"Too bad yer angels can't swim," Jack laughed.

His voice carried poorly, distorted by the water. He either did not know how to speak underwater or didn't have the right equipment for it, but it released air bubbles that floated lazily to the surface. Fenning grabbed desperately for them, but they did him no good, breaking up and slipping through his fingers.

The water frothed around them as he twisted and bucked. They touched the bottom and Jack wrapped the last section of his tail around an outcropping of coral, ignoring the cuts it made. Fenning reached back, clawing at Jack's hair and shirt to no avail. Nothing would make him let go. After a while the body went still, but Jack continued to hold on several minutes more until he was absolutely certain. Only then did he release him.

He undid Fenning's belts and connected them, wrapping them around the body and then looped them through a coral bridge to anchor it. To make certain he would never be haunted by this monster again, he collected his sword from where it had sunk and flayed the arrow's head from Fenning's skull. If ships could have minds of their own, and mermaids and magic pearls existed, there was every possibility this rune provided the beast with some protection. This way at least he could sleep easy, without nightmares of undead Germans rising from the depths to carve him up and steal what was rightfully his own.

He found his trousers and headed for the surface, fearing the approach of sharks he was certain would be arriving to feed. He tossed his hair out of his face and wiped the water from his eyes, reaching under the patch with one finger to do the same. As Jack looked around to get the lay of where he was and hunt signs of shark fins, he heard a voice behind him.

"Now that is something one doesn't see every century."

The voice was sultry and sweet. He spun around, and found himself facing a beautiful woman of middle years lying on her stomach on a smooth rock with her chin resting on her hands as she regarded him with crisp, azure eyes. Her hair was flaxen and reached down the sides of the rock and floated in the water. There was something very familiar about her face.

"C'n I help ye', miss?" Jack stammered, gazing into the crystal blue depths of her eyes.

She smiled, an expression of pure seduction. "I am not sure at the moment. Though you can satisfy my curiosity."

"About?" he asked cautiously, rising higher in the water.

Her smile faded instantly as her eyes locked on his chest. "About why you have my daughter's pearl around your neck."

"Your daughter?" he echoed.

It clicked why she looked so familiar.

She sat up, her rock turning. A giant sea turtle's head came up, looking at her in concern. She ignored it, and slid off its back. A second later, she surfaced smoothly in front of Jack, the pearl in her hand, and though she did not break the chain, she used it to pull him to her.

"Aye, scoundrel: my daughter. I see the rumours are true and she *has* been keeping poor company, blood though they might be." Her voice was cool and clipped, her manner like an iceberg.

Jack kept his calm. "I beg yer pardon, ma'am, but yer daughter gave... *loaned* me this bit o' shine. An' it happens to have just saved my skin."

She looked everywhere but at his eyes for a moment. She even glanced several feet outward beside him before she smiled and let go.

"In this case, young one, we need to talk. Follow me," she said, and turned.

He obeyed, diving with her, followed closely by the enormous sea turtle. The sunlight filtered down through the rough water and glittered across her silvery white scales. She was a little darker along the top, and there were tinges of blue to the filmy dorsal fin that began at the middle of her back. Her tail was larger and fancier than Sirene's, and there was a golden cuff adorning it just above where the fan began. She was a breath-taking beauty, and her voice seemed to have a power out of the water that her daughter's did not, though he could not put his finger on what it was.

She led him around the outskirts of the island and down into a cavern that spent half its time submerged. There was a large pocket of air and a small, white sand beach lit by a gaping hole in the ceiling. It was here that she beached, lowering her dorsal and stretching out on her belly. She propped her chin on one hand

and patted the sand beside her with a smile as Jack surfaced. Obediently, he pulled himself out of the water and rolled over, sitting up and watching her.

"Now," she began, annoying a fiddler crab that was picking itself free of her hair. "What are you to my daughter?"

"Her lover," he said, bluntly. He grew angry with himself at that, scowling, which only made her laugh.

"You cannot lie to me, so do not try."

Her voice was very compelling, but he remained indignant. "I'd no intention o' lyin', ma'am. But I prefer t' be more tactful."

She nodded, shooed off the crab and sat up, straightening out her hair with her long fingers. "Well said. That you are her lover does not upset me, but..."

She sighed and flexed her tail which became long white legs easily. Jack was aware that she was a very naked woman. He deliberately looked in her eyes, which made her laugh again.

"Go ahead, look if it pleases you. That is what the Good Sea gave them to me for. Well, that and other things," she admitted.

"Why are ye here?" he asked. "Sirene said ye were in Madagascar."

She waved her hand dismissively, curling her legs beneath her. "Oh, that was twenty years ago. I've been cruising more northerly waters lately. But I heard very disturbing stories from some whales returning from breeding season. Tales of my daughter in some villain's grasp and badly used," she said pointedly, staring almost through him.

"That'd be Price," he answered. "We rescued each other from that one. Tell me something. We tangled with this fish thing we brought up from th' deeps..."

"How deep?" she interrupted.

"Deep enough Skilly couldn't join us. Abyssal deep. Sargasso Sea."

She nodded for him to continue and he described the hideous creature and the wounds and reaction it caused.

"If the wounds are healing, it will only be a matter of time," she answered. He relaxed at this news. "There is poison to burn out of her body and your foresight to keep her in seawater was inspired. You probably saved her life. At this point she does not need to remain in it, most likely, but it will speed her wakening. It should not be long. Those creatures are dangerous and aggressive. It would have killed a normal man. Now tell me about this hagfish Price."

For the next half hour he told her how they met and what Sirene told him had transpired since leaving her mother's waters. She listened with great attention, braiding her hair absently. She was silent for several minutes afterward.

"Tell me about your parents," she said, suddenly.

"*My* parents? What's they got t' do with anythin'?"

"Just answer the question," she replied calmly.

"My father's Captain Robert Dunning. My mother was Mercy Ellen Wyndlam," he grumbled.

She regarded him with tilted head. "You dislike your father."

"Despise," he spat.

"But your mother... I do not recognize her name," she mused.

"Ah, but ye recog' m' father?" he snarled, now in a rotten mood.

She nodded. "Lucky Robbie Dunn. Charming man." Jack scowled, and she set a hand on his. "I distrust charming men," she added.

"An' well ye should," he snapped. "Wait... *I've* been called charmin'."

"And you've been called handsome, too. But that's never stopped you."

His jaw dropped. "Ye've heard o' *me*?"

She nodded. "From your father. He's quite proud of you, or he was about five years back, when I met him. You were all he could talk about," she sighed. "I am pleased to note that he lied about most of it. Well, exaggerated, really."

Jack didn't know what to make of that. "Not meanin' any rudeness, but may I ask yer name. Ye know mine."

"Lorelei."

"*The* Lorelei?" he asked, stunned.

"Umhmm," she said, as if it were of no importance.

Jack forced himself past those implications. "And why did ye have to bring my parents inta this?" He tipped his head. "This... isn' some mermaid thing preludin' marriage? Findin' out m' background?"

She rolled her eyes. "Your background is obvious and irrelevant really to that sort of thing. It's your soul that matters. And we don't marry. I was just curious, that's all."

"What d'ye mean ye' don' marry?" he asked, suddenly interested. It had never occurred to him that it might not have been an option to use to keep her close to him. "What do ye do when ye fall in love? Or... can ye?"

She eyed the panicked flexing of his tail with a cocked brow and smiled. "When we find that one person that lights our darkness, we are little inclined to leave their side for long or far. Beyond that," she shrugged, "we mingle where we please. Now," she added, standing. "I would like to see my daughter, if you would?"

She searched around the rocks of the cave until she came up with a large enough section of cloth that was part of some shipwreck or sacrifice washed ashore, and tied together some kind of clothing to cover those parts that would raise questions. She called out, and said something to the turtle who turned around and swam away. She put her hands on her ample hips, and frowned down at Jack.

"Well, Amberjack, are you going to just flop there, or are you going to take me to your ship and my daughter? She may not be dying, but she does need tending... and it has been a very long time."

He pointed to the lagoon. "Don't we need t' go back that way?"

"No, silly. How would it look if I am brought wet to your ship? You can get away with it. I can't. So, put your legs back on and we'll take the back way. You can fabricate some story about me being a shipwreck survivor."

She hid her smile as Jack slid half into the water and blew on the pearl, turning his back to her and sliding into his trousers as quickly as he could. "Shy?" she asked, when he stood in front of her, adjusting his sword under his sash.

He flushed. "Yer her bloomin' *mother*," he protested. "Since ye be knowin' th' back way, will ye be so kind?" he asked, with a wave of his hand.

They emerged not far from the point Jack and Fenning had disappeared into the jungle. He stopped on the edge of the beach, and grabbed a tree to steady himself. He was not pleased with the sight that awaited him. The *Griffin* was fully scuttled in the shallows, her top-gallant lying ten feet from their current position. The *Mercy*'s mainmast lay in the water and several sailors were dragging it to shore where they could salvage from it what they could. There were a few holes in her sides, but nothing that could not be repaired. The *Widow* patrolled nearby, her nose angled out to sea, while a handful of her crew helped with the repairs. She had her share of damage. There was no sign whatsoever of the *Ambition's Price*.

Chapter the Fifteenth

Before they had crossed half the beach, Tortuga leapt from the longboat he and several others were rowing ashore and began to manhandle Jack, inspecting him for injuries before clamping him in a crushing hug.

"Was beginnin' to t'ink da worst, Capta'n. T'ough I hahf expected ya from a diffaren' direction all togeddah," he added in a lower voice.

Jack shrugged. "I got sidetracked," he said, nodding toward Lorelei who stood by surveying the damage.

"What is it wid' you an da white women? You collect dem like ivory. So who is dis *fotsy*?"

"This is Lorelei," he explained, beckoning her over. "Sirene's mother." Tortuga's eyebrow shot up. "I know, she don't look old enough. But trust me, she's prob'ly older than..."

"Quite a few things," she finished for him, and offered her hand to Tortuga.

She was a little bit taller than Jack, though standing next to Tortuga she seemed even more so. Her grip was surprisingly strong.

"This is my quartermaster, Tortuga. He is also from Madagascar."

She smiled winningly. *"Really? I never would have guessed,"* she said in Malagasy, though her tone indicated otherwise. *"Miss home much?"*

"Only when I'm drunk, and forget it was my own people who made me a slave," he growled.

"Understandable. You must have been quite a threat to the chieftains."

Tortuga actually laughed. "Aye, Ma'am. An' to his daughtars' virtue. If ya will excuse me, *vehivavy,* I have some scavahgin' to do." With that Tortuga walked off to join Marklain in examining the *Griffin's* mast.

"He called ye Lady," Jack grinned. "I think he likes ye."

She smiled softly. "Most men do."

"That bein' th' case, watch out fer his wife," he chuckled.

Jack helped her into the longboat whether she needed it or not, and let the crewman row them back to the *Mercy's Ransom.* They passed under the prow to the larboard side where the ladder was and Lorelei looked up. He noticed her admiring the figurehead and smiled proudly.

"Beautiful, ain't she?"

"And so familiar somehow," she mused. "Those wings look out of place to me." She brushed her hand along the painted wood and smiled warmly, her eyes closed. "Interesting," she murmured.

"She's th' likeness o' my mother," he explained. The crewman shipping the oars raised an eyebrow, but was wise enough not to say anything. "Now, why did I tell ye that?"

"Because I asked you to. And it explains everything," she added, as she reached for the ladder and scaled up the side of the vessel.

Jack waited until she cleared the rail before he scurried up after her, turning his head and making sure the oarsman did the same. "What be that supposed t' mean?"

She held out her hand to steady him over the rail whether he needed it or not. *"It means, I know damned well your mother taught you to speak more properly than you do,"* she said, falling back to Malagasy, and dropping her voice so that only he heard.

Jack felt his belly turn to a ball of ice. *"Just tell me yer no' m' grandmother."*

She leaned into his ear. "No. But I know her."

The ice melted instantly, though it left behind a trickling in his veins. "We'll discuss that later. This way," he gestured, leading her to the companionway. "An' out here, ye fall into familiar patterns. I can be as snooty an' proper as I want t' be."

They did not get far, as the hallway below was blocked by Anjali. The look on her face instilled panic in him. Beyond her, the door to the cabin was battered off its hinges and lying haphazardly across the sea chest that blocked it. He tried to push past her, but she snagged him and, through force of leverage, and connecting with one of his numerous injuries, arrested his charge.

"You don't want to be doin' that, Captain."

"Like hell!" He twisted free, stumbling over a body in the companionway.

He shoved the chest and the door aside and charged into the room, past yet another body. The table was broken and overturned, the bookcase empty and its contents scattered. Some of the bed curtains were torn down and the remainder was billowing in the wind from the open windows. The barrel bath/bed was on its side and, lying broken in front of it in a pool of blood was Hare. There was no sign of Sirene.

Jack fell to his knees beside the boy, and pulled the still warm body into his lap. His cutlass was locked in his left hand and both pistols lay, fired, beside him. There were several injuries on him: a dark mark the shape of a cutlass guard on his cheek, a bullet in his right shoulder, other cuts. The fatal wound was a stab to his side, under his left arm. The body was pale, the eyes open. Jack closed them.

"Why didn' ye keep yer guard up?" he whispered. He wept, curling the boy close and rocking him, barely aware of others in the room.

"He made an accounting of himself," came a soft voice behind him.

He ignored Lorelei, and forced himself to stand, still holding the body with the cutlass locked in its fist. The doorway had been cleared, and he paused to look down at the dead man in the companionway with a bullet between his eyes. He laid his cheek tenderly against Hare's forehead.

"Fair shot, Seamus," he whispered.

Silence and stillness spread like a plague around Jack as he stepped out into the sunlight and carried the small body over to the others, laying him out as tenderly as if he had been his own son.

"Ye've earned a full share, mate," he whispered.

He turned then to survey the ships. Crewmen stood about, in the midst of pulling down damaged rigging, clearing the decks and laying out the dead. The two ships were bound together, and hands had been crossing from one to the other effecting repairs. On the higher deck of the flute, two women stood with buckets poised beside Mary where they had been pouring them over her head to wash the blood away. All stood frozen.

Nearby, the doctor knelt over a man, pulling a lead ball from his shoulder. Jack's eyes narrowed. The sailor was one of those who had left the *Mercy* to sail with Towers.

Jack felt a volcano boil up inside, and let it erupt. He stalked over, shoving the doctor out of the way and grabbed the sailor by the arms. He lifted the man off the deck and slammed him back against the bulkhead, his thumb digging into the open wound.

"What happened?" he growled.

The man was unable to articulate more than gurgles of pain and Jack dug deeper. "I know ye were with Towers. I know he fled th' fight. I know his men are dead in my cabin and come hell or hot pokers, by God ye'll tell me what happened!"

Nobody interfered. Jack was in high colour and even Tortuga would not have touched him while 'Mad Jack' held sway. His victim managed to choke out an answer and Jack eased up the pressure on the wound.

"He... had a plan."

"Go on," he said between his teeth.

"Fennin' an' him came up with it... t' get t' you."

The thumb drifted over the wound again. "An' this had what t' do with th' woman?"

The man hesitated and Jack reapplied pressure. "A trade!" The man took a second to get his breath and control the pain. "We were set upon by the *St. George*. Towers saw a man he recognized on board and fancied a bargain, tried a twist. Claimed t' know where summat he wanted lay hid and if granted a few considerations he would retrieve it."

The man flinched as he heard the sound of grinding teeth. "Price," Jack spat.

"Aye, I think. Some naval man. He rescues the girl and returns her; Towers gets the *Ambition*, a pardon, and a letter of Marque." He gasped as the grip on his shoulders tightened. "I swear it's the truth. On me muther's grave! We steal the white haired woman, return her to Barbados, and we're pardoned."

Jack let go and stepped back.

"When we ran into the *Griffin*, Towers an' Fennin' hatched the plan t' lure ye close and give him the opportunity to grab her. No one was supposed to be left behind, but we were. I was disc..."

His sentence ended in a gurgle as his throat erupted in a fountain of red. Jack wiped his blade clean and turned as he put it away.

"If they ain't ours, chop 'em up and feed 'em t' th' mako. Shroud our own an' lay 'em out. We'll bury at sea when we're far enough out t' give 'em rest. Tortuga!" he bellowed, spying the man standing at the rail with arms folded and a tight expression. "What's th' skinny on th' mast? M' deck's lookin' a mite bare!"

"Two choice, Capta'n. We can take two day t' make da *Griffan*'s fit, or we can take t'ree or four to find, cut, haul, and prep a new one."

There was no emotion in the man's voice, and he kept his eyes on the captain, pointedly avoiding the growing row of bodies.

"Make it fit," Jack snarled, and stormed toward the bow.

He stayed there all day, one hand on the upraised wing as he watched the sun set and the seas grow dark. Behind him the crew followed the orders of others making haste to salvage what they could from the scuttled ship and get the *Mercy* seaworthy again. No one dared come near him, and even Lorelei kept her distance, for a while.

It was nearing midnight when she finally approached. "Go to bed."

There was something compelling about the way she said it, but he fought it off.

"No."

The tone changed, less forceful. "Then come and talk with me."

He stared down at his feet. "There is nothing to talk about."

She set a firm hand on his shoulder. "There is plenty to talk about. You will not be able to rescue her if you are weak from starvation, lack of sleep, and exposure."

He turned his head to meet her gaze. Her words echoed back to him in the voice of another; which reminded him of a question he had been meaning to ask. "Why is it that you can compel men with yer voice and yer daughter cannot? Or is each mermaid's power unique?"

"See? There is something to talk about." She took his arm and led him to the cabins. "My daughter is not fully of the scale, as we say," she explained as they went below.

The starboard cabin had been appointed for their guest. Tortuga and his wife had found other quarters for the time being. Why she was not berthed aboard the more comfortable *Widow* was a question he forgot to ask when he saw the table. She had a modest dinner waiting for them both, and made him sit and eat before she would explain more.

"Full-blooded mermaids are rare these days. The male of our species are a bit short-lived, barely two-thirds that of a maid. So, we take what we can get. It wasn't always this way."

Jack frowned over his wine. "So her father was just a breeder." This did not bode well for his relationship.

She laughed softly, and he caught a hint of sadness in her voice. "No. I knew her father was my love the moment I saw him. I would have spent my life on land for him," she sighed, toying with thc rim of her untouched glass.

"So why didn't you?" he asked, regarding her with a keen eye.

"Sirene had to be born in the sea."

"And he could not go with you," he finished, nodding.

"No. He could have. It is within our power to change one person within our lifetimes. To give them some of ourselves."

This was interesting, he thought, perking up. "Again, why didn't you?"

She shrugged and picked up the glass. "He didn't want it. So we both agreed. But this is irrelevant. Tell me about my daughter."

"No," he said, reaching for more fish. "You tell me about my grandmother."

She raised an eyebrow. "Ligeia. She always was something of a... oh, how do I put this politely?"

"If you can't, don't," he shrugged as he swallowed a mouthful of bread and reached for a second helping. He was hungrier than he had thought.

She sighed. "I love her as the waves, but... she can be a bit of a bubble-head at times. Never settled, never paid attention to the right things. She got herself landlocked at the worst possible time: in the middle of a war. We knew she had a baby, but when we saw her again she was alone. Gave birth out of the water and had to leave it behind was our assumption. She refused to talk about it and swam back to the Mediterranean. I suppose the romance was merely a dalliance. She is famous for those. Your mother, I would guess, was that child, if that figurehead is any likeness at all."

He chewed thoughtfully. "Mother used to tell me she dreamed of the sea. Her father was an Englishman doing business for his company, in Poland I think it was, when war broke out. She said her mother died there. As soon as they were able to escape, they returned to England. Grandfather suddenly decided to get into shipping."

She smiled. "Sounds about right." She gazed into the bottom of her cup, swirling the wine and watching the patterns. "Tell me about your mother."

He shrugged. "Not much to tell. She ran into my father at some dance and was swept off her feet. Probably literally," he added, bitterly. "He stole her away to sea. I do not know how much of their relationship was her using him to take her to sea and how much was actual love, but they travelled happily for a while. I was born in the South Pacific on one of my father's voyages. They stayed with the natives the last month or so, and delivered me in a sheltered lagoon, the way the natives do. 'From mother's water to Mother's water,' they call it. They claim it easier on both mother and child."

"It is," she injected. "But go on."

He pushed his plate away, and refilled his glass. "Not much more to tell," he answered, though with slightly less sullenness than earlier.

"That's what you said about your mother, but there was a wealth to tell." He still seemed reluctant. She leaned forward, and propped her chin on her fist. "Humour me."

He narrowed his eyes and waved his wine cup at her, one finger pointing. "I know what yer tryin' t' do, wench," he slurred. "An' it won't work. I'm unreadable," he humphed, taking a drink.

She chuckled. "Oh, really?"

"Sirene's always complainin' she can't make headpins out o' what I'm feelin'. Though she can read the rest o' the crew like a bloody book."

"Oh, does she?" she smiled knowingly.

He glared at her. "Wha's that supposed t' mean?"

She leaned back with a sigh. "Tsk. And you were doing so well."

"What th' devil?"

She laughed. "Your manner of speaking. You were doing so well. And then you shifted back into your... sailor's vernacular."

He shrugged, drank. "I told ye, ye fall t' familiar patterns out here."

"But you are an educated man, why lower yourself?"

He eyed her over the cup. "What makes ye think I'm an educated man?"

She breathed in frustration. "I've seen the contents of your cabin, Amberjack. You own Shakespeare."

"Look," he growled, leaning forward. "Aye, I've a bit o' book learnin'. An' I've me manners when I needs 'em. But noble talkin' gentlemen don't earn th' respect o' pirates. Their kind don' sell their loyalty cheap or easy. An' as long as I sound like one o' em, I am one o' em, and th' fact what I *bought* this ship rather than commandeered her is water under the bowsprit."

She smiled, apparently having wheedled something she wanted out of him. "Ah, but you are still marauding after twenty years *because* you are a gentleman."

He snorted into his cups. "Jest 'cause I act like one, don' mean I haf ta talk like one around th' crew. An' afore ye say it, it's easier t' avoid a slip if ye stick to it constant. Besides, what in the underside of a pelican's tailfeathers does a bloody mermaid care fer grammer?"

There was a knock at the door. Lorelei turned in her chair and called, "Come in, Anji."

Anjali opened the door with a surprised look. "How'd you... no, nevah mind. Oh, good, you got him t' eat."

Lorelei smiled. "It wasn't easy. But you wanted something?"

"Oh, forgive th' interruption but have you seen my cat?"

Lorelei cast her gaze around the chamber, settling upon the bed. She gracefully crossed the room, knelt at the foot, and began calling. Even Jack felt the urge to come to her, but held his ground; though he took note as he watched her that she was wearing the first set of clothes that Anjali had loaned Sirene: the ones that had been too big. They almost fit her.

When Flagstaff crawled out from under the bed fussing and fuming, Jack dropped his cup in shock. The animal was limping badly, his black eye was severely damaged and he was missing part of his ear. As Lorelei gathered him in her arms to Anjali's relief, he saw the cat's whole right side had been shaved to allow them to sew up a wicked gash that cut from mid-back and across the shoulder to the paw he was favouring. He crossed to them as the mermaid handed the cat to his mistress.

"What th' devil's happened t' th' devil?"

"It seems everyone got involved," Anjali growled. "Stoopid rattah couldan' keep his tail to himself. Miss Lorelei found him in your cabin under a broken cabinet. From th' wicked claw marks on th' dead man, he got his licks in, too."

Jack stroked the cat's chin, had to fight back tears when the broken purr tickled his fingers. It brought forth too many un-wanted thoughts. Mr. Flagstaff licked his fingers, and wiggled in his direction, anything to escape Anjali. She held him back as Jack started to reach for the animal.

"Oh, no ye don't. Sorry, Captain. Maybe later. He needs his wounds looked at. As do you," she added, looking him over.

Jack glanced down at the scabbed cuts and shrugged. "They've been cleaned."

Technically they had been... when he went into the water. They were starting to ache, however. Lorelei opened the cabin door for the first mate.

"Don't worry, Anji. I'll make sure he gets some sleep."

The Indian woman glared over her shoulder at her captain. "If you need help, call me. I'll bring th' belayin' pin."

Jack scowled. "Conspirin' wench!"

"I'll be back foah th' dishes latah," Anjali said, and left, Mr. Flagstaff growling in her arms, knowing what she was up to.

Lorelei went to the cabinet and pulled out a bottle of rum hidden there, poured two glasses, and bade him to sit. Reluctant, he accepted the cup from her.

"Ask."

"Ask what?" he sulked.

"You have unanswered questions."

He stared into the liquor. "So is that what she did? Give me part of herself?"

Lorelei looked him over intently. "No. It was not necessary in your case."

"Ye mean me tuna-tail is natural?"

She giggled. "Aye. Your powers are greatly weakened, but the pearl allows you to change."

"I see you don't have one, but you change," he pointed out.

"I don't need one. I am full scale. My daughter, and you, are not. I gave her that pearl so she could."

"And me mother could have?"

"No," she interrupted, refilling his mug. "You were born in the water. She was not. Even with a pearl, I doubt her blood would have allowed it. It might have killed her. Those born on land cannot be anything else.

"All right then. Why was me mother dark, an' not light like ye an' yor'n?"

She tossed back her head and laughed. "We are as diverse as men. Colourations differ by area and lineage. My grandfather was red. And I have an aunt who very much resembles a lionfish.

My family is of northern descent, yours... Mediterranean. And then there was the injection of whatever your father and grandfather added to things. Ligeia is a dark beauty, with a classic face, a lot like your mother; although she has vertical stripes," she mused, remembering. Then she rest her chin on her hand, and gazed out the window. "I wish things had been different for her. I would have liked to have known her."

Jack grew thoughtful. "She was an incredible woman. ...Not at all a bubblehead."

She smiled. "I should hope not. I'm sure she got quite a bit of grounding from her father."

"She was always distant, though. Especially after father flitted off. She returned to grandfather and raised me there. He tried to give me the best of everything, but all I ever wanted was a ship. Finally, after sailing aboard his merchants for nearly ten years, I found the *Mercy*."

Lorelei brightened, refilled his mug. "Ooo! Do tell."

He shrugged. "My father attacked the ship we were on, and as soon as he realized who I was, he took me on board. I only sailed the once with him." He scowled. "Bloody arrogant man. The only good thing that came of it was the *Mercy's Ransom*.

"She was weather-worn and being decommissioned, as they say in the military. Truth was, the Spaniard's son who inherited her wanted something larger and sleeker and was going to scuttle her. I took what I had earned with my father and bought her for a song. The rest, as they say, is history. After I got her fixed up I showed her off and mother begged to go on her maiden voyage. She died standing on the bowsprit three days out. She had been so weak and sick. She seemed to get stronger at first. She was so happy. Then she just ...passed away."

"You buried her at sea?"

He nodded, staring into his cup. "And now I have to bury a ten-year-old boy."

She set her hand on his. "Did he want to come with you? To be a pirate?"

"Aye. He was an orphan, a pickpocket... and a lousy one at that."

"And you asked him to guard Sirene while she... healed?"

He stared deep into her bright blue eyes. "Aye. I thought he'd be safe there. If they got that far, we'd all be dead. I never thought they'd kill a boy."

"Did he like my daughter?"

He frowned, wondered why she was asking. "Everyone did. But he... I think he worshipped her."

"Then he gave his life for something he believed in. He shot one man and managed to kill another, probably while he was down."

"What makes you think that?" he asked.

"The doctor looked at the body of the dead man in the room. He had minor nicks and cuts, and a bullet graze. And one deep slice to the groin. My guess is they beat him down and he refused to stay that way."

"Damn it all! I killed him!" Jack swore, throwing his mug across the table, then buried his head in his hands. "I told him t' guard her wit' his life."

"Obviously he thought it worth it. *You* did not kill him. The man who stabbed him, killed him. Now, you need to pull yourself together. The crews need you. My daughter needs you. You cannot allow his death to be in vain. Trust me, the crews are taking this just as hard as you."

"*They* did not order him to his death," he groaned. "*And* armed him for it."

"They loved him. They will miss him. His vengeance is theirs, and I think they would follow you into hell to obtain it. Your bosun will make sure of it, I think, to hear him talk."

He nodded, though still not convinced. "Mr. Marklain was fond of him and Sirene both."

"Good. Use that... tomorrow. Tonight, rest. Tomorrow, plan. And, when the ship is ready, do what must be done."

He grabbed the bottle and saluted. "Aye," he snapped, and staggered out of the cabin.

She watched him until he disappeared through his newly re-hung door.

Jack stood just inside, stared numbly into the room. There was no evidence anything had happened in here. The floors and bulkheads were washed, the curtains re-hung and replaced where needed. The books, papers, and furniture were put in order. In fact, the only thing out of place was the decided lack of woman and the missing table.

He staggered over to the bed and fell into it, propped himself up at the headboard and drained the bottle. Frustrated, he threw it. The bottle hit the curtain and then rolled, intact, under the bed without giving him the satisfaction of hearing it shatter.

Groaning, he reached for Sirene's pillow to pull it to him and his hands found fur. Teeth embedded in his fingers and Jack pulled back, squinting at the cat. Flagstaff growled and wrapped his tail around himself, burying his nose in its tip. Sighing, Jack curled up around the injured animal and the pillow and drifted to sleep to the scent of her.

On the morning of the third day, the two ships stood side by side on the open sea far from sight of land. A distance of a hundred feet between them formed a safe little harbour. The doctor's voice droned on, reading funeral passages from a small leather-bound prayer-book.

"And thus we commend the bodies of our brothers and our sister unto the deep, that their bodies may rest forever in the bosom of that which they loved so well and their souls return to heaven in peace to watch over those of us who remain behind."

Jack prowled past the row of bodies on their raised planks. One by one, he stopped and whispered something into their shrouded ears, slipped a coin on a thong around their necks, and one by one, they were tipped into the sea. On the *Widow*'s deck the bodies of one man, and one woman were similarly treated by Genevieve and Mary. Jack stopped by the fifth and last body on his deck, smaller than the others, but no less treasured. He pressed a kiss to the boy's forehead.

"I'm sorry, lad. Ye'd have made a fine pirate. May th' angels welcome ye with open arms... and mind their pockets. Fair winds and following seas, mate."

Those words: 'fair winds and following seas', echoed from person to person from one ship to the other as Jack himself tipped the board that slid that small body into the sea. From the *Widow*'s decks came the sound of open weeping, not that there were many dry eyes on board the *Mercy*.

On the bowsprit, Lorelei stood, wearing borrowed clothes, and began to sing. Her song, wordless and haunting, carried more power than her daughter's. Her voice crept into each soul as they listened. The sorrow each felt began to swell within them until it was too great to bear or remain locked away. Then, just when it seemed hearts would burst with the weight of their grief, the melody drew it out of them and separated the sorrow from their souls. They could almost see their pain transformed into the tropical blossoms she cast to the winds.

They watched the breeze spin the petals between the two ships, some settling upon the waves, others floating away across the sea. Ever so subtly, her melody changed, the rhythms falling into familiar patterns, until someone began to sing words. It was an old Irish song of a dying sailor dreaming of home. The tune was picked up and spread throughout the crews as they returned to their duties, aiming the ships for Barbados.

Chapter the Sixteenth

Slowly Sirene's mind began to stir. The first thing she was aware of was being warm and dry and lying on something soft. Hands were upon her wrist, fingers pressed to the underside, and everything hurt. Her muscles were stiff and sore and the very thought of moving caused her to think twice about actually trying it.

"I think she's waking, sir."

She forced herself to open her eyes, trying to focus on the grey-haired man beside her. "Dr. Laurence?" Her throat was sore and her voice hoarse.

"No, child," the man said. "Dr. Antwerp."

As her vision cleared, he was replaced by another figure. Sirene had to be dreaming. Then the man laid his hand on her cheek and smiled and she knew she wasn't.

"Margaret," he said tenderly. "It is I, Ambrose. Are you all right?"

"You... are dead," she choked, and tried to escape, but her body was incapable.

"No. You were in a fever. You've been dreaming," he insisted gently.

There was a dark light in his eyes, though his face showed all due concern. She tried to shift her vision but things were hazy, unresponsive. She needed more time to heal.

"My name is Sirene, you black-hearted monster," she croaked. She sank down into the pillows, exhausted by even that small exertion. She heard the doctor just beyond her line of sight.

"I told you, Vice Admiral. She has suffered a tremendous fever. She has been hallucinating for some time and is still likely to believe her delusions. Give her time and do not expect too much too soon."

Price saw the doctor out. The moment the bedroom door closed, she exerted all her strength to sit up, ignoring the screaming of her body. She grabbed the bed curtain and used it to pull herself upright. Her legs tangled in the layers of night-gown that were wrapped snugly around her under the blankets. Her weight was too much and overbalanced her. Feeling herself falling, she grabbed tighter to the heavy velvet. There was a great tearing noise and the whole curtain came with her, sending the nearby water basin and pitcher crashing to the floor.

Price ran back into the room and lifted her into his arms. Looking her over for new injuries, he hefted her up and carried her into a different chamber. It was one Sirene remembered all too well. He set her in the middle of the huge bed and sent the curious servants to clean up and repair the other room.

"Margaret, Margaret," he moaned, as he tucked her in, fluffing up her pillows to make her comfortable. "Why must you torture me so?"

Sirene could not believe what she was hearing. "I torture you?"

"You don't remember any of it, do you?" He sighed. "Of course not. Well... not correctly anyway. Dr. Antwerp said the fever held too much reign for too long."

Sirene, unable to escape, decided to play along. "Remember what?"

"Your kidnapping, of course." She stared at him, trying to bore a hole through his head, but he went on as if nothing were amiss. He stroked her hair tenderly, straightening out the silvery locks. "You were kidnapped by a pirate. He stole our ship and sailed away with you." His expression darkened, "I cannot begin to imagine what horrors he has subjected you to."

"That is not quite how I remember it," she whispered.

"Probably not, my heart," he said. "Dr. Antwerp said that in your fever you might have dreamed what occurred as something far more pleasant. That you might even... assign your captor's baser characteristics to my own person... out of some displaced anger at me for not protecting you as I should have, or as a means of making what happened to you less... traumatic. It's the fever talking."

"I am not fevered," she insisted weakly.

"Not now, but you were. I was afraid I'd lose you."

She turned her head away, shivering under his touch. "Afraid to lose your favourite toy?"

"Margaret, you wound me," he said, almost sincerely. "I love you; surely you know that?"

"Then explain what you've put me through," she spat. "The whips, the chains... the rape, the prostitution." She balled her fist in spite of the agony the movement provoked.

He rubbed her arm tenderly. "Oh, Margaret. You have had such a history of attracting abusive men."

She tried to jerk her arm away, but it would not obey. "Please, Ambrose, don't tell me you're about to get all noble on me," she said, rolling her eyes.

He went on as if he had not heard her. "That pirate, the late Vice Admiral Trask, Governor Forsyth of Jamaica, your brother... your father."

Sirene jerked her head around. Her entire body seized with pain, the muscles tensing and refusing to release. "You are not worthy to speak his name," she hissed through the agony.

Her voice crescendoed into a scream of pain. It was choked, hoarse, the pitch nowhere near dangerous. Price tried to hold her down, to straighten the body trying to curl in on itself. He yelled for the maid, a girl Sirene did not recognize, and between them, they forced a bitter liquid into her mouth. It took several moments before the medicine began to work. Her body became heavy and numb, though different than before. Her eyes drifted closed against her will. Before she passed out, she heard him give the servant girl instructions.

"Julia, sit here and watch her. If she wakes, notify me immediately. If she grows fevered again, keep her brow cool and alert me. I have to go meet with my future father-in-law and cannot have her making a scene in her deluded state."

Sirene opened her eyes again to the same curtained room in which she had first awakened. Everything had been repaired. She was relaxed, but there was still the ghost of an ache in her body. She was healing, however slowly. She tried to move her hand, but was still very weak. The poison had run its course, but it had robbed her of her strength, and somehow her voice.

She caught the glimpse of movement through the filmy inner curtains, near the window. The heavy velvet drapes had been opened to provide her with light and some air, but the fine inner netting remained closed to out keep mosquitoes. The tall windows were open and a figure stood in them, staring out over the sea she could hear at a distance beyond them. The view from that window had always made her homesick. She closed her eyes, refocusing, and opened them again. Now, all she could see was darkness by that window.

"He's not coming," she said in a hoarse whisper. The figure turned his head. When she did not respond, he turned back to the view. Sirene raised her dry voice. "I said, he's not coming."

This time he heard her and crossed to the bed. There was something odd about his gait. He parted the curtain and sat on the edge, took her up hand and kissed it. The touch of his lips on her skin made her stomach turn.

"You are awake. How are you this morning?"

"Still not listening to me, are you? You never did unless I was saying something you wanted to hear."

"Why would you say things like that?" His grief was written all over his face, but his eyes were cold.

"Because they are true. And he will not come for me," she repeated, not sure at the moment how much she believed it.

"Who?" he sighed, clearly deciding to indulge her. "Who is not coming?"

"Him. Jack. Why would he?"

He groaned. "That again." He brushed tendrils of her hair out of her face. "Why *wouldn't* he?" he asked, rising to the bait. Not liking the heat from her skin, he took a cloth and wet it in the new basin, wrung it out and placed it on her forehead. "If he loved you, or even merely desired you, he would. I did. I tore these islands apart for two months looking for you."

"Because he is a pirate, and he now has everything. The ship, the treasure ...and my pearl."

He looked up. She tried to read his expression, but the look on his face could mean anything. "Your mother's pearl?"

"Tell me, how is it you have me, but don't have him and what he took?"

"Because I got lucky. I'd been looking for you, as I said, for two months. I had you once, and then that other damned pirate attacked. That's how I lost my leg, in that fight." He lifted his right foot up, rapped his knuckles on the boot. It made a hollow, wooden sound. "They killed the Vice Admiral, nearly killed Lord Hamilton, and threw me to the sharks. The honourable Lieutenant Malcolm Reese saved me by killing the shark that took my leg and getting me to shore. I've made him a captain for that, and his father is quite pleased."

"You got lucky?" she reminded him, pulling him back on track.

"Ah, yes. A sailor on another vessel found you in the middle of a multi-ship battle. He rescued you while the pirates were otherwise occupied. His captain realized the value of you and fled the fight without staying to risk your life. I have properly rewarded the man. I am at current, however, sending ships to hunt down this accursed Mad Jack, and will see him properly hung for all he's done. The price on his head will be so high his own men will turn on him."

She gave a dry laugh. "Not bloody likely."

"Margaret! Such language. The damage, I see, runs deeper than I thought."

She looked at him, took a gamble. "If you love me so much, why haven't you married me?"

He pulled away. "Margaret, we've been over this. A man of my position cannot marry the illegitimate daughter of a fisherman. Especially not one who's the sister of a known pirate, and has the reputation you've suffered. Be satisfied with what I can give: my love and devotion, which will not change just because I'm married to another woman."

"You think she will take meekly to your keeping a mistress?" she asked. "In her own house, no less?"

He sat down, leaned near, a trace of the Price she remembered creeping out. "She will, considering what I bring to her impoverished, if minorly noble, family. I granted her brother a captaincy he would never otherwise have gained. My family's fortune will enrich her own."

"And hers will advance you to the position you've always longed for."

He brushed his fingers along her cheek. "Yes. I will not deny my ambition. Never have."

"Aren't you afraid she will eventually rebel? Run away with some bold young lover who will pay exclusive attention to her? Especially if you ignore her in all but public ways?" she taunted.

He laughed. "The honourable Veronica Reese is a very homely girl. No one is likely to look twice at her. She is grateful for my interest, on whatever level that may be. I will give her a child, no more. She can turn to him for love. You are the sole object of my affections."

She fought the urge to retch. He pulled away, bellowing for Julia. "You must eat. That should settle you. When I get hold of that pirate I'll rend him asunder with my own hands."

She tried to laugh and choked instead. "Not likely, 'Captain'," she managed when she could breathe again, throwing the title he had always forced her to address him by in his face.

He gave the tiniest smile. "You've been gone a long time, Margaret. I'm the Vice Admiral now."

She was unsure how many days had passed. The doctor had come again, prescribed poppy syrup for her near constant pain and it kept her in a fog. She managed to convince Julia to secretly swap out the water in the basin for bathing her with seawater by telling her it was a beauty secret and the girl swore to tell no one. Sirene noticed she had even begun to wash her own face in it. It would certainly do the girl's complexion some good, even if it did not give her the same benefits it gave Sirene. With this small change, she was able to recover from the poppy juice more quickly, need it less.

The next afternoon, she was able to get out of bed without anyone knowing. It was painful, but she forced herself to continue, and after a few steps the muscles loosened a little and the ache slacked off. She slipped out of the room on bare feet, and headed for the servants' staircase. The descent caused renewed pain in different areas, and muscles threatened to seize up in protest. She paused, took several deep breaths and made herself relax and move, took it one step at a time.

She did not see anyone, strangely, and moved through the back corridors wondering just where she thought she was going. It had begun as an attempt to see if she could manage it, but then the farther she got, the more she wondered how much farther she could get. All the way to the sea, perhaps? Not that she had any clue what to do from there. Call a dolphin maybe.

Just outside the servant's door to the parlour, she found a chair, set there to keep a servant near enough to be immediately available when entertaining. She sank gratefully into it, pausing to catch her breath.

If she believed what Price and the others had been telling her, she was just a fisherman's daughter and the mistress of a fairly important man. A woman who had been kidnapped, then rescued and was now very ill. Everything he said happened could contribute to hallucinations. But could she believe him? That he loved her and that she was only a human woman and nothing more? If that were true then Jack was the one who had abused her.

She remembered chains, some rough handling... and that she had enjoyed every minute of it, had deliberately provoked it. She remembered swimming in the sea, without legs, by his side, his glow lighting up the undersea world like the sun; long nights in the deep spent curled around him in that eternal embrace that unites souls.

She listened for the sound of the waves beyond the walls, and heard nothing, though she might have imagined that she could feel them pulling her toward them. The feel of salt on her skin invigorated her. Surely that was not a dream. And surely she would not feel sudden, instinctive loathing for a man she supposedly loved, nor love the man who allegedly kidnapped her. In fact, the way she remembered it, *she* had kidnapped him.

If this were true, the only option for her was to reach the sea somehow. Once there she could call for aid, dolphin or whale. If

Price was right, then nothing would come to her call and she was mad. If he was lying, as she was almost certain he was, then Skilliweha would be able to take her to Jack.

Her mind made up, she stood, a bit unbalanced at first. She set her hand on the wall to steady herself. But then she heard the sound of voices inside the parlour and stiffened. Someone was being shown in, someone Price was not happy with. She could hear him growl as he dismissed the butler, telling him they did not wish to be disturbed. She relaxed a hair, now that no one would be coming to this side door to serve the guest. Intentions to look for a way out of the house melted away when she heard the guest's voice raised in anger.

"Damn ye, Price! We had an accord!"

A chill ran down her back. The voice belonged to Towers, the black-hearted man they had taken on in Basseterre who had left the *Mercy's Ransom* to Captain the *Ambition's Price*. She paused to listen.

"And I kept it," Price responded coolly.

There was danger in that cold voice. It was a tone that began to tickle Sirene's memory, reasserting that this new Price was indeed the illusion.

"Bullocks!" Towers shouted. "Ye hanged me entire crew."

Price never once raised his tone. "Our agreement was that you bring me the woman and I would pardon *you*. I said nothing about the pirates who sailed under you." Towers was stunned to silence for several long minutes. Price filled the gap, pouring a drink from the sound of things. "You brought her to me near to death."

Towers found his tongue. "And in a mental state yer takin' full advantage of, so I hear."

"You also brought my ship back in a similar sad state."

Towers ground his teeth. "That's another thing, Vice Admiral. Ye promised me that ship."

"Oh, you'll captain her," he assured him. "Once she's repaired and I have a suitable crew for you."

"And a letter of Marque."

"Which you have already."

"The fact remains, Price, ye've yet to fulfill all o' yer obligations whilest I done everything I promised."

"These things take time, Captain," Price said silkily. "You have left me little choice in the timing. Had the ship been in better condition..."

"How the hell was I supposed to know he'd started a bloody fleet? That other ship came out of nowhere. We were lucky to escape a'tall. As it were, I lost two o' me best men getting th' woman out o' that damned cabin and left another third behind fightin' on th' beach."

Price harrumphed over his drink. "Should have been more secretive, or more sneaky, I suppose."

"Secrecy had little t' do with it," Towers snorted. "We got in with none th' wiser. It was that damned Irish brat. Shot m' first mate and then stabbed m' best friend. Nearly took me arm before I put 'im down."

Sirene choked. It took all she had to not scream or fall. She stumbled back, avoided the chair, her mouth covered as Price chuckled.

"You were almost crippled by the cabin boy?"

There were shouts within and Sirene heard footsteps coming down the corridor. She ducked into the next room in time to avoid being seen by the manservant coming to investigate a crash from the parlour. There, she sank to the floor, her muscles screaming in protest at the sudden movement she had forced from them. She sat there, breathing heavily, blinded by tears. Hare dead, murdered by that man. The thought was agony. Who else did he kill to steal her away? Jack? No, Price would have gloated about that. Anji? Penn? Marklain? The lovable Mr. Forrest?

She took a deep breath, trying to control herself, and noticed something in the darkness: the smell of tobacco. Price only kept his pipe and supplies in his private study, a room no one but the

butler was allowed in. She had only been in here once, by accident, and had paid dearly for the mistake. She tried to stand, but
her back froze, fire spreading throughout the places her wounds
had been. Curled up, she tried inch by inch to straighten. Tears
in her eyes, she managed to pull herself to her feet by holding
onto the desk.

Once upright, she began to feel about the cool wooden surface, trying to find the drawers. She counted down to the second
one and slid it open, felt around inside until she touched the cold
steel of the flintlock pistol she had seen him put there. Anger
blinded her to pain; sorrow clouded her judgment as she closed
the drawer and staggered towards the thin line of light below the
outer door.

Out in the main hall she startled a maid dusting a shelf by
the staircase. She ignored the girl and went into the parlour
where the conversation had taken a different turn with the addi-
tion of an important visitor. Sirene was oblivious to the presence
of another man enjoying a brandy on the settee. All she saw was
Hare's murderer making small talk over a cigar, laughing with
Price, and dressed in the fancy clothes appropriate to his new
command. There was a large swath of white over the shoulder of
the uniform, which she barely registered. She only had one ball
and two choices. She raised the pistol to Towers' chest and fired.

He turned as the door opened, saw her standing in her flowing nightdress, glowering at him. Then he saw the pistol and
moved in panic. Sirene's bullet missed his heart and bit into his
upraised arm instead. There was a dull crack and the spray of
chalky white dust, but no blood. She screamed, flipped the pistol,
snatching the barrel out of the air and raised it, lunging for him.
Behind her came the shattering of glass and then she hit the
floor, something heavy wrapped around her. She saw Towers trying to escape and screamed again, varying her pitch as she raised
her volume, trying to find the right note to shatter his ears and
every glass object in the room. If Price was damaged in the process it would be an added blessing.

Unfortunately, a few seawater sponge baths were not enough to heal her whole. Long before she had reached the necessary pitch, she choked. Her cry ended in a coughing fit and her body began to tighten, leaving her lying on the floor curled up like a dying spider struggling to breathe. What had propelled her to the floor now lifted her from it, maintaining its grip on her.

She leaned her head back, tears streaming down her face in pain both physical and emotional, and found herself sitting on the floor in the arms of Lord Hamilton. He held her wrists firmly, but not painfully tight, crossed in front of her, pulling her back against his chest. He was making soothing noises, rocking her slowly. Sirene found herself bathed in a soft blue and yellow glow. Then that was snuffed out by a blackness that threatened to suffocate her. Stifling her panic, she looked up into Price's face. It was twisted in a mask of outrage, embarrassment, and concern. Towers remained on the far side of the room, whimpering, holding his white bandaged arm desperately.

"Margaret!" Price cried. "You have truly gone mad. What possessed you?" he demanded, pulling at her arms to determine if she had another weapon somewhere.

She yelped when he touched her, sending her body into renewed convulsions as she moved the wrong way trying to escape him. Lord Hamilton's voice rang out with authority.

"Back off, Vice Admiral. I have her!"

For some reason, Price obeyed. "She is my responsibility, Governor," he replied. The title did not come easily off his tongue, and Sirene paid as much attention to him as she could while gasping for relief.

"Your mistress she may be, but she tried to kill a man in front of an agent of the king. Now stand down and I'll get to the bottom of this."

Reluctantly, Price sat. Governor Hamilton took several minutes speaking in soft tones to Sirene to calm her before he realized that her spastic state was not rage-induced, but caused by something else entirely. He looked up as a servant peeked through the parlour door. "If she has any medicine, fetch it," he ordered. "Relax, my dear," he purred to Sirene, as the sound of running feet retreated. "Just let it go. Is it the falling sickness or catalepsy?" he asked Price. He never took his attention off Sirene, only his change in tone indicated who he was speaking to.

Price shook his head sullenly.

"No. The doctors are baffled. She was severely wounded when we," he glanced briefly back at Towers, "rescued her. She has been unconscious for nearly a week with some injury-induced fever. Frankly, I am surprised she managed to get out of bed, much less get this far." His manner spoke volumes of his displeasure in that arena. "This must be a relapse of the fever."

"Oh, I don't think so," he said, still rocking her. He did not seem to mind sitting on the floor. "When motivated by the right forces, one can make the body do miraculous things. This woman has a grievance. See how her eyes bore into him even now."

Towers glared across the room at her. "I want t' press charges, Governor," he said, summoning up his most imperious tone. He managed only a shaky sneer. "She tried to kill me, ye saw it."

"Run. Run as ffar away as you can, ddog," Sirene panted. Her whole body was trembling. "Find the ddriest... hhighest... point you can, the ffarthest... distance you ccan... from any water, hhowever small... because I *will* ccome for you. And I *will* kkill you."

He gave a choked laugh, a counterfeit show of bravado.

Governor Hamilton continued soothing her. "Now, now, Miss. Calm yourself. We will get to the bottom of your grievance. If it is legitimate..."

"He killed a boy!" she screamed, half in pain half in rage. "A cchild! Jjust so he had ccurrency with which to buy a pardon."

The Lord looked up at the other two men. "Is this true?"

Towers stuttered, trying to think fast and speak properly, "He... he was a pirate, and not as young as she professes. He was old enough to kill two men. He was preventing her rescue," he said, pulling himself together. "She was in chains, ...bound naked to the bed and bore bloody marks of ill use."

"Liar!" she cried. She lunged for him but her body contorted inward instead.

"That pirate boy broke my arm," he insisted.

Price gestured to the gypsum-encased limb with his cigar. "Ask me, that pirate boy just saved your life."

The servant returned carrying a dark brown bottle and a spoon. For once, Sirene wanted it. She tried to hold still, but could not.

"Help," she gasped, shivering.

The lord-turned-governor nodded and held her mouth open, braced her head back against his chest long enough for the thick, bitter liquid to be poured in. She leaned back as he let go and dismissed the servant with an actual thank you.

The poppy syrup burned through her body, weighing her down, turning her limbs to lead. It took several minutes for the trembling to stop, for her pained muscles to relax. Meanwhile, Price sat smoking his cigar, and Towers grabbed the bottle of medicine left on the desk by the servant and poured some into his brandy when he thought no one was looking.

"There, better?" the governor asked gently.

"Yes, ththank you," she breathed, struggling to remain lucid.

He shifted his weight to his knees, and gestured for Price to help. Between the two of them, she was placed on the settee Lord Hamilton had been enjoying when she came in. Price handed the governor a carved, ebony cane and helped him to his feet. The lord then limped over to another chair, which he pulled closer to Sirene, favouring his hip heavily. She felt guilty, and it must have shown in her face because he put up his hand.

"Don't you worry about me. I caught the bad end of some pirate chainshot to the hip. I was lucky, I'll walk again on my own two soon enough," he said, then glanced over at Price's wood filled boot. "Sorry, Vice Admiral." Price gave a dismissive wave, and the man turned back to Sirene. "Now, you wish to tell me what this madness was about?"

"I heard," she began, finding speaking difficult, spoke with slow deliberation. "He stole me from my love. He killed the cabin boy no doubt left to guard me."

"Who stole you? From whom?"

"Price... Towers... stole my Jack. Me *from* Jack," she corrected. Thinking was becoming difficult.

Hamilton looked at the two men, then down at her again. "Isn't this Jack the one who hurt you? Caused the wounds, the fever?"

"No!" Sirene shook her head violently, and paid for it with a wave of dizziness that threatened to drown her. "I did... it... the fish. Saved his life from the devilfish. It was in the treasure. Only a mermaid could survive the ...poison, but not a man... had to... had to save him."

"Lord Hamilton," Price interrupted with a worried frown. "The woman is clearly delusional, maybe even a touch mad. She cannot be held responsible...."

The governor held up his hand for silence, and bent nearer to Sirene as she began to lose the fight for consciousness. "Tell me, Miss Margaret. If I let you go, when you are well, what will you do?"

"Go home," she sighed, her eyes fluttering closed. "Return to the warm seas I was born in and take my lover with me. But first... first I will kill Jacob Towers for the murder of Seamus Hare."

When Sirene awoke she was in a small, unfamiliar room. The bed was narrow, though well-stuffed and made with extremely fine linen. There was a single, small window and a solitary door. The room looked much like a servant's garret except that what little furnishings were here were of exquisite quality. Sitting just beyond the mosquito netting was a woman in a grey dress uniform calmly tatting lace. She looked up as Sirene moved, then rose and approached a set of drawers. Taking a key from her pocket, she placed her lace work and tools within a drawer and then locked it behind her.

"Ye jest relax there, Miss Margaret. I'm gunna fetch th' doctor," she said with exaggerated calm, and a distinctive lowland brogue, then unlocked the door.

Sirene was startled that there was a second, barred door outside the first and a guard seated across the hall from it. This man got up and unlocked the second door to release the woman and then locked it back behind her. Sirene sat up, stunned by her elaborately comfortable prison. It was only then that she noticed the padded leather cuff locked around one wrist, which was tethered to the bedpost on a long leash. She gave it a tug to test its strength. It held easily. She didn't even make the headboard thump against the wall.

She was still in her nightdress, every infernal layer, and her hair had been brushed and braided. Most of the ache was gone, though there was a lingering weakness in her muscles.

She made herself get out of the bed, and found a pair of silk slippers waiting for her on the carpet. There was a chamber pot within easy reach, which she took advantage of.

She was just exploring her limited tether when the door open again. The woman was back with clothes in hand, and closed the inner door behind her. She came to a stop several feet out of Sirene's reach.

"Miss Margaret," she began, in a formal tone. "Ahm Mrs. MacPherson, yer nurse. Ahm quite capable of manhandling ye if need be, but let's not get ta tha', shall we? Ah've here clothes sent by yer... by Vice Admiral Price, tha' he insists are yer own, though I dinnae see how, wee as they are. I'm t' get you dressed fer an audience with th' governor. Doctor Fiedler will be here in an hour or so."

She bobbed a curtsey. "Pleased to meet you, Mrs. MacPherson. My name is Sirene, but no doubt you have been instructed to call me Margaret, so please, if you would call me Miss Taft I think that would satisfy the admiral of vice."

The woman's bushy eyebrow rose, though the smile in her eyes did not touch her lips. "Miss Taft then." She nodded, and crossed the remaining distance. She dropped the clothes on the bed and took Sirene's manacled wrist in hand. She paused, the key held behind her back. "I'll tell ye noo, Miss Taft, there is nae escape fra this room save that door, and James will'na let any past. If'n ye manage it, ye've a whole garrison near enough t' cause considerable trouble."

"I assure you, Mrs. MacPherson. I have no intentions of jumping willy nilly without knowing how deep the water is."

Satisfied, the woman unlocked the manacle, and helped Sirene to dress. It was one of her old day dresses and, due to its size, there was no way to wear it without the corset. Until the nurse laced her into the brand new busk, Sirene had not realized how much weight she had gained. The Scotswoman muttered something that sounded like complaints while she pulled at the laces. From the shape of her own ample frame, it was unlikely she was wearing more than light stays. Even with the corset laced as tight as they could manage, the dress was snug. Having spent months without the whalebone support, Sirene felt stiff and light-headed now that she was in it once more.

"Who needs iron bars," she gasped, "when one parades about in a portable prison."

For the first time the nurse chuckled. She put on a straight face quickly, then sat Sirene on the edge of the bed, and unlocked the inner door. She said something to a servant waiting outside then set up a chair in front of the bars. Returning, she helped her to the door, setting her in the chair to wait for her audience, before going back to her own chair by the bed and picked up a darning ball and a sock. A sewing needle, Sirene supposed, was a less dangerous weapon than the tatting hook.

She did not have to wait long. Five minutes later, another chair was placed opposite the bars and Governor Lord Hamilton bowed formally to her.

"Please forgive me for not kissing your hand, Miss Margaret, but..." he gestured lamely to the bars.

"You are forgiven, Lord Hamilton, on two conditions."

"Name them."

She gave him a tired smile. "One, you call me Miss Taft or Sirene, as I despise the name Margaret. It isn't mine."

That broke the ice. He gave a soft laugh. "I had an aunt named Margaret. She hated it, too." He bowed again, and seated himself. "Very well, Miss Taft. And two?"

"You explain to me where I am and why?"

He appeared genuinely distressed by the situation. "You are in a private, renovated room in the governor's mansion, my home. You will be attended by my own personal physician, and given the best attentions I can manage."

"I understand I am under an arrest of some sort. But why this? Why am I not in the common prison?"

He shifted his feet. "Well, for one thing, you have yet to commit a crime."

"Then why?"

"I said 'yet', Miss. You confessed to me that, given the chance, you will commit murder."

Sirene relaxed as much as the corset would allow. "I was... overwhelmed at the time I made that statement. I am, at this point, capable of awaiting proper justice."

"And if witness cannot be obtained?" he asked carefully.

She regarded him steadily. "That man confessed to the crime, in front of you no less. Ask him point blank, when he is not expecting it, whether or not he killed a ten-year-old cabin boy while he was on board the *Mercy's Ransom* and determine for yourself whether he is lying should he deny the act. Unfortunately for Jacob Towers, he is a very bad liar. All I seek is justice."

"But if the boy *was* a pirate..."

"Boys are stolen all the time by pirates to serve as cabin boys. I can and will stand witness that the boy committed no act of piracy before me. And I was with him his entire career aboard that ship." Watching the governor's reactions it seemed doubtful that her word would be enough. "Besides, I wish to press charges of kidnapping against Towers, if indeed he is the one claiming to have rescued me."

"He and Price," he said, nodding.

"Do you really think Price was actively with him at the time?" The look in his eyes said no. She shrugged. "But if he insists, charge him accessory. It is long past time he paid for his cruelties."

"Tell me about your kidnapping," he said, making himself more comfortable.

"I know virtually nothing about it. I was not conscious at the time," she sighed. Had she been, she might have been able to save the boy's life. It was, after all, her fault he was on board in the first place.

"Forgive me. Not that kidnapping. Tell me how you came to leave Barbados in the company of Handsome Jack."

She told him, leaving out the details regarding her true form and the nature of the jewel she had sought. She was careful to omit anything that might reinforce the thought that she was mad, as well as the improper details, though she did tell him that she and Jack had become the most passionate of lovers. She had gotten as far as Hispaniola, when she had gone ashore to get the information needed, when she saw something flicker across his light and his face that bothered her.

"What?" she asked.

He seemed reluctant, but relented. "I have been told you would say such things. You have deluded yourself that the man who loves you is your enemy and the man who terribly abused you is the love of your life."

She narrowed her eyes, leaned forward the tiniest hair. "Is he the only one telling you that?" He hesitated and she nodded. "Get a second opinion."

"Who? Gladly I will ask."

She thought a moment. The only people she trusted to tell the truth in the matter were on the *Mercy*, which precluded their testimony. And then there was the Governor of Jamaica, but could he really be trusted to reveal that he was being blackmailed by Price? Most of the servants who had suffered under him she had not seen since her return, and the ones she did recognize would not dare betray him.

"Jeanette! There was a slave, a dark, native girl who suffered as much from him as I and was witness to his many cruelties. She often tended to me afterwards. I have not seen her around the house, but I doubt he would have sold her. If she is still alive, he might have shipped her off to his family estate in Fairlane's Cove."

He nodded. "I will investigate this matter fully. If what you say is true..."

"All that and more. Price is guilty of blackmail, as well. And I have been the unwilling instrument in that. In fact, I was sup-posed to seduce Vice Admiral Trask, or just sleep with him in ex-change for his recommendation of Price as his replacement. Ask any one of Trask's servants: Morton, his butler, and a maid named... Bernadette? No, I think it was Henriette. They will verify that I was in his house for dinner, alone, the night I was 'kidnapped'. And that there were no plans for me to return home before morning."

He was thoughtful a moment, the yellow body of his glow flickering with anxiety and unanswered questions. "Tell me about the late vice admiral, Trask. You were taken to his cabin with Price on the HMS *Redoubt* that night. What happened? Did Price kill him? Or was it the freak accident caused by the storm that Price claimed?"

He seemed eager for the event to be Price's fault and Sirene grew pensive. She fiddled with her hands in her lap, picking at something on the edge of one nail with another.

"If I tell you the truth, you will think me mad."

"Then only tell me what I will believe," he suggested, shifting to the edge of his seat.

She gave a choked laugh. "Then you will hang me."

He chuckled in disbelief. "Are you saying *you* killed the Vice Admiral?"

She nodded. "I am a singer." He shook his head slightly, not understanding how this mattered. "It is within my vocal range... to shatter glass." Her hand drifted to her throat, still a little hoarse. "Or at least it was. The Vice Admiral was standing too close to an object when it shattered."

Lord Hamilton laughed. "An unhappy accident. How can you blame yourself for that?"

"*Happy* accident," she corrected. "He and Price were conspiring to arrange your silence in the matter of me. They had intended to hang the *Ambition*'s crew regardless of the truth, but you began to ask questions on deck. Once you had a plausible explanation there was no way they could. That and my comment of 'mistress or ward'."

Lord Hamilton sat thinking.

Sirene was loathe to interrupt him, but needed answers. "Your Lordship? May I ask you a question?"

He looked up sharply. "Certainly."

"What do you remember of that night?"

"Not much, I fear. I witnessed the interviews of the two officers, not that I was wanted present, but I exerted my position," he grinned. "Their stories backed yours up completely. Then we were attacked by the pirates led by that German horror. I was taken out early, caught a length of chainshot to the hip after it ripped through the mast. Luckily it was slowed down by that, or it would have shreded me, as well. I was brought below and tended by the doctor. The next thing I knew, I was taken to a longboat by British sailors working side by side with an obvious pirate, and not under sword point," he commented wryly.

She chuckled. "That must have disturbed you considerably."

"I'll admit. I was justifiably incensed. Once we were set ashore on Saint Christopher, I confronted the man who was then in charge of the HMS *Redoubt,* a lieutenant who stepped up after her captain had been thrown overboard. He explained it was a second pirate, your Handsome Jack...."

"*Amber*Jack," she corrected.

"Pardon?"

"It is AmberJack now."

"Oh, well." He thought a moment. "That actually suits him, what I've heard of him, at any rate. As I was saying, *Amberjack* apparently came aboard and challenged the German pirate to a duel and won. He then arranged pardons through the lieutenant for those pirates that had been forced to join the German's crew, and behaved like such an extraordinary gentleman that the lieutenant felt compelled to be as cooperative as possible. I understand a great many lives were saved by that action. All of which confirmed all you had said of him. So, yes, I find it hard to believe that such a man would do to you the things Price has attributed to him. But then some men can be perfect gentlemen with his fellow man and be right beastly with women. I've known men like that."

"He is not that kind of man, I assure you. Nor could he be if he sails with women in his crew, which he does. But tell me, how did Price survive? I was told he was thrown to the sharks."

"A second lieutenant swam ashore with him. The man was missing a leg from a shark attack, but dolphins swam in and ran them off. What happened after that, I do not know. Carriages arrived from a nearby plantation, sent for by some enterprising young ensign, and took us for medical attention. We ended up in different places. I returned to Port St. Charles as I was being sent there as the new governor, not that I had informed anyone on the *Redoubt* of this."

"Why are *you* governor? What happened to Governor Rhodes?"

"He has begun to suffer episodes of catalepsy. He did not want anyone to know, and with his family situation..." At her questioning look, he elaborated. "His son was nearly killed by pirates the night you were taken. He thought it best to retire from public life and return to England with the King's good graces." He looked her over carefully. "Are *you* all right, Miss Taft?"

"I'm getting there." She explained about the fish in the treasure chest, only telling him that they had been swimming when they found it, and that she was getting over the poisoning. "I shall be right as rain soon."

"I mean in other ways, my dear," he said patiently.

"Oh. I suppose. I just want to go home; to wear comfortable clothes again. These are far too small."

"The Vice Admiral assured me they were your own," he said, glancing at the near impossible slimness of her waist.

"Oh, at one time they were. But given the opportunity to choose my own garments, I am more inclined to have them sized for my natural frame, not one artificially narrowed. I am having difficulty enough with weakness and body aches without confining my ribs in the jawbones of a poor, unfortunate whale," she replied, wincing as she made a minor adjustment at her waist to make her point.

"You are probably right. I am sure the doctor would disapprove. I shall see what I can find."

"I don't care if they are servant's clothes. I would rather be comfortable than fashionable. Like anyone is going to see me up here."

"Oh, speaking of which, about visitors..."

"If you mean Price, I would rather not see him."

He smiled. "That I can arrange." He looked sideways down the hall at something she could not see. "Now, I believe Doctor Feidler is here to see you, so I fear I must abandon you." He stood and bowed. "If you will excuse me? I have a great deal to investigate. If you need anything, ask Mrs. MacPherson. If you are allowed to have it, I shall leave instructions for you to be given it. After all, this," he gestured to the bars, "is merely a formality at this point."

"You are too kind," she said, curtseying. "You will make a fine governor, your Lordship."

His light rippled with warm yellows over the blue, tingeing faintly green where the two colours met. Smiling, she moved back to the bed to await the physician.

Chapter the Seventeenth

Sirene stood by the window taking in what air it provided and watching the ocean far away. She could barely hear it, and could only see it because the governor's mansion stood on a hill and overlooked the whole town. She could just make out the masts of ships in the harbour in the early morning light. Behind her, Mrs. MacPherson sat doing her lacework.

Sirene jumped when there came a knock at the door. The nurse got up, locking away her tatting in the drawer before crossing to the closed door. "Wha'tisit, James?" she sighed.

"A visitor for Miss Taft."

"Ye know she's no' wantin' visitors, James," she reminded him. There had already been a few attempts by Price to see her.

"She'll be wanting this one, ma'am. It's a lady."

Mrs. MacPherson sighed. "Verra well, but if this upsets her..."

She left the threat hanging and opened the door, fetching the audience chair. When the well-dressed woman moved to take the chair opposite the bars, Sirene was drawn to her instantly. Although it was not until she settled her voluminous skirts, and the broad hat was no longer covering her face that she realized why.

"Mother!" she exclaimed, and ran to the door, ignoring the chair and the concerned nurse.

Lorelei rose to touch her cheek. "Hello, dear. It's all right," she told Mrs. MacPherson. The woman relaxed and fetched her lace.

"What are you doing here? How did you find me?" Sirene was bursting with questions. She dragged the chair closer to the bars and sat on the edge of it.

"The usual way: I asked. And I came looking for you after some rather disturbing rumours swam my way. I take it you found your father?"

"Yes. He was everything you said. He had a wife, a new family. She was a wonderful woman, very friendly. But we can discuss father later. You are here to get me out of here?" she asked hopefully. "To take me home?"

"What? And spoil his chance to be the hero?" she exclaimed, in mock horror. "Not enough spiny sea urchins in the world oceans!" she laughed.

"He?" she asked, her heart skipping several beats, her breath catching in her throat. "You've seen Jack?" she whispered. "How is he? Where is he?"

Glancing at the guard and the nurse, Lorelei shifted to a tongue she was certain neither of them spoke, though should not raise too many questions. "*Quite mad, actually. Beside himself and determined to see this through,*" she said in Polynesian, shaking her head.

Those words made her worry. "*See what through, Mother? What is he up to?*"

"*Don't worry about it. I'll keep you company here for a little, then make my report. Care to explain this? Or is this what you were stolen for?*" she frowned, indicating the bars.

Sirene forced herself to be patient, and told her what had transpired.

Lorelei was thoughtful. *"This new governor is a good man, you say? Where is he now?"*

Sirene shrugged. *"Probably Fairlane Cove, investigating."*

"And Price?"

"Near," she spat. *"He tried to see me yesterday. But thankfully, Lord Hamilton gave orders that he is not allowed."*

"To our benefit. The captain is not in a mood to leave anything unfinished."

Sirene was quiet a moment. "Is Hare actually dead? Or was that a lie as well?" she asked, shifting back to English. This was a conversation she wanted overheard.

Her mother's eyes took on a look of shared pain, as if she would have spared her daughter this. "How did you find out?" she asked.

"A confession," she growled. "Jacob Towers killed him. How did... how did Jack take it, and why was he even in the fight?"

Lorelei related what she had been told, being careful not to give away truths that were best left unknown. "And that is all I know. He took it hard, both your kidnapping and the murder of the boy."

Sirene shifted her chair so she was leaning back against the door-frame, her head resting on the bars. "Tell me something. What does it mean when they are golden?"

It took her mother a moment to realize what she was referring to, and then a knowing smile spread across her face. "So you found him, did you?"

She looked her mother full in the eye. "Found who? What haven't you told me?"

Lorelei was evasive. "Your father was golden," she answered.

"No, he wasn't," she said, shaking her head. "He was blue."

"Not to me," she smiled, dreamy with the memory. She refocused her eyes on her daughter, watched the epiphany erupt.

"'*Your crown of gold to light the way, a joining of souls where dark holds sway*'," she quoted, her face bright. "I never understood that poem until now. But he's... not one of us. How can it be possible?"

"Oh, it's possible. And yes, the Gift will do him good, though it is not wholly necessary. He is *of the scale*, though less than you, and the Gift will balance many things for him. Years for instance. Now," she said, getting up, "I must be going. Mustn't miss the tide." She kissed her daughter's cheek through the bars. "*Listen for it. And don't let this one swim away*," she warned. "*A human willing to live in our world....*"

She left, smiling at the guard and the servant who escorted her out. Sirene sank back into the chair, wondering what she could have meant. What exactly was Jack up to? Whatever it was, chances were it would not happen until nightfall. He would not be foolish enough to try to rescue her in broad daylight.

She was wrong....

Just past the noon bell the next day, a pale grey ship flanked by a larger, black ship with a veiled figurehead sailed boldly into the harbour as if they owned it. It was not until they were in the midst of the harboured ships that they raised their pennants. The grey ship ran up a grey flag sporting a pair of crossed sabres below a half skull in black. The black ship flew a black flag bearing a skeletal woman with arms out to the sides holding sabres.

The other vessels around them motivated instantly, and shouts could be heard across the water as they scrambled to their guns and raced to move the ships into firing position. Several of them quickly found their sails 'in irons' as they caught the wind awkwardly, one mast full, the other plastered against the yardarms, useless, as they struggled to get their helms to respond. Foolishly it seemed, the two pirate vessels glided past heavily armed frigates presenting tempting broadsides for target practice. Cannons were swiftly loaded, as out of courtesy, all ships kept their guns unloaded in port.

The pirates lined the rails armed with pistol and cutlass as if prepared to board, but made no moves. They sailed side-by-side into the lion's den and laughed as the call to fire was heard from numerous ships.

Nothing happened.

Investigating, the enemy ships discovered busted oilcloth bags between the cannon balls and the now wet gunpowder. It would be hours before they could be safely fired. One ship managed to remain moving, a large frigate that wove in between the disabled ships aiming for the pirate vessels.

On board the *Ransom*, Penn aimed old Betsy, and then discharged the single shot. Two balls exploded from the forward gun, orbiting around each other like mad moons by the length of chain between them. They struck the main mast of the active frigate and chewed through the base. Sailors scattered as the structure fell, timbers screaming. The sails collapsed, cracking the mizzenmast and covering the ship's entire larboard side. The vessel floundered, and was struck by one of the other ships in the harbour that had managed to sort out its own sheets and spring forward under the brisk wind.

The commander at the fort swore in frustration, unable to fire upon the pirates without hitting the vessels under his protection. Instead, he ordered every soldier available to swarm the wharfs.

The pirates dropped longboats, and rowed toward the docks, armed to the teeth. Any other ship that did the same found itself targeted by four riflemen on board the pirate vessels. The soldiers waited smugly on the wharf, weapons aimed. The pirates rowed on, dauntless. Then the *Widow* aimed the swivel gun on her deck for the main brace of the dockside hoist and fired.

The long bar of the loading arm swung as the whole crashed through the back end of the dock, cutting off the soldier's access to the land and sending some into the drink. The longboats split up, going around the stranded soldiers, laughing as they swarmed the remaining docks. A few of the red coated soldiers fired at the boats, but then a cannonball struck the first piling on the end of the pier. They looked across at the pirate manning the swivel gun. He held up the torch threateningly, pushing the re-loaded weapon into position, aiming for the centre of them. weapons were immediately stowed.

The pirates dealt with resistance on shore with threats and blunt blows. Most of the dockside workers got out of their way. Jack led the small army up the narrow streets with grim determ-ination, seeking out their target. Citizens ran, doors slammed shut, and bars were dropped ahead of their path. A few ladies of the nighttime persuasion called out from their garret windows, shouting propositions while hanging over their sills. But all else scattered like chickens.

One young maid found herself in their path with nowhere else to go as market goers made haste with their own escapes. Left standing in the street, she faced the oncoming army, shiver-ing. Jack stopped. His followers stopped behind him. He took her hand and lingered over it, never taking his eyes off hers.

"Vice Admiral Price," he said.

She hesitated, and then pointed down the street and up the hill with a shaking hand. Halfway up the slope was a stately manor house with a high, black iron fence. She pointed beyond that to a taller house on the crest of the hill. He gave her a saucy bow, and drew her behind him, eyes still locked, and set her hand in that of another.

"Tortuga," he said, and then headed up the street.

The girl looked up into the face of the black behemoth and fainted dead away. Tortuga swept her up and kicked in the nearest door. He walked up to the master of the house; a round, slightly balding man bravely standing before his family with a broken antique rifle. He glanced beside him to his strapping young son armed with a fireplace poker and dropped the uncon-scious girl in the son's arms and left, closing the door behind him. Catching up to his wife, he found her grinning.

'Vieve and Mary were part of the mob, battling what soldiers found them and blocked their way. The pirates used whatever came to hand, including chicken crates and rain barrels to stop the soldiery, saving their bullets for the retreat. They ran up, wading into the fray. The soldiers were no real match, easily distracted. Then Mary heard feet retreating down an alley. She followed, certain the person was running to report and she intended to take them out. 'Vieve saw a flash of curly brown locks disappear around the building and followed.

Mary tailed the footsteps through a back alley and down a short flight of steps to a tavern door. One of the kind that never really closes. Inside there was drink being poured and wenches being groped, as if word had not yet reached them of the invasion. Mary's eyes met those of a man too well-dressed to be in this establishment; a blonde man in a captain's coat and his arm in a sling. She grinned, hefting her belaying pin in one hand and her cutlass in the other.

She stalked forward, and people scrambled out of her way. The man drew his pistol and fired. She looked down at the hole in the side of her bodice below her ribs. The ball only grazed her. She looked back at him and grinned. With one kick of her knee-high boots, she knocked over the table between them.

"Still a bullacky shot, Mr. Towers," she spat. "Ye'll not find me as easy a target as a green little boy," she taunted, circling him.

The patrons of the tavern pressed to the walls and behind anything they could see over. 'Vieve walked into the bar as Towers drew his sword and lunged for Mary. The redhead skimmed the room, and then leaned back against the doorframe, snatching a pint from the man next to her. He started to protest, but one look at her in trousers and an open sailor's shirt splattered with old blood, wild red hair half-bound in a topknot, and changed his mind.

"Gut 'eem, Marie! Rip out 'is child murderin' 'eart t'rough 'is ears!" she shouted.

Towers risked a glance behind him to see the menacing French woman in the doorway and Mary cut the straps to his sling, taking a deep slice of his chest with it. He yelped, turning back to the fight, lifting his broken arm to use the cast as a shield.

"Do not take too long, *mon amour*," 'Vieve called. "We 'ave a job to do."

"Don' worry, luv!" Mary laughed. "Th' captain ain't gonna need no help wit' Price. But this dog…. This dog be mine!"

The crowd paid attention to the exchange and their participation grew after that. Drinks were passed through the crowd as they watched, and a fresh one was pressed into 'Vieve's hand. She looked across at the bar and saw the tapman raise his mug in toast. She smiled, and drank deep.

Outside, she heard the regular tramp of a soldier's boots. She hefted the previous mug in her other hand, a heavy, polished pewter piece and watched the opening in its dull, mirror-like surface. The moment the red-coated soldier was framed in the doorway, she swung backwards, soundly clocking the unfortunate in the face. He went down in the stairwell with a spray of blood from his nose and 'Vieve returned her attention to the fight.

The man next to her, whose drink she had confiscated, bent close, dared to ask her: "Who is that woman, and what did he do to her?"

"Zat," she said proudly, "ees Bloody Marie of ze pirate sheep *Widow*. We sail wit' ze *Mercy's Ransom,* under Amber Jacque Weendlam. And zat dog keeled our cabin boy een cold blood."

They danced around the centre of the room, Towers using chairs and tables, anything he could to trip her up and slow her relentless onslaught. Escape was out of the question. He was caught between the devil and the red-head. He lunged for her, realized too late that he had left himself open. Oddly, Mary settled for a surer cut along the extended arm. It was not until the third such opportunity was passed up for a nick that he realized what she was doing. He fought his panic. The crowd was against him, cheering on 'Bloody Mary' in ale-soaked voices as she proceeded to take him apart, piece by piece.

The bulk of the pirates still followed Jack. Some lagged behind, finishing off small groups of soldiers that tried to stop the procession, but they all caught up eventually. Anything left in the streets where scuffles occurred lay broken in their wake, and soldiers sprawled unconscious on the cobbles, tied up in their own coats with their arms confiscated. A cart vendor, having abandoned his wares for a safer haven, had his apples raided, and cores were crushed underboot several streets up.

Price's house was enormous. It towered above the small town, dominating the landscape with a wide balcony on the upper floor for watching for the approach of ships. There was a large courtyard with a circular cobbled drive. The wrought iron gate was overturned easily with so many determined to topple it.

As they swarmed toward the front door, someone with a rifle on the upper walk began taking shots at them. Backhand Luke was hit in the shoulder and the pirates pulled back, taking refuge behind the elephantine stone gate posts. Jack began searching through those gathered for his best shot. Anjali tapped his shoulder.

"You want no blood?" she asked.

"As little of th' wrong blood as possible," he said.

The Indian woman hefted a hard green apple with a grin. "Den you get no blood."

The gathered crews roared and yelled as if they were charging, and Anjali grabbed someone's broad brimmed hat and threw it into the open. The feathers were sliced off by the shot and, while the man reached for another loaded weapon, she took the opportunity to dash to the house, taking refuge behind a rose hedge. She feinted left, making it look as if she were coming around that side, then ducked right, and aimed. She threw the apple as hard as she could. As the man straightened with another weapon in hand, the fruit connected solidly with the side of his head and he slumped to the balcony floor.

Cheers went up among the crew and they swarmed across the lawn. They took precautions this time, in case there were others waiting inside with loaded pistols. They went in every way but the front door, crashing in through windows along the front and sides of the house. They were met with no other resistance. They tore through every room, but there was no sign of Price.

Jack grabbed up the first person he found, a petite maid hiding in a second story chamber. He pulled her close and laid his finger on her lips. Pressed close to his chest, she shivered in his grip, and not entirely in fear.

"Shh," he whispered. "Tell me where yer master is hiding an' no harm will come to ye."

She gave a squeak. "Ah'm sorry. The master's not home."

Jack growled, releasing her. "Where did he go?"

She caught her breath as she backed away, affected by the nearness of him. "Only the butler knows f' sure. An' he won't tell the likes o' you. Though I think he went to see his fiancé."

This was unwelcome news. Lorelei had said that Sirene was a prisoner of the governor. She had said nothing about her being engaged to Price. Jack's mind raced.

"Where is she?" he snarled in frustration.

She shrugged. "I dunnow where the Reeses live, sir."

"Reeses?" He stalked closer. She shrank back, genuinely afraid of the look in his eye. "What is the unlucky girl's name?"

"Her honour Vveronica Rreese, sir. Hher father's Bbaron Berkeley."

Jack fumed. The bastard stole *his* woman for his own, and *still* intended to marry another. He stormed out to the gallery and looked down to the main room where his crew and 'Vieve's were milling about, searching the house.

"The villain's not home! Lads, ladies, sack the house. No harmin' th' help unless they ask real nice. They become a problem, lock 'em in a closet."

There was a distant booming of cannon. Jack ran to the outside balcony, where Luke had tied up the unconscious butler and was reloading the rifles. He looked out over the bay. Several ships had managed to get out of the way of the two pirate ships, though they were not capable of much manoeuvring. The fort, now having a clear shot, was taking what it could at the offending vessels. Penn and Williams, the chief gunner on the *Widow*, were giving them hell in return, while Marklain moved the vessels into better shielded positions. He cursed. He would have to act faster.

He ran back inside, skidding down the hall and slid down the curving banister. On his way out the door he paused by Anjali, issued orders, thankful her husband was nowhere in sight.

"I'm off t' pay th' Governor a visit. Take what ye can of value, then burn 'er down. I want this house o' horrors in ashes. If I don't find his scurvy arse, at least he'll have nothin' here t' come back ta. Just make sure all th' servants are out. I only want one corpse in this whole damned town. Then I want ye t' go back to th' ships and make sure ye round up any o' our strays. We seem t' be missin' a few."

"Aye, Captain." She turned to the crews and began directing traffic. "You heard him, lads!" she roared. "Get t' work! Take dem curtain down, an' use dem for hauling. You!" She pointed to a cowering slave girl trying to hide beneath a lamp table. "Come heah." The girl crept forward. "I need you to search de house an' get everybody out. All th' servants, all th' slaves. Need any help, just ask. Our ordahs don't extend t' Price's livin' property. T'ough any o' ye fancy freedom on th' high seas, help out an' hang close."

Jack walked out the front door. He was too determined to care whether the ground swayed or not. Lorelei had said something when she came to report her daughter's location and condition, something he barely remembered, but he knew his 'land sickness' would not affect him now, not for this battle, not for this purpose. As far as he was concerned he was still on a rolling ship's deck and comfortable with the world.

The governor's house was on the slope below him. There was no road that led straight down. Instead, it curved away along the side of the hill and came around. All that remained between them was open property and a large garden. Jack took the short-cut.

Sirene was soaking in the saltwater bath Mrs. MacPherson had brought up for her. She had been concerned that it was too cold, but Sirene assured her that it was part of her beauty regimen and had never caused her ill before. Mrs. MacPherson had heard of ocean bathing spas and merely grumbled, but allowed the luxury to be provided. That was when she heard the first spout of cannon fire from Ol' Betsy.

Sirene jumped out of the water, and ran, dripping and naked, to the window despite the Scottish woman's protests of impropriety. Her heart leapt at the sight of the two ships sailing into the harbour. She swiftly dried while muttering to herself about how crazy he was to try pulling this off in the middle of the day. She threw on the simple black, ankle-length frock, worn without the white bib and apron.

Then the cannons stopped. She watched from the window, worried and hopeful, while Mrs. MacPherson fussed with her hair whilst she clucked at her like a hen.

They were in the midst of an argument about Sirene not wearing the underpinnings when they heard shouting. They heard the footsteps of James as he ran down the corridor, and then a fight. They froze, listening to sword on sword followed by a gunshot and the breaking of wood. Moments later, Sirene heard keys rattling and ran to the threshold, throwing it open as the barred door swung wide.

Prepared to throw her arms around Jack, she was brought up short, face to face with Price. She reached instead to claw his face. He caught the hand and twisted her arm behind her.

"None of that, my dear." He jerked her out into the hallway before the nurse could cross the room, and slammed the door. "You will be safer here," he said, locking it and pocketing the keys. "You will come with me."

"Like hell!" she screamed.

She struggled in his grasp, kicking and thrashing, trying to reach him with her free hand. She was much better, but she had no idea how long her newfound strength would last. He dragged her down the narrow hall in spite of her attempts to hold onto things to prevent it, and down the dark staircase to the second floor.

The stair opened onto a balcony that overlooked the atrium of the house and the grand staircase. Sirene grabbed for the rail and locked her arm around it. He had to release his hold on her to pry her off, and she took the opportunity to kick him and bolt, screaming for James.

She got halfway to the staircase when she saw part of the balcony rail was missing. She stopped, horrified to see James' broken body lying on the main floor amid the rubble. She raised her voice, aiming for the dangerous pitch; but Price pounced on her, jerking her back from the gap and backhanded her.

Mary reeled back from the blow, her hand pressed against her cheek. She looked across at Towers with a shocked expression. "Ye hit me? Ye'd strike a woman?" she gaped. Her words had the desired reaction amid the gathered patrons. "What kind'a man are ye? Ye kidnap women, murder children, an' now yer beatin' a lass? What? Do we threaten yer manhood? Do ye even have one? Or d'ye save that attention fer yer crewmen!"

Towers roared, charging her. Mary deflected his sword and swung her foot, connecting with his groin with all the force of his charge and her strength. He dropped like a stone. The crowd groaned and laughed at the same time. Mary scratched her cheek where blood was dripping from a cut and causing an itch as it dried.

"Hmph, that answers that question. They jest mustn't be very big," she chuckled.

'Vieve roared with laughter. "If zey were, zey aren't now!"

Towers swung blindly at her legs. She took only a nick to her boot. Pissed, she dropped a chair on him. She went to the ring of patrons, appropriated a mug and took a long swig of ale. She turned swinging as he got to his feet and took a more guarded lunge for her. She dodged out of his way, and took a chunk out of his cast. He nearly curled up again, howling in pain, fighting off the wave of nausea that followed. He held the broken limb back, trying to keep it out of the way.

They traded blows for several minutes, dancing around the cleared circle. It was an even match. Almost nothing landed on either of them until he managed a slice to the top of her arm. She lashed back and he trapped her blade against his, grinning in triumph. She grinned back, and punched him with her free hand. He reeled.

Outside, 'Vieve heard the activity in the streets above. The regular stomping of booted feet told her that the soldiers had escaped the docks or arrived from the fort and where hunting down the pirates.

"We are running out of time, *mon chou*," she warned.

The two combatants staggered, covered in their own blood and that of their opponent. Towers took the risk of using his cast as a club. He feinted with his blade, luring her into a parry, which opened her up to the bludgeon. White lime dust rose up from the contact as the cast cracked further and part of it sifted to the floor. He screamed in pain, and grabbed the wounded arm. Mary stumbled over the remains of the broken chair and landed on her back. The crowd shouted, egging them both on. It was all 'Vieve could do to resist interfering.

Towers staggered over to her as she struggled to reach her sword. He stopped in front of her, sneered and raised his blade. As he stepped forward to stab her, he saw her foot draw up and quickly blocked his groin. Instead, she aimed for his knee. There was a sickening snap as the joint bent backwards and the man toppled.

Mary lunged for her cutlass and jumped to her feet. She walked around behind him, and stood at his head as he rolled on the floor cradling the broken joint. She grabbed a fistful of dull golden hair, pulling his head back against her.

"All men are dogs," she whispered in his ear. "Some are noble, loving and treasured companions. You... yer a tick, sucking on th' blood o' others t' feed yer own ambition. How's it feel t' taste yer own?"

Towers gurgled in response, unable to react through the pain threatening to make him black out. He could not even lift his hand as she pressed her cutlass to his throat.

"This is for our bonny wee Hare," she snarled, and drew the blade slowly and deeply across his throat.

She stood over him as he flopped and spurted, not minding the blood. She did not move until 'Vieve touched her arm, and she became aware of the crowd roaring around her and the money changing hands. She fell into her arms, holding the French woman tight, 'Vieve whispering French endearments.

One of the barmaids stepped over the dead man's hand and lightly touched their arms. When they looked at her, she grabbed hold and guided them through the throng of patrons toward the side of the bar. There was no way she would be heard over the shouting, so she did not try, instead she urgently pulled them into the kitchen. Behind them, in the taproom, they heard the patrons fall quiet as an authoritative voice bellowed for answers. The girl reached into a broom cabinet and handed them a pair of skirts, helping them into them.

"These should disguise ye o' bit. Ye should be able t' run through th' streets in a feigned panic fairly freely. Jest be careful."

'Vieve grabbed her wrist. "Why?" she asked.

She laughed. "'Cause that pig was migh'ily unpop'lar down 'ere. Now wait 'til I signal." She picked up a bucket of slops and opened the kitchen door, which led up another staircase into yet another alley. She looked around, and when the coast was clear, waved for them to come out. "Good luck," she whispered.

As they headed out one end, a pair of soldiers peered in from the other. The barmaid threw the contents of the bucket toward them, and then bobbed a quick apology, loudly claiming she hadn't seen them. Grumbling, they moved on.

Jack found slipping into the governor's mansion easier than expected. There were no servants, and the garden doors were unlocked. Still, he crept around corners and stuck to the shadows. Lorelei had told him where Sirene was being kept, but she had been taken up the front way, which required him to cross the open entrance hall of the house. Anyone could be lying in ambush. He was prepared to fight his way up there, but would rather avoid it.

Outside, the cannons were still firing. In between shots, Jack heard a noise behind a door and crouched next to it, waiting. When it opened, he grabbed whatever came out. It was a maid, and a pretty one at that. She squealed, squirmed in his grasp, and started crying. Jack spun her in his arms and pinned her to the wall, his hand covering her mouth.

"Stow it, luv," he warned in a whisper. "Keep yer head about and I promise no harm will come by my hand. Now, promise ye won't scream?" She shook her head, her eyes wide and tearing. "No, ye don't promise?" he growled in exasperation. She started to shake her head again, then nod, unable to make up her mind, mumbled something into his hand. "What?" he asked, pulling his hand back an inch.

"I won't scream," she whispered. "Just... just don't ravage...."

"I don't have t' force women inta me bed," he sighed, glancing over his shoulder. "Where are all th' servants?"

"A navy man came; said those capable of fighting were needed outside. The rest o' us hid in the basement."

He gave her a stern look. "An' why aren't you?"

She blushed. "Privy."

He looked at the door, and cocked an eyebrow. "Indoor privy? Such opulence."

"Do ye want me t' take ye t' the silver, sir?" she asked, changing the subject.

He looked down at her and grinned. "Yes, but not that silver. I'm interested in the silver-haired lady."

Her eyes grew wide. "The mad woman?" As his eyes darkened, she shrank under his gaze. "That's what we were told, sir," she answered meekly. "She's with the nurse in the garret. Upstairs."

"I know where she is. I need ye to take me th' shortest route, one least likely to be seen."

"The only way besides the grand staircase still goes past it on the upper gallery; but there yer less likely to be seen, sir. Um... well, ye'll have to let me go, sir. I can't show ye if I can't move, sir," she whispered.

Jack hesitated. "Just keep this in mind, little bit," he warned, tipping her chin up with a gentle finger. "I have no intention of seeing ye hurt, but if we are noticed I *will* use ye as hostage. Don't do anything stupid, or ye'll run th' risk o' injury. Don't try to alert anyone or turn on me, or I'll be forced t' knock ye out. Savvy?"

She swallowed, and nodded. He let her up and she led him back the way he had come. She crept along on quiet feet, and Jack stayed close enough to grab her if necessary. They encountered no one inside the house, though they had to duck to avoid being seen by liveried man-servants bearing arms outside the windows. She took him down the servants' corridors and up the backstairs to the third floor.

Halfway up he heard indistinct noises ahead. He pushed past the girl, and rushed to the top.

As he rounded the corner he saw Sirene on the far side of the gallery in a black dress, staring down at something. She screamed and he put his hands to his ears. Out of the corner of his eye he saw Price bear down on her, yank her back from whatever edge she was standing at, and strike her. Sirene slammed against the opposing wall and fell limp. Jack went livid.

The hallway was filled with his roar as he charged Price, blade drawn. Price looked up. Panic and fear crossed his face for a moment before it was swallowed up by grinning triumph. He stepped in front of Sirene, met Jack's charge with aplomb, parrying his strike and pinning his weapon to the wall.

"Unusual sword for a pirate," he said, admiring the long blade trapped beneath his. "Having difficulty getting used to it?"

Jack kicked Price back, releasing the swords. "Not at all. Fenning's already christened it for ye."

The pair danced across the broad gallery, blades flashing: lunge and parry, advance and retreat. They traded biting insults and violent threats as easily as they traded blows.

"If ye've harmed her," Jack warned, glancing at Sirene's still body.

"You'll do what? Anything different than you're trying to do now?" Price sneered. "We see how well that's turning out."

Jack brought his blade down. Price dodged back, missing the parry, and the length of Toledo steel bit deeply into his leg …and lodged. As Jack struggled to pull it free, shocked by the lack of blood and soft tissue, Price hammered into his back with both fists. Jack went sprawling. Price jerked the sword loose and tossed it out of reach.

"A gift from a shark and one of your crewmen. I was never actually grateful for it until this moment. How ironic."

Jack rolled onto his back. "I'll take th' rest o' ye bit by bit," he snarled, dodging as Price swung for him.

Price laughed. "With what? Your charming good looks?"

Jack sprang to his feet, ducked under the swinging steel and charged him, taking him in the mid-section with his shoulder.

They tumbled down the stairs together, Jack tucked into Price's belly to protect himself from the fall. Price lost his grip on his sword near the end of the first flight and Jack continued the combat before they'd come to a full stop on the landing. He punched and kicked, turning the previously civilized sword duel into an all-out brawl.

Price was no stranger to combat, but he was more used to fighting with weapons than outright fisticuffs. He made several connections with the pirate's head and body, but left no impression. The smaller man, however, knew how to throw a punch, how to put his slight weight behind his fist and knee to add power without extra movement or effort. Price, on the bottom and unable to get enough leverage to change the situation, grabbed a pistol from Jack's belt. Holding the weapon behind Jack's back, he turned it as best he could and pulled the trigger.

The pistol backfired. When the spark hit the pan, the firing mechanism exploded. Jack bellowed, arching his spine as fragments of metal burned into his skin. Price dropped the weapon and pulled his hand back, putting out the fire on his lace cuff. His hand was blackened and bloody.

Jack's shirt was on fire. As he twisted in pain, his hold on Price shifted. Price wiggled his foot free and kicked Jack in the chin with his wooden leg. The pirate fell onto his back, his head reeling, but it put out the fire.

Price jumped to recover his sword and stood over his fallen foe.

Jack opened his eyes to find the tip of a navy blade in the soft underside of his chin, and then felt the man's foot on his lower belly, the heel grinding down on his groin. He grabbed the boot, but had neither the leverage nor the position to do anything about it.

"Did you think you could ever have beaten me? In anything?" he sneered.

Jack thought his head was going to explode with the pain, but he refused to give Price the satisfaction of screaming. If

Sirene could bear it, he could.

"I won her heart," he choked, trying not to think of the heel crushing his tender parts or feel the pressure designed to intimidate him.

Price actually laughed. "I never wanted her heart. Just her body. Though I might have won even that eventually, but you had to interfere yet again!" He applied more weight to Jack's groin, tempted to squash out of existence that which had outdone him. "I don't know which will give me more satisfaction," he said, drawing blood as the tip of his blade pressed into the skin. "Killing you with my own hand or watching you hang."

Price arched his back and roared as Jack's blade sliced through his coat and shirt and drew a long stripe of blood.

"That is mine!" Sirene cried as she swung. "And the only thing you ever did by your own hand was torment the helpless, you great bloody bully!"

He rounded on her. Jack curled up into a ball as Price's foot twisted against his groin. His knee came around, trying to connect with Price's leg as it folded over to protect his injury. He missed. He tried to grab at the booted ankle, but his body was flooded with white-hot pain that overwhelmed even the burns on his back.

Sirene stood above them on the stairs, looking unsteady, but holding the Spanish sword as if she knew what she was doing. There was a red mark on her face from his hand and blood from her scalp where she had hit the wall, but her eyes were clear.

"I'll hang you both!" he roared, and charged her.

She retreated back up the stairs, parrying his strikes desperately. When his blade bit into the banister, she struck, catching him along the shoulder. He jerked the sword free and batted hers aside, driving her back relentlessly. He sliced into her below her collarbone, from shoulder to shoulder. She tried to parry again, but he pinned her blade, and then kicked her. She fell at the top of the stairs, and back-pedalled out of his reach.

From the corner of her eye she saw Jack get up, and she turned to run, to lure Price away from the sword. He caught her easily by the hair, throwing her to the floor. She flipped over, backed away, put up her arm to defend herself as he raised his sword to stab her.

He heard something behind him and turned to parry. Jack stood there, sword at the ready, though barely on his feet. It was all he could do to make his body stand up, fire still shot through his veins from his bruised groin and his singed spine, but her life was at stake. They stared at each other for several unsteady seconds.

"Why won't you stay down?" Price roared.

"I could say th' same o' you, dog," he spat.

Price attacked, and Sirene scrambled to her feet. She could see Jack had not yet recovered. She jumped on Price's back, clawing his face, biting into his shoulder. He howled, and grabbed her by the hair with his burnt hand, pulling her off. Jack lunged. Price defended himself, retreating. Knowing Sirene was behind him still, he swung his off arm backwards to clear the path. It connected solidly.

She fell back against the balustrade, her hip striking the wood. Her foot slipped off the edge of the gallery, cutting her ankle on a broken rail. She tried to maintain her balance, but the fighters were moving toward her and Price's elbow came back again. She lost the fight.

Managing to grab onto the surviving half of one of the spindles, she ignored the splinters biting into her fingers. She refused to cry out. If she did, it would distract Jack's attention and that could get him killed. All she could to do was hold on. She was not strong enough yet to swing her foot high enough.

Jack and Price struggled down the hall into one of the rooms. Price grabbed the first vase he saw and threw it at Jack's head. It was apparently someone's opulently appointed bedroom. There were plenty of things to block with and throw.

Price managed to get a table between them, setting them at an impasse. They stared each other down, tensing for the slightest movement of either. That was when they heard a cannon fire and then silence. Price grinned.

"Your ship has been taken. There is nowhere for you to go, pirate, but to the gallows," he crowed.

Jack laughed. "That last gun was Ol' Betsy, which means yer fort has fallen."

In a fury Price, overturned the table, causing Jack to jump backward into the dressing table. He pressed the attack, pinning him awkwardly against the mirror. Jack grabbed a powder pot and hit him in the head with it. Price flailed, trying to clear his vision. Jack coughed and attempted to wave away the powder in the air.

He dodged around the white cloud and flanked his enemy. Price, still unable to see clearly, barely dodged. He backed up, rolled onto the bed, and threw the curtain closed to buy himself time. Jack grabbed the fabric by the bedposts and pulled the whole canopy down, began stabbing every lump he saw. Price managed to roll off the bed in time, but got clipped in the head by the canopy frame. His senses reeled as he grabbed the fallen bedside pitcher and poured what remained of it on his face. He blinked, clearing the powder from his eyes. Jack was still stabbing the bed.

As Price was sneaking around the side of it, Jack jumped back, beginning to suspect that the man might have crawled under it. Price leapt at him, but Jack spun, bringing up his sword. Again, the two danced. Price gained the upper hand, and threw Jack against the other door, pinning him with the swords crossed to his chest. Feet tangled as both men sought to knee the other. Then Jack reached down with his free hand and turned the handle. The door swung open under their weight and they tumbled to the floor in the hallway. Ready for it, Jack was able to recover faster, and got his knees up enough to use Price's momentum to kick him off and over his head.

Sirene felt the nails on the balustrade starting to give. The wood had been jarred too much recently for it to hold much longer. She looked both ways, but there was nowhere to move. She tried to pull herself up to the gallery floor, but the more she struggled, the more the nail gave. To her left, she saw Price tumbling down the stairs. This time, he was alone, and did not stop at the landing. There was a loud crack from beneath her hands. She could not wait.

"Jack!" she screamed.

Jack looked down the gallery from the top of the stairs, but there was no sign of her. Then he noticed the missing section of rail and the hands desperately clinging.

She heard his footsteps pounding along the balcony, moved one hand to the balcony floor, and clung to the edge with all her fading strength. Her fingers were cramping. The nail gave another fraction of an inch and she risked the floor with her other hand.

Jack threw himself to his belly along the remaining spindles, using them to brace himself as he reached for her. The moment that iron grip locked around her wrist she grabbed it with her other hand. Jack pulled himself up to his knees, dragging her out of danger. She lay, gasping in his arms, holding tightly to him. He sucked wind as she applied pressure to the burns on his back.

As she sat up, shaken, her skirt brushed against the broken spindle. It fell away, tumbling to the floor below where it landed with an echoing clatter. They glanced over the side at the rail and the body beside it, and she shivered.

He pulled them back, held her tighter; breathing more heavily from the nearness of losing her than from the exertion of the fight. There was sound below, and he gripped his sword tightly. He did not see Price coming up the stairs or down the gallery. He leaned forward, rising up enough to see Price's body halfway down the last flight and beginning to stir. Then the front door burst open and men poured in.

He pressed his mouth close to her ear and whispered, "There is a back way out. Can ye stand and run?"

Something downstairs alerted her senses. "There is no need," she breathed.

Jack prepared to stand and fight anyway. The men below were privately armed and wearing the same livery as the dead man directly below them. They were quickly followed by a well-dressed gentleman with an equally well-dressed woman on his arm.

"My lord, up there!" one of the men shouted, pointing at Jack and Sirene.

Lord Hamilton looked first at the man trying to sit up on the stairs, then to the pair on the gallery. "No," he said, and then pointed to Price. "Arrest him, and help them."

The servants moved to obey. One of them cried out. "James is dead, my lord!"

Lord Hamilton looked up at Jack. "Did you kill my servant, Master Pirate?"

The maid who had led Jack upstairs came up behind the governor. "No, my lord. He couldn't have. The balustrade was already broken when he an' that man there," she pointed to Price, "started fighting."

"What do we do now?" Jack asked warily.

Lord Hamilton spread his arms. "That depends upon you. Your reasons are justifiable. Granted your methods were unorthodox, but so far there have been few casualties to my knowledge and only so much damage. You are not yet outside the realm of a pardon."

Sirene stood. "You spoke with Jeanette?"

He smiled. On his arm, Lorelei clung happily. "I spoke with Jeanette, and she has been confiscated into protective custody until I can bring this matter into the courts."

"I'd rather kill him myself," Jack growled. "Court-martials take too long."

"Oh, but Henry has a much better idea, don't you Henry?" Lorelei trilled, straightening his lapels.

"Henry?" Sirene repeated with her eyebrow raised. "Mother," she began in a warning tone.

Lorelei shrugged. "I like him. And it has been oh so long. I'm entitled."

"What idea?" Jack persisted, refusing to be sidetracked by a domestic issue.

"Well, you see," Lord Hamilton explained, "if Miss Taft brings a grievance against him in open court, along with a few others she can help me round up... seeing as he has no living relation and she is the primary victim, not to mention the reason he has most of it; it is within my power to request all his holdings be turned over to her." Sirene gasped. "A stately sum, in spite of the house burning on the hill."

She looked at Jack. "Burning house?" she accused.

He shrugged. "The dog wasn't home. I let th' crews have a little fun." She glowered with disapproval. "We came this far without significant property damage. I wouldn't stay captain long if I didn't let them sack *something*."

"Well, I thank you for leaving my town otherwise in one piece," replied the governor.

Price was being taken off the stairs as he came to, protesting the irons being clapped onto him. Another servant came in from outside and bowed to the governor.

"My Lord, there is a large woman shouting from a window on the third floor."

Lord Hamilton sighed. "Will someone please let Mrs. MacPherson out of Miss Taft's room?" He gave Jack a half bow. "With your permission, of course?"

Jack shrugged. "It's your house."

"And again I thank you for leaving it and my staff *almost* intact," he said, eyeing the damaged balcony.

Jack held up his hands defensively, "Hey, I didn't do *that*."

"The keys are in Price's pocket," Sirene offered.

Lord Hamilton gestured to another servant who moved up the stairs to the shackled Price.

"What about 'im, m' lord?" asked one of the men holding Price as the servant searched him.

"Well, if the good captain would be so kind as to call off his fleet, I would say take Price to the fort and lock him up."

"That would depend on what be in it fer them. I mean, they have what swag they've sacked from th' Price residence, but there be..." Lorelei glowered up at him, and he sighed, changed his manner. "There *is* a lot remaining between that conflagration and their ships."

Lord Hamilton waved them down. "Please, let us talk like civilized men. I have a proposition for you... and your crew."

Jack came downstairs with Sirene's help, his wounds taking their toll. "You would just let us walk to our ships and sail off?"

"Better than that, mate," the governor grinned boyishly. "I will give you license to do what you do best."

Sirene caught the look on her mother's face and frowned. "Did you have something to do with this?" she hissed.

"Oh, I sowed a few pearls. A lot of it was his idea," she answered evasively.

Jack stopped. "What do you mean license?"

"I mean, have you got anything against your homeland?" he asked.

"My home is the sea," Jack said. "But I have no particular beef with my mother's homeland."

"Good. Then have you ever considered privateering?"

Jack stood on the dock in Fairlane's Cove staring out at the broad ocean beyond the protected lagoon. He wore a heavily embroidered, honey-brown dress coat, with gold silk cravat and tawny new trousers. He still insisted, however, on wearing boots and a sailor's shirt, though both were new and finely made, and belted with his old golden sash. His dark brown and sun-gilded hair was neatly tied back in a queue and shone in the morning light.

He sighed. The earth beneath his feet was still again, though the world surrounding it bobbed and heaved with the ocean swells. Or at least, it seemed to. Whatever Lorelei had done to him had vanished with the sun. The ocean was inviting, but there was much yet to be done before he could stand on his deck again. He heard footsteps on the planks behind him, listened until he identified the gait.

"Aye, Mr. Marklain?" he asked, as the footsteps stopped behind him.

"Captain, the lady begs a moment more and then she will be ready."

"Remind her we don't want to be late," he said, staring out to sea, his hands clasped behind him. "Not for this."

He made certain his English was proper as befitted the situation and his dress. It would not be long before he could regress into the comfortable speech patterns of a common seaman.

"I have, sir." Marklain started to walk away, but Jack spoke again.

"Are you sure," he asked, half-turning. "About not taking her?" He inclined his head towards the *Ambition*, anchored nearby and newly rechristened the *Lorelei*. "You would make a fine captain."

He shrugged. "I thank you, sir, really I do. But I'm happy as a bosun; my hands on the lines, my feet in the shrouds, the snap of the sheets." He sighed, content. "That's my love, sir. Besides," he said, blushing. "I've grown to love the *Mercy*. One doesn't see her kind often, nor gets t' sail her like. And I think giving her," he said, indicating the small brig, "to the governor was the right thing t' do, sir. He'll treat her proper. Too many bad memories on her, anyway."

They were interrupted by a distant whistle over the water. Both of them looked out over the cove and saw a black dorsal skimming the surface, then the flash of white belly and golden cheeks as the dolphin jumped. Jack stepped to the edge of the dock, bent down as the dolphin squealed to a halt below, rolling on her back and laughing up at him.

"Skilliweha." Jack scowled. "And just where did you skim off to? I needed you. Sirene needed you," he scolded.

The dolphin clicked and chattered, and Jack was not sure if she was explaining or fussing. Then he saw a long black form, lightly banded, swim below her and hover near the bottom. He redirected the dolphin's attention with his hand.

"What is it, sir?" Marklain asked, bending nearer.

Jack waved him back, and he obeyed, though he loosened the sword in his scabbard just in case. Skilly did not seem concerned about the possible shark and ducked her head below the water, whistling. Suddenly, the other creature arched upwards.

Jack moved back, wary. The hand lingering on the Spanish sword at his hip stopped when the head broke the surface.

The woman washed back the screen of crinkled black hair and peered at him with great, honey-brown eyes. Her features were classic, with a distinctive, aquiline nose and deep olive skin. She wore a clutter of shell and pearl necklaces around her neck and in the front part of her hair. There were gold and ivory bracelets on her arms of ancient origins, and several rings on her hands. She stared at him for a long moment.

"You must be Mercy's boy," she said, beaming.

Her voice was not as sultry as Lorelei's, but just as compelling, and accented with Greek or Italian.

Jack gave her his lopsided grin. "And you must be Ligeia."

She gave a small frown. "Someone's tattled." She held up her hands to him, and Jack pulled her out of the water. She perched daintily on the edge of the dock, shifting smoothly to legs as she cleared the surface. She noticed Marklain and turned, leaned forward on the docks to admire him, her naked body on full display. "Ooo, hello."

Marklain turned dark red, made helpless gestures, and averted his eyes. "I... I'll, I think I'll just check on the lady." He beat a rapid retreat for the house and Jack tried not to laugh. Ligeia had no such compunction and giggled freely.

"He's cute all pink like that."

"So why are you here?" Jack asked, sitting down beside her. Since the tide was out, he could swing his feet without getting his boots wet.

She rolled her eyes. "Weren't you listening?" she asked, gesturing to Skilly who whistled sadly at her.

"I don't speak dolphin... yet," he added.

"Oh. Sorry. She said she had a... family issue to deal with and got called away. Then, when she found you again, Lorelei asked her to go find me. She's been going on about you since the Baleares. And I must say, you look just as she described, though a bit more... stuffy.”

He self-consciously pulled at his collar and cravat. “I have something important to do on the other side of the island. I have to dress for the occasion. You are welcome to come with us if you like.”

She pulled back, putting up her hands. “Oh no! I’ve had my fill of the dry still, thank you,” she shuddered. She gestured at her long tanned legs. “This is the first time I’ve shed scale since Moldavia.”

“I understand. Lorelei explained. I don’t like land much myself.”

“Lorelei? Oh, that’s who tattled. Explains everything. Well, at least I don’t have to go into detail,” she sighed, playing with her hair. She reached out and turned his face toward her. “Oh, how much you look like him. You have his eyes,” she murmured with sudden tenderness.

“Who?” he asked quietly, afraid she would say his father.

She gave a dry chuckle. “Jonathan’s. The same odd blue and brown. The same crooked smile that melts a woman’s heart. The same blue-golden glow. Skilly tells me you have a tail,” she said, drawing her hand back and changing the subject.

“Aye. Sirene calls me Amberjack.”

“I’m surprised that any child of Mercy’s line *can* change. She couldn’t, you see, so I never told her... though her father might have... hmm. Wait. Did you say Sirene? Lorelei’s girl?”

“Aye, grandmother, I did.” He glanced at her and laughed. “God, that’s awkward. You don’t look more than thirty,” he complained.

She laughed a deep, wave-like sound. “Try closer to four hundred. She’s a good girl, I hear. Level-headed. Is she as strong-willed as her mother?”

“Not quite as domineering,” he admitted.

She nodded. “That’s the Voice, dear.”

“You’ve never met her?” he asked, curious.

"Oceans, no, child. It's a big world out there. I mean, I saw her when she was just a little fry, but... I went straight back to the Mediterranean first chance I got. I'm strictly a home girl. And she's never swam my waters." She sighed, shifting tracks yet again. "I wish I had been able to stay and raise your mother, but things were not to be. I'm surprised she had the foresight to bear in the sea."

"That was the natives' idea."

She perked up. "Oh? Where?"

"South Pacific," he explained.

She deflated slightly. "I think there was one or more of our kind out that way. Probably lots of interbreeding with the natives. Something had to filter down. Lucky you."

"Why did you name her Mercy?" he asked, staring out at the bay, watching the dolphin chasing a parrotfish.

"I was in the middle of a war," she said, as if it was obvious. "I thought it might inspire mercy in others. Far too little of that back then."

"Not much more of it now," he muttered.

Up by the house, they heard the whickering and stomping of the horses as they were being hitched to the carriage. Jack glanced back.

"Well," she announced, perking up, "I should be going. Dry land gives me the shivers nowadays. You take care and I might see you around."

"Not going straight home?"

"I'm on holiday," she simpered. "Besides, there are plenty of islands for me to explore out here."

"I thought you didn't like land," he chuckled.

She rolled her eyes. "Not the dry bits! I hear the seas here are full of sunken treasures. Oceans of lovely reefs and underwater 'islands' for me to poke around in," she said excitedly.

"Be careful near the Sargasso Sea. In the deeps there swim poisonous fish," he warned.

"I'll keep that in mind," she said, flexing her legs as she put them together. They shifted into a beautiful, dark tail with light grey bands and a lacy caudal and frilly side fins. But before she could slide down into the water, Skilly squirted her and squealed. "What?" she complained. She listened, and her face lit up. "Oh, yes. Sorry."

She sifted through her necklaces. "Now which one was it?"

Skilly rolled her eyes and whistled.

Ligeia looked down at her hand. "Right." She grabbed Jack's hand, held it up to hers, comparing sizes. She picked a finger that was about the same size as his forefinger, took a ring from it, and placed it on Jack's hand. "There. That will let you scale. Just dive in," she pinched the fabric of his trousers, "without these, and you'll shift. Just blow on it when you want your danglies back."

Jack looked down at the dark gold band set with a deep golden, Tahitian pearl. Hearing voices at the house in the distance, Ligeia hopped off the end of the pier and slipped into the water without a splash. Skilly did not follow as they watched her skim along the bottom of the cove until she was out of sight. He looked down at the dolphin, not knowing if she would understand him or not.

"Meet us at the ship," he said.

Skilly rose half out of the water and swam backwards, laughing, before she flipped and dove. He turned to go as Sirene approached. She was breathtaking in a steely blue dress that set off her complexion perfectly, the ruby and pearl necklace he had given her gracing her throat.

"Who were you talking to?" she asked, reaching up to kiss him.

He resisted the urge to bury his fingers in her silvery hair and undo the intricate pinnings. "Skilly," he mumbled against her lips. "I sent her to the ship; ...and my grandmother."

She pulled back. "Ligeia?" She looked out across the water. "Why didn't you introduce us?"

"She just came to give me this," he said, showing her the ring as they walked to the waiting carriage.

Sirene caressed his fingers as she admired the jewel. "It's beautiful. So, does this mean no more borrowing?"

He slipped his arm around her waist. "No more borrowing." He ran his hand over the fabric. "And you aren't wearing your corset." He feigned a scowl.

She humphed. "That's not all I'm not wearing."

"How absolutely scandalous."

She pinched his flank. "As if you wouldn't go without these if you thought you could get away with it," she teased.

"Damned straight," he admitted, helping her up into the carriage. "'Vieve has this idea for a pair of tie-on breeches that might work. Make it easier to shift back to my 'danglies', as Ligeia put it."

"Oh, that should be nice." She kept chattering, knowing how little Jack was looking forward to t6he four-hour carriage ride into Port St. Charles and hoping to distract him. "So, what was she like?"

Jack tapped the side of the carriage to alert the driver, and leaned back in the seat. "A complete bubblehead."

The hanging of former Vice Admiral Ambrose Price was a hot, formal affair, and went off without a hitch.

It seemed as if half the island showed up. Even people from outside Barbados came, including Governor Forsyth of Jamaica. He stood near the platform where Governor Lord Hamilton and his new wife, Lady Hamilton, stood overseeing the proceedings. Forsyth glanced at Sirene, smiled, and tipped his hat. When he saw Jack glowering beside her, he gave him a nod and Jack settled down.

Sirene had met with the Jamaican governor earlier, assured him that she had no desire to take part in the blackmail scheme, and was happy to forget it ever happened. This seemed to please him and he listened to the lengthy list of crimes and abuses of office with utter glee.

Price never said a word during the whole affair. He kept his eyes locked on Sirene through it all. She met that gaze with an outward calm, though it was not until the doctor confirmed the death that she relaxed. She sank into Jack's arm with relief as a roar of celebration went up among the crowd. Price was a grossly unpopular man, especially once word had gotten out and his hold was broken. The courts were swamped reviewing his shipboard hangings, to confirm whether or not the men he killed were, in truth, pirates.

Once the crowd dispersed to whatever festivities they had planned, Sirene and Jack made their way to the docks. They were not the only ones. The *Mercy's Ransom* sat proudly moored at one of the piers, sporting a fresh coat of paint, new sheets, and flying the Union Jack below the grey Jolly Roger. Across the pier stood *The Widow*, also spruced up and under British colours. They stopped between the two gangplanks, and moved aside to allow three porters on board carrying the last of the water barrels. From the deck, Tortuga leaned over the rail and called to them.

"We ar ready to sail at yahr word, Capta'n!"

Jack nodded, then turned as Genevieve strolled down the planks with Mary on her arm. With a grin, he bowed to the ladies. "Captain, Miss Mary," he teased, kissing the latter's hand.

'Vieve narrowed her eyes. "Capitane," she growled.

Jack clapped her arm in his in a manly shake. "You look good," he said, indicating her sharply tailored Captain's coat, not unlike his own, with new trousers and boots.

"Why could we not 'ave milled wit' ze common folk?" she complained, stretching her neck uncomfortably.

"Because you aren't," he answered, pulling her closer. "And tell me ye did not enjoy yerselves immensely."

Mary, dolled up in a pale yellow dress, giggled, and nudged her companion. Finally 'Vieve gave in, and chuckled.

"Oh, but ze looks we got!" she crowed.

"I'm sure we'll be th' talk fer quite th' bit," Mary said with a laugh. "One gentleman..., I swear, I thought he'd break his neck tryin' to get it straight who was what."

"See, I told you."

"Oui." 'Vieve sighed. "Poetic justeece, you ask me. I would not 'ave wanted to miss zat 'anging for ze life of me."

Mary shivered, clinging tighter to 'Vieve. "It very nearly was."

Jack set his hand on her shoulder to comfort her. "Nearly is not a noose, Mary. Though you have the governor to thank for that."

"And you are most welcome," said Lord Hamilton, coming up behind them with Lorelei. He bowed to Mary, kissed her hand, then shook 'Vieve's. "Miss Mary, Capitane L'Rouge," he said. "*I trust you have all your papers in order, Captain?*" he asked in French.

"*Yes. Thank you. They are right here,*" she said, patting her breast pocket.

"*Good. I trust you will have no trouble working for England*?" he asked hopefully.

She shifted back to English. "I am an expatriate, *mon seigneur*. My ship eez my country and 'as been for a long time. And, for now, we are not at war wit' England," she grinned.

"Good," he said, stepping back. "I would hate to have you at war with us. Anyone who can disable a harbour full of ships, hold an entire city hostage, and with so little property damage is a dangerous enemy and one I most certainly want *for* our country. Luckily, the king agrees with me." He turned to Jack. "You *must* tell me how you did it."

The women looked at each other and giggled. Jack just grinned.

"Ask your wife," he dodged.

They looked back to where Lorelei and Sirene had their heads together. Lord Hamilton rest his arm on Jack's shoulder, observing the two pale-haired women. "So, tell me, do you ever plan to marry that stepdaughter of mine?"

Jack gave him an enigmatic smile. "Oh, but we already are, your Lordship. In a way that laws can neither define nor disseminate. You, with your title and peerage, need legitimacy. We don't. I still don't know how you got Lorelei to agree to it."

Sirene was asking her mother the same question. "Are you sure about this, mother? This marriage thing?"

Lorelei waved off her concern. "Oh, it'll be fun. I haven't done this since... oh, since Barbarossa."

"Just be careful. Some of these noble women can be real barracudas."

"I eat barracudas for breakfast," she replied. "Besides, once I have a little talk with them..." She smiled.

"Voice will only get you so far." Sirene gave up. It was a pointless argument, anyway. "Enjoy yourself. You can do what you want with the house. I want nothing that man touched."

"I understand, dear. Now, you two need to go," she said, giving her a last hug and passing her off to Jack. "Just be sure you come see me if you start to 'swell'." She patted her daughter's flat belly suggestively. "Oh, and if you see Naoa, tell him where to find me. That turtle will get himself eaten looking for me, otherwise."

"I will."

They bade their farewells and boarded the ship. The *Widow* pulled away from the docks. As soon as the gangplank was stowed and the mooring undone, Jack gave one last wave to the pair on the wharf and headed for the quarterdeck. As he surveyed the work, he promptly made himself comfortable, boots first. Mr. Lucas was immediately on hand to receive his coat, waistcoat, stockings and boots and took them below to the cabin.

Jack pulled his cravat loose, and then wrapped the golden silk around his forehead, letting the tails dangle at the side. He adjusted his glass eye patch beneath it.

"So that's where you were hiding it," Sirene chuckled, coming up the stairs.

She had changed into her favourite choli and sarong, and taken her hair down. She crossed to him and slipped into his arms. She laid her head back against his chest with his arms around her, and gazed out at the sea opening up before them. She basked in the golden glow that was Jack, brighter than any sun, and breathed truly free for the first time in fifteen years. "It's good to be home," she sighed.

"Aye," he agreed. "Glorious, indeed."

He turned to the helmsman, issued his orders, and shouted other directions to crewmen further down. They scrambled, climbing up the rigging as they dropped canvas and adjusted lines. He listened to the creak of wood and hemp, the snap of sail, and the crash of waves on the hull; the squeal of dolphins at play in the ships' wakes. The air was full of salt and the fading stench of city, and the stale heat of unmoving land. The sky opened up before them, the horizon clear and inviting, the winds fair, and the sails full. The world was all ocean and the oceans were his. The crew sang to keep their time, and Sirene joined them; their combined voices carrying from one ship to the other as they made for open sky.

Note bene

There were a lot of hard decisions to make with this book, to make it as authentic as I could and yet still readable. It hasn't been easy. Mistakes have been made and will probably stay at this point.

The accents were the worst. Trying to balance giving you the feel of a character's voice while making them legible was not easy. I know I failed in a couple of places. Tortuga is a Malagasy, and it was easier to keep his accent in mind. Simple switches of pronunciation (that pesky 'th' dipthong for instance). Anjali…. Hoo boy! She is Hindi, through and through, and far too often I started leaning more towards her husband in my head and she ended up sounding half Jamaican half Cajun.

The basic Indian accent usually trades 'th's for 'd's, especially in the middle of words, but she ended up reading more like her husband, so I nixed that for the most part. Also the w/v trade off. With the two Germans in the book being heavy 'v' for 'w', they started to blur there, so I made a sacrifice of consistency versus accuracy. My apologies.

In any case, I know I'm going to break my tongue trying to manage these in the audiobook!

Other Books By
S.L. Thorne

Love In Ruins
The Speaker
Fang and Bone

The Gryphon's Rest Series:
Lady of the Mist
The Gloaming

SHIFT Books 1 & 2
Stag's Heart
Dragon's Bride

All Available in hardback, paperback and ebook at:
Thornewoodstudios.com/books
or
Amazon.com